red on a rose

red on a rose

a novel

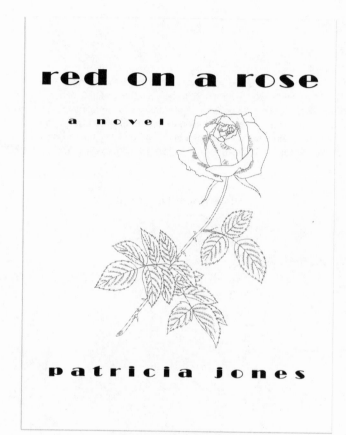

patricia jones

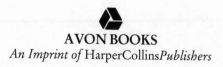

AVON BOOKS

An Imprint of HarperCollins*Publishers*

RED ON A ROSE. Copyright © 2001 by Patricia Jones.
All rights reserved. Printed in the United States of America.
No part of this book may be used or reproduced in any manner whatsoever
without written permission except in the case of brief
quotations embodied in critical articles and reviews. For information
address HarperCollins Publishers Inc., 10 East 53rd Street, New York, NY 10022.

Designed by Jo Anne Metsch

ISBN 0-380-81730-6

red on a rose

chapter one

I T WAS THE kind of infernal heat that could addle any mind
and cause a gentle soul to turn against its very nature and kill,
either physically or metaphorically, but equally as tragic. And it
covered all of Baltimore for nearly a week with an unrelenting
anger that revealed no end to its passion. One thing for sure,
this was no kind of heat for old people, and Lila knew as much
as she watched her husband, Jack, move his stethoscope over
Mrs. Chalm's back while the wilting old woman inhaled and
exhaled, inhaled and exhaled.

And it was this kind of heat that could always get her thinking about what she wanted to think about the least. But heat
begets nothing but heat, she supposed, and right now, it was
the heat of her mother bearing down on her. Or rather, her
stepmother, as she'd more precisely, in her current incarnation,
found herself thinking of Eulelie, though to avoid conflict, she
continued to call her Momma, as she always had. But, despite
Eulelie's wishes to the contrary, Lila could no longer deny the
existence of the woman who gave her life. There was only one
mother, only one *Momma*, and she was Gloria Giles. But she is
dead. God keep her soul, Lila prayed whenever the thought of
her mother crossed her mind. Usually, when Lila thought of her
stepmother, it was in patches of memories that would flash,
quick as lightning, then leave, as if it had another mind to get to
and possess. But now, Eulelie's image, though distracting to her,

did not envelop her in its heat. Instead, Jack's smile penetrated her haze and triggered the memory of the first time she realized that she had fallen in love with him.

Jack's smile was magical for Lila in the way it could sometimes transport her whenever she saw it, and she simply had to let it take her. And now, she watched his smile start with the slide of the right corner of his mouth out and up toward heaven, followed by the left corner, until his lips were framing his teeth into the kind of perfection that could stand alone as art. As he smiled with the pleasure of hearing Mrs. Chalm's healthy heart, and looking, at least to Lila, as manly as a man could be, she realized that she had been indulged with something that came from some centered place inside him. And this time she let his smile lift her right out of Mrs. Chalm's living room, where too much silence melded with the heat into a stew of unintelligible nothingness. She followed it across town, and back to her own home, and her kitchen, where her stepmother's presence, generous and all-consuming, filled every corner, even after the passing of two years.

Lila remembered how she thought, in those moments when she was being as adamant and stubborn as can be, that it would actually be a good idea for her stepmother to stay with them for the week before she would leave Baltimore forever for Florida. Then, Lila remembered the exact moment, after one night and one day, she knew it was the worst thought her mind had ever conjured. Eulelie got on Lila's back, and Lila thought the woman would just go right ahead and ride it out of town.

Still, everything her stepmother said while straddling her back, Lila remembered, was always said in that decidedly wily way of hers that made it difficult for anyone to know, much less speak on behalf of, their umbrage. And to make things all the more ridiculous, it all started when Lila handed Jack a bowl to wash out.

She said it kindly. It wasn't an order, or a demand, or a command at all. Lila handed Jack the bowl with a hand she couldn't spare for too long. "Jack, honey, would you wash this out for the salad, please?"

Her stepmother snapped her head to attention, her intense stare at Lila making the disbelief clear. Then she pressed her lips together in disapproval and said, "Well, I guess you young wives do things differently. In my home, when I needed help in the kitchen, your father and I just hired somebody."

"Momma, I'm certainly not going to hire somebody to wash out a bowl."

"Well, Lila, I'm not suggesting you do that. I'm just saying that in my day, women didn't ask, or even expect, their husbands to help out. I'm just trying to figure out when things changed."

Lila looked at Jack while he washed out the bowl, rinsing it over and over, as if to keep himself as far away as possible from Lila and Eulelie and the torrent of their tension. He was absolutely refusing to meet Lila's eyes. And Lila could see that his bearing was that of a man who did not want to be present. So, knowing that she was alone with Eulelie, Lila said, "A long time ago, Momma. Things changed a long time ago. Catch up."

"Well, maybe that's why the divorce rate is so high." Eulelie took a nibble of cheese into her mouth, chewed it, and then said, with her eyebrows raised in judgment, "I don't know, dear. Maybe you should be careful."

As if she didn't hear Eulelie, Lila said to Jack, "You know what, Jack? I think I'll go down into the wine cellar and see if I can find something that will go with dinner." She tore off a paper towel and dried her hands. Without tarrying or looking back, she walked to the cellar door and said, "Of course I could be a while, since I really don't know as much about wine as you." It was the cue she hoped Jack would take to follow her, although it was obtuse.

But his mind was right there with her. "Maybe I'll come with you to help. You'll excuse us, won't you, Eulelie?"

"Oh, of course. Don't worry about me. I have to tell you, I didn't know you had a wine cellar. You never showed it to me, but it sounds very impressive."

"Well, it was built in down there by the previous owners," he said, drying his hands on the dish towel and then making his way to the cellar door. He stopped only to tell his mother-in-law, "And it just so happens that I like collecting wine, so I guess it all worked out. I guess you never saw it because we hardly ever think to take anyone into the basement. Anyway, it's hardly the showpiece of the house. It's just a wine cellar," and then Jack did what his wife wanted and followed her down to the basement.

"What is wrong with her?" Lila said before Jack could close the wine cellar door behind them. "God, why does she do this to me? Why *can* she do this to me?"

"Do what?"

"Drive me out of my freaking tree. She is driving me nuts, Jack, and she hasn't even been here a full twenty-four hours yet," she said, wringing her hands and pacing back and forth, to and from Jack, between the rows of racked-up wine. "Can you please tell me how I'm going to get through this week? It is going to be full-tilt Eulelie for one solid week, and I'm telling you right now, Jack Calloway, I will be down here in a drunken stupor every evening when you get home, because I will need to stay as drunk as a skunk just to deal with her. And you know I'm not a drinker, but by the time this week is over, I swear to you, Jack, there'll be a room waiting for me at the Betty Ford!"

Jack fought back the smile he thought would surely lead to laughter. But then his face took on a completely sober sternness that seemed to pay homage to the fact that Eulelie wasn't *his* mother, and that this was serious to Lila. So he replied, "Lila, Eulelie is who she is. It took her a lot of years to get this way, and you can't expect to change that." Jack pulled up the stray crate that had always been there and sat down on it. He took in a breath, then sighed it out and continued, "Now, you have to decide what you want to do, and you have to be honest with yourself about it. If you can't do this, Lila, you need to say it now and I'll go up there and tell her to leave, because this could be the longest week in your life if Eulelie's going to be getting to you this way. Personally, I don't like to see you like this. I *won't* see you like this, and so as far as I'm concerned, if she can't respect you in your home then she needs to go."

"Well, you know I can't do that, Jack. I can't just tell her to go." She went to the far end of the aisle and hoisted herself up on the wine barrel that sat there for atmosphere, just as it had for the cellar's former owners. "It's just that my father's dead, and Lucretia's moved to South Carolina, and Gil has his own life, and I'm married, and Linda, well, she'll always be with Momma, but still, now Eulelie has left home and it's as if with all of those things that defined her removed from her life, she's forgotten who she is and is trying to remember herself by trying to make my home what her home once was for her. That's who Eulelie is, Jack. She's one of those women who leaves home and then forgets who she is the moment she gets where she's going. And you know, even if she's only going to be gone for a minute, she's leaving the only thing that can define her. She can't impose her life on me and my home."

"No, Lila, she can't. And she certainly can't do it in a week." Jack got himself up with an older man's grunt and slid the crate back into its corner. He went to where Lila sat perched atop the wine barrel and got her down. "So let's go on upstairs. I have a solution that, I think, will make all involved happy."

"What is it?" she said with the animation of a child.

"Well, I can't tell you that, Lila, because if I do, then you won't be able to respond with the requisite surprise that's going to be needed. If you know, or if you even appear to know, it might look to Eulelie to be a plot, and, well, in her words, that would just be bad manners." Then he smiled.

And every part of her became liquid. His smile gave her no choice other than to trust without question. So she didn't question, she simply slid her arm around his back and let him and his smile blind her, then seize her, then lead her.

Jack stopped, and in so doing stopped them both where they strode. "Don't you think we need to take a bottle of wine back upstairs just so Eulelie won't know for sure that we were down here talking about her?"

"Yeah, that would make sense." She grabbed the first thing her arm could reach without having to let go of Jack.

Jack looked at the bottle. "Blanc Fumé. You're making lamb, right?"

"Yes. Why?"

"Well, you should put that back." He let her out of his grip only long enough to reach up and pull out what he knew they needed. "This merlot would be better."

"Well, I'm going to take this upstairs anyway and chill it. I figure with Eulelie around for the next week, I might need this entire bottle of wine to anesthetize myself."

"Fine, Lila," Jack said, laughing. "That's just fine. And who knows, maybe you'll both need it by the time this week's over."

Lila landed on the top stair and heard the water running. She couldn't imagine what Eulelie might have been doing. Maybe she was washing a piece of fruit. But as soon as she pushed the basement door open and stepped into the kitchen she found Eulelie washing the few dishes that had collected in the sink. "Momma, what are you doing? Will you stop that, please!"

"I'm just trying to wash up some of these dishes so that you won't have to ask Jack to do them."

Lila went to Eulelie, turned off the water, then nudged her out of the way. Had Eulelie been a frailer woman, Lila could have nudged her right on her bottom. That's how determined a push she gave her. "That's enough, Momma. These dishes are our problem. You're our guest, so please just sit down and rest yourself." Lila was making her best effort to sound undisturbed. She squeezed the dishwashing sponge to damp, set it aside, and went back to chopping her garlic. "Jack, you need to fix the salad. There's the spring mix of greens in the refrigerator and then in the crisper there's a head of romaine that you can mix in with it."

Jack headed for the refrigerator and got only paces from it when he was stopped by Eulelie's shrill squeal. It seemed to shock him so, it was as if he didn't know what there was for him to do but stand still until the storm passed; because without a doubt, a storm was brewing right there in the kitchen.

"Oh, Lila, now that's enough," Eulelie said, getting to her feet. She headed for the refrigerator and said, "If you need the salad made, I can do it. Why are you treating your husband like this? You were not raised like that, and I just don't know what to say."

"Momma, please don't say another thing," Lila said, her hands trembling so under the strain of her frustration that she had to put her chopping knife down. "Will you please come away from the refrigerator and go sit down? I have never been more serious about anything than I am right now. Just stop it, please. I said Jack will make the salad, and that's what Jack will do." Lila looked behind her to find Jack frozen where he stood. And for just that instant she'd become as annoyed with him as she was with Eulelie. Why was he stilled by the nonsense of a fool? Because that's exactly what Eulelie was being right now, a fool, talking and spreading foolishness all over her fool-free kitchen. "Jack, fix the salad, please," Lila snapped. And only when he got moving again toward the refrigerator did she turn and say to Eulelie, "We don't have one of those Stone Age marriages where the wife is supposed to race around the kitchen preparing her husband's meal while he puts his feet up, Momma."

"Okay, well, I'll just ask Jack how he feels." She went back to the counter and climbed on her stool. "Jack, tell me the truth. How does it make you feel to have your wife order you to do this and do that? Does it make you feel as if you're not the man of your house?"

"Momma, nobody's ordering anybody to do anything!" Lila said, fully embracing her annoyance. "And stop putting words in my husband's mouth."

"Lila, come on now," Jack said with the calm the kitchen now needed. "Nobody's putting anything anywhere. And, Eulelie, in answer to your question, well, I have to say that two things come to mind right now." Jack paused as he took the salad greens from the refrigerator, walked to the sink, and put them in the colander. "Number one is this: I don't do anything I don't want to do. Number two, and this is the most important number, Eulelie, so I need you to really hear me: a big distinction needs to be made here between the running of Lila Calloway's kitchen and home, and the way Eulelie ran her kitchen and home. That distinction needs to be made, Eulelie, or else this might as well be your home."

Eulelie took him in with just the right amount of incredulity on her face that seemed to leave her speechless. But then she answered, "Oh, well I'd like to think that my daughters' and son's homes are like my home away from home. I'd like to think that I'm as welcomed here as if it were my home."

"And you are, Eulelie," Jack said.

"Of course you are, Momma," Lila said, nearly back to the center of her calm. "You just can't come in here and try to run things your way."

"Lila, I'm just trying to tell you—"

Jack interrupted before both Lila and Eulelie could set themselves off and running in a circle, trying to resolve a dynamic that was on a course set in place so long ago that it was now too solid to shake. "The bottom line, Eulelie, is that you will always be welcome in our home," Jack said, with only one corner of his smile. "But you're going to have to leave your rules on running things down in Florida at your own home. But I have something that will make you forget all of this." Jack took a business card from the inside pocket of his jacket. He handed it to Eulelie, saying, "This is for you."

She regarded the card for a few seconds before responding. "Harborcourt Hotel. Jack, is this supposed to mean something to me? I mean, it's a lovely place, but why are you giving me this card?"

"Well, Eulelie, I decided that it might be nice, for your last week in Baltimore, for you and Linda to stay in the lap of luxury. And since you were so impressed by the place when Lila and I got married down there, I've booked a suite for you and Linda to stay there until you leave for Florida. And their restaurant is fantastic, so you just charge all your meals there to the room and I'll pay for it. It's all on us. We'll come down a couple of nights during the week and join you for dinner, and then on your last night, we'll have Gil come down, and we'll have a big dinner and toast you farewell with champagne and all the works."

"Oh my, Jack," Eulelie said, her mouth scarcely able to close from the shock of such a gesture. "Thank you so much. Lila, did you know about this, honey?"

"No, Momma, I didn't," Lila said, unable to move from where she stood due to her amazement. Even though Jack hadn't told her exactly what the surprise would be, the edge was taken off of it somewhat simply by knowing that something would happen; yet she was still astonished, and overwhelmed, and filled up with love that he would save her in such a way. When she got her legs moving again, Lila went to Jack and put her arms around his back, squeezing him close. She landed a kiss lightly on his cheek and said in a whisper: "Thank you for being such a generous man, Jack. This is really so sweet of you. Really. Really." And then she giggled so reflexively she almost gave away the ulterior motive.

Jack turned to Lila at an angle where Eulelie wasn't welcome, and gave her the other corner and then the full frame of his teeth. In his smile, which showed no fear of the woman who had given Lila plenty in another lifetime, Lila's mind tripped back for the merest second to other lands with fearless warriors, defending lives and territory with nothing but glistening skin in its deep blackness covered sparsely with cloth and animal, made as impenetrable as any metal armor by bravery. Skin. Cloth. Animal. This was Jack, her knight, her warrior. There was no doubt that for now, and for the rest of her life, Jack would be her knight when the damsel in her needed him, her equal when she needed balance, and her lover when she needed love to touch her in the flesh.

"I love you," Lila mouthed to Jack.

And he said the same without words, but with his eyes, and then that smile.

SO NOW THAT she was present again, back in Mrs. Chalm's living room, Lila paced the rug, needing to free herself from heat and thoughts, and the heat of her thoughts—flashing memories of Eulelie, and now the remembrance of Sandra Hightower, the woman her brother Gil nearly married. She wasn't exactly agitated by remembering Sandra, but it was certainly a memory she could have done without in this heat, with Sandra's dash of streetwalker-red fingernails and toenails, and flash of smile that seemed to hide more than it revealed. Lila had been taken captive by the thought of Sandra, which came from out of nowhere, and it would not let her loose. And what the memory of Sandra let Lila know now, more than she'd ever known, was that Lila Calloway's life, the former Lila Giles's life, the full circle of things, could be summed up by one of her father's sayings: "Don't ever point your finger at anyone in blame or shame," he'd say, "because there'll always be three more pointing back at you."

She paced, without realizing that she was making herself hotter. But that house was too quiet, and the heat was too intense, and all Lila wanted was to stop thinking and in the process lose herself in a blank mind. Only momentarily. But she couldn't, because now, as she watched Jack, she was struck by irony. And she remembered, with the heat of shame rising in her, made more present by the heat of the earth rising around her, the way she once believed as strongly as the rest of her family that Sandra was not good enough to be a Giles; the way she once believed, as her stepmother believed, that water must find its own level. Her feelings about Sandra, not so many years before she met Jack, were like the deepest, most shameful part of herself she could never reveal to Jack. What would he think of her? Jack, with his unprivileged past in stark opposition to the man, the doctor, she watched in the present as he jotted down notes about the beating of Mrs. Chalm's heart.

And so now, she had to smile at herself, and at life, and fate as well, since that finger she pointed at Gil for the dishonor of bringing East Baltimore into the Gileses' purebred respectability ended up sending three fingers pointing back at her not so many years later when fate sent her the love for whom it had been preparing her to be worthy to receive.

"What's so funny? Why the smile?" Jack asked, grinning for seemingly no reason other than seeing her smile and having it lure him to joy. He unfolded the blood-pressure cuff as his eyes squinted at Lila in complete bemusement.

"Oh, nothing," Lila said, flustered by his interruption of her thoughts. "I was just thinking, for reasons only God knows, about something my father used to say about not pointing fingers. He said you should never point your finger at someone in blame or shame, because there're always three more pointing back at you." And she pointed her finger at Jack to show him that there were indeed three more pointing back at her. "You see?"

"Sure enough," Mrs. Chalm said through a throaty laugh. "Sure enough. Your daddy was a smart and wise man."

"Yeah, he was. But it's mighty funny, isn't it, coming from him, since his life's work was to judge people and point his finger at them, so to speak. Maybe judicial fingers don't count," she thought aloud as she went to the chair and sat, without taking her eyes off of Jack, who now reminded her that he possessed nothing the old Lila ever dreamed she'd want. Yes, he was the doctor she'd always seen in her imaginings of her married self, but the other side of Jack was that he was real in the way he now, and had always, lived—too real. And yet, Jack didn't love her for all those reasons she'd thought important— not her breeding, not her name, not her family, nor her family's home. But even more than that, Jack was unimpressed by Eulelie, and nearly irreverent regarding matters of class and place, which charmed and vexed Lila all at once, at least in the very beginning. After all, Jack's brand of don't-give-a-damn irreverence was still coming very slowly to her when they met. In that way, he put her in mind of a private eye she once knew named Pick, who challenged everything she knew to be true about the insular world in which she was bred. But with Jack, everything was so different, because she knew that he was headed to the core of what he saw from the moment he saw her—her goodness. And now, sitting in the home of a woman Lila's former self would not have dreamed of having in her life, Lila was able to let him get to her goodness, because she had already found the best part of herself that had nothing to do with her stepmother, and less than nothing to do with the legend of the Giles family.

"Here you go, darlin'. Here's your pie," Mr. Chalm said, handing Lila a slice of the blueberry pie Mrs. Chalm had made just for Lila.

"Thank you, Mr. Chalm," she said, smiling with a forced desire to eat pie she didn't like on a day that was far too hot for food. She watched him make his way to the corner where he always sat, like an obedient pet. And it wasn't until she watched him sit in the ritualistic way that was his own—leaning the chair back on its two hind legs, as if it were the only way he knew to sit in a chair—that she picked up her fork to force-feed herself for the sake of the communion.

Lila took a bite of the blueberry pie perched on her lap before Mrs. Chalm could have a chance to order her to eat, then Lila studied the blueberries bulging from between the flaking crusts and wondered who the first might have been to have the wrongheaded idea to bake these things into a pie. It was hardly her favorite fruit pie, but she smiled sweetly and ate, as if the pie were a slice of heaven on earth, because that's what Mrs. Chalm wanted to see. But in spite of the blueberries, the pie was good enough for Lila to eat only because she knew that it was made by hands where love flowed through the tips of fingers, and with palms that kneaded with a heart too beholden for words.

What Mrs. Chalm didn't know, could not possibly know, is that her debt was repaid each time Lila saw the peace on Jack's face just from being there, and it was in every fraction of his way. This was his passion, and in so being had become her passion as well.

They were medical missionaries of sorts, with Jack bringing the medicine, and Lila on her mission to cheer the ill and forgotten. Jack had to be more than a doctor, and she had to be more than a doctor's wife. This was all quite plain to her before they married when Jack told her that his medical degree allowed him a sacred entrance to the world of the poor as a healer. He cared nothing for the world, hallowed by most, from which she hailed. And so every Saturday morning, sometimes into the afternoon, Lila followed her husband from one old person's home to the next while he listened to hearts, or palpated livers, or checked the sugar levels in diabetic blood.

Actually Lila did more than eat pie and smile prettily and make small talk. She was his secretary, nurse, assistant, and chaplain all at once, scheduling appointments when desperation called, taking an occasional temperature or holding a nervous hand while Jack drew blood or gave a flu shot. And she was positively indispensable when those old men and women wanted a communion of faith as they'd fall to their wobbly knees in prayer for their soul, or the soul most complexly entwined with their own. The only pay that satisfied them both were the smiles, no longer careworn, on the faces of all the elders who once packed a lunch and punched a clock and poured every drop of sweat into their work, into living in this city, day after day, only to reach their years of twilight and end up cast aside.

So the pride with which she watched him now was about more than his dedication, though that could have been enough. It was also about the energy that was driven by his dedication, which always got him up with the sun on a day that was his own after sometimes being in surgery from the sun's high straight through to its low the day before. Jack knew who needed him, Lila thought as she smiled at her husband, who had just shot a quick love-look at her after taking Mrs. Chalm's blood pressure. He was a man with the clarity of his own purpose and the good sense to see it through, and for this, Lila couldn't imagine loving anyone but him. And even though she was now a Calloway, Jack's purpose made her become a true Giles.

A true Giles, she thought. That family name of hers always

had the power to raise eyebrows or induce deference whenever she claimed it, and in the life she'd left, where Eulelie ruled, Lila had claimed it more times than she could count—sometimes only for the rush of importance she'd get from watching eyebrows raise, or hearing the *oohs* and *ahs* of sycophants who craved entrance into the world that was merely her life. Lila never imagined there would come a time when she would so easily relinquish the name. When marriage was only something that lived amid the things in her hope chest, her mind had things fixed in such a way that any name to which she'd marry would have to fall in behind Giles, and then defer to it; unless, of course, it could hold its own next to it. She would forever, and always, as her former mind knew, be Lila Giles, otherwise who would know her? And who would know that she was set apart? But on the day when every last thing she called her own was moved out of her stepmother's home, the Giles home, and into her safe land, her apartment in Charles Village, Lila Giles became an entity. She became a woman who did not need the renown, and did not want to be set apart, at least not for her name alone. And as she now remembered the morning when she awoke from her first night's sleep in her very own place, Lila knew that she was no longer a small part of a whole. She was Lila, and then Giles, but mostly a complete being.

Just as Jack finished his exam, the sound of Velcro tearing through the room when he ripped the blood-pressure cuff open to free Mrs. Chalm's arm, Lila smiled at the woman, who had given her an impish wink. And then how Mrs. Chalm's eyes twinkled and pranced after the wink. Her eyes, like brown brilliant gems set in the depth of her smooth, midnight face, had the natural shine of the moon. Lila just loved watching those eyes dance over whatever surface they lit upon. Through Lila's mind played the melody of a song, though she couldn't remember the name, but she knew the words of that one line, *Yours are the sweetest eyes I've ever seen. . . .* The song could have been written only for Mrs. Chalm's eyes, because hers were truly the sweetest eyes Lila had ever seen. The flickering light that spread out from them was dazzling in the way it flatly defied her old and ailing body. And Lila supposed those eyes were what made it seem as if an electric stream flowed between Mr. Chalm and his wife whenever he walked into the room to find her smile.

"Did you like that pie, honey?" Mrs. Chalm asked.

"Oh, I sure did, Mrs. Chalm," Lila said, eating the last morsel on the plate. "But Mrs. Chalm, we tell you every time that you don't have to go to all this trouble."

"Honey, it's the very least I can do for the two of you. Ain't that the truth, Chalm," she said to Mr. Chalm, who sat in the corner, still leaning the chair back on its hind legs.

Mrs. Chalm was certainly not the only old woman Lila had ever heard calling her husband by a surname only, but Chalm just seemed somehow awkward, even forced; as if she were thinking of another word altogether like *charming*, or *chum*, but *Chalm* is what slipped out instead.

"And stop that, Chalm, you're gonna fall and bust your head wide open."

"Well, if I do, at least I won't have to go far to get patched up, will I, Doc?" And he rasped a laugh up from his chest filled with years of smoke.

"Mr. Chalm, I can hear you're still smoking," Jack said as he folded his stethoscope back into his bag, then took it out again and unfolded it with a sudden yank. "As a matter of fact, why don't I listen to your lungs right now. I'm not even going to waste my time telling you that you need to stop smoking, because I've told you so often even I'm tired of hearing it, but you really do need to stop."

"I thought you wasn't gonna say nothin'," Mr. Chalm said, cracking himself up as he walked over to the sofa to sit next to his wife.

Jack put the stethoscope to Mr. Chalm's chest, asked for deep breaths, and listened. He lifted his eyebrows in a way that could have meant almost anything. Then he moved the stethoscope to the man's back, asking for more deep breaths, and listened again. Jack smiled ironically, nodded his head, and said, "Well, Mr. Chalm, I don't know how you do it, but your lungs sound good. When was your last chest X ray?"

"Oh, let's see." Mr. Chalm thought, looking up at the ceiling for the answer. "I think it was sometime around Christmas. Ain't that right, Violet?"

"I think it was right before Christmas."

"All right," Jack said, finally folding his stethoscope into his bag and then his blood pressure cuff. He closed the bag with a zip that overtook the room. "The next time I come I'll make arrangements for you to get another one. I'd really like to see you getting a chest X ray every six months or so."

"Sure thing, Doc."

"And Mrs. Chalm, I want you to keep doing what you're doing by taking your blood pressure medicine. Your blood pressure is probably more normal than mine." He then laughed heartily at the possibility of this being true.

"Oh, yes, I take it religiously. I never miss a pill," Mrs. Chalm said, squeezing Jack's hand. "And I want to thank you, Dr. Calloway. And thank you so much for bringing that beautiful bride of yours." Then she looked at Lila and reached for her hand and when Lila took it, said, "I'll tell you, you're as pretty as a painted flower."

And Lila said nothing but smiled her appreciation. She supposed that having her and Jack there as a couple meant more to the old woman than any conversation they ever had, which was always very thin. Mrs. Chalm was more of a sweet smiler than a talker, though she seemed to observe everything in her silence. Like the time Lila and Jack had come there one morning on the heels of an argument over Lila's leaving the car on empty after having driven it all over town the day before. Jack was angry that she'd done it, and she was angry over his anger. What was the big deal? Just put some gas in the car and stop complaining, was Lila's thinking. Besides, she had driven it all over town shopping for groceries that *he* would eat. Somehow, though, Mrs. Chalm knew that something was wrong that day, and Lila could tell she knew by the way the woman's sympathetic eyes pierced Lila's sad face as the old woman was being examined and the way she smiled so coyly at Jack when he took her blood pressure. So just as they were about to leave that day, Mrs. Chalm told them both something that Lila would never forget: "Jesus forgives us no matter what we do, and nobody's above Jesus, so forgive each other." And she said not another word after that except to say good-bye. Lila and Jack took her powerful maxim with them that day and tucked it in their hearts for every argument thereafter.

Lila stood to leave, but just before she got completely to her feet, she bent to give Mrs. Chalm a peck on her cushy cheek, not so much for the compliment the woman had just given her, as for the wisdom from so many months ago. And before Lila knew what was happening, Mrs. Chalm had slipped Lila's hand into Jack's. Lila laughed like a shy schoolgirl. She felt Jack squeeze her hand, as if he were holding on to it for his life, and she laughed even harder, overcome by a quiver that went through her every now and again when she remembered just how much she loved him.

"Mrs. Chalm, you're just too much," Lila said, blushing.

"I am indeed," Mrs. Chalm said with a giggle. "You two have a blessed day, and I'll see you next time."

And with them still joined at the hand, Mr. Chalm saw them out.

"They're a great couple," Lila said after Mr. Chalm had closed the door, leaving them alone on the stoop.

"They sure are. I think that's how we'll be one day, you know," Jack said, smiling at Lila. "We'll still have it bad for each other," and he placed two soft pecks on her lips.

They hurried to the car, Jack following Lila, because even though it was hot, she knew there was a better chance of getting cooler, eventually, in the car, than standing out on the sweltering sidewalk. At least the next stop was home at last, Lila thought with a smile that vanished all her cares, where there were even greater possibilities of cool comfort. She smoothed out the lap of her dress after Jack closed the door, and then, overcome by the thick heat and sparse air, fanned herself furiously, without realizing that she was making herself hotter with the wasted energy. When Jack settled in next to her, all she could do was talk about the obvious. "My God, it's hot."

"It sure is." He wiped a line of perspiration that had started its run down the side of his face. "What do you think it is out there, ninety, ninety-five degrees?"

"Oh, no. It's easily closer to a hundred out there," Lila said, smoothing back her sweat-soaked hair. "Maybe even more. All I know is that it's miserable. At least Mr. and Mrs. Chalm are keeping cool."

"I know, but I keep thinking about the Swans."

"Oh my gosh, yes," Lila said, closing her eyes as if to shut out the thought. "It sure was hot over there this morning, and it was only the morning. Can you imagine what it's like there now? And they've got that little one-month-old great-granddaughter of theirs living with them. I think you should call them when we get home, just to check on them." Then Lila fell silent in thought about the Swans. The very old and the very young together in what had to feel like an oven by now. When you're ninety-two and ninety-three years old like Mr. and Mrs. Swan, she thought, you know what's happening to you. You know why you can't catch a cool breath. And you know why the air is thick with enough water to drown. But when you've only been in the world for a month, my God, she thought, how in the world do you understand the notion of soggy air when there's no rain in sight?

"You know what, Lila, every time I walk into the Swans' house, or the Chalms' house, or any of my weekend patients' houses and open my bag to start an exam, I get—I don't know, I guess really proud of myself. I mean, when I was a kid coming up down in Cherry Hill, it was the absolute worst the way my parents had to use the emergency room as our doctor because we didn't have health insurance. We didn't have a family doctor, or anything like that, you know. And everybody in our neighborhood lived the same way, so you would think I would have thought that it was normal, since it was all I knew, all I saw." Jack stopped as if the reality of his memory was too full in its displeasing color for him to continue to ponder. He looked out the window, checked the mirrors, then shook his head, seemingly with the pain of a recollection in which he'd never find good times. "But I've gotta tell you, I knew it wasn't normal when I saw, and could feel, the way they'd treat us in the emergency room when we went in there compared to the way they'd treat people coming in there with health insurance. Oh, we'd get seen and get treated, and all, but only after all those insured people were tended to. And there were never any niceties, you know. Nothing like, 'Oh, little Jack, you're such a sweet boy.' Or, 'Jack, do you like baseball?' It was just fix us up and move us out. Like we were cattle or something. And they always gave us that skeptical look, as if they thought they just might have some part of themselves stolen away if they came closer to us than duty called. More than anything, though, I remember feeling overwhelming shame. Ashamed of being poor, ashamed of being black."

The only new sentiment in this story—that Lila had heard more times than she had heard about the happier times—of his childhood was his shame at being black and poor. She still responded empathetically. "I can't even pretend to know how that must have felt. It must have been horrible to be ashamed of something you can't help. You never told me about feeling shame before."

"Be glad that you can't imagine it. And yeah, it does something really bad to a kid's spirit when he's made to feel as if he should be apologizing for the very essence of himself, and apologizing for conditions into which he was born. You know, over here on the west side, some people complained about the old Providence Hospital with horror stories that may or may not have been true, but all I know is that at least at Providence, black people had a place they could go for medical care and at the same time be treated with some dignity by their own people." Jack curved around onto the Lake Park Drive, then sped up only to have to slam on the brakes after getting caught by the light.

"Well, Jack, you should feel proud of yourself. You know, if your career were suddenly to end next week, you still will have done more in the years you've been a doctor than the majority who've been doctors for most of their lives. I really believe that, so you have a reason to be proud. And we both know that the doctor you are right now has everything to do with the shame you felt back then. Thank God for those days, because had your life been any different than it was, the Chalms and the Swans and the Jacksons and all the others would not have the dignity that you give them."

Jack took his eyes from their watch on the red light only long enough to smile at Lila. "You're right, Lila. I guess there was a reason for the shame." When the light changed and Jack started off again, his face grew sullen once more. "I still get really anxious, though, when one of them has to go into the hospital, because the hospital's been really good at giving pro bono treatment on the few occasions when I've had to hospitalize someone. So I'm right there with them, you know. But one of these times they just might say no and then they'll end up in Liberty Medical where I don't have privileges. I'm sure they'd be treated well there, but still, some other doctor could possibly give them conflicting information on their condition just because they don't have a history with them." It seemed that Jack was thinking out loud more than he was talking to Lila. "I guess it helps to know that what I can do for them is help to prevent them from having to go in the hospital in the first place."

"Exactly," was all that Lila said before she was distracted by the Druid Hill Park reservoir, and how inviting it looked, especially with that fountain throwing gallons of water into the air that just had to be cold, she was sure. She wanted to drink it, wanted to be in it. Lila wanted its cooling faculty in any way she could get it. And just like that, her oasis was gone as Jack curved around onto Twenty-eighth Street, leaving her with only her fantasies of finding a cool spot anyplace in this city that was burning.

"I'm going to stop here at this store and get a Coke," Jack said, pulling the car over to the curb.

Lila regarded, for no longer than it took her to blink, three pink-faced, pink-necked men bumbling around the store, but staring with intent at the car, before she said frantically, "No, no, Jack! Please don't stop. I just want to get home and sit under the air conditioner. This air conditioner is doing nothing. Besides, this place looks so scummy. You'd actually want to buy something in there?"

"I do all the time on my way home from the hospital," he said.

"Well, thank God you've spared me till now. Please, let's just go home." Then she blew out a frustrated sigh, realizing that after nearly two years of marriage, this was one of those quirks she'd once found endearing, almost charming, and certainly part of what put stars in her eyes in their six months of courting. The innocence of his being hooked on Coca-Cola. How absolutely sweet and childlike. Now, though, thinking about the nearly two years of their marriage during which she'd shared him with a libation she was not terribly certain he wouldn't choose over her if it were ever to come down to that, she wanted nothing more than to go home and hurl each and every bottle and can from their home and into their front yard in a fit of maniacal, low-down rage. And it would not matter who saw.

"Lila, I'm only going to be a minute. Probably not even that. I'll leave the air on for you, okay? I'll be right back." And with that he was out of the car.

All Lila could think of was the heat as she sat in the car outside the small package goods store under the heavy arm of the noonday sun, trying to cool herself in the air blasting from the vents. She turned them all, every single one she could reach, to blow on her, and still she seemed to get no relief. Beads of perspiration dripped from her temples, lines of body water slid down her chest to disappear beneath the scoop of her sundress. She was damp all over and felt as if she'd just been dipped into a pool of warm water. Jack had left her in the car no more than five seconds ago, and already she was impatient for him to get back. Somehow, Lila believed, with the car standing still, she was certainly hotter.

Coca-Cola. He loved Coke and had to have one; just couldn't wait until they got home, where there'd be cases of the stuff. And then there was this part of Twenty-eighth Street, which she just hated, that added to the heat. It always made her heart sink, made her feel the longing in the desperate souls of all those white faces, made pink under the sun's fire, going here and there, some in rubber thong sandals, others in cheap vinyl imitations of leather sandals, not abjectly, or even indecently, poor but still longing for a better life, to which some, possibly all, may have thought their color entitled them. Stuck with the hope of release. As if in purgatory.

As Jack appeared from behind the back of the car, Lila put her face squarely at the window to get his attention. Hurry up, she would tell him. It's hot, she would let him know by fanning herself. But Jack couldn't see her, wouldn't see her. He had his head, his eyes, set straight ahead of him, on the store, even though those three pink-faced, pink-necked men standing around outside the store were trying their best to engage him. Maybe, she thought, Jack wouldn't look at these mutts because of the one pink man who wore shorts that were so short and so tight that they showed his gittels, as Lila had come to call a man's private parts, pilfering the euphemism from old Mrs. Chalm. Those gittels were like a magnet in all of their repulsiveness, so no wonder Jack wouldn't look at any one of the men. If he even looked in their general direction, those gittels were certain to draw his eyes to them.

Lila noticed that there was one man in particular, the largest and pinkest, who seemed to be the most vociferous, saying something to Jack that did not provoke the smile that started her every day. This was odd, she thought, for her husband who under most conditions conducted himself with the Southern courtliness of a man straight from the age when men tipped their hats and called womenfolk ma'am. What could they have possibly been saying to him that would have set his jaws so tightly and cause his bearing to become so intractable? But to put the window down to hear, or to interrupt, would have let in more heat than would ever dissolve in the car's barely coolish interior.

Jack was nearly at the door of the store now, but hurrying him on was no longer her concern. Something was not right, and she could see it in her husband's stiffened body and that vein that she could not see yet knew had risen up on his right-side temple. There was something wickedly repugnant on that corner in front of that store, as fetid as raw chicken in the sun; this she could discern without hearing because the tension was sturdy enough to push through glass and steel. But mostly she knew something was wrong from the men's gape-mouthed laughter, laughter that did not seduce Jack. And just as she saw Jack, from the corner of her left eye, pull the handle of the store's door, she saw the words, clearly formed and spat from the red-mustachioed mouth of the biggest, pinkest man—*Dr. Porch Monkey*, he said.

Lila's mouth hung open with incredulity, because he couldn't have possibly said something so base. No one, she thought, could still be living with the kind of insipid loathing that would bring him to say such a thing. But this was all she needed to see to know that her husband was quite possibly, quite justly on the verge of losing himself in the heat of the moment, in the heat of this day. Lila shot her eyes at Jack, who didn't even seem to miss a step as he glided like smoke through the door and into the store, and only then did she snatch her face from the window and try to calm her heart, which was pounding for her life, and with the prayer that they'd make it home with their lives intact.

She thought about those words, and their like, which she'd never actually ever heard hurled at her, or for that matter, at anyone she loved. They were the kind of words that had been so used up in the South of decades past as a tool for maiming that they should no longer have teeth. By now, they should have simply found their way into extinction, or nonuse, as had *thee* or *thou*. They shouldn't be able to bite, or sting, or hurt anymore. So why did they? And why did *porch monkey*, particularly, strike at her so viscerally? Possibly, she presumed, because it was so descriptive, so graphic, coming from the depths of a particular kind of white mind and conjuring in her own consciousness the images that they must see of beacon-white teeth shining out from the faces of indolent happy darkies of all tones, rocking on any porch, anywhere in America, from any walk of life. And what was it about sitting on porches? Oh, how something so innocuous and ordinary can be turned into something so ugly in a mind incapable of seeing otherwise. So now, she was stuck pondering what one does when one is called a porch monkey in the twenty-first century. Does one riot? Fight? Sue? March? But what would not leave her mind were the most appealing of her musings on requital, and they were so vast, so vicious, so completely against her nature that they raised her temperature, both physically and metaphorically. Cursing. Socking. Burning. Stabbing. Interminable and sadistic torture. Every extreme was within the realm of plausibility for her.

He was dead in her imaginings, his fat belly heaving up and down, his face in slack-jawed shock at Lila the meek, slayer of the North American Redneck; and as he took his last gurgled breaths, she'd stand over him, maybe kick him once or twice, then she'd twist the heel of her pump into his shoulder until it pierced, or he passed out from the pain. Yet, she would not laugh, because vengeance is not at all funny, and vengeance, like a thick membrane, would certainly cover her cold, steely eyes. Then Lila would walk away with the same detachment from any and all human relativity with which he'd uttered those foul words.

And her plea would be so simple: *She simply blanked out, Your Honor* is what she imagined her attorney, more than likely her brother, telling the judge. *Mrs. Calloway was rendered mentally incapacitated at that moment when she thought her husband was under attack by the victim and she did not know what she was doing when she stabbed, then shot him. She was temporarily insane, Your Honor.* She'd pretend to be genuinely disgusted by her act once her mind was back from its deranged journey, but deep inside she'd be comforted by the thought that vengeance belonged to her.

Lila sat deep in thoughts of the hypothetical for only seconds before Jack reappeared through the door, and when she caught his form from her eye's corner, she turned her face back to the window to watch him, to will him safely back into the car beside her. And with his face, his manner, still set in stone, yet somehow seeming to float above the mire, he glided back to the car and slid in beside her.

Lila looked at Jack expectantly. Surely he'd have something to say about the vileness through which he'd just walked. But he merely sat there, to her amazement, opening his Coke and then taking a long swig with such pleasure, with so little care, that just watching him made her wonder if perhaps she had read the wrong words slithering from that man's lips. She waited until she could wait not a second longer. "Jack, who are those men?"

Jack looked at her with a side-turned smile that showed no teeth. "Lila, who do you think they are?"

"Rednecks. I think they're rednecks, Jack," she said with flat absoluteness.

"Okay, then. You didn't need to ask me."

"Jack, did that man call you what I think he called you?" Lila shook her head with a closed-eye disavowal. "I read his lips, and I just hope that I misread what he said."

Jack swigged more of his Coke until the bottle was only half full. He let the rush subside, then said, "What was it you told me your father used to say? Something about what does a cracker call a black judge? And then you said he would answer it by saying *nigger*. Well believe it, Lila, believe it. Your father's old saying is old enough for it to not still be true, yet it is."

Lila slid down into her seat and pondered her anger, wondering with whom she was angriest—at the pink men for being so unthinkably backwater, or with Jack for being above it all. Just look at him, she thought as she watched him drive, turning this corner, then that, humming to the music playing low on the radio, drinking his Coke as if it were some sort of antidote for hatred. It's only Coca-Cola, for God's sake! she screamed in her mind. It cannot make this go away! It happened to him, yet she was the incensed one. He endured the kind of contempt whose depravity could have dissolved into calamity, yet she was the one who could have killed. And Jack, with his lightness of being, was so irritating. Irritating in the way it made her doubt herself, because Jack was acting as if the vileness was long forgotten or maybe hadn't even happened at all. "Jack," she finally said in that whispery voice she used when she was just not going to let something lie. "How can you—"

But Jack said, "Lila, I'm serious now. I do not want to talk about that cracker back there. It's over."

But it wasn't over. How could it be over with something so obscene swimming around in her mind? It harkened back to a darkness of which she had no real memory, and it was inexcusable, unforgivable. So Lila would not press, but it was far from over for her as she sat staring at their house while Jack parked in front of it. She thought about what she could do, once in her refuge, to heal her agitated soul, because there was no end to how deeply she was wounded; wounded enough for both of them.

But the walk through the heat from the car and to the house was what turned her mind from the pink men to her aggravation with nature. "Thank goodness I don't have to come back out into this heat again until Monday," she said to Jack, who did not respond but simply opened the door so she could walk through. "There's no way I can make it through church tomorrow with this heat being like it is and the church having no airconditioning. I just can't do it. On the news last night they said the heat and humidity should break by Monday. That's what I'm waiting for." Lila walked past Jack and over the threshold into the front hall to find that it was surprisingly cool enough to make her feel more than a bit refreshed. But when she went to the living room, the illusion was gone. She slipped out of her sandals, stretched out on the sofa, and wished for Monday to bring with it the hope of claiming Baltimore back from what had seized it. But as she closed her eyes all she could see was pink. Three pink faces, and one pinker than all the rest.

c h a p t e r t w o

LILA WALKED WITH Jack up Calvert Street with a stillness imposed on her by the drag of Monday morning, and it mingled with the heat that still hung—its promise to acquiesce broken—over Baltimore like a wet wool blanket, threatening to suffocate. She would have taken his hand, wanted to take his hand, the way she always did on any ordinary morning, but the mere thought of touching anyone, even Jack, made her hotter. In spite of their not touching, she was pleased by their morning ritual of Jack's walking her to work.

When Jack and Lila met, she had enthralled him completely with her dream of being a sort of female Mr. Rogers of cyberspace. *Miss Lila's Neighborhood*, she jocularly told Jack. She had this vision of an Internet story hour where millions of children all over the world would visit *Lila Lilly's Story Hour* site and listen to her very own stories of mythological proportions as well as the children's stories of other black writers—they had to be black writers because they needed a break. And once a week, with one of her stories, she'd stop short of the ending, allowing the children to write their own endings.

She got the idea from some woman who put a camera on herself every evening at six o'clock so that anyone who logged on to her site could watch her cook dinner. The woman was such a good cook, and her site and her recipes were so popular, that the woman actually got a job as a chef in a posh Los Angeles restaurant. Well, Lila didn't want anything like that to happen to her, but she believed the Internet was the only way to fulfill the creativity screaming to break free of the bondage of a classroom.

Lila had tired of teaching by her second day on the job, but duty and a will not her own forced her through the seven-year-long sieve of making a sensible living. When she met Jack, all it took was one simple question from him—*What would be your dream job?*—to get Lila talking about a dream so vivid it was clear that she could actually see it, and that she saw it in more than just theory.

She had every minute of her days planned out up until the moment when she'd turn on her cyber camera and enchant little ones without having to scold them constantly to stay in their seats, or stop talking, or spit out the gum. And even though the incentive was that she could reach children without ever having to deal with their unpleasant sides, it was Jack who had to push Lila out of the classroom and into her dream. So, without telling her, he rented a studio apartment over on Calvert Street, two blocks from where they lived, and set it up with every cyber thing she could ever need, or imagine she'd need. It was beyond generous, what he did. To Lila, what Jack did came from a place in him where deep, abiding respect for her lived, and on that day when he walked her, blindfolded, into her dream, she believed that no other man could ever love and respect another woman on this planet with as much intensity as he loved and respected her. Lila imagined being ninety-five years old, senile as a nanny goat, and still never forgetting that feeling, and it was particularly poignant on this special day.

When they reached the steps of the row house, Jack took her hand and pulled her to him. Then he put both hands on her waist and asked, "Do you even remember what today is, Lila?"

She gave him a crooked smile with her head cocked sideways. "What do you think? Of course I remember what today is. Two years ago on this very day, at this very hour, fresh from our honeymoon, you were walking me, blindfolded, up these steps, into the house, and up into my office." She threw her head back and laughed with the heart-rushing giddiness of that two-years-ago moment. "I had no idea where you were taking me, but with the blindfold and all, I was certain you were taking me to some wacky surprise party, even though there was no reason for one and—"

"And it was nine o'clock in the morning," Jack said, laughing just as heartily as she. "Who in the world is gonna give you a surprise party at nine in the morning?"

"I don't know," Lila said, laughing so hard in the thick, still air that she had to work to catch a breath. And when she grew serious, she confessed, "You know, the faith you showed in me by doing all this, setting all this up, is what helps me make it work."

"Naw," Jack denied, shaking his head modestly, almost shyly. "You're making this work because it was already real for you. All I did was give you the hardware."

Lila looked into Jack's eyes and a rush took over her as she thought about his mother, Cordelia, and her dream to be a dancer. She would dream out loud, she remembered Jack told her, about dancing on Broadway like Debbie Allen, or Ann Reinking, or with Alvin Ailey like Judith Jamison. The life he had growing up, Lila knew, was not a life in which dreams could be fulfilled. But this life was, and so he realized hers.

Jack lighted a soft kiss on Lila's lips, and said, "Anyway, you go on. I've got to run. I've got two surgeries today, and so I may be late tonight. I'll call you and let you know."

Lila squeezed his hand, then trotted up the steps to the porch. And once she got the door open, she turned to Jack, still standing on the sidewalk watching her, protecting her, and said, "I love you." Then she watched him merely smile and walk on his way before she closed the door with the slam and hip bump it needed in the humid days of summer.

Lila climbed the first flight of stairs, then the second in the stale air of the row house. When she reached her office, she turned the key in the door, and it wasn't until the door was open just beyond a crack that she could hear Nell, her assistant, already at work. Lila stepped into the office and took in the cool comfort of the room. She gave the door a soft push closed, then

looked around and found Nell on the set, fussing over the fresh
flowers she'd brought in for the vase that sat just beyond Lila's
left shoulder during *Lila Lilly's Story Hour.*

"Oh, Nell, you are wonderful," Lila said, breathing out a sigh
of satisfaction. "This feels so refreshing. Thank you so much."
She took in Nell as she left the set and crossed the room,
headed purposefully for her desk.

"What?" Nell said, staring with round-eyed puzzlement. "Oh,
you mean the air conditioner? Oh, well . . ." she trailed off then
smiled naturally and added, "You're welcome."

Lila smiled as she thought of the comfort she felt with Nell.
To Lila, Nell was a woman who stepped into her life straight
from another era, when children regarded their parents' friends
as Mr. or Mrs. So-and-so, or when milk came in homey glass
bottles left on the front porch by the door. And when she
looked at Nell, she could scarcely believe that they were con-
temporaries, because Nell had honed so well the art, lost to so
many women their age, of how to take care of things. Mostly,
though, to Lila, Nell was a woman who had been a mother and
wife for so long that she didn't know what else to do but take
care of things, and she had most likely, most certainly, forgotten
how to let anyone take care of her. "So how was your weekend,
Nell?" Lila said, settling in behind her desk and turning on her
computer.

"It was good," Nell said, placing a plastic tumbler on Lila's
desk and pouring lemonade and ice cubes into it from a thermos. "I made this lemonade for us today. I figured we could use
it because you know that this is our much-dreaded E-mail Monday. I downloaded all the E-mails from the kids who wrote their
endings to Friday's story. Most of them are really good, but
there are a lot, Lila, a whole lot. I sifted through them all and
put aside the ones I think we should choose to read today, and
then the rest we can just post on the Web site, but it still leaves
us more than enough. So this is what I think we should do.
Instead of reading stories for the first half hour, I think the
whole hour should be devoted to reading the endings. Trust
me, with all this mail we got, you'll be certain to fill the entire

hour with just this alone." Nell screwed the top back on her thermos, then continued answering Lila's question about the weekend as if the thought had never been interrupted. "Anyway, all I did this weekend was more of the same, you know, take the boys to their softball games, take my daughter to her piano lesson. Lila, you know my weekends never change from one to the next."

"Yeah, well I asked because you never know when something different might happen."

"So, what do you think about today? Do you think that will work?"

Lila looked over at a stack of papers in the middle of Nell's desk and widened her eyes, as if it were too much to take in with just a glance. "All those are the responses we got for the end of the story?"

"Yeah, that's what I'm telling you. We got a lot."

"Okay, then, I guess you're right. We'll just spend the hour reading the endings. That's best anyway, because I haven't finished this new story I started writing over the weekend. I'm trying to get it just right because I want to read it on Friday." She took a long drink of lemonade, closing her eyes in rapture as the cold liquid slid down her throat. "God, Nell," she finally gushed, "this is great. Nobody can make lemonade like you. Thank you so much. You think of everything."

"You're welcome," Nell said with a humble smile as she sat behind her own desk facing Lila's. "It's a necessity on a day like today."

"Well, you know what happened to me and Jack this weekend? We were coming back from Mrs. Chalm's house—you remember, I told you about old Mrs. Chalm, one of Jack's elderly, Saturday patients." Lila waited for Nell's confirming nod before continuing with the story. "Okay, so anyway, Jack pulls up in front of this little store over near Twenty-eighth and Howard to get—what else—Coca-Cola. So, on the corner are these three white guys, you know those kind of people who live over in that area. Anyway, they're saying something to Jack that I can't hear because I'm sitting in the car and the windows are up and the radio's on and so is the air conditioner. Still, something doesn't feel right to me about the way these guys are looking at Jack and talking to him, and Jack's not responding at all. Then, this big old fat white guy calls Jack Dr. Porch Monkey just as Jack is going into the store." Lila paused to take in Nell's complete slack-jawed astonishment before continuing. "I'm telling you, Nell, I didn't know what to do. I was scared, then I was crushed, then I was angry enough to kill that fat son of a whore."

"So what did Jack do?" Nell asked eagerly, as if salivating for a good-conquers-evil ending.

"Get this." Lila inched her face across her desk, in Nell's direction, as if her neck could stretch it clear across the expanse. Then slowly, and overarticulating every word, she said, "Jack did nothing."

"What?"

"I'm telling you, he did nothing. Zip. Zero. He just got back in the car after he got his soda and we drove home. Can you believe it? I was so mad at him."

Nell sat for a second, thinking, then smiled matter-of-factly and stated, "Well, Lila, Jack is a peace-loving man. You know that. He doesn't start trouble and he doesn't go looking for trouble."

"Yeah, Nell, but this time trouble came right up to him and spit in his face. How do you just not do anything when something like that happens? I mean, I'm all for keeping the peace and steering clear of trouble, but come on. This kind of thing pushes those boundaries way beyond what's acceptable."

Nell got up and walked across the room again to pour more lemonade into Lila's nearly empty cup. She went back to her own desk and poured more in her own cup, and when she sat down at her desk again, she took a sip, then asked, "Lila, have you ever been called that word, or anything like it?"

"No, Nell, because growing up, my world was so insulated. Anything I ever needed or wanted I got either from my family or other black families like mine. And I think that's what makes me so mad. Who does that guy think he is, Nell? Who does he think he's talking to?"

"It doesn't matter who he thinks he is, or for that matter, whether he knows who he's talking to," Nell said without a trace of passion. "It doesn't even matter who he is at all. The fact is, Lila, you have been called that word and worse, you just don't know that you have because you've never heard it. But trust me, it's been said about you. About your family. About your husband. And when you have children, it will probably be said about them. But let me ask you something. Assuming that you have been called that word without your knowing it, has it made any difference in your day-to-day existence? *Does* it make a difference to your daily existence?"

"No. But, God, Nell, what are you saying? That most white people think that way?"

"All I'm saying is that whether you're a child, or a wife, or a mother, that word can still loom in your life, whether it's actually said to you or not, and it's up to you to determine just how much it's going to touch you."

Lila drank her lemonade, thinking about what Nell had just said, then she asked, "So, have you been called that word before?"

"Yes, many, many times." Then she laughed ironically, reeling back in her chair. "And look at me, Lila. I'm little. I'm plain. I wear not an ounce of makeup. I look like a mom. A car pool mom, at that. I'm about as nonthreatening as you can get, but I've been called that word, out of anger, out of fear, out of hatred, out of all of it. Who knows? To me, though, that word just sounds like *it*, or *the*, or *wall*. I don't feel it. You know, when you get hit in the same spot enough times, eventually you just don't feel it. Maybe that's Jack, Lila. Maybe he doesn't feel it."

"Well, I feel it." Lila stopped and stared off at nothing. She gave Nell a pressed-lipped smile and said, "I guess I just haven't been hit enough. Or at all."

"Oh, I almost forgot, Lila," Nell chirped, nearly panicked.

"You've got another E-mail from that woman, Barbara Gallagher. Do you want me to print it?"

"Yes, would you please?" Lila got up and went to Nell's desk to watch and wait over her shoulder. "You know, she's such a big fan. It feels kind of nice to have this kind of constant validation from a parent."

"Well, I'm a parent, and I say that what we're doing is great. Doesn't my opinion count?" Nell asked, her eyes trained on the computer screen.

"You're hardly objective, Nell. After all, you do have a vested interest here."

"True," Nell agreed as she plucked the letter from the printer tray and handed it to Lila. "You know, though, there's something odd about the fact that when she writes, she never mentions a child. Have you noticed that?"

"Yes I have, but I didn't really think anything of it until after her third letter." She paused long enough to skip her eyes across the page, looking for key words, and then noted, "And this is her fourth letter to me and she still doesn't say anything about a child. How odd."

"Are you going to write her back?" Nell asked with eyebrows raised.

"Yes, of course. I always write her back."

"I didn't know that."

"Well, yeah, I write her back, but my letters are nowhere near as in-depth as hers. I just keep mine very simple, thanking her for supporting what we're trying to do, and talking about our interest in educating children in a way that makes them want to learn. Stuff like that." Lila went back to her desk, reading the letter as she walked. And when she was halfway through, she sat, looked at Nell determinedly and said, "But you know what? This time, I'm going to write to her, really write to her. I don't know for sure, but I think she's more than just a bored, childless housewife with too much time to kill."

"Maybe she's trying to pick our brains to become competition," Nell said.

"Or she could be someone who has always wanted to write

children's stories but never had the chance and now sees us as a good opportunity to do some writing. She could be just what we need, Nell. I think it would be nice to have more original stories other than mine. I know it would take some of the pressure off me. And maybe she's a writer *and* an illustrator. It could take some of the load off you, you know."

"My load's just fine, thank you."

"Well, anyway, I didn't mean it like that." And Lila settled back into her chair and started the letter again from the beginning, afraid she might have missed something in the intermittent distraction of talking to Nell.

Dear Lila Lilly:

I hope you're not tired of my saying this, but it just makes me feel good to know that there are people like you on the Internet who're really committed to children. The way you speak to the children, not talking down to them, lets me know that your love for children is the genuine article. When I think of the sinister minds that children can so often fall prey to, it makes me sleep better at night knowing that there's someone on the Internet who's not trying to sexually victimize children or brainwash them. Your site is good, clean, wholesome fare. A mother can let her child log on to it and then walk away without anxiety or fear for one solid hour.

I know you must have a child or two of your own, just by the way your love for your little cyber kids is so warm and sincere. How old are your kids, and how many do you have? Do they ever come there and watch you while you're doing Lila Lilly's Story Hour? I know they must be so proud of their mom.

Well, good-bye for now. I look forward to tomorrow's story. And thank you, again, for giving yourself to children.

Most sincerely,
Barbara Gallagher

Lila put the letter down and then leaned over her desk on her elbows, thinking about what she might say to Barbara Gallagher.

Would she simply tell her that she doesn't have any children, and then leave it at that? Or would she tell her that even though she doesn't have any children, she's more ready than she's ever been to be someone's mother? And if she were to go that far in revealing herself to this cyber friend/stranger, she'd also have to tell Barbara Gallagher how, nowadays, she can scarcely pass by a baby carriage without looking in to see the baby. Just the mere sight of a baby, she would tell her, can make her heart smile. But then she wondered if she'd tell Barbara Gallagher how just seeing a baby is slowly growing to be not enough.

"Boy, she must have said something that really got you to thinking," Nell said. "You're way gone."

"She thinks I have children, Nell," Lila said, very close to melancholy. "Do I really look like a woman who has children?" Lila asked, trying to suppress a shadowy smile that couldn't help but reveal her thrill at the thought.

"Well, let me see," Nell teased with a humorous lilt. "No, you don't look like you could have children. You don't have that far-away look in your eyes that says you just might be right on the edge of insanity. When you get that look, you'll look like a mother."

"I'm serious, Nell. I mean, I look at you, and even if I didn't know you, I think I would know that you're a mother. In fact, the first time I met you and Chuck I could tell you were a mother. There's just this special look that mothers have that the rest of us don't."

"Lila, what are you talking about? I was just joking with you before. And besides, you knew I was a mother the first time you met me because Jack probably told you before we met. There's no special look that mothers have that other women don't have. I guess one telltale sign to let you know for sure is if she's hauling around a big old diaper bag. Now that's a sure sign that she's a mother. Other than that, Lila, there's no look."

"No, Nell, I'm telling you that there is a look. And that's another thing. Women with children carry larger purses. Whenever you see a woman with a big purse, you can rest assured she's got children. You'd never catch a mother carrying around one of these little cutesy, girly, tiny bags like this one." She held up her dainty black purse, no bigger than a large wallet, with a perfectly curved handle. "This is not a mother's bag."

"Okay, that's probably true, Lila. But on the other hand, I've seen plenty of childless women hauling around big purses. I don't know, Lila. All I can say is that you shouldn't be worried about whether you look like a mother or not, but you should be asking yourself seriously if you want to be a mother. Do you want to be a mother, Lila? You say you do, but have you really thought about how motherhood would change your life, considering you're married to a heart surgeon and would probably end up feeling like a single mother most of the time, as I do?"

"I think about it all the time, Nell, and I've thought about all of it. It's easy to hire somebody to help, you know. But I think about having a baby more and more, and I think about it nowadays more than I seem to think about anything else. This time last year, having a baby hadn't crossed my mind. Now, a baby can pop into my mind at the most unexpected time. And I know that I'm ready, Nell, because my concept of myself as a mother has grown from just being the mother of a baby to being the mother of an older child."

"Well, it sounds like you are ready, Lila, because most women, and that would be myself included before I had a baby, think about having a baby and then don't think about that baby beyond those really young years. I'm telling you, my boys are a challenge, Lila. And I'm not even ready for the hell that girl of mine is going to take me through once she turns thirteen and those monthly hormones start kicking in. I'm telling you, girl, I'm scared. But if you want to make sure you're ready, spend an afternoon with my kids, and then let me know. If you can survive an hour with my boys the way they argue with each other, then you will have earned your stripes."

"Okay, well just bring them to me."

"Don't say what you don't mean, girl." And Nell laughed heartily.

"Oh, I don't. And you forget, I taught in the Baltimore City

public schools. I think I'd surprise you." And Lila smiled, knowing that what was most important is that she would not surprise
herself. She thought about what she'd say to Barbara Gallagher
as she turned to her computer. Nothing came to her in a tight
and complete form, but what she knew was that she'd take her
first step beyond the general politeness that she'd always given
the woman. What would have to come across, what Lila could
not close the letter without giving, was her thanks for being
mistaken for a mother. So she pointed and clicked her way to
her blank E-mail page, and once she started typing, all that she
needed to say, all that was appropriate, came to her seemingly
without thought or hesitation.

Dear Barbara:

   Again, I thank you so for your kind words about Lila Lilly's
Story Hour. *In my mind, I know that what we do here is good
for children, but it always feels reassuring to have validation
from someone like you.*
   *In your letter, you said that you could tell that I have chil-
dren. Well, I thank you, Barbara, for the compliment, because
I think it is high praise to have someone tell me I look like a
mother, given how badly I would like to be a mother. The truth
is, Barbara, I don't have any children. Maybe one day I will be
so lucky as to have my own child watch me put* Lila Lilly's Story
Hour *together, and maybe he or she will be very proud. Until
then, I have to be satisfied with the smiles and love I get
through the children who log on.*

                         It's always good to hear from you.
                                        Lila Calloway

She clicked, and it was gone, just like that, on its way to Barbara Gallagher. Lila smiled with thoughts of the possibilities.

THE CITY WAS still caught in the heat wave, and though Friday
brought the week's end, it offered no relief. It was almost *Story*

Hour time, as Lila went over to the set. It had been designed to give viewers the feeling of the sheltering warmth of a grand-mother's living room, with the promise of cookies still steaming on a plate from the oven. She settled herself on the sofa in front of the camera with her story in one hand, Nell's illustrations to the story in the other. It was less than a half hour before Nell would turn on the cyber-cam for *Story Hour,* and Lila was still touching up her story-with-no-end. Nell began poking and combing straying strands of Lila's hair, and Lila sat, stiff as a rail, trying to read over her story, making marks here and there. She put Nell's illustrations beside her on the sofa when they threat-ened to slide from her bony lap.

"Are you almost ready?" Nell said.

"Yeah, I'm ready."

"Okay. I'm going to see how you look on the screen." She aimed the camera at Lila, then fidgeted a bit. "You look great." She stepped away from that camera and turned to the one pointed at the easel where her illustrations would stand. She picked them up from the space next to Lila on the sofa, and when she went to order them according to the story, she saw that Lila had already done it. So she went to the easel and propped up the whole stack.

Lila placed her story in her lap with a look of satisfaction that said she was ready. She watched Nell focus the camera on the illustrations, then said, "Nell, I wish I had half the ability to paint the way you do."

"And I wish I had half your talent to write. The stories you create, I'm telling you, are just incredible. I read your stories and think, Where in the world did she come up with this idea?" Nell let out a quiet laugh, mostly to herself. "Although, I have to tell you, it's not hard to figure out where you got this story. It's pretty obvious that this one came from what happened to you and Jack last week."

"Is it that obvious?" Lila said with an abashed smile, turning her face away with diffidence. But today had to be the day for this story, because it allowed her to live in one of those rare but hallowed moments where the morals of fresh souls are molded, and Lila didn't take lightly her responsibility, albeit in part, for shaping the characters of children.

"Oh, Lila, come on. Of course it's obvious."

Lila looked off in a daze and thought about her story of the Boochies, magical nymphs who look like regular people except for their long earlobes that almost touch their shoulders, who'd come in the night to the homes of villagers who want impossible wishes to come true. But nobody knows it's the Boochies making the impossible happen, so they mock them and say cruel things to them because of their unusual ears. So one day, a mean villager begins taunting the leader of the Boochies, slapping at his earlobes and telling him that since his ears look like donkey ears he should give the villager a donkey ride. So the mean villager jumps on the Boochie's back to ride him like a donkey, and all the people in town watch and laugh and join in the mockery by hee-hawing like donkeys. When the taunting is over and the Boochie is sent on his way, he goes with a broken heart. How could all those people the Boochies only want to help treat them so cruelly? And so the question, the ending Lila would ask her children to create, is: what should the Boochies do?

When she came out of Boochie-land, Lila looked up at Nell, who was still looking at her, as if waiting for some sort of answer. "You know, Nell, I guess Jack and I *are* the Boochies."

"Yeah, I know." Nell looked over at the grandfather clock, which was a clock that really worked instead of simply standing against the wall as a prop, and got to her feet. She checked Lila through the camera one last time and said, "Okay, it's time." And with that, she turned on the camera and gave Lila the cue to start the story hour.

"Good afternoon, young minds. If you come to visit me regularly, then you know what will happen today. It's Friday, which means that you get to finish my story. Today's story is the story of the Boochies." And Lila paused to smile at herself, because maybe on Monday, she'd finally know what to do.

chapter three

 HE NEXT MORNING Jack and Lila stood on the Belamys'
porch, waiting for the door to open. It always seemed to be an
interminable wait, between the time they'd ring the bell and the
time it was answered, for Mrs. Belamy to hobble to the door
with her walker, or for half-deaf Mr. Belamy to realize it was
actually the doorbell he'd heard and not some other indistinct,
insignificant sound. There was a noise coming from some distance on the other end of the door, so Lila knew that shelter
from the sun, bearing down hard on the porch, on her back,
baking her skin—sun that had by now become positively insuf-
ferable for Lila—was on the way. The door crept open with the
slowness of the old woman's hand. But Lila craned her neck,
trying to see which half of the couple had opened the door, as
the faint light in the gloomy house only backlit the stooped figure, which did not come fully into the door's frame, but stood
back, as if afraid of the heat certain to rush into the house. Since
both Mr. and Mrs. Belamy were of equal size and equal hunch,
Lila didn't want to make the mistake of calling one the other.
And the beveled glass in the storm door didn't exactly make for
clear vision, but Lila was almost certain there was a glint from
the sun on the rounded edge of a walker.

"Mrs. Belamy?" she called.

"Yes, darling. Come on in," the woman said, her frail voice
chipper with her delight at seeing them.

Jack followed Lila across the threshold and closed the door as Lila walked slowly beside Mrs. Belamy into the living room, her arms seemingly on their guard, as if expecting the feeble woman to crumble to the floor at any moment. Lila's gait was tentative, and she couldn't speak, since her preoccupation with the need to keep the woman walking erect was overwhelming for her. But when Mrs. Belamy reached her chair and eased into it, Lila finally said, "You look terrific, Mrs. Belamy. I swear, you're about the only one in this city not wilting from this heat."

"Oh, this heat is nothing. Why, I can remember way back when I was a girl in Savannah, and for three solid weeks straight that city baked like a pie in the oven—a hundred and two degrees, it was. And it was muggy, oh my goodness was it ever muggy. You haven't felt a muggy day until you've spent a summer in Savannah, child. I pray we never see anything like that."

"Well, it's close to it, Mrs. Belamy," Jack said, coming into the room. "Already it's been a little bit over a week that we've had this heat, and I don't think it's going to let up anytime soon. And they say it's only been ninety-five out there, but I'd swear it was over a hundred."

"Oh, honey, you haven't seen a hundred degrees until you've lived through that summer I lived through in Savannah."

Lila's face perked up, struck by a sudden thought. She grabbed her purse, which still hung on her shoulder, and rummaged through it until she came out with a white paper bag. "Here's Mr. Belamy's medicine, Mrs. Belamy. I picked it up for him, just like always."

"That's my medicine?" Mr. Belamy asked, as if everyone else were the ones who couldn't hear. He shuffled into the room from the front hall and sat on the edge of the sofa.

"Yes, Mr. Belamy, it sure is," Lila said, loud enough for him to hear her, but without shouting. She handed him the bag.

"And you mean to tell me that the five dollars I give you for this stuff is all you need to buy this medicine?" Mr. Belamy said, looking at Lila with a suspicious squint. "Because I was talking with this fella at church last Sunday, and his wife takes the exact same thing. He says that this stuff costs him fifty-six dollars every single time he has to get it."

"Oh, really," was all she had the wits to say. She looked imploringly at Jack for help. She had thought about telling the old man that they went to a special pharmacy that gave doctors a lower rate for prescriptions, but along with it's being patently untrue, the thought of it was eminently vulgar. And to lie about this at all was to insult this proud, old man. So with her eyes, she passed the responsibility onto Jack to explain.

Then Jack said, loudly, to the old man, "Well, what it is, Mr. Belamy, is that I know how to get prescriptions subsidized, so that's what I did with your prescription. I got it subsidized for you."

And that was that, Lila thought with a sigh heard only in her mind. It wasn't a lie. It was a vague truth. Mr. Belamy's prescription *was* being subsidized—by her and Jack. And if he just happened to think that his medicine was being subsidized by the government, or some philanthropic corporation, it was due to nothing that Jack said. Lila smiled at Mr. Belamy, as if to confirm Jack's explanation.

"Okay, Mr. Belamy," Jack said, not so loud, now that he was right upon the man. "Why don't you take your shirt off so that I can examine you."

"All right," Mr. Belamy said as he unbuttoned his shirt.

"Have you had any pain?" Jack asked. "Any tightness in your chest, or shortness of breath, or exhaustion?"

"No, none at all," Mr. Belamy proudly answered. "But I've got to tell you, son, that pericarditis is something else. I'm telling you, though, if having a heart attack feels worse than that, then I'm one lucky son of a gun to just have this thing."

"Well, I wouldn't call you lucky, but it is good that it wasn't a heart attack. That's what we're trying to prevent."

Lila watched her husband get to work on Mr. Belamy, and she remembered how sick Mr. Belamy had been when she visited him in the hospital. He looked so small, smaller than usual, but oddly peaceful, with that glow that said he had reconciled with this world. Before she could see it, she felt movement somewhere near her. "Mrs. Belamy, are you okay? Is there something I can get for you?" Lila said, rising to her feet.

"No, darling," the old woman said, steadying herself with her walker. "I just thought you and I could go in the kitchen and have some iced tea. Let's let the boys do their work." And she blinked three swift times, playfully.

So Lila followed Mrs. Belamy into the kitchen, far enough back so that she wasn't right on her heels, but close enough to catch her if need be. When they got through the dining room and into the kitchen, Lila sat only after Mrs. Belamy was settled into her chair, which had to be her chair for breakfast, lunch, dinner, and just plain sitting.

"My darling, would you get the iced tea for me out of the icebox?" Mrs. Belamy said.

"Oh, of course," Lila said, nearly halfway to the refrigerator, which was only steps away. "Where are your glasses?" And Lila went to the cabinet over the sink, where the old woman pointed. She brought the tea and glasses back to the table saying, "Mr. Belamy certainly looks good."

"Oh, yes, he does. I mean to tell you, he came back from that thing so nicely, but he sure was sick. Oh my goodness, I thought I was going to lose him, you know. So, right now, I'm thinking more and more about what I would do if something were to ever happen to him. I guess I would just go and live with my daughter and her family in North Carolina." She laughed with a throaty chuckle, then said; "Can you imagine? I've been living in Baltimore all my womanly life. Moving out of here after all these years, well, it would be like I'm making a fresh start, or something."

"Well, you don't have to think about that for some time, Mrs. Belamy. Your husband is in good hands with Jack and is going to be just fine."

Mrs. Belamy took a sip of the iced tea Lila had poured for her, then said, "Your husband is just a wonderful man, darling. And you, you're the best, too. You don't find too many young people like both of you. Here your husband spent all that money going through medical school, and what does he decide to do with his weekends? He gives free health care to people like us. I'm telling you, he was sent from heaven, is what he was. The both of you, sent from heaven."

Lila's face flushed with a blushing heat, so much so that had she been a shade lighter, her face just might have turned like a Japanese Maple leaf in autumn. She lifted her glass to her lips and drank for lack of anything else to do in her embarrassment. "Well, giving to others lends our life meaning. And for Jack, he feels that if good health care isn't available to everyone, then the time and money he spent becoming a doctor is pointless."

"Well, this is what I'm talking about. Young people just don't think like that anymore. It's all about *me, me, me* for so many of them."

Lila looked off into the corner of the ceiling, snatched away from the company of Mrs. Belamy by those pink men from last week. Why, of all times in the day, did they have to come to her right now? Maybe, she thought, it was because of all that Mrs. Belamy was saying about Jack's generous spirit. He was so connected to the human part of being that to strike at his soul in such a way was to try to annihilate that connection, for Jack and for anyone ever touched by his altruism. Those men are murderers.

"You're thinking about something," Mrs. Belamy said.

"Yes, I am," Lila replied, pulling herself from the corner of the ceiling. "I was thinking about something that happened to Jack and me last Saturday." And so Lila proceeded to tell Mrs. Belamy about their run-in with the pink men over on Twenty-eighth Street. And as she spoke, as she let the details of the worst encounter she'd ever had with a white person spread out over that kitchen, her eyes welled with the tears that had been needing to fall all week. So she bent to their will, letting them flow and fall and drip into the lap of her skirt. She cried with the brokenhearted pain a child could only share cradled in the arms of a grandmother. The words seemed to shoot from her mouth only to reverberate off the walls, as if they were in a room with nothing to absorb her voice, make it softer. And when she felt Mrs. Belamy's hand slip into her own, Lila was overcome by her inappropriateness. She wasn't supposed to be there unloading her pain on this old woman. She was there to help, to give succor, not to seek it. Lila took her hand back from the old woman to wipe her tears with and whispered, "I'm sorry, Mrs. Belamy."

"Sorry?" she asked, her eyes surprised. "What's there to be sorry about? You haven't done a thing wrong. Don't you worry about these tears, you just go on and get it all out. That's a terrible thing the two of you went through. And that old dog probably ain't half of what your Jack is, darling. You have a right to be upset with some trash like that saying something to a man like Jack."

"Yeah, well, I guess I just lost it for a minute because I haven't been able to talk to Jack about it. He just doesn't want to discuss it, so I don't mention it."

"Well, men try to be strong like that, but believe me, darling, it's hurting him just as badly as it's hurting you. You just try to be there for him when it hits him."

"If it ever does hit him," Lila said despondently, then drank the last of her iced tea.

"Oh, believe me, it will. He's a proud man, darling, but when you least expect it, something will trigger the memory of that man saying that horrible thing to him and all that hurt will come gushing back at him. Just help him not to let it take over his soul."

"Lila, are you ready to go?" Jack called from the living room. "I'm finished with Mr. Belamy, so we should get going."

Lila got to her feet as if sprung. She took Mrs. Belamy's hand and squeezed it, then planted a kiss on her cheek, and said, "Thank you, Mrs. Belamy, for listening to me."

"Oh, that's all right, darling." Mrs. Belamy stood and began her trek into the front hall with her walker.

When she met Jack in the front hall, Lila said, as if just barely a moment ago she was not sitting in the kitchen with eyes soaking wet with the water from her core, "Okay, ready to go back out there into that heat?"

"No, but let's go anyway," Jack said, taking her hand. Then

he spoke over his shoulder to the Belamys. "Please don't bother seeing us out. You just stay in here where it's cool." And, on a whim, he turned to face Mr. Belamy fully. "Listen, Mr. Belamy, I know you don't like air-conditioning, but I'm telling you, this heat's going to get a lot more brutal, so in the high heat of the day, I want you to turn that air on."

"Yes, that's okay," the man said.

But Lila saw a look in the man's distracted eyes that said he had heard very little of what Jack had said that made any sense to him at all, so she said, filling the hall with her voice, "Turn the air on, Mr. Belamy. You don't want to risk either of you getting heatstroke, or worse. Okay?"

"Oh, yes," he said, nodding as with a sudden awareness. "I understand. I certainly will turn on that air."

So they said their good-byes, and Lila and Jack stepped through the door and into the heat, with Jack pulling the door tightly closed behind them. Lila adjusted her purse on her shoulder, the heat already oppressing her, and said, "So now on to East Baltimore to Mr. Rawlings's house."

"Well, actually, no," Jack said, looking at Lila as if waiting for something. "Don't you remember? Mr. Rawlings is in the hospital, and since I saw him in the hospital yesterday, our next stop, my beautiful wife, is home. You can actually have me to yourself for the rest of the day."

Lila let a grin spread across her face, then followed Jack to the car, and just before she got in, she said to her husband, "So, does that mean you'll fix your tropical rum drinks?"

"Sure, I just love watching you get drunk and pass out on the sofa."

And once Lila was settled into the car, just before Jack closed the door, she gave him a shy smile, gazing at him with lowered eyes. "I don't get drunk. Besides, you're the one who makes them so strong."

It only took seconds, meager seconds before Jack got in the car next to her. As he pulled away from the Belamys' house, Lila looked around and was in awe of the way all those children played up and down Park Heights Avenue, as if there were no heat, as if the sidewalk were not melting beneath their feet. Their parents chatted across porches or sat on their stoops, every now and then barking an order for a child to behave; and they all seemed, parents and children, as if there were no other choice than to accept the heat. Would it have been that much hotter indoors? she wondered. Some of the houses had air conditioners in upstairs windows, she noticed. So why weren't they up there escaping? All the way down the street, it was the same scene, but different children, different porch chatters. Something close to envy came to her as she watched the way everyone seemed to be almost impervious to the heat. Maybe, she thought, if she had their tolerance, their fortitude, she wouldn't have had to tell Jack *no* on those nights during the heat wave when his desire for her would rise. The hot and sticky nights seemed to make him far more amorous than they made Lila. And she felt so poorly about rejecting him, but the last thing she wanted on those nights of stale steamy air was another body against her own making more stale steamy air.

Jack whizzed through the junction where Park Heights, Reisterstown, and Liberty Heights converged, and when he made that turn to go on to Auchentrolly Terrace, she knew where they were headed. It was actually no surprise, since the most direct route to their home was Twenty-eighth Street, and it wasn't the actual street that troubled her. It was whether or not Jack would stop at that store where trouble loafed. Lila squirmed where she sat, then looked over at Jack, and when she saw his set jaw, his stone face of battle, she knew they'd stop. Lila's heart pounded in her ears with the fate of what was ahead. She caught a breath, let it out, then said, "Jack, please don't stop at that store. It's so hot, Jack, and I just want to go home and get cool."

"I want a Coke."

"Jack, we have cases of soda at home. Please. Please, Jack, I'm begging you not to stop." For as much as Lila wanted to avoid those corner-hanging louts, she also wanted to be in the cold comfort of her den's air conditioner. "Jack, look at me.

Have you ever seen me looking as flushed as this? I'm telling you, I cannot bear this heat, so please take me home."

She knew Jack was not in a place where reason could touch him. He had his eye only on proving a point, though she believed that if he had to give voice to it, he wouldn't have been able to give her one specific about that point. Whatever it was, though, it flowed in and around his pride, which lived at his center in false modesty.

"I want a Coke right now, and I want a cold one right now, so I'm stopping at the store. If you're so hot, I'll get you one, too."

Lila squirmed where she sat again, and watched the reservoir as they sped, like a lion toward game, to Twenty-eighth Street. Once they turned onto the street, Lila could even feel the car speed up. "I don't want a Coke, and Jack, slow down, will you?"

But Jack would say nothing until he reached the store and parked. Sure enough, the same pink men from last week were sitting there. "I'm going to leave the air on for you. I'll be right back."

"Jack, why are you doing this?" Lila asked with a face so sweet in its innocence.

"I'm simply thirsty, Lila, that's all," he said without his eyes once meeting Lila's. "I'll be back." With that, he was gone.

Lila turned to face the men, and it was haunting. Déjà vu. As if they hadn't left the corner all week. Even those shorts, showing that man's gittels, were still the same. Did he ever change those shorts, or were they his Saturday shorts? Either way, they needed a good washing, a good washing with lots of scrubbing. And even though those shorts, those gittels, made her glad for not having anything in her stomach that could have resurfaced, she couldn't take her eyes off of them, off of all that pink flesh. She stared, with flat eyes that seemed dazed by it all, yet her mouth contorted to show the magnitude of her disgust.

Her gaze was broken when she saw Jack passing the men from behind the car, and that's when she leaned forward to see what would happen. She was aware of her pounding heart as her chest heaved with double-time beats, and it seemed as if she would never catch her breath. Her eyes were stuck on the biggest pink man, because he was the one. Lila cracked the window, only an inch, only wide enough to hear, but not enough to let in his pollution in its entirety. What she heard was general taunting. The kind that emanated from the mouths of children on school playgrounds, children too stupid to get good grades, too empty to do anything but what they do best—harass smarter children.

Hey boy, where's your watermelon? the man with the shorts said. And Lila thought, My God, is that the extent of his wit? It was less insulting to Jack than it was shameful for the shorts man. But then the next foul words were spat by the fat pink man, like poisonous venom that slimed both Jack and Lila. *Is that bitch there your whore or your momma who had you when she was nine?* and the corner burst into a chorus of their loud belly laughs, replete with back slapping and foot stomping. The thinnest of them all, the quietest of the three and possibly the only one to make it to fifth grade, lobbed a wad of spit into the gutter while shiny dribbles of it got caught in his beard. She couldn't look a second longer at him and his spitty mouth.

And that was when she saw Jack's gait slow to a near stop. Did she want him to stop, or did she want him to ignore it all? Lila didn't know. How could he walk on by? But how could he do anything else, considering what were certain to be dire consequences if he were not to walk on by? This could dissolve into a desperately vicious encounter. That's why, in spite of all the savagery she could have personally heaped on that pig of a man the week before, her heart was most grateful for Jack, who floated above the mire and continued to walk toward the store. But again, déjà vu. Just as he pulled the handle on the door to walk through, it came: *Hey, Dr. Porch Monkey? Can't you hear me, Dr. Porch Monkey?* And just as he did last week, Jack disappeared through the door and into the store.

Lila turned herself around and planted her back smack against the seat. She was seething so bad that her hands were shaking. Shaking as if they were itching to be in a clutch around that pink man's neck, squeezing the life out of him that he shouldn't have had in the first place.

Then, through the tiny crack of the window, Lila heard a disturbing sound—one she knew she'd heard before—and it conjured a memory of death. It was the thwack of flesh hitting earth, and choking gurgles, which could have been almost anything, given the base ways these men entertained themselves. So it wasn't compelling enough to turn her around. It took only a second before the song on the radio took her mind from those men, and that corner, and that sound. And she was content in the reverie of the song and the few words of it she knew until she saw the haste with which Jack flung open the door of the store. She couldn't begin to fathom what was the matter—what was on his mind.

Because Jack opened that door with an urgent yank. Despite the power in his action, and the immediate focus of his attention, he could only stare at the unbelievable. From inside the store, he had seen the man on the ground and found the suddenness of it all to be amazing. And so what was on his mind was the fact that he could scarcely believe it was happening at all, as he stepped from the store as if drawn by something other than his own will, his eyes downcast and unable to look away from the sight before him on the ground. Of all the ways he had imagined fate stepping between himself and this man, so fat, so pink, so repugnant, it had never occurred to him that things could come down to what was happening right now. And without being fully aware of what was right before him, without realizing that this was not some sort of dream state or otherwise altered reality, Jack still knew that in whichever realm, he would be forever inextricably involved in the man's life, or death. He heard a voice that seemed to come from some distance but was clearly directed at him.

"What're you just standing there looking for?" the man in the red shorts said. "Help him! Help us!"

The fat dying man called out in a garbled voice what sounded to Jack to be the name Ernie. And now Jack knew that the man in the red shorts was named Ernie or something close to it. As Ernie assured the man that he was there and going nowhere, Jack's eyes locked with Ernie's wide, frightened eyes, as they each listened to the unmistakable gurgle of a painful death emanating from the figure spread out on the sidewalk in need of a man who had come to be the last doctor on earth for him. Still, Jack felt fear in empathy, both as a doctor and as a simple man without an ability to heal, as his own heart pounded with a heaviness that seemed to pump sweat from every pore in his body; heat's sweat commingled with the secretions of his conscience. And in those seconds that their eyes were locked in the only one of life's ironies capable of connecting disparate souls, Jack was almost able to see outside and above himself. In one second, his higher self was being beckoned when he looked compassionately into the face of a man with whom he had a wretched history, who was trying to speak, trying to call out for mercy from anywhere, but in the very next second it seemed reality was slamming Jack down to earth.

"Goddamn it, get over here and help him, boy, 'stead of standin' there wit your thumb up your black ass. It's his heart! You're a doctor, right? If you're a doctor, then you gotta help us! If you ain't, then get the hell outta here!"

And that was the moment when Jack's mind split so completely, so consciously into two parts. The part capable of rational reasoning told him to run, not walk, to the trunk of his car and come back with the defibrillator that would shock the man's heart out of the seizure. But then the other half, also thinking quite rationally, but barely reasonably, told him that no amount of shock to a heart so black would ever bring it into the light, as it had never known light. So, just as he was about to answer the man's question to affirm that, yes, in fact, he was a doctor, Jack simply stared at the man with eyes too blank to read as the word *liable* flashed through his mind. Jack took his eyes from Ernie's to see that the man on the sidewalk was now unconscious, and his breaths, if any at all, were too shallow to be detected from where Jack stood. Then, for a reason he'd never know, and certainly didn't know at the moment, Jack turned to look at Lila with expectation in his eyes. Surely she was watching it all unfold. Maybe she even saw the fat man crumble to the ground. Though he didn't know what he'd hoped to find, he was looking to her eyes for something, but her face was as flat as the glass through which she peered, with the same horror he felt; so he found nothing, and perhaps, he thought, that is exactly what he wanted to find.

So once Jack had made up his mind, he moved past the men, who were so close he nearly had to step over them. He thought of saying something like, Sorry I can't help you, but I can't seem to get my thumb out of my black ass. Or saying mockingly in broken English and Southern drawl, Sorry, y'all, but dem ain't teach me 'bout savin' no lives up in porch monkey school. But then he thought that the mere fact that he was simply leaving the man to rot and die under an inhumane sun, and leaving Ernie and the other man to watch, would say all that he needed to say, and reveal his loathing for them, which was quite separate and detached from his oath to first do no harm.

Once he got past them, it was easier to leave them behind, to forget what he'd just seen and go about his life with the comfort that there would be one less redneck in the world. Just as he got to the door of his car, though, his conscience tweaked him in the gut. But when he heard what he thought was the man's gasp for life, Jack stopped for the barest second, and turned his body in a millisecond's change of heart. Saving lives was as natural to him as his jerking knee when tapped in just the right spot. In spite of his pride, he believed he would go to this man at this, the eleventh hour, and save his sorry life. Then, as he looked over the top of the car at that fat belly, that red mustachioed mouth that never failed to set free the derelict thoughts from an adulterated mind, Jack reeled in his conscience and opened the car door.

The man with the spitty beard, stricken with panic, shouted over his shoulder to Jack, "You're a doctor, right? Come on, you've got to help him." But by now, Jack was already beside Lila, and just before he closed the door, the last thing Jack heard was, "Damned nigg—"

And those were his thoughts—thoughts to which Lila was not privvy in the seconds it took tragedy to invade both their lives in ways she never dreamed plausible. Yet Lila had not moved from the moment when she saw Jack nearly step over the afflicted man, as if he were stepping over a heap of bothersome garbage in the middle of the pavement, wondering what he could have been thinking. She sat there with her face still in the window as she heard Jack fastening his seat belt, keys jingling with his every movement. But over all those real and immediate sounds, her mind replayed the frightful sound of all that pink flesh hitting the ground with a slap and thud. The way he clutched his chest and writhed in pain while his two friends, or brothers, or cousins—who knows how they knew one another—knelt beside him. In the moment after he'd fallen, it occurred to her that it could have all been a part of their school-yard pranks—feign illness to make Doctor Porch Monkey look like a fool when he rushed to help. She wanted with everything in her to believe this, because the niggling thought, which she could not chase from her mind even with shame, was that she could not bear to watch Jack save such a life. In complete conflict with this, though, was Lila's feeling that if this were not a prank, she was left, now and forever, with the burden of the dilemma of loving a man who slacked on his moral covenant to another human. More than that, though, if the man were indeed slipping from life, she would never know another moment without guilt. So, she wanted it to be a joke at Jack's expense.

The only problem, the only thing that didn't quite fit in this drama, was that his companions didn't have a trace of humor in their faces, in their bearing. They weren't acting, and her mind would always remember with vivid exactness their faces, which were in the desperate throes of sheer terror. It was the same look of deep anguish boring straight into the heart that she remembered seeing in her sisters' faces, and which must have completely overtaken her own face, when they watched their father die right before their eyes the day something came from out of nowhere and seized his heart. The helplessness. The feeling of wanting it simply not to be so. She saw herself in those men as their fat friend—or brother, or cousin, or whichever he was—thrashed with the agony of a pain they couldn't possibly know; and now he simply lay there, dead or alive, while the rest of life, with time leading, moved on.

Lila whipped her head around to Jack. He hadn't started the car yet, hadn't even tried to leave this horrid scene, and with his Coke cast aside, unopened, in the beverage holder just in front of the gear shift, she thought, Maybe now is when he'll go to the man and honor his oath. She knew things were grave, with the way he pressed his lips, and blinked his eyes with the intensity of a facial tick, and clenched his jaw with the tension of death, cometh; so he was certain to help. And just as a smile of relief almost claimed her tightened face, Jack started the car.

"Jack?" she said quietly.

But he wouldn't answer.

"JACK?"

"Yeah?" he answered flatly as he turned the key in the ignition.

"What's wrong with that man?"

"He's having a heart attack is my guess."

Lila looked back at the man, at the scene of the men imploring someone to help. Jack pulled the car away from the curb, and Lila flung herself around to face her husband.

"Jack, you need to go back and help him. If he's having a heart attack you've got to help him. You're a heart surgeon, Jack. This is your thing. You've got to help him," Lila said, as if she had to remind him.

"They'll get help from where they want it. Let them call 911 and maybe some nice white-boy paramedic will come along and save his fat ass, but it won't be me."

Everything around Lila, even what she could hear, turned to white, and everything in her turned cold, clammy, as if she had passed, body and soul, into another realm where there was no heat, no color, no day or night. Through her haze, she looked over at her husband, who drove them home without a care, without a trace of the conscience she knew he owned. How angry was he? How hurt was he? What had those words done to him, and would he ever come back to her? And whatever those words had done to him, had they done it just this time, or had they built up over time? Jack had gone to a place, Lila believed, from which not even a Coke could coax him back.

"Jack?" she said so quietly she was almost whispering, "I know what that man called you, but as wretched as he was in saying that, you have to honor your oath, Jack. Don't you remember? Don't you remember how you told me about the time when you were a resident working in the emergency room and that drug dealer guy was brought in who had been shot by the cops after he and some other drug dealer decided to open fire in a playground full of kids over in East Baltimore? When they wheeled that guy into the emergency room you still went to work on him and you helped save his life. Shooting recklessly into a crowd of innocent children was the worst possible thing a human being can do, if you ask me. And no, he probably didn't deserve to live, but you saved his life. Don't you remember that, Jack?"

"I remember, Lila. In fact, I'll never forget it, because for as much as all of us wanted to let him die, we had to shut down every part of us that makes us human in order to save him." Jack laughed drolly, coldly, then said, "Yeah, we saved his life, but let me tell you, those nurses didn't find that vein for his IV on the first shot, not even the second or third. And when I had to insert his trachea tube . . . Well, let's just say that the tube didn't go down his throat as smoothly as it would have gone down somebody else's. We saved his life, though. But this time, Lila, with that guy back there, it was personal."

"Oh, God," Lila said, futilely turning herself to look back, to see if she could still see the large pink man on the ground, but mostly to see if someone, maybe the law, was in hot pursuit of them. "Jack, please, go back. I know how angry I was about what he called you last week, and I really, really wanted to hurt him . . . and okay, secretly, I even wanted him dead, but now I see that you were right in being the bigger person by not answering him last week. That's why I'm telling you, Jack, if you don't go back there and save that man, you will never forgive yourself."

"You think so?" Jack said with a cynical chuckle, and with a coldness she had never heard in the two years she'd been married to him.

Lila slumped down into her seat with the most distressing image slowly making its indelible impression in her memory: the face, the large pink face, contorted, forced to the limit of what it could bear of the unceasing pain from a heart under siege as his body writhed on the ground grunting, perhaps like the pig she knew him to be, for the breath of his life. He was dying, if he hadn't already died. And the only conjecture in which she could potentially find solace was the possibility that even if Jack had tried, the man still would have died. Or perhaps he would have lived in harrowing pain long enough to get to the hospital and then he would have died, in which case, by not going to him, Jack saved the man the torture, the indignity of dying in the grip of a wrenching pain. But none of this supposition quieted her heart. It still beat as if it were not a part of her, as if it were like the heart that wrestled the large pink man to the ground. She just wanted to feel normal again. How could it be that in only the scarcest of minutes her worst problem went from staying cool in the heat to a dead man on the sidewalk? From petty to epic. Before she could realize it herself, Jack had gotten them home and parked right in front of their house. Her daze was broken when she felt Jack's eyes upon her.

"Look, Lila, I don't want you to stress out about that guy back there," he said, slipping his hand into hers. "Besides, let me tell you that he got what he deserved. I stop in that store, from time to time, you know, on my way to or from the hospital, and almost every time, that lazy good-for-nothing is hanging somewhere around that store. Ever since the time he saw me coming home dressed in my scrubs, he's been calling me Dr. Porch Monkey. And you know, I could have stopped going there, but why should I? The guy who owns the store, a white guy in fact, is as nice as he can be. Besides, this isn't 1952. This is 2001, and this is America, and some uneducated backwoods creep is not going to keep me out of any place my rights as a human being tell me I can go." He took his hand from her hand and slumped onto the steering wheel with his head on his folded arms. Jack inhaled deeply, then let it out and said, speaking into his lap, "You didn't need to see those guys, Lila, and I was stupid to bring you around them last week and especially today. But I don't know. In a way, you know, there's a part of me that looked at him on that ground and didn't even see him as human. A whole different species. I couldn't save the life of a dying pig or dog any more than I could have saved his life."

Lila looked at her husband through squinting, fearful eyes. He could have possibly lost his mind in this heat. "Jack, what are you talking about? You *couldn't* save the life of a pig or a dog because you're not a vet and you wouldn't know how. You *chose* not to save that man's life. There's a difference."

"Look, Lila, I let it go, I let it go, and I let it go. I wouldn't say anything to him because I was better than that cracker, you know. And I knew that one day, Lila, he would get his. One day he was going to get in the face of the wrong black man."

Lila thought for a second about what he was saying, but then she had to say what he had omitted. "And today, Jack, *you* were that wrong black man. You should have helped him, Jack, no matter what. That's the man you are. You know right from wrong, and it was wrong to just let him die like that." When she realized what she'd actually said, she smacked her hands in hopeless angst against her cheeks and said, "And, oh God, Jack, what if that man did die? If he died, Jack, what then? You're liable for his death. At least that's what I *think*."

"And you're right. In a lot of people's eyes, I am liable for his death, but Lila, those are just the consequences I'll have to face, and I'll have to face them like a man. It's just that sometimes a man has had enough, and for a black man, sometimes enough can be too much." Jack took the key from the ignition and got out of the car without another word, without even taking his Coke.

Mostly due to the reflex of not wanting to leave anything behind that would junk up the car, Lila took the Coke from the cup holder and got out. She tucked it under her arm and walked down the path to climb the steps to the porch, where Jack was waiting with the door opened. She was dragged down by the perspiration that had been on her so long it seemed as if it belonged there, slowing her gait, disquieting her spirit. But she couldn't blame it all on the sun. Guilt had claimed her. As she passed Jack, who was holding the door for her, she only half looked at him, unable to look into the eyes of the man she was uncertain if she knew at that moment. Lila heard the door close behind her as she headed into the kitchen.

"I'm going to take a nap in the den" was all Jack said.

And all Lila could do, with the heaviness of heat and tragedy upon her all at once, was sit at the kitchen table and let questions fly through her mind without any prayer of resolution. Lila wanted to move, she wanted to get up from that chair and go to where Jack slept in the air-conditioned den and read a book, or watch the television on low, or nod off herself. But shock and heat combined was a powerful paralyzing entity. Lila wasn't certain if she would ever read or sleep again. So she sat there, doing nothing but spinning Jack's unopened bottle of Coke and staring like a catatonic through the kitchen window; she sat there for hours.

When the dinner hour approached, Lila righted the soda bottle and got up from the chair to turn on the small television that sat on the edge of the kitchen counter. Jack was still sleeping in the den. She blasted the six o'clock news, not wanting to miss a minute of it, just in case the man's death would somehow make it onto the news. It was doubtful, reason told her, that anyone would find newsworthy the story of a poor, possibly drunk redneck's death on a street corner in northeast Baltimore, but on a day when the only news was the heat, it was hard to say. So she glued her eyes to the television while her hands worked, by their own volition, tossing the salad, then turning the chicken on the stovetop grill, then tossing the salad again. Slowly, she began to watch, and not watch, as her mind drifted to the previous week, which seemed so far behind her now, like a run-over possum on the side of the highway that gets smaller and smaller in the rearview mirror until it resembles something trivial and not something that once drew breath. It was a place where she simmered in the kind of unadulterated loathing that could have caused her to do just about anything to that pink man, had she had the heart. In the heat of that day, in the heat of her anger over such insolence, Lila wanted to attack in some way. She wanted him to suffer, and she remembered every imaginable way in which she could have made him suffer. And so now he was suffering, or maybe not anymore; the possibility that he could be in a place where he felt no pain is what panicked her heart most, because though in her wildest imaginings, she could see him dead, that's not at all what she'd wanted.

As she stood there, pondering her spirit's musing, which truly did cause an equal and opposite reaction, Lila had that tingle on the back of her neck telling her that the dead pink man's red blood was on her hands. Something told to her by a man called Pick—who seemed to have passed through her life so long ago, but actually it was only a few years now, that in reflection it almost seemed as if it were not even her life, but someone else's lived in another place—had Lila thinking about the nature of evil and where it lived. Did it live inside or outside the soul's core? And if indeed it does live at the core, how can it do so without its master's knowledge, or will?

IN THE FAMILY room, only steps from where Lila cooked, all of Jack was stretched on the sofa, except one leg, bent at the knee, holding his foot flat to the ground, as if it were poised to spring him to life on his feet at any moment's whim. He lay, somewhere between his dreaming mind and his mind that could remember; remember the day when he turned to find Lila standing on the threshold of their new home only a month after they'd said their "I do's," as still as immaculate beauty and with a peace he knew he had given her. It was moving day, and they had passed each other in the wind more times than he had been able to count, and with each passing he'd forgotten how he'd wondered, when they dressed together that morning, why anyone would put on a dress, a white dress, on moving day only to chance soiling it while unpacking boxes and putting things in place. But seeing her perched in the doorsill, in the dawn of their new life in their new home, Jack knew why that white dress on that day called to her.

And all he could do was freeze where he stood, and stare at the love that he hadn't even seen coming. He heard her call to him through her resplendent smiling lips, "What're you doing?" It was only then that the weight of the box he held while in his trance made its heft known. So, Jack turned and shut the box back up in the trunk, then locked the car with the bleeping touch of his thumb on the remote. He ambled down the walk, as if uncertain whether he should approach this woman for whom his worthiness was doubtful. According to the spinning of the universe, where for every action there's a reaction that's sometimes virtuous and sometimes not, but always equal, Jack couldn't know specifically if he had actually put out the one virtuous action that brought to him the equal reaction of Lila. He couldn't imagine how it could have been comparable in any way to the never-ceasing gift that nearly stopped his heart with thankfulness at moments like this one—which came to him just as she had, from seemingly nowhere—when he could actually take in all that Lila would always be to him.

Standing there only for his eyes, she could have been a nymph. Or maybe she was the personified image of a painted woman rendered in her most simplistic loveliness. She could have been so very much, but much too much to capture. And so, as he got closer, his eyes were glued to hers with an intensity that seemed to him to wrench their hearts one notch closer, but had he seen what was really there, Jack would have seen bewilderment.

"Jack, what's wrong? Why are you looking at me like that?"

she asked with an anxious giggle that made him smile with want. She was positively breezy in the way she knew nothing of her power.

When he finally reached her, he smoothed a lock of hair back from her forehead and kissed the spot where the hair had lain. Then he gasped, then exhaled and inhaled quickly, as if to desperately take back the breath he was slowly losing to her. "You are so beautiful in every conceivable way, and you're my wife, and this is our home, and I'm remembering a boy in hand-me-downs on the streets of Cherry Hill whose mother had to send him out to borrow fifty cents from the neighbors for a loaf of bread for his family, and he, I, couldn't see past the humiliation of those two begged quarters clenched in my angry little hand to know that this, here, right now, you, were in store for me. And even if I had known, I wouldn't have believed that I was worth someone like you, back then. I can barely believe it now." Jack pulled her to him and wrapped her up in his arms so tightly that they seemed almost to double around. He slackened his hold a bit, closed his eyes tight, then said into her ear in a whisper, "It doesn't matter, though, because whether I deserve you or not, whether somebody up there made a mistake or not, you're my blessing for the rest of my life, and so no matter what happens, even if this house falls to the ground around us, I'll happily step over the whole heap of rubbish as long as I'm carrying you in my arms."

Jack pulled out of the embrace to see her face, and it was one he'd never seen. Still, he knew he'd touched her in a place he'd never been before, because tears were filling her eyes by the second.

She blinked furiously, as if to keep them from falling, but it was too late. They fell, and her voice broke in pieces when she said, "You just spoke a love letter to me. I have to believe that I'm the only woman alive who's been loved so much that they've had a love letter spoken to them."

Then, with a suddenness even Jack didn't expect, he scooped her up, as if she were a mere sack of feathers, and carried her into the house. Once they were over the threshold, he looked into her unsure eyes and said, "Don't you trust me?"

"Yes, of course I trust you."

"Well, don't look so afraid. You look as if you're expecting to hit the ground at any second. Don't you see what I'm doing? I'm carrying my bride across the threshold," and then he laughed at his own corniness as he put her back on her feet.

"This is real sweet," Lila said as she steadied herself. She followed Jack into the living room, where he headed to the only clear corner, maybe in the whole house.

Jack folded down onto the floor, then reached out his hand for Lila and pulled her to him. "We can take a break now." He cradled her in his arms as she melted into him. Pressing his lips to the top of her head, which had grown musty with the day's work, he said, "I figure our Christmas tree can go right here where we're sitting. What do you think?"

Lila laughed with a sweet affection. "Jack Calloway, we haven't even gotten unpacked yet, let alone arranged the furniture in here, and you're already thinking ahead to Christmas. You're too much."

"Well, you know how I am. And besides, this house is everything I always pictured. I can remember the first time I went into a Colonial house. It was the home of my physics professor at Hopkins, and he invited some of his star students to dinner just to talk about our futures, and all. I'm telling you, Lila, I was just a freshman then, but when I walked into that house I knew that it was the kind of home I wanted to live in with my wife and kids, and then, when I saw your house, you know, the one where you grew up, I said to myself, Ah, man, this is it. She knows what it's like to live in something this beautiful. Even though you took it for granted," he said, tweaking her arm playfully. He kissed her head again, then said, "Anyway, I know I've told you all this before, but I still have to tell you, that center hall and staircase is really what did it for me, and the fireplace, too. And I knew that in my home, this home, the Christmas tree would go right by the window, just to the right of the fireplace, which would be right here where we are. Oh, and on the fireplace mantel we'll put that silver box I gave you when we got married where we'll keep all our special pictures and keepsakes that we'll look at every Christmas Eve on the sofa, with nothing but the Christmas tree to light the room." Jack laughed self-consciously and hung his head bashfully. He pressed his lips to her head again with a lingering kiss, then wondered, "It sounds silly, doesn't it?"

"No, of course not," Lila said, sitting up to look him square in the face. She touched her fingers to his cheek. "It sounds sweet. It's like your fantasy, and I'm a part of it. And in a way, you know, as I look around and see it all through your eyes, it's becoming my fantasy, too. So, I'll finish that Christmas picture for us. The next morning, the kids will come in our room before the sun's even up and wake us to come down to see what Santa Claus brought them. Then—"

"Since it's so early in the morning, do they walk in on us making love?" Jack asked, squeezing her closer to him with a devilish glint in his eyes.

"Jack!" Lila giggled through a blush, swatting him playfully on his thigh. "Stop that, now. Anyway, like I was saying, then our four kids—"

"Four?"

"Four. Our four kids, two boys and two girls, will pull us downstairs and we'll watch them open their presents and play with their toys, and then I'll fix hot cocoa with our oldest girl— she'll be the oldest child as well—and then we'll all go back upstairs and dress for church."

"Wow, you've really thought all of this out," Jack said, still smiling devilishly at his wife. "And so does this oldest daughter of ours have a name? I mean, you've planned everything else out."

Lila looked up at the ceiling, as if to give the question honest thought, then said through a funny-faced grin, "Oh, I don't know, I was thinking about maybe Hannah Cecile, or something like that."

"I see," Jack said, rising up closer to her face, as if approaching for a kiss, or some such overture to passion. "Well, why don't we get started on little Hannah right now." But then he went without dithering, and without as much as a smack on her lips or a nibble on her ear, to that spot on her neck that never failed to soften her beneath him.

JACK'S EYES OPENED as if they'd never known sleep. He looked around the room, comforted by the muffled sounds of Lila's busyness just a room away in the kitchen. And he smiled. He smiled because, more than anything he'd ever strongly desired, Jack wanted to relive the afternoon of their moving day, which was still in his memory in primary tones of vivid color. And he wanted to relive it right in the original spot, even though it would mean moving a chair and a table out of the way.

He sat himself upright, so that both feet were planted on the floor, and then he rose. By the time he got his hand on the doorknob, he could hear the seriousness of the news coming from the kitchen television, and thought it was odd, since Lila rarely watched the news. But none of it would linger long on his mind, because Jack had a passionate interlude to re-create with his wife.

"So, you know what I've been thinking about?" he said as he walked into the kitchen. Then he squinted his eyes, as if in pain, at the television and said, "It's a little loud, don't you think?"

"What?" Lila said, so startled that she tossed some of the salad out of the bowl and onto the counter.

"The television. It's a little loud."

"Oh, yeah. I guess it is," Lila said, turning it down only a few clicks with the remote. "I'm sorry. Did it wake you?"

"No," he said, stretching his back out in a yawn. "I didn't hear it until I woke up."

"I'm just trying to listen and see if they say anything about that man from today. I have a bad feeling, Jack, that he died."

Jack didn't say anything but stared straight ahead at the television. He didn't seem to think one way or the other about Lila's

portends, and she could see it in the way he held himself neither stiff nor slack; he was simply there without caring. He went
to the table and plucked from it his Coke he'd gotten from that
dreaded store, which Lila thought he would now drink. Instead,
though, he went to the sink, opened the cap, and poured the
whole of it down the drain.

"Why are you throwing that out?" she asked.

"Because it's warm now" was all Jack said.

"Then just put it in the refrigerator, Jack. Why waste it?"

But Jack wouldn't answer, as his attention had been snatched
from her, from the soda. His eyes grew wide, and his eyebrows
nearly jumped high enough to blend with his hair. Something
had struck him.

"What is it, Jack?" Lila said, startled.

"Turn it up."

And as she did, the salad tongs tumbled onto the floor. "Oh
my God," was all she said as she listened. Listened to the
reporter, live from that corner, talking about the man who suffered a heart attack and died, right there on the sidewalk of
Twenty-eighth Street, in the heat of the day. They blamed it on
the heat, that is until the reporter cut away to an interview with
the man in the red shorts that showed his gittels, who turned
out to be the dead man's son, Ernie.

His Baltimore drawl dragged through the room at top vol-
ume: "One minute we was sittin' here talkin', you know, about
nothin', then he's clutchin' his chest and fallin' to the ground.
We didn't know what to do. Alls I know is that there was somebody here who coulda saved him." Then he rubbed his stubbly
head and said, "I don't know, maybe he wasn't a doctor. We
sure thought he was a doctor, but maybe he wasn't. I've sure
seen him dressed up like one before, you know, with the green
getup and all. Alls I know is that he walked right by him and
left him to die on the street here like a dog. That just ain't right.
And I think he let him die 'cause my daddy's white and he was
black. It ain't right."

In the next blink of the screen, a face appeared that was
strange to Lila. Underneath his face was a name that she

wouldn't retain as well as she would what was written underneath the name: store owner. And he said, "Well, I'm not sure if he's a doctor or not. He stops in here every now and then, and sometimes he's got on them hospital clothes, you know, so I guess maybe even if he ain't a doctor he still prob'ly knows enough to save somebody's life, or keep 'em alive till help comes. Alls I know is that even though he died in a way that nobody should have to die, Jimmy wasn't no angel in all this. He would call that black fella all kinds of awful things, callin' him porch monkey and jungle coon. All kinds of things that nobody with any sense would call another person. I would hear it all the way in here. Still, though, if that black fella was a doctor and could have saved his life, I don't know, maybe he shoulda done it."

And then, when the reporter came back on the screen, he said in that fake-serious voice he must have rehearsed in the shower for years before his big moment: "So we've just heard some pretty serious allegations, if indeed there was a doctor on the scene at the time of this man's heart attack who did not offer medical assistance. For now, though, the summer's heat appears to have claimed its first victim, and we're warning . . ." He went on and on about staying out of the heat and the Baltimore Gas and Electric Company's plea that people keep air-conditioning use to a minimum.

Lila clicked off the television and looked down at her salad for several long seconds. The only sound the kitchen held was the fizz of the Coke, desperately gurgling and burping to make its labored way through the slow drain of the sink. She wanted to get to the sink, make it stop in some way. But getting to the sink meant looking at Jack, which she could not do, not yet. So Lila turned from him and snapped over her shoulder at Jack to turn on the water, and in the first seconds of the rush of water from the faucet, Lila knew that water would make the burps and gurgles worse. At least, though, the fizzing would stop. The fizzing of that soda in the sink would have nearly the same effect on her as looking at Jack; because if she had looked at Jack in that moment, even caught a glimpse of him, she just might scream, or break down in sobs beyond anyone's control. So she stayed with the salad until she could meet his eyes without fear of calamity.

And when their eyes met, not at all purposefully but by the happenstance of both being startled by the ringing phone, not a word had to be spoken for her to understand that their life had morphed into something beyond what either of them could comprehend. And the fear, or the heat, or the ringing phone, but most likely the fear, pounding with an unrelenting heaviness in her ears, on her chest, all through her head, weakening her knees, put her on the floor in a dead faint.

c h a p t e r   f o u r

AFTER LEAVING THE store across from the university track, Jack opened the bottle of Coke he'd just bought, then started to cross University Parkway. He took a long swig, and it was so soothing in the pouring-down sun that he could have finished the entire bottle in that one gulp. Instead, he took it from his lips and closed it back up with the cap, so that he'd have more to drink on his walk home. It was comfortingly cold in his hand. As he waited for the light before crossing, he opened the bottle he'd just closed up and was about to drink again, when he started across the street and saw her.

Way on the other side of the street stood a small girl with brown skin that had nearly faded to gray. She couldn't have been more than twelve, and the sight of her distracted him to the point where he saw nothing or no one but her. Either from chemotherapy or the cancer for which it was meant, it didn't much matter which, the child was a most chilling sight. To be so young with something only the old should get. She had to have cancer, he thought, or some other awful disease that was slowly trying to take her. The sight of that little girl hit him somewhere very, very deep, because she caused his mind to flash on the times during his pediatric rotation as an intern when he was nearly brought to tears after examining more children than one man should have to; children who were made, seemingly, of nothing but papery skin stretched over frail bone. Who could pay much attention to their footing under such circumstances? Who could be mindful while under attack of such memories, and in her presence? And so he stumbled, without seeing it coming, without seeing the glass in pieces, jagged, rugged, strewn on the ground. So just before his descent to the ground, he saw nothing in his path but those hollow sockets that once held the eyes of her soul's innocence.

In the seconds it took him to fall to the ground, Jack's mind traveled back through the last twenty-four hours. It wasn't exactly as if his life were flashing before his eyes in the prover-bial sense, rather, he thought about the decisions he'd made, the decision he was about to make. Once he realized he had a choice between saving his bottle of Coke by falling, or avoiding the fall altogether by letting the bottle go and grabbing hold of the car next to him, he accepted his fate with grace—he saved the Coke and met the earth. Three people saw and not one of them so much as snickered at his absurd choice. In Jack's mind, it was out of their respect and awe for the eloquent way in which he held on to the soda bottle without spilling a drop. There was dignity in his trip and fall.

Not even Jack could explain his relationship with Coca-Cola. He knew that for Lila, his thing with Coke was one of those lit-tle quirks that she once found endearing when love was so fresh they could smell it. But now each and every time she saw him with a bottle of Coke, he could see in the faint glint in her eyes that she probably wanted to pour that soda over him from head to toe, then pummel him unconscious with the empty bot-tle. Still, it was what he had to have. There are people, he believed, who talked of being addicted to things like coffee, or chocolate, or ice cream, but compared to him, they simply used it as nothing more than another uninteresting tidbit to fill their repertoire of dinner-party small talk. He, on the other hand, never spoke of his problem, for it was something personal and private and frankly, part of a neuroses that did not belong out in public.

On this day, he was due. In the highest heat of the day, Jack had tried to shake the ghost that had been on his trail since the day before by taking a run around the track across the street at Johns Hopkins. He had run that track nearly every day of his four years at the school. And even when he had passed on to the medical school, he still managed to make a pilgrimage all the way from the hospital, all the way from East Baltimore, to that track to take a run; sometimes once a week, sometimes once a month, but it was always enough to fill him up with his own pride of how far he'd come to this place. So now his homage to this place was his home, directly across the street, proudly facing Johns Hopkins—the university, he always felt compelled to make clear, not the hospital where he worked—and he would have no other home. Jack would live and die, he believed, right alongside the campus, this Homewood Campus, which had upon it the steps, his steps, that had brought him so far.

Jack was helped to his feet by a kind-faced young man with shocking pale skin set against a thick mane of deep brown, neatly cropped hair. Jack looked into the young man's eyes, which wore the shock and horror that perhaps Jack's should have had, and that's when Jack fully understood the extent of his injuries.

"Sir," the young man said with an accent that came from somewhere deeply south, "maybe we should get you over to the hospital."

When Jack looked down, his legs were covered with blood, and so were his sneakers. A thumping that could only have originated in his chest sounded in his ears, and his sweat was now the spawn of panic when he found that out of his right knee stuck a shard of glass about an inch long. His right elbow and hand didn't take as brutal a scraping, though there were bits and pieces of glass set shallowly in both. What was most incredible is that he felt no pain. It wasn't shock, because he did feel the fear of seeing his own blood and responded to that fear with loud cries of anguish laced with expletives. Calm overcame him, though, as soon as he looked down and saw the Coke still in the bottle. He took a long gulp and smiled a sideways smile, more to himself than to the young man, then looked around for the bottle cap, which had been lost at some point during his fall. Just as well. All the more reason to drink it till it was gone.

"Sir, I'll help you get to the hospital. I don't mind, you know. With you being in so much pain and all you really should go."

"Damn! I didn't even see that glass," Jack said into the face of this man who showed such genuine care. Then he let out a chuckle, mostly to set the young man at ease, and said, "Besides, who would expect to see broken glass on a street as clean as University Parkway, so close to the university? Anyway, thanks so much for your concern, but I'm a doctor, and I can take care of it when I get home. I live right around here. Thanks again." And that was Jack's cue for the man to get on his way.

"Okay, then," the young man said warily. "As long as you're sure. I hope you're better soon." And with a hesitant gait, and doubt on his face, he turned to leave Jack to hobble his way home. "Bye, now," he called over his shoulder.

Jack's limp worsened as the pain began to set in and throb. He thought about the glass, and wondered how he could have missed it, and when he remembered the eyes of that child he couldn't chastise himself for the distracted stumble, but his decision to fall was quite another matter. What most disturbed him as he limped down the street and toward home was not being able to do a thing about that part of his mind that possibly would have, *probably* would have, still made the decision to save the bottle of soda even after seeing the glass. There wasn't the element of having just spent his last dollar on it. There was plenty of money in his pockets to buy another one or twenty, but Jack knew he still would have consciously, with all good wits about him, chosen to spill his own blood rather than lose the Coke. And that is what flashed before him as he tumbled down—how this fall, which he refused to stop, was a metaphor for every decision he'd made within the last twenty-four hours. He'd nurtured his immediate need but compromised his general, long-term need to be whole, unscathed.

So, Jack was making his way home, limping along and swigging Coke when he saw a newspaper walking toward him, hiding the distracted eyes of the reader. He recognized the pants,

and the gait, moving along at a clip that showed it was so intimate with the path that it could walk it blindly; a walk familiar
enough for Jack to know. But if there were any doubts at all,
the hands clutching the newspaper gave away the man's iden-
tity completely. Those hands the color of coconut shells, the
texture of coconut shells, sometimes so dry they seemed to
flake scales, left no doubt in Jack's or anyone else's mind that
when Chuck Teague says that he worked his way through medical school, he clearly wasn't saying it for a dramatic, rags-to-
riches effect, nor did he mean that he worked at some bookish
academic job. Those hands were the hands of hard labor. So,
certain that these were the hands of his friend, Jack set his voice
low, and mocking the formality of a stranger said, "Excuse me,
Dr. Teague, but you'd better look where you're going, unless
you can see through that paper."

Startled, Chuck jerked the paper away from his face. He
looked to find Jack standing in front of him and let out a low,
easeful laugh, then he gave Jack his soft smile that always
seemed like a gift. "Hey, Jack. What's up, man?" And he
embraced Jack like a missing brother. When he stepped back,
he looked down at Jack's bloodied leg and said, "Man, what in
the world happened to your leg?"

"Ah, it's not so bad. I cut it when I fell after my run. I was just
over at the track."

"That leg looks bad, and I can't believe you ran in this heat.
Man, you're crazy."

"Yeah, I know. But I really needed to clear my head. I've
been working like a dog."

"I can't give you a hard time for that. I've done the same
thing. Anyway, it's better than running through the streets.
Somehow, it doesn't seem so hot when you're running around
that track."

"So, what's that you're reading?" Jack said, pointing with his
head at the newspaper.

"Oh, check this out. You'll be interested in this. It's an editor-
ial this guy wrote in the *Sun* this morning about medical ethics.
He's talking about the man who died yesterday over on

Twenty-eighth Street, and how there may have been a doctor there who could have saved the man's life. Did you hear about that?"

Jack nodded his head with so little movement that his yes was nearly imperceptible.

"So, anyway, this guy is saying that no matter what went down between the doctor and the dead man, the doctor still had a moral obligation to save that man's life. Huh. You know what I say? I say that considering some of the white folks you can find over there, there's no telling what went down. That man might have said, or even done, almost anything to that doctor. Hell, the son finally admitted that his father had had some pretty uncouth words with the doctor, but he didn't say what they were. So, depending on what those words were, I might have left him there to die myself." Chuck looked into Jack's blank face, which would give away no part of his mind, or conscience. Then Chuck laughed awkwardly and said, "Well, anyway, I know that you'd never do something like that. You're so dedicated to medicine. I'm not saying I'm not dedicated, but I guess I'm saying that I would be more inclined to submit to being human. You, though, you're one of those exceptions who can rise above it all."

Jack smiled distantly and looked off at the passing cars. In that one instant he could have told it all. He could have admitted to Chuck, who had been a part of his daily life since freshman biology, who held confidences that Jack wouldn't even have shared with his brother, that he, too, was as human. Jack could have just blurted it out—I'm the doctor who left that cracker to die like a rabid dog. But there was something about saying it aloud that simply wouldn't ring true, Jack thought, neither to Chuck nor to himself. So instead he said, "Yeah, well, I guess you can't make a judgment call unless you were there."

"That's right." Chuck glanced back at Jack's bloodied leg. "Hey, are you sure you don't need that leg sutured?"

"No, no. I'm okay, really. It looks a lot worse than it is, but it still hurts like hell. I can take care of it when I get home. Anyway, let me get on. Tell Nell I said hello."

"Yeah, sure. And you tell Lila hello for me, too. Say, we've been talking about all four of us getting together for dinner downtown. We should do that, you know."

"Okay, we *should* do that. Maybe one night this week. I'll tell Lila and she and Nell can work out a night when you two can get a sitter for the kids."

"Good. I'll see you." And Chuck walked on, opening his paper to the story of some doctor's slacked ethics.

With Chuck still on his mind, Jack crossed Charles Street midblock. Chuck had a charm that was indiscriminate in that it was equally slathered over men and women. It was in the way he could stroke anyone's ego without being sycophantic; as he'd just stroked Jack's with the way he put Jack above the mire of being human. And while Jack knew that such a charm left Lila cold and guarded, he, on the other hand, found it engaging, almost refreshing. In the freshest seconds after leaving Chuck, though, Lila's words whispered in an echo in Jack's mind: *I'm telling you, Jack, that man's charm will lead him down a truly unholy path.* How many times he'd heard this Jack could not be sure, but this he knew: Lila was adamant in her judgment.

IT WASN'T THAT Lila disliked Chuck, or even mistrusted him in the larger sense of not trusting him with her life, she thought as she watched from the living room window as Jack parted company with Chuck and crossed the street. No, she didn't dislike him at all. She was simply worried about Nell's heart in the midst of so much charm, for charm did not disarm Lila but kept her ten paces away—its exact intention. It always gave her the oddest chill of hidden secrets, though she believed she knew at least one of Chuck's.

In the upstairs hall of Chuck and Nell's house, there was a runner carpet. Now, Nell, Lila knew, shared with the children the bathroom that connected her bedroom with the boys' room.

Chuck, on the other hand, had his own bathroom, which sat off that hallway. So whenever Lila had the occasion to be upstairs in their home, which was rare, she never failed to notice that the runner was never centered in the hall, but pushed against one wall, the same wall that happened to hold the door to Chuck's bathroom. Though it never bothered her aesthetically, she still wondered about the off-center carpet each time she saw it until the day Nell had led her upstairs to see a pair of shoes she'd just bought and Chuck stepped out of his bathroom and onto the runner that was so conveniently right at his door, just for his feet. From the cold hard tile to the warm comfort of carpet. And that's when it struck her—thanks to his charm, no one would ever have the slightest inkling of Chuck's selfishness; a selfishness that would let him take a runner meant for the use of the whole family and use it merely for his own comfort, even if it meant skewing, if only slightly, the clean, sparse beauty of an otherwise perfect center hall. This was Chuck's secret, Lila believed, and nothing could make her believe otherwise.

But right now Chuck's excessive self-indulgence wasn't what plagued her. That contemplation was for another day. Her only interest was in knowing where Jack had been. Lila looked at the clock on the mantel to mark the amount of time she had been keeping a vigil for her missing husband, and she discovered that she had been standing at that window in that one spot for going on an hour. She thought about how her nerves had grown increasingly jangled in increments of five minutes with worry and horror over Jack's fate, and she couldn't help remembering that there was a time when she wasn't like this. Lila could sleep with the peace of a well-fed baby, of a soul untroubled, in those nights when an emergency bypass surgery kept Jack at the hospital longer than expected. She'd awaken only by the connected passion of Jack's presence in the room, or next to her in bed, or even coming through the front door, untouched in the least by haunting night scenes of Jack stepping out of the doors of Johns Hopkins Hospital into the middle of the worst part of East Baltimore.

But this morning, everything changed when she awoke to an empty space next to her in bed. "Jack!" she remembered bellowing. "Jack, where are you?" She was scared out of all reasoning, which would have told her Jack was indeed somewhere in the house. But he wasn't there next to her, and that was her fear. And when Jack ran to her, she could see the fear of what he might find in his troubled eyes, his tightened face. Jack didn't understand it then, she knew, any more than she understood herself now. Maybe it was the fainting spell of yesterday, or perhaps it could have been seeing death so close it seemed ten times its enormity, but whatever it was, Lila believed that something had definitely rewired her brain.

During her watch at the window, Lila had been certain that Jack had met some sort of calamitous fate. That was the only account she could think of for what could have possibly kept him so long. Where had he gone? she had wondered and worried at the living room window, searching up then down the street. No one could run this long in the kind of heat and humidity that was just beyond her, on the other side of the window. So what else had he done, and why wasn't she made privy to his whereabouts? It's not that she thought he'd done something, or would ever do something untoward, like meet another woman for a romp, or sell stolen hospital drugs from an abandoned crack den. Her mind would never travel to such ignominious places with him in tow. Where she did allow her mind to go, though, was to the middle of a street, University Parkway, mostly, flattened by a driver who would not know to call her; where he'd lay desperately injured, maybe even shrouded with death's black cloak, his mind calling for her help or for one last look at her face. And though, as she stood there, she heard not one ambulance screaming its way to some nearby tragedy, she still feared the worst. She was soberly aware of time's passing, sometimes not even allowing a full minute its due before gawking angrily at the clock as time did only what it knows to do—pass.

The churning in her gut grew up, and out, and for the scarcest second she thought she just might vomit. She leaned her bony bottom against the high arm of the chair that sat slanted in front of the window, hoping that partially sitting would stop the churning, and stop the burning that had begun just behind her eyes. The burning did stop, extinguished only by the tears that were hell-bent to well and fall.

She plucked a tissue from the box that sat atop the antique chocolate server—a Giles heirloom that did not fulfill its purpose in the Calloway home, but merely sat aside the chair as a side table holding a lamp, the box of tissues, and a small frame with a picture of Lila and Jack in Greece on their honeymoon. Lila wiped her tears in a smear, then nervous fingers picked and pulled at the tissue until it was nothing but shreds on the floor. Tissue after tissue met the same fate, so that by the time she had Jack in the grip of her view, at her feet was a pillowy pile of white. But it was only seconds before she saw him across the street with Chuck that Lila had determined that she would give her husband only five more minutes before she'd leave home in search of him, like some pioneer woman leaving the homestead to trudge through the heat of hell to help her man and bring him home.

So, just as Jack approached home, and her heart settled back from her mind's foray into tragedy, it seemed to stop again. Blood, Jack's blood, seemed to her to be all over him. She ran to the door and threw it open. "Jack, what happened?" And in that short time, before she had come to know why he was bleeding, Lila was beside herself with fret and fright. "Oh my God! Look at you! What happened? What happened to your legs?"

Jack limped past her, instinctively placing a carefree kiss on lips that were shocked apart by terror and not at all prepared to receive such affection. He went to the living room and eased himself into the chair by the window as Lila closed the door and hurried to his side. "Well, I was crossing University Parkway coming from the store, and when I got to the other side of the street, I tripped over the curb and fell on some glass." He paused only to take in Lila's face, heavy with dread, before he assured, "It looks a lot worse than it is, Lila. It's really not so bad. I can take care of it."

"How, Jack? You fell in glass, for goodness sake! That can't be good. You need to go to the hospital." And she went to leave the room in haste to get her purse and her car keys.

"Lila, come on. Get back here, now. I don't need to go to the hospital. I have everything right here in the house that I need to clean this up." He looked off to his side, to find the pile of shredded tissues. He asked, "Lila, what's that?"

Distracted only briefly, she glanced at the pile of white fluff, then answered, "Nothing. I'll get it later." She glared at him again, then went back to the point, folding her arms across herself in judgment. With a voice rife with sarcasm, she said, "And so you think you have everything you need, do you? What about a tetanus shot? Can you give yourself one of those? Do you have that in the house?"

Jack slouched back in the chair and ran his hand across his head, as if pushing back an invisible mane of hair. He drew in a breath and looked over at his wife with perplexed eyes. She was worked up, and he didn't know why. "Lila, what is wrong with you?"

"What's wrong with *me*?" Her eyes were angry, accusatory, frightened. "What's wrong with me is that I was sitting here worried half to death about where you were and what might have happened to you and here you come, limping back here with your legs covered with so much blood it looks like you've been shot. That's what's wrong with me! What in the world took you so long? Where in the world were you?"

In the second it took him to blink, Jack gazed at her with uncertainty. His eyes squinted into her eyes as if he was wondering why she was standing before him asking where he'd been. "I went over to Hopkins for a run," he said with the measured rhythm of uncertainty. "I told you that before I left."

"The hospital?"

"No, Lila. I went across the street," he said impatiently.

"Well, I had to ask, because you took so long. Nobody can possibly run that long in this kind of heat."

"Lila, are you accusing me of something?"

"No!" she said with bugged eyes and a nervous giggle that

originated not from humor at all but rather fear. "I'm just saying that I was worried that you had passed out over there from the heat, or something. I didn't know what could have happened."

"Well, it was too hot for a run, but I needed to run. That's all there is to it. And anyway, I've been over there many times, Lila, running just as long as I did today, some days longer, and you've never worried like this."

Lila looked past Jack and out the window at flashes of the sun's reflection sliding from one passing car to the next. Though she did not have an actual question before her, she could feel it, see it, smell it, hear it, as it hung in the room with the high hopes of a hummingbird. And so she felt obliged to answer, to come up with something, though she didn't know what, to make rational the irrational. She lowered her eyes, then her head followed, and as she turned to leave the room, she mumbled barely loud enough to be heard, "It's just this heat, that's all."

When Lila came back into the living room, she found Jack slumped down in the chair with his eyes shut. "Jack?" she called out in a panic. And when his eyes opened with a shock, she didn't need him to answer her call. She struggled with the weight of the first aid kit, which was no white box of ordinary size with a red cross emblazoned smack on top. Rather, it was a brown suitcase, the fraying at the edges telling of its years. Placing it on the floor in front of Jack, Lila knelt and unzipped it, and when she peeled back the top, revealed were bandages of varying types and sizes, and bottles and jars of liquids and salves of what, she did not know. "So, which of this stuff do you need?"

"No, I don't want to do this in here. Let's go upstairs to the bathroom," he said, pushing himself up and out of the chair.

Lila watched that leg of dried blood move past her and tried her best not to think of gangrene, or lockjaw, or amputation. She zipped the bag closed, stood with it, and followed her hobbled husband up the stairs, wondering if there was anything in the big brown suitcase that would prevent gangrene, lockjaw, or amputation.

She watched Jack put the lid down on the toilet seat and sit, and even though she knew his physical comfort would only come from his cleaning, disinfecting, and patching his own wound, all she wanted right now was the peace in her own mind that would only come from her cleaning it up. There'd be no real harm, as she saw it, since he'd already gotten the glass out. She still knew that later, maybe later in the night while she slept, he'd sneak off somewhere and do it again his way.

She saw him studying her every movement as she followed him into the bathroom carrying the first aid kit and a basin tucked awkwardly under her arm. She noticed his eyes squinting at her in bewilderment and a certain concern, as if he were expecting everything she carried to come crashing to the floor. "Why are you looking at me like that?" she asked defensively.

"What? Oh, no reason. Well, I was just wondering why you have that basin there."

"So that you can hold your leg over it while I clean it with water. I'm also going to need it to catch the Betadine solution when I pour it over the wound. You know that, so why are you questioning me? I think I've watched you enough times to know what I'm doing when it comes to doing this."

"No, I'm not questioning you at all, Lila. I guess I just forgot, that's all." And Jack sat back, while Lila went about patching him up. Then he said, "Listen, sweetie, we need to talk about why you were freaking out just because I was a little later than usual coming back from my run."

"It was hot. I was worried. You could have passed out somewhere from the heat, unable to tell anybody who you are or where you live."

"Yeah, but that's ridiculous. Nothing was going to happen to me. I keep good and hydrated when I'm running, and you know that."

Lila froze where she was and looked at him sideways. "Jack, you can honestly look at me patching up your bloodied leg and say that my worrying was ridiculous? That nothing was going to happen to you?"

"Okay, okay," Jack said, with a breath of exasperation behind it. "You're right. The fall is really what slowed me down and kept me from getting back sooner."

"I didn't need you to tell me that," she said as she went about the business of washing his wound.

"So, what all were you doing, aside from crying, while I was gone?"

"Thinking. And watching for you. But mostly thinking."

"About what?"

"About what happened yesterday. Jack, we've got to talk about it," she said as she stopped washing in midstroke to look at him. "Yesterday was so bad, Jack, and as much as I want it to just go away, I think we need to talk about what we're going to do, and what's going to happen."

As his eyes retreated, Jack looked at Lila, his glare only skimming the side of her face and said, "What is there to do, Lila? He's not Lazarus and I'm not Jesus. I can't raise him from the dead."

"No, you're not Jesus, and what you did, Jack, what *we* did was ungodly, leaving a man to die like that."

Jack took in a breath so deep it seemed that he would explode, in one way or another. He tapped his finger nervously on his one good knee, and nodded his head, as if to a rhythm only he and dogs could hear.

Then he offered, "Lila, Jesus came to this earth fully human, and fully divine. I'm only fully human." Then he gently slid his leg from her, and even more gently took the cloth from her hand. "Look, I'll take care of this, okay? You can just go. I'll finish up."

Lila relented and handed over the cloth, but then stood and planted herself firmly. It would have been quite reasonable, she thought, simply not to say another word to Jack. But reason taking on the life that it takes in a marriage, becoming twisted, and conditioned, and abstracted, silence would not be within the realm of reason. So she said, "I'll let you finish, Jack, but I won't go." And when he didn't respond, she could nearly hear every muscle in him clenching, clamping, locking him up. "Your argument, Jack, about divinity seems to suggest that because we're not fully divine that we are excused from taking the part of God that lives in us and doing something divine with it. And if you're saying that, then you just might as well stop being a doctor, because there's no point to it."

"I'll tell you what there's no point to, Lila. There's no point to this conversation. Now if you won't go, then I will. All I want to do is bandage my leg and then relax for the rest of my only day off. All I want is peace in my home. Can I do that, can I have that without you being on my back about me and my ungodly act?" Jack held his leg over the basin and poured the Betadine solution all over his open wound, letting it run off. He salved his leg with a topical antiseptic while Lila's angry eyes lit into him as he did it all. Once he settled the gauze under the water-proof patch that secured his wound, Jack hobbled to his feet, still under Lila's watchful eye, and poured the basin of bloodied water and Betadine solution into the sink. And just as he hobbled past Lila to leave the bathroom, he turned with a start when he heard Lila shriek.

"Jack!"

"What is it?" he snapped.

"Where the hell do you think you're going? We are not finished. Be a man, damn it, and deal with what you've done."

"You want me to be a man?"

"That's right, I want you to be a man," Lila said with the heavy breathing spurred by a heart racing full of fear.

"Okay, well, I'll be a man. And right now, this man's going downstairs to his den to relax under his cool air-conditioning, and this man would want nothing more than for you to leave him the hell alone."

"Don't you dare, Jack," Lila said with a rising fury that she was trying desperately—more than she had ever tried to do anything—to have power over. "You'd better be very careful what you're saying and what you're doing, and you'd better decide if it's worth it." And as she watched Jack move closer to the door without so much as a mumble under his breath or a grunt from her gut, Lila saw her hand move, as if independent from her mind and body, over to the vanity that was right by her side and clutch something. She could hear nothing and could only hazily see anything. So, when her jar of bath salts flew with a force that had come from some unfathomable rage and crashed against the door—the door that Jack had scarcely gotten closed for his own protection—then broke to bits on the floor, she had to look in the mirror to find the irate woman who'd thrown it. It was only when she saw the anger, the seething wrath in her own eyes, that she awoke from the fiendish stupor that had claimed her will.

"You're crazy, damn it," she heard Jack say through the door as his voice faded down the stairs.

"Maybe I am crazy!" she yelled until her voice cracked, "but I'm not so crazy that I lie to myself and believe it! You think about that and then tell me who's CRAZY!!" Tears burned where they were born, and then fell as if they had always been falling, as if they'd never stop. She was so filled up with every conceivable emotion that up until that moment, she had only known one at a time. Now, anger, frustration, fear, and even a twinge of hatred all piled up in her tiny self to rage in a hellish war. She slid down to the cold tiled floor, with her back against the tub, and pulled her legs to her chest. In her childlike ball, she let her head rest on her knees, and she cried the way she had wanted to cry when she and Jack, almost exactly twenty-four hours before, had driven farther and farther away from any hope of their own salvation.

And after she got every single tear wrung from her eyes, something intoxicating had filled the room with the smell of brightness; bright enough to stop tears. Was it the soap in the tub's soap dish? She picked it up and sniffed, but that wasn't it. Then, just as quickly as she had forgotten, she remembered, and her eyes were guided, more by olfaction than by the memory of her fury, to the scent of exotic flowers that had now completely overpowered the bathroom. When her eyes could focus through remnant tears, she saw the bright blue crystals, mingled with glass, scattered on the floor at the door. How could she have forgotten, in the barest second, that she had nearly pulverized Jack's head with the jar of bath salts? And could anger, she wondered, have made her act against her very nature, and then forget? It was too frightening to think about, because if she could come a hair away from seriously hurting the only man she'd ever loved, it could make her do anything. She could kill.

Lila crawled over to the remnants of her ire and picked out the large shards of glass, tossing them into the trash. And as she scooped the bath salts, chucking handfuls into the trash, she wondered if she would have ever said *I do* had she known that she'd one day end up on her hands and knees, cleaning up a jar of broken bath salts she'd tried to break against her husband's head the day after they had left a man to die. Probably not, she had to believe. Probably not.

chapter five

ILA SAT AT her desk with no sound filling the studio except the hum of her computer and a click, click, clicking as she searched for anything she could find on lockjaw. Her imagination had taken her to a place where she saw the disease, minute by minute, squeezing Jack's jaw, pulling, clenching, tightening it through savage pain until his only means of communication would be the mmmm's trying to slide their way frantically through his locked-down lips. Never again would the power of speech reign so prominently in his life, in his mind. And in the final seconds of the wrenching pain that would render him mute, he would pray for the impossible chance to relive the moment when he could have heeded her warning and gone to the hospital for a shot. Actually, she didn't know for certain whether he had an up-to-date tetanus shot, but given that he took better care of his patients than he took of himself, she had to believe that he didn't. Still, she read on, about extremely painful spasms, and how lockjaw could incubate for two days, or two weeks, and how there should be no delay in getting the shot. They had cleaned the cuts and scrapes completely, and Jack drowned his leg in antiseptic, but how could she be sure this was enough? Lila's chest boomed with dread, because considering everything she was now reading, Jack, she believed, would be dead in a day.

She logged off while grabbing the phone and dialing Jack. Most likely, she thought as she dialed, he'd still be at home, just about to walk out the door. But instead she heard their answering-machine message, too cute, with Jack's voice, *This is Jack* . . . and her voice, *This is Lila* . . . and then in sickening unison, as if she were sitting in his lap in a baby-doll nightie, . . . *And we're not home*. . . . If it were any phone message other than her own, it would be enough to make her want to hang up and never call again. Yet, after two years of marriage, it was one of those things she endured in quiet embarrassment because it simply seemed like the prerequisite show of affection that told of their fused oneness—like steadfastly holding hands while maneuvering through a throng, where walking detached would be far more prudent, or *I love you*'s that could be prompted by nothing more than passing the bread at dinner. Lila did hang up, though, but only because to leave a message would be absurd. And just as she was about to pick up the phone again to get him at the hospital, Nell's key slid into the lock.

"Hey," Nell said with surprised eyes. "This is new, you here when I get in. What brought you here so early?" Nell gave Lila one of those smiles that seemed to try its best to be as easy as a summer Sunday.

"Oh, I just wanted to look something up on the Internet," Lila said, placing the phone back where it belonged. She didn't want Nell to see her in such a panic. "You know, Jack took a bad fall yesterday and cut his legs up something awful. He insisted on treating himself and not going to the hospital. He needs a tetanus shot, but you can't tell him anything."

Nell closed the door and locked it, then went to her desk to relieve her arms of the bag of bagels and thermos of lemonade. She plopped into her chair with seemingly wearied legs, breathing only slightly heavily from the climb up all those stairs. "Well, that's a common problem with doctors, you know. Chuck will do the same thing." Her lips formed into an exasperated twist, and her eyes rolled all over the room. Then she said with mocking sarcasm, "They know what's best. Even if body parts start falling off, they're the doctors and they know what they're doing. Sometimes I think it would serve them right if they ended up in bad shape because of their arrogance."

Lila tilted her head, her eyes lively, her lips parted, at the ready to harmonize in this song of frustrated wives until she thought about what she was about to do. It would serve them right, she thought. Would it really serve them right? No, it wouldn't, it couldn't possibly. What a despicable way to prove a point.

But instead of offering up an amen and hallelujah, which she felt Nell fully expected, Lila said, "Nell, have you ever wished something bad would happen to someone and then it happened?"

"Oh, Lila," Nell said frantically, with deep apology in her squinting face. "I'm not at all saying that I *want* something bad to happen to Jack. I'm just saying—"

"Oh, I know, Nell. And I'm not talking about that, anyway. I'm just saying have you ever wished something horrible would happen to a horrible person, and then it happened?"

Nell looked to the ceiling, then replied, "No, I can't say that I have. Why?"

"Because I wished death on somebody out of anger, and now they're dead, and I just have this tremendous weight of guilt on me."

"Oh, that. Well, the closest I've come to something like that was when Princess Diana died."

"You wished she was dead?!" Lila said with a near-deafening pitch, scarcely able to believe what she'd heard. "But she wasn't a horrible person."

"Of course she was a good person, and of course I didn't wish her dead!" Nell said in a snap, glaring at Lila, as if to wonder how she could have assumed such noxious darkness secretly lived in her friend's heart. "What happened was that when she was killed and all this hoopla started up over her death and what she'd done for the world, and blah, blah, blah, I said to Chuck one night when we were watching all that news coverage, 'If Mother Teresa were to die tomorrow, nobody would be carrying on like this.' Well, the very next day, Chuck called me from the hospital and said, 'Well now you've done it. You've killed Mother Teresa.' The woman died the very next day, Lila. The very next day! To this day I still feel responsible for that sweet old sainted woman's death."

"Oh, my God," Lila said, covering her mouth with astonishment, but mostly trying to rein in the smile that was a prelude to laughter. "How awful for you, Nell. You never told me about that." And now, laughter was complete.

"Well, why would I, Lila? I couldn't tell anybody about that. And stop laughing!" she snapped, with a faint smile on her own lips, as if she knew her command was futile. "As it is, Chuck still thinks it's just the funniest thing he's ever heard. But there's nothing funny about it at all, to me."

"Oh, come on, Nell," Lila said, her laughter uncontrollable. "You have to at least find some humor in the irony. I mean, there we were, sitting around mourning and shaking our heads and filling all of our small and big talk with what a shame it was that this tragic, fallen princess died who had done so much for the world, and the world had to lose her in such an untimely way, and oh, how the world would miss her, and everybody cried. 'I didn't know her, but she just seemed like an angel here on earth.' How many people did you see on the television saying something like that? And then you offer up a chunk of reality, asking if the world would be mourning in quite the same way for a far less glamorous humanitarian, and then fate comes stepping in to prove your point. The irony is hysterical, Nell."

"I guess it is," Nell said, with a shadowy smile beginning to grow full. And by now she was chuckling when she added, "I mean, after all, it's not like I wished her dead, like you wished someone would die. And who is this dead person you wanted dead, anyway?"

And the light, whose life on Lila's face, on this day, was only temporary, slid away like the melting driblets from a candle. With slowness. And seemingly of its own will. In an instant she could have told Nell. But in that same instant, Lila knew that to give it a face that was already too real to most of Baltimore by now, and have that face attached to her own in Nell's mind was much too much shame to bear all at once. So, she smiled crookedly, and cutting her eyes sharply from Nell's, said, "No one, really. I mean, someone actually died, but I guess I didn't really want them dead. I just wanted something horrible to happen, that's all, and the horrible thing turned out to be death. I would never wish anyone dead, no matter how awful they are." And as she said it, Lila was glad she was not looking Nell square in the eyes.

"No, most people wouldn't. But even if you did, I just don't think it works like that. I don't think you can say something like 'I just wish he would die!' and then God complies. If that were the case, people would be just keeling over on a daily basis because somebody wished them dead out of anger, or frustration, or whatever. It just doesn't work like that."

Lila lowered her eyes doubtfully. "Maybe it depends on how strong, and how ceaselessly, you wish death to fall."

"Maybe." And Nell left it at that. "Anyway, Chuck told me that he ran into Jack yesterday. He said that we should plan for dinner out one night this week. I know I can get a sitter for the kids on Wednesday, so how does that look for you?"

There was no answer, not even a hint that Nell's question had fallen onto ears that heard words in any particular order that made sense. Poor me, Lila thought, as she mired in her heart's musings of being made an untimely widow. Here she sat, she thought, worried about the health of a man who believed his degree told him all he ever needed to know, compounded by the fear that her black desires were actually powerful fate. But she couldn't just sit torturing herself with self-sorrow. Lila finally came out of her deep momentary stupor long enough to snatch up the phone and dial furiously.

"Lila, is Wednesday okay for you and Jack?"

"For what?"

"Dinner with me and Chuck, Lila. That's what I just asked you about."

"Yeah, Wednesday's fine," she said distractedly. Then, into

the phone she said, directly to the humorless, cool-spirited nurse on whom chit-chat and niceties were always wasted: "Hello, I'm calling for Dr. Calloway. This is his wife. Is he there?" And while she waited for Jack to come on the line, she smiled easily at Nell, as if her behavior in the last few moments had not been the least bit odd. Then she beamed as she said, "He is?! Oh, that's great! Thank you so much. Would you just let him know that I called, please?" Lila was so elated by what she'd just learned that she'd lost sight of all of her manners, forgetting to bid the nurse good-bye. She let out a hoot of a laugh, then said, "Nell, my husband is in with your husband, getting a tetanus shot." And as if she'd just been given a reprieve from her own imminent death, Lila slumped with relief over her desk. "This is great, you just have no idea, Nell." She was certain Nell would truly have no idea, certain that Nell had never had fate threaten to plunder her life in retribution for ignominy. Nell had never known, Lila was sure, and would never know, she prayed, the fear of what can be exacted when karma, without a warning, becomes questionable. So she beamed at Nell's innocence.

But then Lila saw Nell's close-lipped grin, as if she were holding back a truth. She wondered if her friend had any memory whatsoever of when life was uncomplicated and lives and hearts were merged tightly enough to make Chuck's pains her own. And now, as she sat breathing for Jack, feeling for Jack, living for Jack, Lila felt a blush of warmth, yet an oddly congruous deep mourning for the way things might not always be. She watched Nell unscrew the thermos of lemonade and pour her cup half full, probably for something to do that would distract her from the melancholy that had taken over her face. Lila wondered if her face, which was by now nothing but the sun, had placed an envy in Nell's heart for this kind of love, still so new. As she watched Nell sip her lemonade, Lila studied her friend with eyes flattened by a mysterious heartbreak that had come from left of nowhere to claim her. And she wondered when it would end.

chapter six

How could it have happened, Lila thought as she stood motionless, listening to the racket of chat rising from the living room, that her sister Linda, her stepmother, and Jack's parents would actually all be visiting Baltimore and landing in her home on the same day for the same four-day visit? It was all so very surreal; it was definitely unfair, but mostly it was fate at its sinister best. And there was only one morsel that Lila could hold on to that could get her through the balance of the evening—they weren't, all four of them, staying at her home for the four days. Her stepmother and Linda she was dumping on her brother, Gil. In fact, where was Gil, come to think of it? she thought. He'd better not try to pull a fast one and change his mind about putting them up, she suddenly feared, because she and Jack were long on space for all four of them, but quite short on patience.

That they were all in there together talking was astounding enough for Lila, considering her stepmother and Jack's father were as likely to be in comfortable conversation together as a lion would be to share his den with a tiger. Same family, different animal. Jack's mother was another story, since she was a reasonable woman. And Linda, well, Lila was certain she was distant and fashionably bored in the corner of the sofa, but somewhere very near to her stepmother's side. But when Lila thought about Jack's father and the way he thrived on pushing the rowdy envelope of contention as strongly as her stepmother lived for her upright gentility, Lila couldn't be certain, but she would bet that maybe not all of hell, but at least a part of it, would break loose before the night was through. She'd just stay low, duck and cover, and keep out of the line of fire.

Well, for now it all seemed sane in there, as voices and words danced with one another in midair to make an unintelligible mix that only they could understand; at least all was calm, or so it seemed from where she stood, way back in the kitchen. The cloud of their chatter came rushing in to her when Linda pushed open the kitchen door and walked through.

"Momma wants more of those stuffed olives," Linda said, putting an empty bowl down on the counter.

"They're in the refrigerator," Lila said without looking up from the broccoli she was putting into a serving dish. "How's everything going out there?"

"Oh, God! So boring," Linda said, as if exhausted by the thought.

"Come on, Linda," Lila said, laughing because she knew Linda had to be telling the truth. "What's happening?"

"Well, Momma's in there talking about the prizewinning rose garden she's grown down in Florida, and how she took that class to get the title of master gardener. And then, as if that wasn't boring enough, Cordelia and Dub start talking about how they grow all these vegetables on their plot of land out back and take them to town to sell them, and how one day a polecat got chased into their vegetable beds by their old hound dog and 'dang near spoiled the whole bunch of it.' And then, 'Dub had a devil of a time,' Cordelia said, 'gettin' that ole polecat out of those vegetables.'" And she managed to mock Dub and Cordelia, and even Dub's name by drawling it out, without even a trace of a smile. She slumped herself up on the stool at the counter where Lila stood, then continued, "Of course Momma had to lean over and whisper to me that a polecat is a skunk, as if I even cared. I just wanted something either to drop through the ceiling and lift me out of that room or shoot me. Oh, and then it got real crazy, you know, with the three of them, but mostly Momma and Dub, trying to outdo each other with how good they are at growing their gardens. Momma was actually in there making up stories about how people stop their cars, asking if they can photograph her roses. That's just a lie, Lila. And then Dub starts talking about how he grew watermelons so sweet and juicy that people were fighting one another over the last one. I don't know for sure, of course, but that sounds like a lie, too. So, I'd had enough, and that's when I saw that the olives were gone and I told Momma that I'd run and get more. And here I am."

"Well, we'll be eating soon. Maybe the conversation at the dinner table will be more interesting," Lila said through a laugh she was trying hard to suppress.

"Don't count on it. That Dub, he just never shuts up. And what kind of a name is Dub, anyway? It's the stupidest name I've ever heard in my life."

Just then, before Lila could explain, Jack pushed through the kitchen door, letting it swing dramatically behind him. He looked, to Lila, the way Linda felt, and his strain couldn't be missed. "How're things going, Jack?" she said, without a need to ask but wanting him to have his say, let it out.

"Oh, just fine," he said with an unmistakable disdain.

"What does that mean?" she said, looking up and becoming stilled by the strain that was more intense than she'd assumed as it tightened every part of his body. She knew that when his jaws clenched in the way that made words struggle to slide from his lips, tension radiated to every muscle.

"It means that aside from the fact that my father and your mother have to comment on everything the other says, as well as what anybody else says, things are going quite well. I just need to know how close we'll be to eating once Gil gets here?"

"See, I told you," Linda said to Lila.

"Once Gil gets here we can just sit down and eat, Jack. In fact, why don't you go ahead and get everybody in the dining room. We'll just start without Gil." She was as anxious as anyone to have the evening over.

"No, we can wait for Gil. It'll be okay, I guess," he said, his demeanor softening considerably.

"Okay," Lila said, placing a top on the dish she'd just filled with broccoli. "Well, let me get the olives and then I'll be right in."

"Good," Jack said as he moved toward the kitchen door. "I hope your brother gets here soon so we can eat, because maybe with food in their mouths they just might shut up," and he left the room.

For as much as Lila chuckled as she followed shortly behind Jack and Linda, she knew there was nothing funny about their predicament, hers and Jack's. One of them should have been able to have complete normalcy on their side of the family. At least Jack had his mother, Cordelia, Lila thought as she walked into the living room, giving her mother-in-law a smile too warm to be the insincere daughter-in-law kind; but then again, Jack's father was irksome enough for both himself and Cordelia. Lila just tried her best not even to look at him. She placed the bowl down on the coffee table and announced, "Here are the olives."

"They certainly are delicious, honey," Eulelie said.

"Oh, yeah," Cordelia said. "I've never had anything like these before." She leaned over from where she sat in the chair and put a few on her napkin. "Where'd you get something like this, 'cause I ain't ever seen this in the market where we shop down in Virginia."

"I got these in the gourmet section at Giant," Lila said as she took a few on a napkin and sat between her mother and sister on the sofa. "I usually shop at the Safeway farther down on Charles Street, but once in a while I like to break up my routine and ride out to the Giant in the Rotunda Mall. Only once in a blue moon, though, you know, because I just can't take parking out there. That parking lot makes me want to scream each and every time I go. It's too frustrating for me to even want to bother."

"Oh, yes, and it's always been that way," Eulelie said.

"Is that so?" Cordelia said. "So are these expensive, Lila?"

But before Lila had a chance to answer, she could see that Jack's father, Dub, had two cents to add.

"Of course they are. These two don't do nothin' on the cheap. With whatever it is that she does, and Big Time Dr. Dub Junior—oh, I'm sorry," he said in a tone to suggest that mockery was not far behind. He put his hand on his chest as if for sarcastic effect and said: "I mean Dr. Jack Calloway. Dub Junior don't exist no more. It's a little bit too lowbrow for a highfalutin' doctor like him."

Lila rolled her eyes to the ceiling, dismal with the thought of hearing again how Jack relinquished the moniker of Dub Junior. So she simply would not put in his hands the opportunity. "Well, actually they were a little bit more than what you pay for olives in a jar or can, but they weren't that expensive," Lila said, in a tone and manner to indicate that what Dub had to say either went unheard or was simply insignificant.

"As with anything," Eulelie said, pausing to chew and swallow another olive, "you pay for quality. There's absolutely nothing wrong with that, honey."

The bell chimed, and Jack was the first to jump for the door, getting to it, it seemed, before the chimes had stopped reverberating. "Gil!" he said with enthusiasm as he swung open the door. "Come on in. We've been waiting for you."

"Hey, Jack. How's it going?" Gil said, stepping through the door, clutching a bag. He handed it to Jack and said, "I know this is like pouring a glass of water in the well, but I brought a bottle of wine for dinner."

"Ah, that's great, man. You know wine is always welcome by me." He closed the door behind Gil and followed him into the living room. "Gil's here, so I guess we can eat now, Lila."

Lila got up from the sofa and went to Gil. Standing on her tiptoes, she planted a kiss on his cheek. "Hey, big brother." Then, hugging him, she slyly whispered in his ear, "So, are you ready for your houseguests?"

Gil laughed lightly and whispered back to her, "Yeah, I'm as ready as I'm going to be. But we really need to talk about the fairness of this whole arrangement."

"Nothing to talk about, big brother," she said, still whispering and still embracing him. "I've got my in-laws for a mind-numbing four days. It's six in one hand, half a dozen in the other. If you put Momma and Linda back on me, I'll have to send you Dub and Cordelia. It's shared pain, big brother." And she pulled out of the embrace laughing gaily.

Gil kissed her on the forehead and let her loose. Linda was standing nearby, but not too close to have heard Lila's whisperings. Gil stretched out his arms and took her into them.

"Hey, Linda. How's it going?"

"It's going just fine, Gil. I'm really glad to see you," Linda said, hugging Gil as if he were as comforting as an old worn robe.

"Dub, Cordelia, you remember my son, Gil, don't you?" Eulelie said, practically pushing Linda out of her way so that she could get her chance at hugging Gil. "How are you, honey? You're looking so good, so handsome."

Gil simply smiled in thanks at his mother and said, "It's good to see you, Momma." Then he loosed one arm from his mother and stuck his hand out to Dub. "How are you, Mr. Calloway, Mrs. Calloway? How're those vegetables growing? Those tomatoes you gave me last year sure were good."

"They're doin' just fine, son," Dub said. "They keep me goin' from sunup to sundown."

Cordelia cackled with delight and added, "Oh Gil, you're still talkin' 'bout those tomatas? Well, I'll be. I'll just have to send some back for you with Jack and Lila next time they come down."

"I'd certainly appreciate it," Gil said, finally freeing himself from his mother's arm, allowing him to give Cordelia a peck of a kiss on her cheek. "Yeah, those tomatoes sure taste different from the stuff you buy at the supermarket. Taste-wise, you can't even compare a garden-grown tomato to a supermarket tomato." Gil went to sit but couldn't get in the chair before getting the rush from Lila.

"Okay, Gil's here, so I guess we can eat now," Lila said as she stood in the center hallway, trying to herd everyone, with her beckoning arms, across the hall and into the dining room. "Everything's ready, so we might as well eat while the food's still hot."

"Well my goodness, Lila," Eulelie said. "What in the world is the big rush? And where are your manners? Gil just got here and he hasn't had a chance to sit and visit. It's just not proper to rush a meal as soon as the last guest arrives."

Lila drilled an unescapable stare into her mother's eyes and felt something rising in her that she had felt many, many times before with this woman. She's doing it again, Lila thought, she's trying to run my life, my home, my dinner, and I won't have it. "The rush, Momma," she countered, "is that *my* dinner is ready, and *I'm* ready to serve it. It's not like we'll eat in silence. We'll have plenty of opportunity to visit with Gil." She smiled in a rather self-satisfied way as she turned to the rest of her guests. "Dinner is served. Now, if everyone will go into the dining room and sit wherever you're most comfortable," she instructed, "Jack and I will get the food on the table for you."

Jack followed Lila into the kitchen, making sure the door had stopped swinging, before he said, "You really put your mother in her place, huh?"

"You know, Jack, I could have let it go, but then it would be just like old times, with her telling me what to do and me doing it. This is my home and my life, and she's the one who has to fit into it, not the other way around." And when Jack said nothing right away, in agreement or disagreement, she knew that he never would, because she knew that the last place Jack wanted to be was smack in between Lila and Eulelie for any reason, particularly since he had his father, the three-hundred-pound problem of his own, to tackle.

Jack wheeled the serving cart out of the closet and put it next to the counter. He picked up two full serving dishes and put them on the cart without realizing how hot they were. "Ouch! Jesus, that's hot."

"Did you think I was lying when I said the food was hot?" Lila said in teasing sarcasm, but with a vague edge on the side that said maybe she was only partially kidding. Only the presence of her mother, she thought, could put this kind of edge on her.

"Yeah, I guess you did say it was hot, didn't you?" And with the protection of Lila's oven mitts, Jack got the rest of the food loaded onto the cart. "I'll just go ahead and take in the food. You can bring the water and the wine."

When Jack entered the dining room pushing the serving cart with Lila on his heels, the room fell silent in a way that caused a look of bemusement to come across both their faces.

"Is something wrong?" Jack inquired.

"That's a really nice serving cart," Gil said.

"Where in the world did you get that?" Eulelie said. "You just don't see pieces that exquisitely and solidly made anymore."

"Oh, the cart," Lila said, setting the wine down in the center of the table. "Well, it was left by the previous owners." And that's all she said, as she was concentrating on pouring water in glasses.

Looking down at the cart, as if unsure why such fuss was being made over it, Jack picked up the story. "Lila and I found it down in the basement. So I called the former owners and asked if they wanted it. They said no, so I cleaned it up, refinished it, put some new wheels on it, and here it is." Jack regarded the cart again, as if with new eyes. "I guess it is pretty unique, huh?" Then he looked across the table to where Dub sat, because though Jack didn't know what specifically, he knew something was coming.

And without a moment's hesitation, Dub said, "Well, that would be right up your alley, boy. Taking handouts and hand-me-downs from rich uppity white folks."

Jack looked to his mother, who looked back at him helplessly. But she could do no more than he when it came to the stench that had always been between Jack and his father. And then there was the heat of Eulelie's silent stare of judgment boring into Jack, and into Cordelia, and into Dub. Just as he was about to relent to the silence, Cordelia's voice, tiny and sweet, saved him.

"Now, Dub Senior, you shouldn't go teasin' Jack like that. It's just not nice." And then she let out a shrill of a laugh that seemed obvious in its tenor.

Then Jack, just as if nothing had been said, and nothing had been heard, added, "I guess they entertained a lot over their years in this house."

"How is it you can assume that the white people who left it were uppity?" Eulelie asked Dub. "Had you ever met them?"

"Naw, I ain't have to meet 'em. I just look around here at where they lived, and, well, you can tell they was prob'ly uppity."

"You can't assume that a person is uppity just because they live a comfortable lifestyle, Dub. It's ridiculous, and somehow just smacks of sour grapes."

"Sour grapes!" Dub said, rearing his head back indignantly. "What you talkin' 'bout, sour grapes? I ain't got no sour grapes for nobody. Not a soul. Not even for you, and you as rich and uppity as they come." And then he laughed, as if it was meant to be a joke.

So Eulelie stared him full in the face and replied, "Dub, if your life didn't turn out the way you dreamed it would turn out, that's no reason to attack those of us who got the life we worked to get. That's the problem—" And she was silenced in midsentence when Gil held her in a still stare, lips tight, jaw set, his breathing measured and rising as if with every inch he was creeping toward a most righteous anger. Those last words of hers, *the problem*. And how on earth she would complete that sentence was anybody's wonder. Would she sound off on the problem with self-righteous judgment? She could speak volumes on such a thing. Most likely, though, everyone knew what was in her heart. And that was the problem with black people like Dub—and Sandra, whom Gil almost brought into the Giles family straight from the wrong side of town. Eulelie seemed to shrink under Gil's squinted eyes. And in answer to those squinted eyes, could she indeed see the irony in Dub's judgment of the wealthy, and her own condemnation of the poor back in those days when Gil almost married Sandra? But whether she saw or was still blind, none of it mattered because with nothing more than his will, which was mighty through his stare, Gil had shut her mouth and reeled in her commentary. "Well, anyway, Dub," Eulelie continued, her tone softer, more amenable to reasoning with him, "you get my point. It's bad manners to judge."

"Ah, judge smudge," was all Dub said dismissively as he went digging into the broccoli that Jack had just put on the table.

Once all the food was on the table, and the hosts had taken their seats, Jack at the top of the table, Lila at the bottom, the sound of metal tapping against glass took over the room as the serving dishes passed around the table. It was all so very civilized, their family meal, until Linda, with the most innocent of questions, lit a spark.

"So, Lila," Linda said as she put the last spoonful of food on her still sparse plate, "how's *Lila Lilly's Story Hour* coming along? I actually log on some days when work is slow and watch you. It's just so well done, and it's amazing that it's only you and Nell doing it. Everybody in my office is so impressed that you're my sister."

"It's going really well, Linda. It's amazing the number of kids out there actually watching. And it's nice to know that *Lila Lilly's Story Hour* is more interesting to kids than a lot of the other junk on the Net that does nothing to exercise their minds."

"Well, I'd have to agree with that," Cordelia said. "Of course, we don't have a computer or nothin', so I ain't ever seen your little show. But it sure does seem like somethin' that'll keep these kids off the streets. Seems like the chil'ren you see hangin' 'round on these streets, rippin' and runnin', ain't no older than 'bout a minute, and they seem to be gettin' younger and younger. And only the Lord knows where their mothers is at. It's not like it was, I tell you, 'cause my boys and my girl knew that I wasn't gonna have them hangin' on a street corner. They had to get to their schoolwork."

"Well, you were a good mother," Eulelie said. "You had values that you passed on to Jack and Martha and. . . ." Eulelie looked to the ceiling for the name of Jack's brother. "I'm sorry, Cordelia, but I don't remember your other son's name."

"Oh, that's quite all right. It's Buford. Y'all didn't meet him 'cause he wasn't able to make it to the weddin'. He's in the army, you know, and he's stationed over in Germany. I think he's plannin' to make it his home once he comes out the army. He just loves it over there."

"Yeah, he's another one," Dub spoke up. "Thought he could marry his blackness away by marryin' some ole German woman, white girl. Germany's a hell of a place to try to get rid of your blackness 'cause they ain't gonna never let you forget you black. What a damned fool," Dub said, the only one laughing at what he alone found humorous.

"Well anyway, I made sure my kids stayed off the streets," Cordelia said, as if she hadn't heard a thing. But the way she squirmed with an itchy discomfort made it clear that she had indeed heard. "A lotta mothers can't make that claim."

"I'm just glad to do my part for children," Lila said. "They're so ignored in this society, and their little souls are the purest of any human beings." And then where did she go? Her mind glazed over with the cataract of her desire for her own innocent child, for which she now and again—more now than again—pined. Her desire for one had been creeping along at its own measured pace, and now it was trotting, about to become a full-out sweaty dash, and she couldn't deny its call. It was the sweetest distraction for her, right now, taking her from the thought of Dub and what he'd say next. So she let her eyes and thoughts come back to him as she watched Dub take a large wad of beef into his mouth, then settle back in his chair to chew it.

Dub managed to say in between bites, "Well, just what the hell is this *Lila Lilly's Story Hour* thing, anyway? How in the world do you do that kind of thing and call it work? Who gives you your paycheck, the kids?" And once again he had the opportunity to be the only one laughing at his own wit.

Lila drew in a deep breath and blew it out before she put the bite of food that sat on her fork into her mouth. She felt the expectation in the room, all of it directed at her, but she would answer only when she had gathered enough patience, and a little bit of kindness, to speak to Dub. So she chewed and chewed, knowing that ears were perked for what she'd say. But Lila would not hurry herself, because there was no point to it. With the way her life had been unfolding, Lila knew nothing was a certainty, but of one thing she was sure: Dub was the kind of man who, no matter how many times and ways she were to explain it to him, nothing would penetrate his pride.

"Well, as I've explained it to you before, I read stories to kids on the Internet at my *Lila Lilly's Story Hour* Web site. Some of them are stories I've written, some of them are stories by other writers. Every week, I leave the ending to one of my stories off so that the kids can write the ending the way they see it concluding, you see, and that way they get to be creative and feel a part of *Lila Lilly's Story Hour.*"

"So how many stories do you write of your own in a week, Lila?" Cordelia asked.

"I only write two stories a week. Mostly I read stories by other children's authors and then we ask the kids questions about the stories, like when something that happened in the story might have happened to them, and they write back and give us their thoughts. It's kind of like a book club for kids. And every Monday, I read some of the endings to my stories that are sent in."

"Oh my goodness, girl!" Cordelia said with what seemed to be pride in knowing her. "Look out Oprah Winfrey!"

"Well, I still don't see how you gonna make money doin' that," Dub said, looking around at everyone at the table but Lila. "I guess Mr. Money Bags over there, Mr. Big Time Doctor, don't need no wife who works. I guess he can afford to have a fam'ly where his wife don't work."

"I make money, Mr. Calloway," Lila said. She never called him Dub. It just seemed far too intimate for a man whose insensitivity made tedious any attempt at closeness. "I make money through advertisers who buy advertising space from us. I also make money from the parents of children who buy the stories I've written—they pay six dollars to download my stories."

"Uh-huh," he said, chewing on broccoli. "But at the end of

every week they're paying for a story that don't have no endin'. That don't make no sense."

"The stories have an ending, Mr. Calloway. I just don't read it, and I let the kids come up with their own endings. On Mondays, I tell them my ending, and then we read their endings. The story they buy definitely has an ending."

"Well, I gotta tell you," Dub said, smacking his lips with a swallow, "I think the whole bunch of it is a lotta hogwash. I think Dr. Big Shot over there just needed to have his wife doin' somethin' so hoity-toity that nobody else would understand it. I think it's a bunch of hogwash, is what it is. Internet this, and Internet that."

Lila looked into her plate, because if there were any hope of her not letting Dub have it, right there in front of his wife, and his son, and three other people who were certain to think he was one of life's lower forms, she'd need to ponder something pleasant. And so she thought, This broccoli is steamed to perfection, just the right crispness. The sautéed asparagus couldn't have been paired with more complimentary seasonings, just the right amount of chopped red pepper and garlic, and olive oil; not too much olive oil, though. But the roast beef, well, she couldn't really take too much credit for it, because the cut of beef was top. Then she thought about her part, and remembered being inspired by the open bottle of red wine on the counter, compelling her to pour a cup of it over the roast. It wasn't just the cow, after all. Just as she was ready to move on to what good potatoes she cooked, Lila couldn't take it anymore. She had to say it or scream, let it out or burst. So she let her eyes roll up to find Dub, and the sarcasm to come showed first in her eyes before she said, "It's okay, Mr. Calloway. I completely understand your opinion, because it's been my experience that the easiest thing for the feebleminded to do when they can't grasp something is to ridicule it and call it hogwash."

Dub sat stark still and stared Lila down. "Are you callin' me ignorant, gal?"

"No, I'm calling you a fool, and I don't bother myself with the nonsense of a fool. You're a fool because the only things capable of spewing from your warped mind are put-downs. You put down Jack for being a doctor." And then she laughed at the absurdity of such a thing. "You put down your other son, Buford, for finding a better life for himself in the army. Well, you want to know something, as much as I know how badly Jack wanted Buford at our wedding, if I were Buford I wouldn't have come either, if I knew I'd have to deal with your foolishness. You're a mean man, Mr. Calloway, and you're sick in your soul. But your meanness is almost evil, because I can't think of anything but evil that would cause a man to have a man like Jack as a son and still find a reason to put him down. So you can go right ahead and call what I do hogwash, because I consider the source, Mr. Calloway, and I know that it's nothing more than the nonsense of a fool." Lila speared a piece of asparagus on her fork and popped it in her mouth. Before she had even given it a good chew, she turned to Jack, first with downcast eyes, then staring him full on, and said, "I'm sorry, Jack, but I just can't take it anymore, at least not right now."

He looked back at her with blank eyes, smooth face, as if he was well aware of why, right now, Lila couldn't take it anymore. But with a dead man in their lives so freshly dead that the stink of all that he was hadn't even begun to settle yet into something completely and purely putrid, Lila could see in his eyes that Jack knew why *not right now*. Still, in all the parts of her heart that sympathized, all she could do was stare at Jack as he stared back at her. She could read in his eyes the disparate emotions of resentment and pride sloshing through him. She believed he resented her defense of him as if he were some child still in search of his manhood; and he most likely, she thought, resented the word *fool* because the fool that was his father is what had always been the greatest part of the shame he felt for the circumstances into which he'd been born. Still, all the resentment she thought she saw in his countenance, she felt pride in the way in which she called that fool by name, and no one, not even Jack, had ever had the constitution to name him. Still, she knew there was nothing he could say would suffice, with his sympathies as conflicted as they must have been between the two people who, in their own ways, defined his life. So that, she presumed, is why he said nothing.

Dub drilled into the side of Jack's face with a squinty-eyed stare. "So you just gonna sit there and let her talk to your pappy like that?" And when he got no response, at least not the response he seemed to expect, Dub pushed himself from the table and stood. "Well I ain't gonna sit around here and take this. I'm a man, and I won't let no damned body, even my son's uppity wife, sit here and call me a fool. And I sure ain't gonna be sleepin' where I've been insulted. A man knows an insult when he hears it. Come on, Cordelia."

And Cordelia, without looking up from her food, and without budging, said, "I ain't goin' nowhere, Dub Senior. I'm stayin' here for a visit wit my chil'ren, just as I planned. You know you was wrong, so now you just go on and go where you gonna go, but I'm stayin' here."

"Fine wit me." Dub walked around the table and out of the room.

The last they all heard of Dub was the sound of the door closing behind him. There was not one word in the language that could have been the right one for the moment. So everyone sat, and ate, and looked at no one. The room had filled with, not exactly tension, but a clumsiness of unspoken yet contradicting words and emotions.

Then Cordelia, breaking into the silence, said, "Ah, what the hell. He'll be back."

"How can you be sure of that, Ma?" Jack said, and his tone sat on the edge of worry. "He was pretty angry and very offended when he left."

"I know he'll be back 'cause he ain't got no clothes for wherever he's goin', and even a fool needs to change his drawers every once in a while," she said with a giggle that grew to be a full-bellied laugh.

And it grew in everyone else, too, to a laugh in which everyone had to join, particularly Lila, who held her head high, laughing with the contentment of the just.

NELL HAD LEFT for home and family fifteen minutes before, and Lila was left to listen to the quiet of the office that filled her with a loneliness that struck out from a secret hiding place. It was a restlessness, a longing. But for what? Certainly not for home, because if she'd really wanted to be there, by now she would have been turning her key in the door, and stepping through to its silence; silence that at one time comforted but now was simply stillness with the muffled nothingness of imperfection. So, she stared at a pile of papers, wondering if they held anything that would distance her from this restless longing; yet they didn't compel her enough for her to want to lose herself in them. They couldn't even inspire her to move.

But the thought of Barbara Gallagher did bring her into action. She sat up straighter and clicked into her E-mail. There it was, a new message from the woman, which read:

Dear Lila,

You know, I really do know how it feels to want for your first child. I have three children. Two are still living. Before my Sam was born (he's my oldest) I wanted him so badly that I would swear that I could hear his little spirit talking to me from where he sat waiting in heaven to come to me. I can honestly say that I have never gotten over the birth of any of my children. My Gretta is my second born, and she is a delight as well. But there is nothing in this world that can prepare you for the moment when you bring a new life into the world. It's like magic, really. My Sam and Gretta are now eighteen and sixteen, respectively. Way too old to still need me. Oh well, any-

*way, I know that you'll be writing me soon with the news that
you're expecting. And I hope you will share it with everyone
else who's hooked on* Story Hour.

*All my best to you, Lila,
Barbara Gallagher*

Lila scrolled back to the top of the message. *Two are still living.* How could she say that so offhandedly? Lila thought. Had
this woman made the kind of peace with the death of a child
that would allow her to casually mention that child's death with
less emotion than she would that child's birth? This was
mother's love in the raw, Lila thought, and for as much as she
was terrified to the core of everything she called herself when
she imagined knowing that kind of agony of the heart, it fascinated her with equal vigor. And then it vexed her, because she
wondered whether that much love existed in her, to have a
child pass on to the next world without following that child, in
spite of the other children left behind, who made her feel useless, anyway. So right before she began typing her response to
Barbara Gallagher, she said out loud, but in a whisper, "Oh, my
God!" And then she wrote:

Dear Barbara Gallagher,

*I received your last message, and it compelled me to write
you and tell you that you cannot lose heart. Don't confuse
teenage bravado with independence. It may seem as if Sam
and Gretta don't need you, and they may even think they
don't need you, but they do. Just being the mother of teenage
children has earned you kudos in my book. That's got to be the
toughest job in the world.*

*There's something else that struck me about your last corre-
spondence, and if I'm not prying, I'd like to ask about your
child who has passed on. I'm really sorry to know this. I can't
begin to imagine the kind of pain that comes with burying a
child, because, quite honestly, you have experienced the*

unimaginable. Nonetheless, I'd like to know more about him or her, if that's okay.

All my best to you, Barbara Gallagher,
Lila Calloway

And Lila sent it without bothering to check it for misspellings. All she wanted was for Barbara Gallagher to get it and explain to Lila the peace she'd found in the death of a life she'd given. So Lila waited, because she would not leave her computer, nothing else would be allowed entrance to her thoughts until she'd heard from Barbara Gallagher. She tapped her foot fervently, then watched the leaves of the tree out the window. Their movements were so faint, at the whim of the wind. And then a thought came that nudged Barbara Gallagher to the side for the moment. Lila wondered if wind was for tree leaves what the random nature of fate was for humans. It must be, she thought, since wind could take a leaf capriciously, and at every stage of its life cycle, wherever it fancied. And she knew quite well about fate and its caprice in a human life.

"You've got mail," her computer said to her.

And Lila clicked with a fury until she could see it.

Dear Lila,

I just got your message, and no, you're not prying at all to ask about my Matty. That was his name, Matty. After all, in a strange way, I feel so close to you, as if I've always known you. And I hope that doesn't frighten you in any way, because for all you know I could be a nut. I promise you, though, that I am not a nut.

Anyway, Matty was killed instantly in a car crash on June 20 of last year. He was seven when he died. And just so that you don't have to bother with checking the calendar, it's been exactly one year, two weeks, a day, and nineteen and a quarter hours since he died. I miss him so. And just so that you'll know, Lila Lilly's Story Hour *gave him so much joy. He couldn't wait to log on and hear the stories. He sent you four endings to your stories, and you read each one of them on* Story Hour. *It made him so proud. You might remember his endings. Matty was short for Matthew. Matthew Gallagher would be the name. Does it ring a bell? It may not, but just please remember that you brought my son so much happiness, and he even said that he could tell that you liked kids. He actually said that, Lila. And you know, I know that the one thing he misses the most, aside from his mommy's kisses, and the way I would caress his hair until he fell asleep at night, and the strawberry pancakes I'd make him on Saturday mornings, is* Lila Lilly's Story Hour.

> *All my best to you, Lila,*
> *Barbara Gallagher*

Lila saved the letter among her special correspondences, then shut down her computer, put her head on her desk, and wept in silence. She wept for every dead child who was missing *Lila Lilly's Story Hour.* She wept for the pain of how Matty died, because it must be what was too great to bear, since Barbara had never mentioned it until now. Mostly, though, she wept for her empty womb that she wanted full, to fill the void of one dead child in the world.

chapter seven

LILA RAN ACROSS the parking lot at the Safeway to catch Nell. The art of grocery cart selection was thoroughly lost on Lila, and she focused on her bad grocery cart karma as she pushed one that rattled with the tinny discordant racket of a throng of children's feet with steel wheels strapped on the bottoms; cursing her choice as it resisted moving as fast as she needed to go to catch up to Nell. Just before following Nell through the automatic door into the supermarket, Lila looked wistfully across Charles Street at her old apartment, her land of freedom, and she wondered—as she always wondered—who was living freely in there now, and if their freedom was indeed as profound and desperately needed as hers had been. She missed that place. Sometimes she'd drive out of her way in the evenings just to be able to go past her old place and look up to see the soft yellow glow of someone's life radiant in the shelter of home. Safe land right across from Safeway. What more could anyone ask in a flight to freedom? And a flight into safe arms? The safe arms of Jack, whom she met amid the vegetables right in this Safeway, right across from her safe land.

"Nell, wait!" Lila implored her friend. It was always the same scene on the days when Lila decided to join Nell for grocery shopping at Safeway. Nell was the steady shopper, mother of three, wife of one, who could twirl through the market with a purpose, without distraction. Lila, though, could take her time, strolling from broccoli to bread, milk to meat, looking from this to that to the other thing in search of everything or nothing; and she had the luxury of being open to the seduction of the bakery's perfume, and the sale on Alaskan crab claws. She wasn't shopping within the sliver of an open window of opportunity between the end and beginning of work.

Nell turned just enough for Lila to see the side of her face, then said, "Lila, you take forever in the market. I have to get in here and get out." And she went with snappy steps to the roll of plastic bags and tore one off, then another, and another, and she continued until she seemed to have as many as she knew for certain she'd need. And then there was Lila, standing in the middle of the produce, waiting for the inspiration of a decision. "If only I had the luxury of decisions," Nell said with a wry smile, "and the freedom of a deadline that's mine alone. When a man comes home from work like clockwork with his hunger in full roar, it's much too much for a working mother on shift two. But you will learn, especially once you have the baby you want so badly."

"I'm coming," was all Lila said breezily, distractedly.

Nell grabbed up a clump of green beans—who had time to pick through?—and stuffed them into one of the plastic bags, then cinched it with a loose knot. She grabbed two bags of carrots—smaller, but still a better buy than those large loose ones—the color of the sun's good-bye, that looked to be the epitome of pureness with their shock of greens sprouting from their tops. She took a few bags of spinach and tossed them into her cart, then stuffed two heads of romaine into one of the plastic bags she clutched in her left hand, and Lila was still without decision. By the time Nell had picked out her tomatoes, cabbage, nectarines, peaches, and plums, Lila was still standing in contemplation, without inspiration. Nell grabbed and stuffed until every empty plastic bag she'd been clutching was full.

Lila saw Nell moving like lightning through the produce, but she couldn't bring herself to move with such swiftness. This was the very place, the very same section of the market, and where Lila stood was the exact spot where Lila and Jack had met, and

Lila could not simply walk through this holy land as if it were mere produce. After all, Lila and Jack's was the sweetest story ever told of how a man met his woman.

As Lila remembered it, she was doing just what she was doing now, piddling her way through the market without a list, without a clue. Lila turned to pick tomatoes, and when she went to put them in her basket, there were two extra items in the cart, but she didn't notice them. And each time she turned away from her cart, extra items popped up. This went on until she finally discovered the things that she simply did not remember putting in there. Lila stared quizzically at the cart until she saw the culprit—a man's arm attached to a man she wouldn't have minded knowing. Jack was putting a tied-up bag of corn on the cob into Lila's cart without seeming to notice she was at the helm of the cart. With polite indignation, done in such a way that would not offend, she called Jack's mistake to his attention.

"Excuse me, but is there any particular reason why you're putting your groceries in my cart?" Lila remembered saying with a laughing smile, because after all, she was curious to know this man. And of course it ended up being an honest and innocent mistake. At least that's what Lila thought until the night of their honeymoon, when Jack admitted that he knew there was only one shot to meet her, right then and there at that Safeway, and so he took his one shot by pretending to confuse his grocery cart with hers. And Lila smiled magically to herself with the sweet thought that she and Jack went from the grocery cart ruse to the altar in six months.

"Okay, Lila, I'm gone from here," Nell finally said.

But in her reminiscing, Lila had forgotten that Nell was still there so she frantically said, "No, wait, Nell. God, you can at least wait for me to get some vegetables."

Nell blew out a breath that seemed filled with loving exasperation. "Lila, you've been in this aisle long enough to buy and cook every single vegetable here. What's the big deal? Pick some vegetables and get on with it, will you?"

"All right, all right," Lila said, with the quiet giggle of her little girl self as if she'd been gently scolded by a fond aunt. "Geez, Nell, you are such a mom." And she went over to the broccoli. "It's my in-laws' last night in town, and I want to make something special for them. Not that it'll matter to Dub," Lila said, drawing his name out in disrespect. "At least, I guess Dub is coming. I really don't know and I really couldn't care less." Then, as if struck by something that flew at her, all at once, she said excitedly, "I know! I'll make a broccoli soufflé tonight!" She tore off a plastic bag and picked up one bundle of broccoli and put it in the bag. "And I'll make a salad, too. One of those really pretty summer salads with nothing but fresh, fresh greens. That will be good for a day like today." She was, as if without thinking, stuffing the bag full until she had four bunches of broccoli struggling to fit into the already oversized bag.

"Lila, how big of a soufflé are you making, girl? That's just way too much broccoli."

Sheepishly, Lila took one of the bunches from the bag and placed it back on the broccoli heap. She looked down at her remaining three, then asked, "Well, so, how much *do* I need?"

"Only one bunch. And you may not need to use all of that."

Lila was doubtful. This can't be right, what Nell is telling her. She must be thinking of some other dish in which she'd bake broccoli in the oven—with eggs. How does she know this for certain? This is one of those exotic dishes like stuffed jumbo shrimp, or Peking duck; one of those dishes that no one would ever cook more than once a year. Still, she figured Nell, with her magical domestic powers, would probably know best. "Okay," she said, putting all but one back on the heap. "So, I guess I need to get some cheese, and . . . oh, yeah, greens for the salad."

But by the time Lila had looked to Nell for confirmation, Nell had already scribbled a complete marketing list for Lila's soufflé and salad dinner. "Here," she said, handing Lila the list. "This is everything you're going to need for what you want to do tonight. The ingredients for the soufflé are here at the top, and the stuff for your salad is at the bottom. If you find you already have something on the list, I guess I don't have to tell you that you don't need to buy it again." Nell repositioned the strap of her handbag on her shoulder and started out of the produce section in haste as if to make up for wasted time. "I'll meet you on line when you finish."

"Okay, go on, go on," Lila said, amused at Nell's impatience with Lila's love for browsing the supermarket. "You've been itching to get out of this aisle, so I'll see you at the checkout."

When Lila finally made her way out of the produce aisle, and out of her memories, she dallied down the aisle with exotic foods, or at least they were exotic to her, being that they were from faraway lands. She considered buying a can of tahini sauce, except that she couldn't imagine what else she'd do with it beyond spooning it over falafel. And she and Jack would have to eat falafel several times a week for a month, she thought, to use up a can as big as the one she pondered buying. Then she'd have to listen to Jack gripe about eating the same thing over and over again. It just wasn't worth it, so she moved on down and eventually away from the exotic foods. She went over to the seafood counter, because, after all, how could she leave there without a can or two of crabmeat, and tilapia? Ever since she'd tasted that tilapia at Nell's, Lila had claimed it as her favorite fish. Red snapper and orange roughy still held their high place on her list of preferences, but tilapia just seemed to dance all across her tongue the way no other fish ever had, and that's why, even through Jack's grumbling, they ate it once a week.

So Lila took a number and waited her turn, in a sea of fish lovers, for her tilapia. She took a can of Old Bay seasoning from a pyramid display atop the seafood counter. Suddenly she realized that she had been so seduced by the tilapia that she hadn't even heard, hadn't even noticed, the four white women off to the side, possibly waiting for their turn but nonetheless embroiled in a discussion so heated that it had the potential to go terribly wrong. How could she have missed it, the raised voices on the brink of yelling, the finger-pointing, the hand gestures? These women were beside themselves, and what most disturbed Lila was that she got the distinct impression that they didn't know one another, at least not well. "How can you say that?" she heard one of them say. "What has happened in your life that would make you say that that man should have saved that other man's life?" And it was only then that they had Lila's attention. For as much as she could not believe that something so private, so personal, so despicable, that it belonged only to her and Jack had made its way into the lives of four women shopping for fish at Safeway, Lila was still masochistically riveted. Something in her needed to hear the response. "It is my conviction as a Christian woman that tells me not only to say that, but to believe it. It would have been the Christian thing to do." That's when Lila couldn't take it a second longer. Every single one of those women seemed to have clearly set in her mind what she would have done, or what should have happened that day, and not one of them, she would bet her unborn child, had ever had such a dilemma laid at her feet. She didn't need their supposition, and at that moment, she didn't even need the tilapia. Lila crumpled her little pink number, slipped it in her purse, and walked away.

As Lila approached all those other women in the checkout line, who would end up just like herself, spending most of their natural lives on line at Safeway, or Giant, or Food Lion, or Metro, she grew a hazy smile that showed her self-satisfaction at making it to the register with time to spare. Just to make sure she'd gotten there before Nell, she craned her neck, trying to see over or around heads that moved in and out of her line of vision. Nell was not there, and Lila claimed her victory as she released from her mind the anticipated shameful look Nell would give her for being late to the line with not even enough food to cover the bottom of her rickety cart. Turning her attention back to the line of people in front of her, Lila acknowledged that this was not just any ordinary checkout. It was the register that had come to be her and Jack's spot. It was so automatic for her to glide up to the line. It was the first line they'd ever stood on together after they met amid the vegetables. It was where she first laughed from her soul when Jack explained to her his technique for sautéing the leaves of an artichoke. Boy, how she laughed when she realized that he was serious, and that he had actually speared artichoke leaves on a fork and slid them into his mouth and chewed them like they were collard greens, or something. She was powerless over her tears of laughter, which fell in streams, and her stomach ached from the grip laughter held on her when he admitted that he knew something was not right after his first bite. And even now, she had to chuckle to herself, reining in a full laugh, imagining Jack chewing into eternity before realizing that he'd never be able to swallow it.

Oh, and yes, this was the line where they argued into stony silence, two nights after they'd gotten back from their honeymoon, when she told Jack that it was only fair that he clean up the kitchen when she cooked dinner, only to make up before they'd even paid for the cart full of groceries.

And as she stood, nearly in the same spot, remembering, Lila was struck all over again at how easy it was simply to let go. Her eyes glazed over, becoming oblivious to the man right before her smiling for her attention. She couldn't see him. All she could see was that other man, also a stranger, who brought her back to love through his melancholy memories. And as clearly as she heard the supermarket's Muzak, she remembered saying to Jack in the coldest voice she could muster that would serve to get her anger across, "I need tomatoes."

"What kind? Regular or plum?" Jack said with a coldness to match.

"Plum. A pound, please."

So Jack left an empty space, beside and within her, when he went for the plum tomatoes, and she stood alone, thinking about little else but the battle between his self-love and his self-interest. One allowed him to love her, the other allowed him to love only himself. Lila tried to understand, but it was unfathomable to her that he came from a home without a basic understanding of give-and-take. How could he let her cook for him, she wondered, and then just go off to the sofa, loosen his belt, maybe let out a belch, and watch television while she scurried around the kitchen washing dishes, scrubbing pots, and wiping down the counter like a woman who would leave the better part of herself in that kitchen if she didn't clean it.

And, she wondered, had he always believed in such inequity? It vexed her, because it had to end before it would even get a good start. Lila remembered reading in one of those women's magazines, maybe while passing time on this very line, that just as you have to teach a cat or a dog how to behave in a house, you also have to teach people how to treat you. Well, she decided right then and there that she was not about to teach Jack that he should continue to treat her this way—take without giving. She was not going to be one of those women married to a man who was a river of give and an ocean of take. And so she would never apologize, she believed, for having decided right there in Safeway, so that it would forever be set in stone, that if she could come home from work and cook a meal, he could come home from work and eat it, and then put their kitchen back together again. After all, he lived there, too.

And that's when she let him die as her best friend, because how could he, she wondered, be her best friend outside of those romantic moments when they're existing only for each other in a way that they didn't exist for their real best friends? How could he possibly be her best friend and still have expectations of her drawn along gender lines? She had to question the practicality of it all: spouse as best friend. She thought about Nell and their friendship, and the one thing she knew for certain was that if Nell—the closest friend to a best friend she'd ever known—were to break into her house in the middle of the night and scrub the kitchen floor, Lila would thank her profusely, and then never forget it. But if Jack were to get up in the middle of the night and do the same while she slept, she wasn't certain if she'd thank him, or even remember it the next day. After all, it's his floor, too, and his shoes get it just as dirty as hers.

Before she had the chance to take her thoughts deeper, a finger fell on her shoulder, and when she looked around she saw only Jack's eyes, and tomatoes, dangling in midair. "Here're the tomatoes," he said, each word strung and strummed softly in her ears with deep contrition.

And she smiled on automatic because right then, she existed only for him. Big, bright, and showing her soul, she smiled at him, then became locked in a gaze of an apology that needed no words. The words were right there between them in the brief touch of their hands as the tomatoes passed between them. They were there when he brushed against her, trying to get back to his space next to her. They were there, rich, lush, and full throated, in the glances and half smiles. And their unspoken banter was ended only by the live words of a stranger directed at them.

"Boy, that was a loving smile you just gave him," the older man behind them said. In spite of his white hair, thick, full, and nearly a pompadour, he was still not old enough to be an old man. "I can tell you two are in love."

"Yeah," Jack said, tossing a distant smile at the man, scarcely able to take his eyes from Lila.

"You two just got married, huh?"

"Yes, we did," Lila confirmed. "We just got back from our honeymoon two days ago."

"Oh, that's beautiful. I could tell you two were newlyweds. Your wedding band there is so nice and shiny," he said to Jack. Then he laughed and showed his well-worn band, which was merely a thin strip of gold and was so thin that it looked as if the years had withered it down, so that by the end of his life it would simply go with him into dust. "Well, where'd you two go?"

"We went to Greece," Jack said proudly. "It was beautiful. I'd always wanted to go there."

"That's great. Always share your dreams like that. And even when you don't have anything to share as pleasant as dreams, still share it all, no matter how bad it may seem. That's what's gotten me and my bride through. Forty years this October," he said, seeming to fill his chest with a bit more air than it could normally take in, and flashing his thin band of gold at them again. "Yep, you gotta share it all."

Jack leaned in closer to Lila in a way that would have seemed a rude gesture to the man under ordinary circumstances, except that by now, the man seemed to be talking more to himself and his memories than he was to Jack and Lila. So Jack whispered to Lila, "I'm sorry, baby. I don't ever want you to think that I don't appreciate what you do when you cook. I'll clean the kitchen. You're right that it's only fair. If you cook, I should clean. That's just the way it will be." And he kissed her hair instead of waiting for the softness of her cheek or lips.

AND SO, AS Lila remembered that moment when they let the veil of perfect love cast out their fear that had been wrapped in the anger that stood between them, she was actually forced to laugh out loud. And now that she was back in the present Safeway, everything seemed to be magnified to twice its size, like the woman with the grapes in the next line.

There had to be no less than fifteen bags of grapes in that cart with nothing else, and just as she was about to go off, wondering what anyone could possibly do with so many grapes—the only halfway reasonable exception being some sort of extreme grapes-only diet—she noticed that the man in front of her was smiling knowingly into her face. She wasn't certain what bothered her most—that he was staring, or that she didn't know how long she'd been watched. Did she know him? And as she washed his face through her memory, she decided she did not and looked away from him.

"Hi, Lila," the smiling man said.

With that look she gets when she knows she ought to know something, but simply doesn't, she merely returned his hello and continued her search for Nell. But he knows my name, she thought, giving him a second glance. "I'm sorry, but do I know you?"

"Lila, it's me. Don't you remember me from high school? I was at Poly the same time you were at Western. I'm Billy Boots. We used to talk all the time in the quad."

Billy Boots! her mind screamed. Suddenly she remembered that name and how in high school she thought it made him sound hand-drawn. *Billy Boots and His Roving Band of Forty Cats.* Her mind went all the way back there to her teens, then played. Those forty cats following Billy Boots all around the town to regale the townspeople with their musical adventures. This is a man whose wife, if he had one by now, surely did not take his name, because there is no name, invented or traditional, that would ever flow with Boots. How long had it been since she'd forgotten this poor fellow? It was all coming back, those conversations she'd have with him, mostly out of pity, that would all too often end with her having to lie just to get away from him and his talk, which went in painful circles around his passions for botany and physiology. At that very moment, her eyes could have fogged with the tedium of nothing but the memory of those days. Instead, she smiled with recognition and said, "Billy, of course. Wow, I didn't even recognize you at first."

"Yeah, I'm thinner than I was back then," he said as if proud of that accomplishment, whether she noticed it or not.

As if it could have been nothing, a feathery brush fell against the back of her skirt, and she turned, curious at the contact. It was the corner of a grocery cart, and pushing it was Nell. "Oh, Nell, there you are. I made it to the line before you so that you wouldn't have to laugh at me."

"Now you're learning how to shop. In, around, and out. That's my motto." She looked past Lila at Billy.

"Nell, this is an old friend of mine from high school, Billy Boots. Billy, this is my friend Nell. Nell and I work together."

"It's a pleasure to meet you, Nell," Billy said, extending his arm past Lila to shake hands with Nell.

"Hello, it's nice to meet you." She shook his hand, and seemed to be holding back laughter.

Then Lila asked, "So Billy, what are you doing now?"

"I'm a doctor, Lila," Billy replied with a look that asked her what else he would have become. "I was one of those science geeks girls used to laugh at. You remember that, don't you? But you never laughed at me. We always had such nice talks, didn't we?"

"Yeah, we did," Lila said, with barely enough passion to be convincing. "Well, did you specialize, or are you in general practice?"

"I'm a neurologist."

"Well, that's really nice, Billy," Lila said, this time her sincerity without question.

"Yeah, well, thanks, Lila." Billy lowered his head bashfully, regressing to the Billy that Lila remembered, then blurted with a burst of awkward excitement, "But I'm not the doctor who let that man die on Twenty-eighth Street." He laughed heartily at his wit. "Did you hear about that?"

But Lila, her face frozen with the smile that had instantly vanished from her eyes, merely gave a slight shake of her head to say no and prayed nothing more would be said. What was he, a fool? Of course she'd heard, and wouldn't it astound him to know just how she'd heard. There didn't seem to be a person in the market, maybe even in the city, who wasn't talking about the dead fat bigot. But what no one could ever know, not even the Christian fish-buying woman, was that not even in infamy did he deserve to be on everyone's lips, swilling around in everyone's mind.

"Oh, wow, it's unbelievable," Billy said, moving closer to Lila to lower his voice. "This black doctor stepped right over a white guy over there on Twenty-eighth Street. It seems that the two had had words, or something, before. But anyway, I guess the white guy pissed the black doctor off with whatever he said, and when the white guy collapsed with a heart attack, the black doctor walked right past him as if the man was already nothing more to him than a chalk outline. I can't believe you haven't heard about it. It's been all over the television and newspapers."

But Lila hadn't seen the television since everything went black for her on Saturday, and she hadn't seen a newspaper since Saturday morning. "I just haven't heard, that's all," she said quietly with eyes shifting everywhere but into the eyes of Billy, which held her virtue.

"Oh yeah, Lila. Chuck and I were talking about that yesterday. It was in the paper, but I guess you didn't see it."

And it wasn't until that exact moment as Lila, folding into herself, trying to make it all, or perhaps herself, disappear that she knew that Nell knew the truth. She watched Nell's lower jaw drop on its own, and for all Nell seemed to care it could have been down to the floor. Lila saw in Nell's eyes, brimming with empathy, that she wanted to take Lila and keep her safe. Billy Boots was muttering something about how he would never do anything so unethical. She heard him say he was from the school of teaching bigots who's really superior. It didn't matter. By now, Billy Boots right along with his ethics were no longer real for Lila. Her mind was plastered on Nell and what she must think as she watched Nell press her lips together, as if to keep a secret, or to hold back some erratic emotion that could spew any minute. And destroy.

And without connecting in any ordinary way, Lila was sure that Nell now knew about that secret adulterated place too deep in Lila's heart to be seen nakedly; a place that Lila only found when the bane of her recent life became full and always present, but where her soul now wallowed. Then, just as Billy Boots put the definitive stamp of his judgment on the subject by saying, "I wonder how you live with yourself when you do something like that?" Lila raised her head to look into the face of Nell, whose eyes bled.

Lila hadn't had a chance to get through the automated door before the need to confess had overcome her. Nell knew, she thought, but she had to make sure. She had to breathe again with the burden of the secret shared with someone else. So as Lila looked into Nell's face, creased with concern, she said, "Nell, you know, right?"

"Lila, what happened? And why didn't you tell me?"

"It was horrible, Nell. One minute that man was calling Jack Doctor Porch Monkey and the next minute he was on the ground dying of a heart attack and Jack was stepping over him as if he was yesterday's trash. He just let him die, Nell. How could I tell you that? I didn't even want to think about it, much less talk about it." Lila gathered her few bags from the cart then stepped aside so as not to block the door. She plopped her bags in the child seat of Nell's cart and continued. "Nell, I know this is an impossible request to make of you, and I know I can ask it because you are truly the first real friend I've ever had. But I need you to keep this from Chuck for right now. Jack's not talking about this, not really, and I thought that if he would talk to anybody about it he would talk to Chuck, but I don't think he has."

"I know he hasn't, because Chuck couldn't keep a secret if it had handles. He wouldn't necessarily tell the whole world, but he would definitely tell me, and he hasn't said a word."

"Okay, so please give Jack some time. That's what I'm trying to do, but it's hard. The other day, he came home from a run with his leg all bloodied and cut up from a fall, and one minute I was patching up his leg, and the next I was throwing my bath salts at his head."

Nell let go of her grocery cart, which she had ben clinging to as if it were all that kept her upright, and brought Lila to her in an embrace, saying softly, "So what are you going to do?"

"I don't know, Nell. I don't know what there is to do, you know. Are we murderers? I just don't know. But somehow, now that you know, doing something doesn't seem quite as urgent. Still, even in sharing this with you, it still doesn't take away the fact that Jack and I have got to do something." And she held Nell fast, too comforted to let go.

LILA CHOPPED BROCCOLI mindlessly as she thought of Cordelia's words to Dub—You was wrong. They were said so plainly, without a second's hesitation, without a second thought, and they came from a place where the deepest part of Cordelia's forthright womanhood lived without fear of anything. It put Lila in awe, the way they rolled from Cordelia's lips. It was as if those words were on ball bearings heading downhill, the way they came out so smooth and easy. She wondered how many years it took for honesty so raw to roll like a wheel. But she and Jack didn't have the years, and so truth between them would have to come sideways, and maybe stumbling.

In Cordelia, Lila had seen the best of what she hoped to one day become—capable of standing in the presence of Jack and being plainspoken enough to say, You was wrong, and still know that the blunt trauma of those words, and the aftershock, would not be enough to shake them apart. Right now, she wasn't at all certain their bond could take such a blow. For a man to be wrong about something he's said is one thing; for him to be wrong about something horrifying he's done is quite another. This is how she'd come to regard marital honesty in the face of her own marriage. Even so, she couldn't help but feel the anxiety of wanting badly to be there on Cordelia's plateau. When, she wondered, will it be her day?

Cordelia was right. Dub did come back; not completely sheepish, but not at all self-righteous either. And he came back the same night he left. He had a few general words of greeting for Cordelia, with this and that of how one friend or another said hello to her through him. He had fewer words for Jack, and none at all for Lila. That was fine by her, she thought even now, as she prepared a meal for his last night's visit in Baltimore— that is *if* he shows up. Evidently this was the only night Dub couldn't rustle himself and Cordelia a meal up at anyone else's home but hers and Jack's, Lila thought as she beat her egg whites, because every night since the night she lobbed the name of fool at him, he and Cordelia had conveniently had plans elsewhere. So, either there were no more dinner offers, or Cordelia had simply put her foot down and told Dub that they would eat at their son's home, and that was that. And with a smile, Lila thought her bet was best placed on Cordelia. Still, she thought, you never know with a man that stubborn.

Just then, Cordelia came into the kitchen with Dub following behind. He looked to Lila to be most obedient, but then she let that thought go. She knew that ever since the night Cordelia let

Dub know that he was wrong, Lila had begun to imagine far more meaning in Dub's moments of reticence than perhaps were real. "Oh, hello, you two," Lila said. "I'm working on dinner now. A broccoli soufflé. I thought it would be just right for a hot day like today. We'll have a salad with it, too."

"Soufflé!" Dub blurted out. "What's that?"

"It's made with broccoli, eggs, and cheese," Cordelia said. "You'll like it."

"Well I like broccoli, and I like eggs, and I like cheese, but I don't know if I'm gonna like it all together like that."

"Dub, you'll like it, now just be quiet."

So Lila thought about how this was their last night in town and how she could afford at least a little bit of generosity toward Dub. So she said, "I can put a steak on the grill and bake a potato for you, Mr. Calloway."

"Well, I'd like that. It's just that I don't know about that soufflé stuff."

"I understand."

"Dub, you don't make sense," Cordelia whispered.

And even though Lila knew Cordelia wasn't counting on her hearing, she heard. Lila simply smiled with the patience that she regarded as a gift for Dub on his last night in town and said, "It is no problem at all. Ma, can you go downstairs and get a steak from the freezer for me?"

"Oh, sure, honey. I'll be right back."

With Cordelia gone, Lila felt the weight of Dub's discomfort, which walked into the room the moment Cordelia left and sat down beside him. She knew she had to say something when she looked up to find him picking at a spot on his finger that was most likely nonexistent. "Listen, Mr. Calloway," she said gently as she put down the wire whisk. "I'm not going to apologize for what I said the other night, because I meant it. I only hope you can understand how it feels when a person has had enough. It was just too much for me to take, listening to you put down Jack, put down me, put down anything you don't understand. And I'm not trying to change you, or even to tell you that you have to change, I'm just asking that you have some respect for your son while you're in his home."

"Look, now," Dub said, getting up from where he sat, as if he were about to leave in haste. "I ain't gonna stay here and listen to you tell me how I'm s'posed to be with my own boy. This ain't got nuthin' to do wit you, so you's just best to stay outta it."

"Well, you see, that's where you're wrong, Mr. Calloway, because as long as you're in my home heaping that kind of meanness on my husband, it has everything to do with me. I won't just stand by and put up with it. You see, in many ways, I was raised by a mother who was just like you. The judgment, the disdain for people she knew nothing about, the fear of anything foreign that made her judgment even more angry—I know it all too well, Mr. Calloway. And that's why I am hell-bent on not letting you, my mother, or anyone bring it into my home. You think you know your son so well, but you really have no idea who he is and what drives him." And then her eyes squinted at him under the strain of hoping he wouldn't ask her to tell him, because so many of the parts of Jack that she never knew were lurking inside him were just beginning to unfold before her eyes.

Cordelia had come back upstairs empty-handed while Lila was talking to Dub. She took her seat next to him and waited, looking at her husband as if to see what he'd have to say after Lila's unrefined honesty.

"Oh, I know my boy," Dub said with chilly, almost sinister, sarcastic laughter. "Don't you worry 'bout that. I know him so well that I know that if he had a been in the exact same position of that doctor who left that white man to die up here a few weeks ago, he woulda saved that cracker's life just as sure as I'm sittin' here in your face right now. I don't care if they woulda called him an ass-scratchin' nigger, he woulda saved him 'cause he love himself some white people way too much. That's the only way you git where he is. I've said it before, and I'll say it till I die, he done sold his soul to the white man."

Lila looked at Cordelia with a face smoothed over of the frustration that was roiling just beneath her surface. She was aware of her agitation and so tried to reel it in before she spoke, since her vexation was not at all with her mother-in-law. "What happened to the steaks?"

"I couldn't tell what was what down there. I thought everything would be labeled. And it looks like you have more than one kinda steak down there, too."

"Yeah, you're right. I'll just run down myself and get it." She wiped her hands on the bottom of her apron and looked at Dub. Suddenly she found her mind cursing Jack for his silence, for his untruth, for being so wrong, because if for no other reason than to prove his piggish father wrong, she wanted Jack to shout from the top of Baltimore's Washington Monument that he was the one who left that man to die. It would bring Jack an albeit ill-gotten respect from his father, but it would nonetheless be long overdue. The thought of telling him herself, right then and there, crossed her mind as she went to the cellar door. He did it! she wanted to shout out. Jack did leave that white man to die, so what do you think of him now? What do you think of your white-people-lovin', ass-scratchin' nigger now? she wanted to say right in the senior Jackson Calloway's face, letting the spray of each word from her mouth splatter all over his face. But it was not to be. It would be less than prudent. And so just before she descended into the basement, she looked back at Dub with her head held high in the arrogance of what she knew and he did not, and said, "Mr. Calloway, you don't know what you're talking about. You have no idea."

T HE TWANGING HONKY-TONK music, pulsing from the restaurant and smacking against Lila's nerves as soon as she and Jack stepped into the Light Street Pavilion, calibrated her mood at a rather lower level than it had been just seconds before when she'd wrapped herself in the summer sounds of Harbor Place. She brushed her eyes only briefly over the name of the restaurant emblazoned on the window—Jean something or other. She had paid no attention to the name days before when Jack told her, and she paid no attention to it now, as she was too distracted by what she saw underneath. NEW YORK, BEIRUT, BALTIMORE, CHATTANOOGA. It seemed to her such an abstract collection of cities. And so she stared at Beirut, and then Chattanooga, wondering if it could be one of those inside jokes that would only seem to her, and so many other outsiders, off center. Why would anyone, she thought, open a restaurant in Beirut? She let it drift away from her when she decided that for all she knew about Beirut nowadays, it may not even be Beirut anymore.

Jack gave the hostess Chuck's name—Dr. Charles Teague— that's how Jack said it, Lila noticed, and certainly that's how Chuck would have it written down. Not simply Chuck Teague or Charles Teague. It made her smile when she thought of the absolute uselessness of a title in a restaurant reservation. Then she heard the hostess ask if Jack preferred to sit inside or out.

"Outside, please." Lila spoke up forcefully. There's no way she'd be prisoner of this hillbilly-rock music that did not quite fit in a restaurant with *Jean* in its name.

They followed the hostess across the restaurant, down three steps, around a group of waiters, and out a door to the patio. She showed them their table, which was smack against the window of the restaurant and surrounded by nothing but tables and oversize umbrellas. Lila felt enclosed, encroached upon. What's the point of sitting outside if they had to sit here? And when Lila saw the same emotion of ultimate dissatisfaction in Jack's face that was in her mind, she knew it was more than apropos to say, "I'm sorry, but this is not a good table for us. Could we take that table over there?" Lila pointed to a table at the edge of the patio that looked on to passersby, the harbor, everything anyone would want to see while sitting outdoors.

The hostess hesitated at first, but when it was clear that neither Lila nor Jack would so much as touch, much less sit in the chairs the hostess had offered them, she relented with a sigh. "Well, that's fine," she said, leading Jack and Lila to Lila's desired table, where they sat with easy smiles.

"That table made me feel claustrophobic," Jack said, shaking himself out, as if now he had enough space to move.

"I know—me too," Lila agreed, adjusting her thin shawl, worn only for fashion's sake, back onto her shoulders.

The waitress approached them with a smile that gave Lila a start. It was so familiar, so intimate, Lila felt as if she should have known the rest of the face, but she didn't. Yet, this woman had joy aplenty in her smile, and in response, Lila found herself saying hello before the woman could even introduce herself.

"Hello, how are you? I'm Kara, and I'll be your waitress this evening." She paused for their cordiality, then spoke, it seemed, mostly to Lila. "How do you manage to look so fresh and beautiful in all this humidity? I've been wilting all day long."

Lila smiled into the empty space in front of her, and thought, A chitchatter. What else would she be with that smile, those teeth, all that joy? She looked into the woman's beaming face, then replied, "Thank you. It hasn't been easy in these last few weeks with this heat."

"Yeah, I guess you just do what you can and hope for the best, huh?" Kara said.

"Yep, that's about it," Jack said, interjecting his little bit into the banter.

"So, can I get you something to drink to start?" Kara asked, again addressing Lila.

Lila looked blankly at Jack, as if the question had snuck up on her. "Well, let's see. I don't know."

"Why don't you just bring us a bottle of your best merlot," he said to the waitress. "Chuck likes merlot," he then said to Lila.

"I'll be right back with your wine," Kara said as she left.

Watching Lila as she opened her menu, Jack looked at his wife with a smile somewhere between longing and distraction, then stared off at a boat pulling away from the dock. To say she looked beautiful would make the word ring hollow; and tonight, she actually looked, to Jack, to be in a realm just beyond beautiful, where she'd put men in mind of other things far more complex than sex. She was like something they'd want to create in a painting, or merely stare at for hours and contemplate the beauty of only one eye, then the other, or her bottom lip, or the way the light jumped clear from the water to place an enchanting twinkle upon her right cheekbone. She was that vision of which men of ages past spoke in terms nearly ethereal. She glowed. And thinking that this was the woman by his side until he no longer breathed the breath of this life put a rather sizeable mass in the center of his heart. So, he shifted his eyes back to Lila to say the only thing he could think to say: "You look nice tonight."

"Thank you, Jack." And she smiled.

As the waitress turned to leave, Jack saw Chuck and Nell following the hostess to the table. "Here they are," he said as he got quickly to his feet. He embraced Chuck like a brother, then kissed Nell square on the cheek and hugged her hello. "I ordered a bottle of their best merlot for you," Jack said to Chuck.

"Oh, that's my man," Chuck said, slapping his hand into Jack's for a determined handshake. He held Nell's chair as she sat while watching Lila settle back in next to Jack. "Lila, you look lovely. Just like one of Degas's dancers."

Lila aimed a distant smile just beyond him, then said; "Thank you, Chuck."

"We're the envy of every man in Harbor Place, aren't we, Jack?" he said, playfully punching Jack on the arm. "I mean, to be in the company of such beauty, and then we get to go home with them."

Jack simply smiled and said to Nell, "Nell, it's really good to see you. Lila tells me that the two of you have a great partnership. She's said she can't imagine working with anyone else as well as she works with you."

"Yeah, we really do click," Nell said, smiling at Lila. "I think I'm pretty lucky in that regard. Chuck comes home nearly every night complaining about one thing or the other about the hospital. I can honestly say that I have not had one complaint about work since Lila and I have been working together." She would have continued but stopped as the waitress approached.

"Here you are," the waitress said, placing the wine on the table, then the goblets. As she opened the wine, she said, "Well, I see there're some new faces here. I'm Kara, and I'll be your waitress this evening." She tipped the bottle just enough to cover the bottom of the wine goblet with the nectar that poured with the rich color of liquid garnet. She set it in front of Jack. "Here you are, sir."

"Oh, it's best to give it to him," and Jack, motioned with his head toward Chuck.

So Chuck picked up the goblet, swirled, sniffed, then sipped. Very delicately, imperceptibly, he washed the wine over every part of his mouth, then swallowed, and smacking his tongue against the roof of his mouth for the finish, said, "This is just fine."

"I'm always impressed by connoisseurs," the waitress said as she poured Lila's glass half full, then Nell's and then the others. "Personally, I wouldn't know merlot from moonshine." Then she laughed heartily with the others. She shifted ever so smoothly. "I'd like to read you our specials for the evening," and she rattled them off with an enthusiasm that could easily make her listeners believe that she had actually tried each one before they were offered up to the innocent palates of diners.

Lila had the focused gaze of someone present, but she could remember nothing since she'd become so distracted by one thing or another on the menu as each triggered memories of something else, or another time, like the grilled tuna or some kind of pasta that would come in a vodka sauce. By the last one on the list, Lila had given up trying to retain anything Kara, even in all her enthusiasm, had to say. With an involuntary suddenness, she grabbed her menu from the table and opened it flat before her face, as if it were her last hope for anything remotely special. Then she heard Nell say, "The marinated tuna grilled with portabello mushrooms sounds good, so I think I'll have that," and Lila smiled, knowing that if anyone among them would remember anything, it would be Nell, who would remember everything.

"I like a woman who knows what she wants," Kara said jocularly to Nell. "I'll give the rest of you some time to decide." And she walked away, leaving them to their thin, polite laughter.

"Now that's a good waitress," Chuck said, once Kara was out of earshot. "Don't flirt with the husbands because that will just piss off the wives. Connect with the wives and they'll make sure she gets a good tip." He sipped from his wine, then leaned back in his chair with a carefree chuckle.

"Are you disappointed, Chuck?" Nell asked in such a plain way it was hard to tell how she meant it.

He looked sideways at Nell with questioning eyes, then said, "Disappointed? No. I'm just making an observation, that's all. Wouldn't you agree with me, Jack?"

Jack looked off into the harbor and smiled distantly. "I don't think about that kind of stuff the way you do, Chuck. She's a nice woman. That's all I've noticed."

Lila thought to say something, she wasn't certain what, but it would have praised her husband for a virtue she really couldn't name. But as the moment passed, and everyone's interest along with it, she discovered there was no point. So she just smiled at Jack, even though he didn't see it to receive it, and found what would suit her on the menu. "What are you getting? I'm going to get the grilled prawns," she said as she leaned closer to Jack.

"That looks good, huh? But I'm leaning more toward the filet mignon. I haven't had that in ages," Jack said, closing his menu.

From across the patio, Kara took her cue from Jack and started for the table, pen and pad ready. "Has everyone decided yet, or do you need a little more time?" she said.

Chuck closed his menu and held it in midair, as if for Kara to take. "Yeah, I think we've all decided."

Lila ordered her plain green salad—she always had to have a plain green salad, because her mother taught her the importance of several things green at every meal, and she simply couldn't depend on restaurant people knowing to put enough vegetables with their fancy prawns. And as soon as she ordered her prawns, she became immediately distracted by a woman walking by, cursing like a junkyard dog at the man walking with her. He was oblivious, Lila could see, either out of sheer embarrassment, or out of mere apathy; no matter what, he had completely checked out. Or so it seemed. She kept her eyes on them, wondering what might have happened in their lives that could have triggered such all-out disregard of decorum for time and place. Lila knew that to be a couple is sometimes to ache and hate to the core, and she knew what it was like to be so hurt, saddened, frustrated by Jack that she could have screamed a blue streak across the sky at him, but anger had never claimed her so viscerally as to make her act out in public. Mostly, though, as she sat watching this couple play out their life on a stage of their own design, she couldn't fathom what the circumstances might be in her life that she would just cuss Jack a new name, right there in the middle of town for everybody to see, the way this woman was renaming this man.

Then, what would happen next would make Lila want to step

in and take that man down. Out of nowhere, making it clear that he had, indeed, been cognizant of the woman's ranting, the man, in one fell move, hauled off and slapped the woman. Slapped her so hard her head nearly went full around, at least that's what it seemed like to Lila. And something went flying out of her mouth. Those passing by did so with trepidation, as if the two were live grenades, and then once past, hurried on their way before the detonation. "Oh my God!" Lila nearly screamed.

"What happened?" Jack said, grabbing Lila's hand and looking around.

"That man over there," she said, pointing, and still trying to collect herself from the shock of it all. "He slapped that woman so hard that something flew out of her mouth. It looked like it could have been a tooth."

Nell turned to look, and when she saw them, she snapped back toward Chuck and said, "That's the same couple we walked past who were arguing. They were arguing so fiercely people were getting out of their way. She was mad enough to kill that man."

"Yeah, but still," Lila said, disgusted, "it doesn't call for all that public display of their business."

"I guess it depends," Chuck said plainly as he craned his neck to see what the enraged couple would do next. "We don't know what happened."

"Well, none of that matters," Lila said, incredulously. "No matter what he did, or what she said to him just now, it did not warrant his slapping her. I think that is just the lowest of the low, to hit a woman like that, and out in public, no less. How can he feel he has the right?"

Chuck settled back in his seat, his interest in the hullabaloo having waned, and said, "You can't contain passion, Lila, no matter what kind it is."

Nell then turned around herself swiftly, unable to watch another second as the woman was reduced to crawling on her hands and knees in search of whatever it was that was knocked from her mouth. "Please, Chuck. That is *not* passion."

"It's not the good kind of passion, Nell, but it's passion. Passion, good and bad, can drive you insane. That's how that fat cracker ended up dead on the sidewalk. Right, Jack?"

And it was in the way he said Right, Jack?—with a sly arm chuck and eyebrows that rose and fell in a most furtive way that meant they shared the secret—that gave Lila the shock of cold to her brain that comes with the sudden astonishment of betrayal. She slid her eyes into Nell's, certain she'd see shame and feel disgrace. But in Nell's widened eyes that took in all of Lila's wound, a wound that had thickened into scabby layers in only seconds, was the forthright assuredness that all was still safe, and in the shake of her head that could only be seen by eyes trained to see, Lila saw that in spite of the unspoken, unwritten vow Nell had taken to keep no secrets, Chuck had not been told—at least not by Nell.

"I'm going to the ladies' room," Lila said, bounding to her feet and scraping the legs of the wrought-iron chair across the cement and out from under her. With her eyes she told Nell to follow. She asked Jack, "Would you have the waitress bring me a glass of chardonnay?"

"I think I'll come with you," Nell said. "Will you get me a glass of chardonnay, too, Chuck?" She had the face of a woman being left behind, as Lila was practically inside the restaurant already, so she went off to gain her ground, but Lila's path was fierce. It wasn't until Lila reached the door of the ladies' room that Nell sprinted to catch up to her. Just before Lila pushed the door open, Nell said, "Lila, you have to know that I didn't say one word to Chuck."

Lila waited until they were both fully in the rest room, door closed and all, and certain that no one was in either of the two stalls, before answering. "Yeah, I could see by the look on your face back there that you didn't tell him. So how does he know?"

"I'm sure he doesn't, Lila. It's just the way he said it." Nell leaned against the sink only to nearly jump out of her skin when she discovered it was wet, nearly soaked. "Oh jeez, yuck!"

"It's just water," Lila said with flat confusion.

"Maybe. It really drives me insane when I touch anything wet and I didn't see the source of the wetness. This could be almost anything. People can be nasty."

Lila stared at her, holding back a smile that would surely become laughter, but she couldn't let it, since Nell was so clearly vexed. Then she reached up and yanked down an inch-thick chunk of paper towels. "Here," she said, handing them to Nell, "just wipe yourself off with these."

But Nell refused to take even one towel. "I need to wash my hands first, girl. I hope this soap is antibacterial." So she washed her hands with vigor, scrubbing and wringing, scrubbing and wringing, until they were as clean and germ free as any hands could ever hope to be. And only then did she reach out and take the bunch of towels from Lila, saying with an embarrassed smile that said she knew she needed to explain her extreme obsession, which probably had not yet become a compulsion. "Once you have kids, germs take on a much larger role as the enemy in your life."

Lila simply nodded with pressed lips to give the impression of understanding. Then, hoping to leave the topic of germs forever, she said, "So you're sure Chuck doesn't know?"

"I'm positive he doesn't know. He's just been absolutely obsessed with this whole thing. He talks about it constantly. Sometimes I think he wishes he had been in Jack's shoes walking away from a dying racist. All he's done since the story hit the news is sit around fantasizing about how he would have done it, and what he would have said." Nell turned and walked into one of the stalls, and as she clicked the door locked, Lila was doing the same in the next stall. "Honestly, Lila, it's beginning to really bother me the way he's so into this whole the-proud-black-man-has-to-let-these-rednecks-know-who's-really-superior thing he's going through. He has turned the phantom doctor into some sort of mythical conqueror, so believe me, if he knew that Jack was the doctor he's made into a hero, he would have said a lot more than what he did."

Lila said nothing. Someone had walked into the bathroom, and Lila would take no chances on a stranger's ability to figure things out. The roar and swish of first one, then the other toilet overwhelmed the small room. And when they stepped, each from their own stall, into the room, Lila was struck in a rather particular way by the blond black woman standing in wait of a toilet. Skin too deeply brown for blond hair; hair too spanking blond for brown skin. But Lila returned the woman's pleasant smile, washed her hands, and left before Nell. She didn't have a choice.

When Nell met her on the other side of the door, Lila was suppressing a laugh that began oozing out after her eyes connected with Nell's. "You know, I have to tell you that the old Lila, the Lila that, thank God you never got to know, would have looked at that woman and said something like 'I don't know what the circumstances would have to be in my life that would make me wake up one morning and say, Yes, today's the day when I must dye my hair blond. And I have the skin tone for it.' But the Lila here today, the new and improved Lila, makes no judgments." And Lila let out the heartiest, most infectious laugh.

She passed it to Nell, who said, "Well, I do. She looks ridiculous in a way that just makes me sad. It's bad enough when you see these girls with their hair cut off short and dyed blond, but here she comes with a head full of curls falling down to her shoulders. It's ridiculous that we straighten the God-given kinks out of our hair—and I'm talking about myself, too. But when we start dyeing our hair blond, then somewhere along the line we have become terribly confused."

"Now, Nell," Lila said in her nonjudgmental tone, "there are some black people born with blond hair."

"Maybe quadroons, or octoroons, or whatever you call them," she said seeming to unconsciously lower her voice, as if not to offend as they passed the waiters' station and stepped onto the patio. "But you show me one black person as black as the woman in that bathroom born with naturally blond hair, and I'll eat every inch of that wrought-iron chair."

And just as they reached the table, Lila let out a hoot of a laugh that came to an abrupt end when she saw the large shapely glass of Coke that Jack had just taken from his lips and set on the table. Why? Why, with all that wine and water on the table, does he have to have something that served to do nothing but bastardize elegant food? Standing there now, looking at that glass of Coke, she had to make a profound choice between raising hell or sitting down next to it. She sat.

"What's so funny?" Jack asked,

"Oh, nothing, really," Nell said. "We were just talking about this blond black woman we saw in the bathroom."

"Wasn't that the worst sight?" Chuck said in a near whisper. "She's sitting over there with that guy," and he bobbed his head slightly in the direction of a man sitting alone, swarthy enough to be Latino, or southern Italian, or maybe even Middle Eastern. It was hard to discern from his profile. "This is what makes things bad for us. Bigots like that dead redneck don't look at black women like her and think, Oh, she's doing such a good job at assimilating to our ways. She's practically one of us. No, they think, Look at that, will you? They're just dying to be like us. And they're right."

Nell said as she blew out a sigh, "Chuck, why is it that lately you always find a way to weave that dead fat man into everything you talk about? Just leave it alone. Leave *him* alone and let him rest in peace, or go to hell in peace, whatever it is he'll do, but just drop it."

"I can't drop it, Nell. This is a big deal for every single black doctor in an American hospital who has ever walked into an examining room to find the look of absolute terror on the face of a white man because he's certain your black skin doesn't make you the best the hospital has to offer, or even anywhere near the best. Some of those guys would take the high road in a situation like this, but a lot of them are like me and that doctor—we'd walk away from that man in a heartbeat for saying what we can only imagine he said. Isn't that the truth, Jack?"

Jack had so disconnected that he willed himself invisible and deaf. He stared off at Federal Hill and thought about how, just beyond that, was Fort McHenry. All those class trips. Every September of every year of grade school, it seemed, there was a class trip to Fort McHenry. Couldn't everything there was to know about the place have been learned in first grade? Some-

how, though, everything there was to know was collected in a
layer of years, so that by the sixth grade he remembered knowing all there was to know about the fort. So, as he sat there
escaping Chuck's compulsive outrage, he was perplexed at how
little he knew of the place now. Then out of nowhere it came to
him, all at once, what he most remembered about all those trips
to Fort McHenry.

There was always a stiff breeze on the bluff as he stood with
still obedience looking out onto the harbor; not a wind at all,
but a breeze just solid enough to whisper across his face and
make his eyes flutter, he remembered. And as they stood on the
cliffy hill, or hilly cliff, watching boats sail and tiny water ripples
roll, his mind was taken to the boat—a boat Jack had in his
mind, even now, as a rowboat for some reason—in which a
lawyer was seduced into penning words to the notes of a beer-
hall song after seeing that banner with not one missing star or
stripe still waving in the breeze after the Brits tried to blow it
and its fort to bits. And he wondered if the breeze that stirred
Francis Scott Key's muse was the same steadfast breeze that
blew on those class-trip days. A beer-hall tune as America's
national anthem. As his mind scattered all over the country, and
into ignominious faces and places, there was something quite
appropriate about it. Francis Scott Key. National anthem hero,
American barrister, advocate of slavery.

The awkwardness of Jack's disregard of the question was
eased by Kara, when she said, "You're talking about the doctor
and the bigot, right?" It wasn't hard for her to catch enough of
Chuck's diatribe as she got to the table. That's how she knew
that he was talking about the sole subject that seemed to have
the entire city rapt. She placed the oversize tray of appetizers on
a folding tray the busboy had opened for her.

"You know it," Chuck said, looking at his wife as if to let her
know that there wasn't a person around without an opinion,
one way or another, about it.

"That's a tough one, you know," she mused, her eyes serious.
She stood straight, one hand on a hip, the other waving one
finger sagely in the air. It was as if she seemed to forget, for the

moment, that her job was to give them their food. "On the one hand, I certainly understand that doctor walking away from that man, considering some of the vile things the store owner heard the man call him," she said, looking back and forth between Lila and Nell. "But on the other hand, I think he would have been a hero had he saved the man in spite of the vileness. Still, I think if it were me, I would have left him there to die, too."

"That's right," Chuck said religiously. "And if you asked half of Baltimore with any sense, they'd tell you the same thing. Did you hear what she said, Jack?"

And as distant as Jack was, he was equally as present, at least now that he wanted to be. "Maybe she's being a good waitress," he said with flat sarcasm, his eyes still off in the distance, remembering Fort McHenry.

Everyone laughed thinly except Jack, as he felt Lila dig her eyes into him. Jack knew he didn't have Chuck's off-putting charm, for which he was oddly thankful. Still, when Chuck turned on his charm, he always put Jack in mind of the worst part of Lila's mother. And so even though Jack wasn't the kind of man who always knew the right thing to say, the right time to smile even when it didn't start in his heart, he still knew the root of good manners—it was not sarcasm, he knew, particularly when it's unprovoked and spat at a stranger. What he felt was shame, even from so far away on the bluff of the fort. He could see Lila watching him, so he came back to her and asked, "What? What's wrong?"

"That's what I'd like to know," Lila said. "Why would you say that?"

"Because it's true. Chuck even said it himself. Let's just drop it," he whispered, his conscience now needling at the place where shame stayed. Kara shouldn't hear.

But it was too late. Though there was no way for Kara to know that Jack's derision wasn't meant for her at all, it was clear from the creases of her plastered smile that she felt the sting of his words.

"Well, she is that," Chuck said in his smooth-over tone. "She is a good waitress."

Kara placed the last appetizer on her tray in front of Jack, then said, "Enjoy. If you need anything, just let me know." And she walked away, well in her place.

Chuck dipped a shrimp in the cocktail sauce and bit it off to the shell. Then, just as he went to dip another, he said, "You know, man, I think you insulted her."

"Yeah, well, that's clear. But I wasn't really aiming what I said at her. I was aiming it at you."

"Me? Why?" And he bit off another shrimp and chewed it rigorously, then looked questioningly at Jack.

"You honestly have to ask why?" Jack said, looking first at Lila then at Nell. Surely they understood. "Chuck, when you get on your soapbox about anything racial, you tend to run it to the ground. You need to listen to your wife."

And as Chuck seemed to try not to see his wife's eye of shame, he set his own eye of shame on Jack. "Run it to the ground? That's what you think I'm doing with this, running it to the ground? Man, you're way off," he said with an ironic chuckle. "I'm taking a stand. I'm supporting this guy that so many are quick to call morally deficient. I am outraged that a black man with a medical degree living miles and years away from 1952 Mississippi would have to endure so much disgrace. I don't have a problem being outraged, and I plan to keep it that way until either I die or I have the chance to shake that brother's hand and tell him that what he did was as monumentally political as what Rosa Parks did." He chewed another shrimp in a hurry, swallowed, then continued. "What I need to know, Jack, is where is your outrage in all this? Where do you stand? At the hospital, everybody has talked about this thing every which way, except you. You've never taken a stand. What do you, Jack, think about that brother?"

How would Lila swallow without breathing? She didn't know which stole her breath—Chuck's question or the possibility that Jack would answer. Across the harbor, the aquarium was bathed in weak sunlight, and it would have been the perfect deflector. I wonder how much it costs to get into the aquarium these days, she thought to say. Or, Have you ever seen that dolphin show over there at the aquarium? It would have been pathetically desperate, she knew, but somehow she had to take the life out of Chuck's question, drown it in the harbor. She was helpless to save Jack, and so she stared without necessary purpose at the wave in neon, the simple symbol that claimed and named the aquarium without one word. There were not many minutes of sunlight left, she thought, and so pretty soon that wave would be a beacon in the dark night of the harbor. Jack could have been standing on his head juggling plates, but all Lila could see of him was that he was gulping down Coke while everyone else was sipping wine. And then, without actually hearing or seeing that Jack was preparing to answer Chuck, but feeling it, she looked completely at Jack.

Jack took two large swallows of Coke before setting down the glass that was now nearly only ice covered with amber traces of what used to be soda. He regarded Chuck squarely, then shot his eyes off to the large dinosaur head bobbing atop the science center. "Chuck, have you ever stopped to think that this doctor may not be the hero you've built him up to be in your mind? What if he had no idea that he was walking away from a dying man until he saw it on the news? I mean what if he thought the guy was just playing possum? Yanking his chain?"

Chuck looked off into midair as if to think about the possibility for several seconds, then said, "No, that doesn't seem possible at all. I think he made a conscious decision to send a message to this racist society as a whole."

Jack picked up his glass of ice and remnant Coke, rattled the ice cubes, and set it down again. Then he looked back at the dinosaur head before responding. "And all I'm saying is that you need to be careful who you make your hero. If this doctor thought himself such a hero, then we'd know who he is by now, don't you think?"

"Jack has a point, Chuck," Nell said with a plea in her tone. "Now can you please just leave it alone?"

Lila studied Chuck as he sat back in his chair and stared off into the water with the dejected bearing of a young boy just given the devastating truth about Santa Claus or Superman.

Mostly, though, she looked at Jack from the corner of her eye, too afraid to look wholly at him for fear of what she'd see. For when he said all that he'd said about *that doctor*, there was something in his eyes—in the way his hands gestured with such certainty, in the way his face was flattened by indifference—that told her Jack had disconnected from some part of his reality. And if he had indeed separated from such a large truth, what other part of him left with it?

LILA WAS IN the office so early, that morning light had yet to find its strength. There was no point in hanging around her house, now that life was slowly seeping from it. There was simply not enough space, not enough rooms in the house for life and Jack's silence. So, there was only one thing to do. Get to the office and reach out to a woman who may or may not be substantial but who somehow drew her nonetheless. She had a feeling, though—maybe it was that added sense she'd heard tell of—that there was a reason she needed to know this woman to learn the nature of loving as a mother.

As if she had composed it in her dreams, Lila knew exactly what she'd say in the E-mail she was about to send to Barbara Gallagher. Now was the time, she knew, after so many E-mails back and forth between her and the woman, for them to meet. And Lila wasn't certain if what was compelling her to see this woman, touch her hand, hear her voice, was the fact that Barbara Gallagher was the only adult ever to write to her about *Lila Lilly's Story Hour,* or if she was more fascinated than perhaps she should have been with the way this woman could mother a dead child. So she wrote:

Dear Barbara Gallagher,

   Your words last night moved me deeply. I wept for you, and I've never before wept for someone I did not know. I feel very strongly that I'd like to meet you, Barbara. Perhaps if you're not busy on Saturday at noon we could meet down at the har-

bor for lunch, or maybe to just sit and talk. Whatever you're most comfortable with is fine by me. I'd just really like to meet you, since I, too, feel as if I know you. I've never been this adventurous, Barbara, and I'm the kind of person who's always been comfortable with the people who are already in my life, with no interest in letting anyone else in. There's something about your letters that compels me to take this leap and meet you. Let me know when you can if you'd like to meet me as well.

All my best, Barbara Gallagher.
Lila Calloway

She sent it, then immediately felt the shame of her lie, because for as much as she was, in truth, moved deeply by Barbara Gallagher's words, Lila really didn't feel as if she knew her any better than any other woman she'd call a stranger. It was something that seemed to be the best thing to say to flatter the woman into meeting her downtown. But she couldn't worry too much about that right now. Pressing down on Lila was the dilemma she faced of explaining to Jack why this Saturday, the first Saturday since the day they met, she would not be with him on his medical mission. It would hurt him, she knew, but it would also disappoint, and what she knew for sure was that if there were a choice, she would rather he be hurt by her than disappointed in her. Hurt is forgivable, but disappointment whittles away at trust until it just isn't there anymore. Would he ever trust that he could count on her for Saturdays again? It troubled her. Then she thought about why Saturday was the only day that would come into her mind so reflexively, given her obligation on that day. The motivations of her subconscious vexed her, because maybe, she thought, she had claimed back her Saturday since trust had already gone.

"You've got mail," her computer informed her.

Lila's eyes squinted in a perplexed stare at the computer screen, because though she was only halfway waiting for Barbara's immediate response, it still didn't make sense that she would indeed respond with such expediency. She clicked into her E-mail, and read Barbara's message.

Dear Lila,

You are such a dear, and what you said made me feel so absolutely special. I'm really not certain if I have any friends anymore, and I suppose that's something I'll explain to you one day. But it gives me hope to know that there is the chance for a new friendship. I really only leave the house, Lila, to go to the grocery store, or to the bank, but most of the time, I just combine those errands into the same day. Anyway, with all of that said, I would still like to venture down to the harbor to meet you. Lunch sounds just fine, although I'd like to play that by ear, if you don't mind, since sitting in a restaurant for me can be the source of severe anxiety. It's very hard for me to be public these days. But if you'd still like to meet me, I'll meet you at noon in front of Rash Field. I look forward to Saturday, Lila.

All my best to you,
Barbara Gallagher

Lila responded: "Okay, I'll see you Saturday!" And after she sent it, Lila sat back and pondered what she'd just done. She'd just made a plan to meet a stranger who has no friends, hardly ever leaves home, and could well be in a precarious emotional state over the death of a child, and what worried Lila most was that Barbara seemed to be one of those people who spend the balance of their day on the Internet. So now, all she could do was wonder into what adventure she was about to send her nonadventurous self.

chapter nine

ON AN ORDINARY night, Lila wouldn't hear the cars going up and down Charles Street. On an ordinary night, they were an organic extension of the silent sounds of her home that washed the peace of sleep over her. On this uncommon night, though, the third in a row since the dinner with Chuck and Nell, when she watched what seemed to be the last ounce of truth seep from Jack, Lila recognized every sound's unadulterated origin— the sports car sounding more like a lawn mower hurtling down the street, the car with the busted muffler that imitated a truck. Even the arthritic creaks in the walls and floors and ceilings of her old house full of old charm and old character and old stories of the old lives of strangers failed to rest her mind. And as Jack slept beside her into the night headed for the next day, she wondered how, and at what point, he would be jolted awake by reality.

Her mind slipped off to think about their truth-packed love-making. So, if truth had indeed seeped from him, it just might be seeping from his love. And as her mind drifted back to their glory days of lovemaking, her leg shook with the discontent living in every nerve ending that had not been touched, had not been brought to full life in weeks. She glanced past Jack to see the clock on his nightstand glaring 12:23 A.M., and desire, if not the memory of desire, pounded harder in her. Lila had complete recall of every single time, at this very moment of the next day, when she and Jack had come fully together. But now, she lay next to him, as she had lain there for more weeks past than her heart could take in reflection, wondering when he'd touch her again. And wondering when and how it could happen that he'd simply stop wanting her. She'd never had to go to him, because he'd always wanted her. She never had to seduce, because the seduction was just in her being. She had no womanly wiles, because a woman like her, possessing a man's love the way she owned Jack's, did not need them. This is what she'd believed since the day they met. So why now, she wondered, was she lying next to her husband, quaking with a restlessness for his touch, desperate for him to join her?

Even though her mind and body were already as far away from rest as could be, when the telephone shouted into the darkness she still shuddered and shrank into her fear of the broken calm. And her fright was justified when she felt Jack spring up before the first ring was done and before the second ring could barely begin, and grab the phone from where it sat blaring on his nightstand. She leaned close to Jack, hoping to catch a word from the other end that would hint at a voice she would know, then she put her hand to rest on Jack's shoulder, hoping it would help ease the blow of what had to be the bad news of death, or trauma, or loss of some sort. It could be nothing else, she thought, coming so typically, so conveniently, in the middle of the night, as if to prepare the contented for the harsh truth of daylight.

"Oh no; this just can't be," Jack said, moving from Lila's touch to sit on the edge of the bed. He hung his head, cradling it in his free hand.

Something was rising in Lila—an unease, of pure fright—as she watched Jack listen to the details of what had to be a tragic end. It was probably his mother, or perhaps his father. They'd moved down to Virginia more than two years before, right before Jack and Lila married, to live a country, yet one-step-up, life in a house too small even for a family of country mice at the end of a bend in a two-lane country road. Maybe one of those pickups common to rural living had come flying around that bend in the road to run smack into his mother, or father, or both, backing their own pickup out of the driveway. Or maybe one of those same pickups, still flying around that bend, went buck wild right across the front yard and into their living room, and maybe no one was killed, but the cost of that kind of damage could certainly set them out on that two-lane road. And Jack's father was certainly a man far too prideful, far too ornery, even in the wake of plain need, to accept help from his son's prosperous hands.

Watching Jack as he sat in half shadow, half pale light, she felt the churning up, the paralysis from a time when darkness was to her a timeless vacuum. And so it was tonight. She thought of turning on her bedside lamp, yet the tether of darkness would not let her reach it. And she could have moved closer to Jack for comfort, or curled up in his lap as she really needed to do, but how would she ever get to him, being held down as she was by the terror of her imaginings? But then with light speed, as that moment's darkness made lame every part of her that could move, the unthinkable, the positively unimaginable claimed her every thought. Maybe Jack's sister, living there with his mother and father in that matchbox of a house, was too wrapped up in the television to notice that her three-year-old boy had wandered out of the house and into the road—and then tragedy. The worst that could ever be. The kind from which any woman who'd ever known the almighty miracle of growing a mere seed into a human inside her body can simply never recover and live normally again.

It was an unimaginable thought that led Lila to wander back two months to the time she and Jack went down there for a visit and drove around that bend to find the baby playing all alone in the yard, and far too close to the edge of the country road. And where was Jack's sister? Asleep in front of the television. Said she didn't even know the boy could open the door; said she would have died if anything had happened to her baby. She's lazier than a house cat, Lila thought as she grew angry all over again thinking about that day. And so now, all she could do was to sit, and sit, and sit, in painful angst, waiting for Jack to hang up the phone and tell her the awful news about the dead baby. Tears, premature, were about to fall when Jack did finally bid a good-bye and hang up the phone.

"What happened, Jack? It was the baby, wasn't it?" she said through a quivering voice. Lila was shaking through and through. And her eyes were damp with the tears that would free-fall at any second.

"Mr. Chalm died. The guy I was just talking to was the paramedic who got the call." He stood from where he sat, then went into the closet and returned with a pair of pants. And as if he'd just heard her, he looked puzzlingly at her and said, "What baby?"

Lila looked up at him through the pall of her own shock from the news and replied, "Your sister's baby. I thought something had happened to him."

Jack only grunted.

"So, what happened? How did Mr. Chalm die?"

Jack didn't answer. He went to the window and looked out at the few cars passing by at this hour of the night/morning, contemplating whether to tell her outright, or not tell her at all, that his hand was dug deeply in the old man's death. He blew out a defeated breath and said, "He was dead by the time the ambulance got to the house, so it's too early to know until they do an autopsy. Right now, though, based on what Mrs. Chalm told them, they suspect it was pulmonary edema. They believe it was brought on by a silent infarction, and at his age, that makes sense." He ran his hand over the top of his head and turned to Lila. He watched her receding into herself as the shock wore off and the unchanging veracity of death seeped in, and he decided that now was not the time to tell her. Now was not the time, he reasoned with himself, to land upon her the blow that he should have seen it coming, done something to prevent it, put his foot down definitely—even if it meant putting it down on Mr. Chalm's back—about the smoking.

Lila stared off into nothingness, then said, "What does that mean?"

The veil of light from the lamp across the street turned Lila's features positively gray as she stood, watching him. "Well," he explained in a rather common tone that said she should know this much, "it means that he had a mild heart attack, maybe even several over the course of some weeks." He sat down in Lila's chair in front of the window and put his legs into his pants. When he stood to button and zip, he continued. "Pulmonary edema is basically when the lungs swell because swollen tissue in the pulmonary veins dams up blood that should be pumping from the lungs to the heart."

"So, wouldn't he have had symptoms, or something?"

"From the heart attack, or heart *attacks*, maybe not. But he would have definitely felt something from the pulmonary edema. It would have felt like something was sitting on his chest, keeping him from breathing. He had to have ignored it." Even so, Jack thought quietly, that didn't afford him absolution. That would not help him in the moment when he'd have to look Mrs. Chalm in her weeping eyes and offer his condolences for what did not have to be. "I'm going to see Mrs. Chalm."

Those words, his thought, in the first-person singular, stunned her silent. And just as he reached the door to leave, she found voice to ask, "Don't you want me to go with you, Jack?"

"No, you don't have to. Just get some sleep."

And that was that, as he closed her up alone in the night, in a room where death had just phoned. She lowered her back flat on the bed, sensitive to her aloneness. Suddenly, every creak in the house was more than a creak, sounding like something far more malevolent. A burglar who might murder if circumstances forced him, or maybe someone with only murder on his evil mind. She began to believe in such terrible things, which is how she had come to convince herself that someone had been watching their home on that particular night in wait for some emergency to clear the way for murder, her torturous murder, and right there in her sanctum. This maniac could have been the one who called Jack to lure him from the house in order to get to her, she thought. Wouldn't that be the ultimate revenge on Jack, to take from him the one he loved most? Lila's heart beat so furiously she was certain that what she felt was her blood, sloshing, flowing, pumping throughout every inch of her tightened body. And she was tingling, feeling almost electric all over, so it had to be her streaming blood. What else could make her so aware of being alive—except death? It was everywhere, and it was in plain sight, physical, from where she lay, especially in the silver light that slid in from the street and slimed the walls, the ceiling, and a far-off corner with its evil magic that tricked eyes and minds. She couldn't take its trickery a second longer, so she reached up and switched on the lamp—with its benevolent, yellow light of life, of home—and stole darkness's power.

JACK HAD GOTTEN only one foot solidly on Mrs. Chalm's porch when the door opened with some urgency. Behind the screened door stood a woman, backlit in the blackness of the porch by the hallway light inside the house. He didn't know her. But as he moved closer a distant memory told him that he had seen her before, if only once. She was lean, nearly bony, and trying desperately, with her hair shagging all over her face, to look twenty years younger than her age, somewhere quite close to late fifties, if not beyond. Even so, her half smile under the circumstances made her seem pleasant. And he could see as he moved even closer that her rawboned cheeks and nose had conspired to take her too far past pretty and made her just plain odd-looking. He smiled into her face, which was beginning to bring something back to him, then he moved past her through the doorway.

"Hello, Dr. Calloway. I'm Sonia Butterfield. I met you about a year ago. I'm their daughter."

"Oh, yes," Jack said, extending his hand to the woman. It had all come back with a big whump. He remembered wondering why Lila had studied Sonia so intensely that day whenever the woman wasn't watching. He remembered asking Lila why, once they left, and she said that it was because she was trying to figure out who the woman reminded her of, until she finally did. Sonia and her hair, which was too long and shaggy for fifty-five or sixty, and her nose and cheeks pointing too sharply south, Lila said, put her in mind of an Afghan hound. And it would have sounded downright vicious, nasty, and wicked, Jack thought even now, if Sonia had not been far too old for Lila to have considered the woman sexual competition in any way.

He went into the living room, with Sonia following behind, and found Mrs. Chalm smiling peacefully at him from the over-stuffed chair, Mr. Chalm's chair, probably with her memories, but without a trace of anything resembling deep grief. Maybe it hadn't settled in for her yet, since it was all so fresh. Only a few hours old. Jack sat in front of her on the ottoman where Mr. Chalm's feet were often propped, which should have been supporting her feet, considering. He reached to take her hand, catching the keen smell of the warmth of her years. "I'm so sorry, Mrs. Chalm, I really am."

"Oh, thank you, darling. But you shouldn't have come here in the middle of the night like this. And where's your wife? I hope you didn't leave her home alone."

"Yes, ma'am, she's at home. She sends her love and sympathy to you, though." Jack held the woman's thin-boned hand a little tighter, then said, "Can you tell me what happened?" Suddenly he felt smarmy, like an overzealous journalist in hot pursuit of sensation, or an unfeeling detective concerned only with his mission, and he wouldn't have felt so had he not been painfully aware that his motives for asking had nothing to do with helping the woman patch together her ripped-out heart. Jack was in search of every single detail of the old man's death that would inflict on himself his due punishment of suffering, and more torment than one man should ever bear. He thought of all the aged patients he'd lost to the other side of earth, and they were more than he could count in his head. Still, he'd never lost any of them to the divine retribution of knowingly playing God.

"Well, he's been slowin' down a lot in the last week or so," she said, as if unaware that she was speaking with her husband in mind as still present. "Then, tonight, he couldn't breathe for nothin'. And he had the worst cough you'd ever want to hear. Was even coughin' up blood, and everything. That's when I said, 'Chalm, you need to get on to the hospital now,' but he didn't listen to me. Said he would be okay, that he just had to catch his breath, you know, rest awhile. So that's when I went on upstairs, real quiet, you know, and I called Sonia to see if she'd come over here and talk some sense into him."

"And that's when I rushed right on over," Sonia said, seemingly to prove herself, lest there be any doubt, to be the good daughter.

"But by the time I got back down here," Mrs. Chalm continued, "he was sprawled out here in the middle of the floor. Right over there." And she pointed at the very spot that no doubt she would forever remember.

"They were never able to revive him," Sonia said. "I think it had to have been a heart attack, don't you, Dr. Calloway?"

"Please call me Jack," he said. "And I don't know. It's so hard to say. With his inability to breathe and the coughing up of blood, there are a number of things it could have been. I got the call from the paramedic who was here, and he seems to think it was pulmonary edema. It could have been that. It could have also been a pulmonary embolism. Mr. Chalm was such a heavy smoker, so that's a real probability. They both have similar symptoms. When did you say the breathlessness started, Mrs. Chalm?"

She stared off to the side of herself as if trying to remember. "Well, it actually started yesterday morning when we got up, but it got worse tonight. He would lie down, sit up, lie down, sit up. Then he would walk. He walked all over this house till he couldn't take it no more. Nothing helped."

Jack scratched his head, stumped. "You'll have an autopsy performed, won't you?"

"Aw, yeah, Sonia is pushing for one," Mrs. Chalm said, waving her hand dismissively in her daughter's general direction. "I don't see the point. It's like draggin' a dead man to the doctor. He's gone, ain't he? Findin' out what took him ain't gonna bring him back here, is it?"

"No, ma'am, I suppose it won't," Jack said, acquiescing in the delicacy of the moment.

"And I say we need to have one because Daddy was in good health. Strong as a horse," Sonia countered in a way that made clear her firm stand. "For him to have just dropped dead like that without any kind of warning doesn't make sense to me."

"So I guess if I had dropped dead, then it would have made sense to you, huh?" Mrs. Chalm said, her acrimony present in her squinted eyes and tightened lips. "I'm the one who had the stroke. I'm the one with the high blood pressure. I guess I'm the one who should have been carried outta here in one of those black bags, dead as a doornail. Well, let me just tell you something. This should show you, it ain't always the sickest who die the quickest." She sank into soft mush in her husband's chair and wept the quiet tears of a woman afraid and alone in the world.

"Mother, for goodness sake! No one's saying you should have—" Sonia turned her face away and said through deep sobs, "Oh, just forget it!"

Jack didn't know what to do and was even more vexed by the pressing need to say something, being sandwiched between sorrow and guilt in such a way. And there he was in the middle, and beside himself with something of the same. So he decided to rise higher than his immediate needs, which just happened to be the same as Sonia's, and comfort the old woman. "I suppose you're right, Mrs. Chalm. Knowing what killed him isn't going to make him any less dead."

"That's exactly what I'm saying," Mrs. Chalm said.

When she leaned forward and raised herself up to stand, Jack got to his feet instinctively, ready for any command. "Please sit, Mrs. Chalm. Whatever it is, let me get it for you. What do you need?"

"Nothing, darling. I'm just gonna walk you to the door. You should get on home to your wife. I'm gonna be fine. Sonia will be in touch with you to let you know about the funeral arrangements." By now she had already crossed the room, and it was clear that she was giving Jack no other choice.

Jack followed her hesitantly but figured it was best this way, since her wishes were clear. "Lila will probably come by some time later today, and you know we'll both do anything you need."

"I know, sweetie," she said, opening the door, then reaching for Jack for a good-bye kiss. "Don't you two worry about this old lady. I'm gonna be fine."

Jack put his lips to her cheek, which felt only slightly more firm than fresh cotton, then said, "I'll see you soon, Mrs. Chalm. But please, if you need anything, you have all of my numbers, and I want you to call every single one until you reach me. Okay?"

"I'll see to it that she does," Sonia said, standing behind him. "We'll see you again soon, Dr. Calloway . . . Jack, I mean."

Jack only smiled, then turned to leave, hearing the door close behind him once he took the first step off the porch. He dragged himself to his car, weighted down by the heaviness of Mr. Chalm's suffering into death. How could he step lively when his lack of something—he still couldn't know exactly what without an autopsy—had taken from that woman what seemed to him to be all that ever really mattered to her. When he finally got to his car, nothing in him was in a hurry to do anything else. So he slid in behind the wheel, buckled himself in, even put the key in the ignition, but then, inertia. He let his head fall back on the headrest, and closed his eyes, not in sleep, but in contemplation of that fall in slow motion he'd taken that, in a way no one else would understand, had come to portend, perhaps, the rest of his life.

BY NOW, LILA'S mind had taken her to such horrifying places that she had worked herself into acceptance of Jack's desperate fate. The most prominent thought of what most likely had happened to Jack, though, was that he'd encountered the police. Maybe he was speeding, or had run a light, or maybe even been in a minor fender bender. However they'd come to find him, they'd certainly arrested him by now. They'd figured it all out, put all the pieces together in that magical way the police can do, and now he's sitting in a cell but waiting till morning to make his one phone call to her. That's the kind of considerate man she married—a man who'd fester among lowlifes to give his beloved a few more hours of sleep and peace of heart.

Lila's pounding heart got her out of bed and over to the window. She peered out through the sheers, then pushed them aside for clearer vision, but saw nothing other than the usual miscellaneous cars hurtling past. Not one car, not Jack's car, slowed up to turn into the driveway. She had to be near him, feel him, smell him, hear him; and she may never again. Lila went to his closet and pulled from it a dirty white shirt that he'd stuffed in his clothes hamper. And as she slipped into it, she could smell him, his musk, and it enveloped her. She went back to the window for one last look out before she slid to the floor, pulled her knees to her chest, and wept like a motherless child.

For Lila, there was no deeper, darker void in the universe's soul than the hour of four in the morning. That's why, just as Jack's key had come to turn in the door, Lila had already fought the good fight but ultimately was forced by her better judgment—which told her of the ire she'd strike in Jack if she was caught tracking him down amid such circumstances—to put down the phone. She heard him stirring in the front hall and then the living room, once he'd closed the door, but it was with deliberate motion, she could tell. What was going through his mind, she wondered, to leave her there alone in the middle of the night, and then take so long getting back to her side. To do this to her was rubbing so roughly against his natural grain, she knew, because there was no room for cruelty in his heart.

Jack pushed the bedroom door open with the slowness of anticipation, expecting to find Lila sleeping soundly, even in the brightness of the room. But it was the brightness of the room, as it hit him with its immediacy, that gave him a hint that something was amiss. And to find Lila with eyes boring into him in the full awakening of some extreme emotion made him know it with certainty. He stepped inside the room and stood, still as the clear and moonless midnight sky, sharing the gaze with her for several interminable seconds. Jack had no idea why he was being accused, this time. "What's up?" he asked evenly. "Why are you awake? And why are you wearing my shirt?"

"Never mind why I'm wearing your shirt. You can have your shirt," she said as she roughly unbuttoned it, peeled it off, and threw it on the floor. "The question here should be, why am I still awake?" Lila said with stress on every word. "I never went back to sleep. I was left here alone in the middle of the night, while you were gone, and God knows anything could have happened to you. And anything could have happened to me."

"Like what?" Jack said, with widened eyes that really needed to know.

"Well, the obvious, Jack. You could have been in an accident. You could have been carjacked or something. Just anything at all could have happened," she pointed out, her hands gesturing in his direction with a plea for understanding.

"And what could have happened to you?"

"Well, anything. Somebody could have seen you leave and could have come in here home-invasion style, or something, prepared to kill me. *Or* I could have been trapped in this room by a fire." Then she stopped, as if realizing she had reached too far into potential disaster.

"Okay, well, none of that happened, so why are you still so freaked out? I'm home now," Jack said, as if that should have been the end to everything.

"Because, Jack, what took you so long? I have been watching this clock and I know how long it takes to get to Mrs. Chalm's and back, especially in the middle of the night when there's no traffic."

Jack hung his head to stare at his sneakers. She deserved an explanation, he knew. Providing one would involve telling only part of the truth, leaving her with enough pride to know that her husband hadn't outright lied to her. So he said, "I just couldn't drive back right away, so I sat in the car in front of their house until I was certain I would be able to make it all the way back home."

"You could have called."

"I didn't have my phone with me, Lila. God!" he snapped.

And now he was frustrated and confused. He'd told her a version of the truth, or at least as much as she needed to know. What more could she possibly want from him, gushing as she was in that moment like a font of need?

"Don't you *God* me, Jackson Calloway. I'm your wife, and first of all, I should have been with you. Did you ever stop to think that maybe if I had been with you that I could have driven home? Second of all, I don't think it's all that unreasonable for me to have expected a phone call from you if you had known that you would be sitting in your car in a state of exhaustion."

Jack crossed the room, unbuttoning his shirt as he went, in need of something to do to settle the rage that was rising. "Oh, for Christ's sake, Lila, this is ridiculous! How many nights have I dragged in here from the hospital at one, and two, and three in the morning, and not once have I ever had to deal with you in a state like this. In fact, half of those times, you don't even know that I'm in the house. I don't know what this is, or what you're suspicious of, but I'm telling you right now, it's new and it's already tiresome to me, so something's got to give."

"I'll tell you what's got to give," Lila said, grabbing her pillow by one corner and dangling it beside her leg as she crossed the room, past Jack's path, to get to the closet, where she snatched up a miscellaneous sheet that matched nothing else of the bed linens. The sheet unfolded in her clasp, which had grasped it in a rage in the first place, and trailed partly on the floor as she moved in haste toward the bedroom door, looking like a scorned child dragging her blankie behind her for comfort. Without so much as glancing back at Jack, she said, "What's got to give is your arrogance, which actually makes you believe that you're an island." And the door slammed, propelled by fury.

Jack was stilled by expectancy. She would come right back, he thought, she would have to, since there was nothing in the past few minutes that justified sleeping apart. And so he waited, because the sweetness of their fresh marriage simply could not end like this, without warning. And so he waited, because it was clear that she had lost something of herself that maybe she'd find out in the hallway, before she could get so far as the sofa, from where it would be impossible to return. But when he heard her descend the staircase, and then heard nothing else, Jack went to the foot of the bed and sat. There was nothing else he could do, because he had no idea where to find the parts that would put Lila back together again, and fix everything. And he still didn't know why she had been wearing his shirt.

THE NEXT MORNING, Jack walked groggily into the living room and watched Lila as she pretended to be asleep. He had to decide, he knew, if he would let whatever this thing was festering between them from last night stagnate by letting her continue to fake-sleep, or take the high road and wake her up, forcing her to face what took her to the sofa. So he tried to rouse her, which wouldn't actually be a stirring up at all. "Lila," he called to her without a whisper.

She opened her eyes and stared at him, then said, "What is it, Jack?"

"Listen, I don't have a lot of time before I'm due at the hospital, but don't you think we need to talk about last night?"

"Yes, I do, Jack. What I think is that you were wrong, and you should have called me. I don't think I was being unreasonable for expecting you to call me and let me know where you were and how long you were going to be."

"Okay, look, maybe you were right, but what I think is that you were just a little bit out of control with the way you reacted. To me, you acted like Eulelie Giles's spoiled-brat daughter."

"You take that back, Jack."

"No, I'm sorry, but I can't." Jack stood his ground. He was ready for anything. She could bray like a mule, she could hiss like an alley cat, or she could thrash like a fish out of water, but she wasn't going to get her way this morning. And there was no nighttime to allow her the defiant act of running off to sleep on the sofa, so she had to deal with him and his refusal to bend.

"Jack, I'm beginning to question just who I married."

"Oh, yeah? Well, last night I began to do the same." Jack looked at Lila without a trace in any muscle, any crease of his face, that would indicate he was saying something so cruel simply out of spite. He meant every word."

Lila looked at him, up and down, with a fire in her eyes that was sheer meanness. "Oh, really, Jack. Well, I'll tell you who you married," she said, rising up from where she was lying on the sofa. She stood opposite him and on the other side of the couch, planting her feet as if she were a flag of some ill-gotten victory. It was a stand of sheer disobedience that came from nowhere in her that was truth, a place where she just might end up regretting what she was about to say. But she said it anyway. "Do you remember when I told you about how Gil was going to marry this woman named Sandra?"

"Yeah, I remember. And your mother and sisters gave her the bum's rush, so to speak."

"That's right. Well, what I didn't tell you, what I purposefully left out, is that when he first brought her home, I didn't think she was good enough for our family. What do you think of that?" she said, as if to goad a rise out of him. And Lila stood there, wide-eyed, waiting.

"Because she was from East Baltimore?" Jack said flatly.

"Because of everything about her, Jack. Because of East Baltimore. Because her mother worked down at Lexington Market and her father worked at Sparrows Point. They weren't like our family, and I wanted no part of them."

"So you were a part of all that?" Jack said with icy judgment. "You made it seem to me as if you were some sort of an anomaly in your family. And so, what must you really have felt about my family? Because I wish my father had had as good a job as working down at Sparrows Point."

"Well, I'm glad you asked," she said, still so angry her venom seemed to hit every corner of the room. "When I first met you, when we first started going out, and you were so candid about your family's poverty and the way you all lived when you were growing up, and where you grew up—"

"Why wouldn't I have been candid about that?" Jack said, with a sharpness to his tone that shouted his vexation out loud. "There's no shame with me."

"Yeah, I know that. You've always made that loud and clear to me. But anyway, I couldn't get over the class schism between us. It wasn't as strong as it was with Sandra because I had a completely different way of thinking when I met her. But I still had to ask myself, given the differences between you and me, if our different worlds would ultimately end up being a problem in our ability to relate to each other, and our families' ability to relate to one another." He couldn't keep the hurt from filling his eyes by the second, but considering that Lila wasn't completely hard-hearted, she softened her tone when she continued. "Jack, it's just that the way you talked about your life growing up—having to put cardboard in your shoes because of the holes in your soles, and having to take mayonnaise sandwiches to school for lunch—I don't know, it just made me uncomfortable. It made me feel as if I should have felt guilty about my privilege, yet I didn't. I couldn't. And I could not see, for as much as I had already fallen in love with you, how our two drastically different worlds could ever make sense together."

"So, what did you come up with?" Jack asked, his face set in stone and nearly paralyzed by the fear of what she'd say next.

"Well, what I came up with is that none of it mattered because we would make it work out. And it's not as if I didn't see that for as proud as you were of your humble roots, you were proud of them because you had given yourself a better life."

"So why did you marry me?" Jack asked plainly, still trying to hide the bruises inflicted by Lila's honesty and malevolence. His posture became as disconnected as his tone when he said, "What made you look past the cardboard in the shoes and the mayonnaise sandwiches and say yes when I asked you to marry me?"

"I love you," Lila said sheepishly. And as if a different woman was speaking than the one who began with such malice, Lila said to Jack softly, sincerely, "I married you when I knew that what I felt for you had nothing to do with how you made me feel or what you brought to my life. It had to do with putting that glint of pure peace in your eyes when I did the smallest thing that made you happy. And I married you because I could never forget the moment when you and I were laughing together and I realized that for the first time in my life, someone had made me laugh from my soul. That's why I married you, Jack."

But then, as if he hadn't heard the specifics of her love for him, Jack still asked, "Would you have married me, would you have loved me, if I were a garbage collector? You know, a garbage collector could make you laugh from your soul. And little things could make him peacefully happy, too."

"That's an unfair question, Jack, because you're not a garbage collector."

"No, I'm not, Lila. I'm a doctor. I'm the cream of the crop of doctors at that," he said with slightly more air filling his chest. Then he continued, with an arrogant overpronunciation on every syllable, "I'm a cardiothoracic surgeon. So, what, did that somehow cancel out the cardboard in the shoes and the mayonnaise sandwiches?"

"Jack, I think I know what you're getting at, but I hope it's not what I think you're getting at. Because if you're trying to say that I married you just because you're a doctor, you are on the verge of insulting me."

"Well, I guess you're just going to have to be insulted, Lila, because knowing what I know now, I can't think of a damned good reason why someone like you, who felt so *uncomfortable* hearing about my life as a poor black boy, would ever in a million years think about marrying me unless I was able to lift myself up and become something like—oh, I don't know, let's just say a doctor." And his words were rife with sarcasm. So rife that he wanted them to slide into her ears and fill up every other sense so that she could smell, and taste, and touch, and see it in all its putrescence, just as he had smelled, and tasted, and touched her anger.

She would not look at him. "Okay, Jack, in all honesty, yes, part of the reason I married you is because you're a doctor. I don't think that's a crime, and I don't think that makes me any different from ninety-five percent of the women in the world. And the other five percent would just be lying. Would I have married you if you had been a garbage collector? Probably not, Jack. Anyway, I don't even know why I brought all of this up."

"I don't either," Jack said, gathering up his medical bag. "I've got to go." And he was gone.

Lila slid back down on the sofa and put her head in her hands. And when she threw her pillow across the room at the fireplace in self-anger and knocked their silver memories box from its perch on the mantel, all she could do was sob deeply.

chapter ten

THE FUNERAL WAS held on a day that brought enough rain to float Mr. Chalm into heaven. It fell in torrents, and with drops large enough for one to fill a glass entirely, it seemed. And as Lila and Jack sat in the car with nothing but the silent passion between them that sealed their lips, their hearts, and their minds, the thwacks and sputters of the falling rain made Lila feel as though they were heading for something far more morose than a funeral. Lila was well aware of whom her sorrow should flow to, yet all she could feel, and think about, and nearly weep for, was her own grief for her own loss, which was separate and only abstractly connected to her grief for an actual death. She turned her head as much as she needed to fix Jack in part of her vision, and she waited, as he was positioning the car behind the others parking in front of the church, for any little sign he would give her saying that what bound them was heavier, thicker, deeper, than what had shut them both down. But since she couldn't name it, how could she expect that anything could take claim over it?

She remembered the most powerful second of her life, because that's how long it took them to feel the rare trinity of connecting mind, and spirit, and body, and now, miles away from then, some very significant part of that trinity was nowhere to be found. All she had now was the numbness of one solitary ice cube sliding up and down her spine, telling her that it was lost, perhaps for now, perhaps forever. But does the duration of its absence matter in the face of her mourning? What was most disturbing about their silence, Lila now knew, was not in what wasn't being said, rather, it was in what seemed impossible to know.

The awkward quiet pushed Lila from the car before Jack had even turned off its motor. She closed the door, opened her umbrella, and stood on the sidewalk, trying her best to peer through the rain that fell before her eyes like a sheet of lace to find a familiar face, or the face of anyone who looked to be deep enough in their sorrow to pull her from the depths of her own gloom and drop her into the shallow end of another. Between talking heads and hugging bodies, she caught a second's glance of Mrs. Chalm being helped from the limousine by her shaggy-haired daughter. A woman in a yellow dress stood next to a man, and Lila found herself wondering why this woman hadn't worn a more subdued funeral dress.

So that's who would do it for her, she thought, not the man or the two women, but Mrs. Chalm. Lila waded into and through the throng to reach Mrs. Chalm just as the old woman was greeting and hugging the yellow-dressed woman and the man, who could have been the woman's husband. They were a couple, at least that much was clear, but it was only clear through the common look of a leathery life. And they had to have, as Lila's mind had them fixed, come together through the divine cathartic intervention that brought them each, singularly, out of what had to be a hard-liquor life that shone through in their hard-liquor faces and the unbroken connection that seemed to make each the other's salvation. But what mostly gave away their relationship with the bottle was their reverence to a moment-by-moment life that was in every move, every gesture, every smile. So she stood there waiting her turn to offer consolation and studying these two people, wondering how they, each and as a couple, fit into Mrs. Chalm's life.

As Lila saw Mrs. Chalm about to pull out of her embrace with the man, Lila said, "Hello, Mrs. Chalm. I am so truly sorry about Mr. Chalm's passing." And she bent toward the woman with spread arms. As they embraced beneath the umbrella Sonia held over Mrs. Chalm's head, Lila let out a rush of breath that was relief and consternation in one, because what she got in Mrs. Chalm's arms was far more than what she could give with her own.

"Oh, my goodness, Lila darling," Mrs. Chalm said, taking a step back, as if she were making certain Lila was real. "Now don't you just look as pretty as a present. Thank you so much for coming in all this rain, honey. Chalm is so honored, 'cause he loves seeing your pretty face. He knows you're here." She said this with the certainty of God's unchanging hand, then she slid hers snugly into the crook of her daughter's arm and they all moved, even the leathery-life couple, on their way into the church.

All except Lila. She turned, looking for Jack, but could find him nowhere in the rain. Craning her neck to peer into the crowd that was trying to make its way through one open door, she searched frantically for Jack's head, or jacket, or umbrella, taking soggy baby steps inside the slow-moving haystack of black umbrellas, black clothes, black people. This is what they call a good turnout, she thought. Then, as she turned to go toward the car, with Jack on her mind, something came over her that wasn't necessarily dread, but a deep wound of self-reproach that, together with the rain and all that black, brought her back to original devotion. So just as she started off with a gait somewhere between a trot and a brisk walk, she saw Jack, but only his figure, which she had fixed in her memory from touching, smelling, seeing him even when his presence was not physical. Then, as if she'd just run headlong into the will of a wall, Lila was stopped without pause. And there he stood beneath the shallow arch, smack against, it seemed, double closed doors; and he looked as solitary as a man can be without being the one for whom death's bell was presently tolling. He was still, as if stilled by something buried too deeply within for anyone to reach. At least this was the chill it gave Lila. So she waved, but the only indication he gave of being alive in any significant way was the flatness of his glare that followed her, unwaveringly.

The first impulse she had, the only impulse she ever had, was to go to him, because from the beginning of their time it was the only place that seemed to be the truest place she belonged. She went toward him, following what led her, until, without consulting with her mind, a current came along and shifted her course. Before she had a chance to question it, or herself for understanding, Lila was headed for the throng and away from Jack, to find herself among the last of the stragglers squeezing into the church through that one door. And without seeing, she knew Jack would follow.

Inside the church, Lila slid into a pew closer to the back, where she felt most comfortable, terribly appropriate. After all, she was only in Mr. Chalm's life through a roundabout connection, and then, only once a month or so. Besides, with the crowd, there was no possible other choice left for her. She didn't need to look behind her to know that Jack was there, yet she still felt the calming comfort of contentment slide over and through her when he sat next to her. It was whole, her response to him—equally as emotional as physical.

They hadn't been seated a full minute, it seemed to her, before she had to get to her feet again for the pomp of the organ moaning the processional hymn for the priests and the family walking slowly behind the casket. Lila studied the stoicism in Mrs. Chalm's baby steps, the overwrought despair in Sonia's tears, and it was all so pitiful, but somehow Lila couldn't keep her mind from bopping down to Virginia and sitting down at Cordelia's dinner table to listen to the woman compulsively nag Jack's fat father, who could never seem to get his fill—"Dub Senior, I'm tellin' you, you keep eatin' like that and drinkin' that beer as fat as you are and I'm tellin' you, we gonna be walkin' slowly behind you. Your heart's just gonna clamp up and stop." It was meant to scare the flab off of him, Lila knew, but every time she heard it, it sure sent a hoot of a laugh echoing in her head that never seemed appropriate to let loose.

While he wasn't looking, Lila slid her eyes to Jack's face, unformed by somberness. And though she shouldn't have been, she was still at his mother's table after the portends of the sud-

den death of a fat man. Jack's father needed to deflect something somewhere. Why not at his son? So Lila stared into the
fallen face of who had once been Dub Junior, who then
became the more mature J. W., who then evolved, through the
sophistication of the company he kept at Johns Hopkins, into
Jack. It was something that the fat, less urbane Dub Senior
never missed an opportunity to remind anyone who would listen, for the umpteenth time. "Did this boy ever tell you, Lila,
how he used to be Dub Junior, after me, Dub Senior?" Lila
seemed to remember his finding some way to slide this into any
discussion on any topic each and every time she was in his
presence. And then he'd go on to say, "Yeah, he used to be
Dub Junior, that is, until he got too uppity and started callin'
himself what all those white boys called him—Jack. Boy thinks
he's the president of the United States or somethin'." And then
he'd laugh a laugh that sat so steadily smack between natural
and unnatural that it rang in Lila's ears, even in retrospect, as
sinister.

But what Lila found more fascinating than Dub Senior's
repressed ire over Dub Junior's forsaking his name was the origin of such a ridiculous name. Jackson W. Calloway was the
name of these two men, but the W stood for nothing; their middle names were absolutely nothing at all but an initial. So someone, when the senior Jackson was just a boy, came up with the
dim-witted idea to give him the nickname of Dub, short for W,
and as if it made sense, they passed the nickname on to Dub
Junior, who later in life had the good sense to take on the
moniker of Jack.

And so now that the priests were on the altar, and the hymn
was in its last refrain, she had to jump off this path of names she
had wandered down from some misplaced point of origin and
focus on the dead man in the casket—Chalm. She could just
hear his wife calling him by the name she must have called him
for their whole life together; and suddenly, Lila found herself
thankful for Jack's uppity, sensible name change.

Once all the Catholic ritual was done and it looked as if
they'd be sitting for some time before having to get to their feet

again, or kneel, the priest finally got to the point of the gathering. Something very specific—a life alive with one heart, but lived with two. Then, it wasn't clear whether it happened when Lila looked down to her program to discover that this man had a real and sensible given name, which was Melvin, or whether it happened when the priest spoke of the Chalms' sixty-fifth wedding anniversary celebration as a rare and divine experience that made anyone not in attendance part of the unanointed, but whatever it was, Lila was suddenly stilled by Melvin Chalm's overwhelming life's passion: his love for his one and only. She lowered her head to let one untamed tear fall, but ashamedly, as her weeping was both proper and impertinent all at once. Her hand slid from her lap to creep under Jack's hand, where it rested on his lap.

That is until he slowly, tensely, claimed back his hand, his nearly imperceptible head twitch saying to her *Not here. Not now.* He felt her recoil, pull back into herself as if licked by the angry and roiling passion of a flame, wounded, and by him. There was nothing he could do. She was not where he needed to be, and he could not have her in him, though he had gone with her thoughts to the same place. A lifetime of love. Someone he knew had actually done it. Mr. Chalm loved one woman for more years than he didn't love her; many more years. Jack couldn't say that, since their love was so new, and right now sitting next to the loveliest, worthiest woman he could ever be so blessed to love, it seemed to be an impossible dream, reaching a place in his life where he would love Lila for more years than he hadn't loved her.

Jack looked too stoned-in for anything to reach him, but while nothing could penetrate, he could neither see nor feel it all slide under and creep over until it landed in the softest part of him. They were the words that were realized organically in every way in which the old man had lived with his cherished one. It was biblical, and it was simple, and on the day Jack told the Chalms that he had asked Lila for her life with his own, that's when he knew for certain that there was something in that book of God's for every passage of time, and every passage in life—that book from which he'd never, until meeting Mr. Chalm, purposely read one word. And though the priest had just quoted the old man's favorite words from the Word as blatant testimony to what had come to be the all-meaning point of the old man's, the dead man's, life, those quoted words meant not nearly as much as what Jack was hearing Mr. Chalm himself saying right now, in his head: *When one finds a worthy wife, her value is far beyond pearls. Her husband, entrusting his heart to her, has an unfailing prize. She brings him good and not evil, all the days of her life.* That's all he could remember, even though Jack really did go to the Word and read those words— even though they read differently in King James version—particularly when Lila nudged his patience to the edge of any man's reason, and particularly since Mr. Chalm practically challenged him. "Proverbs thirty-one," Jack remembered the old man's telling him more times than would be practical to count. "You need to read Proverbs thirty-one whenever you forget how to cherish your wife."

Jack was snatched from that place where the living dead talked in his head, not by the organ singing as sadly as the mortally wounded, but by what he could neither see nor hear but knew to be true. So, without intent, he looked only halfway at Lila and could still see the stream as if he were staring full at it. She wept beside him, inert except for the tears, like all those statues of Mary weeping the consecrated oil to salve a wounded world. And though some significant part of him was moved profoundly enough to want to hold her until her tears flowed through and from him, he did not know where to find that part of himself where compassion was crying out in echoes. Lost. It seemed so odd and abstract as it immobilized him, much like the tears that had stilled his Lila.

So he leaned into Lila stiffly and whispered, "Lila, this is just not the place for all of this right now. Please get yourself together." And even with being so certain that this was the proper thing to say at the proper time to get her back to the proper mourning for Mr. Chalm, Jack did not expect her action. He wanted to grab her, pull her, hold her, keep her from flee-

ing, or go after her, mostly because of how much of their rawness she was revealing, but he was powerless to her passionate
will. So all he could do was watch as she shuffled past bent
knees to exit like a woman-child, stoical within her righteous
wounds, yet broken down within the same.

And what Lila did next went beyond what even she could
explain reasonably of herself. She walked. Walked blindly the
distance that only sheer fury can compel. Her steps were firm
and pure in their resolve, her gait slowing only the slightest to
step out of the path of four teenagers taking up the entire pavement, and talking about something that had all of them raising
hell. "Damn right I woulda left his ass there to die. Crackers
need to die if they can't give a brother respect whether he's a
doctor, lawyer, or Indian chief," said the most vociferous of the
young men. And Lila wanted to scream. Enough of this already.
Let it die with him, she shouted in her mind. Was there a corner
in this city where no one cared about that dead fat man or the
mysterious black man who left him to die?

She continued on, though, picking up her pace so she'd no
longer hear their ranting, only to have to step quickly out of the
way of a stooped woman with a shopping cart, moving lickety-
split without a clue as to whom or what was in her path and
seemingly unable to move to one side or the other of the sidewalk. The woman may or may not have been old, may or may
not have been homeless, but then again, she passed Lila with
such haste that Lila really couldn't tell. And though the rain was
no longer streaming in torrents, it still fell in an intermittent
spritz that, because she could barely feel it, made it seem as if
she were walking between the drops. Before she could even
know what had happened to her, before she could realize that
she really wasn't walking between raindrops, anger had gotten
Lila across Poplar Grove Street, from Baker Street all the way to
Gwynns Falls. And in the course of her trek, she crossed North
Avenue as if she knew, not exactly as if she belonged on such a
street, in such a low-down part of town, but as if she could certainly handle herself if pushed to do so.

So now she was at the end of the road, in every way out of

options as to which way to go, with nothing in front of her but Hanlon Park—always inviting for the prospect of running free, but not today. She thought about her old home, Eulelie's home, because, after all, she was only blocks away—long blocks, but mere blocks, nonetheless. I could certainly walk home, Lila thought. But walk home to what? There'd be nothing there but the shell that held all her memories, and the new memories of other lives being formed even now as she stood there at a crossroads remembering the parlor, and her old room, and the day her momma and Linda moved out, lock, stock, and barrel to Florida. They were so far from Baltimore, and so far from all that ever mattered to them, yet still hanging on to everything that doesn't, just as she was now, in her moment. And then there was Lucretia, ensconced in her new life in Charleston, so far from home. On that corner of Gwynns Falls Parkway, watching all those cars she believed had to be speeding by on their way to lives so much better than her own—lives without angst. Lila had never felt so alone. There was always Gil, though, she thought. She had to remember to call Gil, because right now, she believed, he just might have been all that was real and constant for her in the world.

She wrestled her phone from her purse, turned it on, but then grew blank as to whom she should call. Nell. All she would have to do is call Nell, and no matter what she was doing she would drop it all, pack those kids in the car, and be right there to collect Lila, with five minutes on her side. But no, she couldn't call Nell, because then she'd have to explain what she could not, what had become so entwined with something wraithlike and intangible. So as fast as the rain that was beginning to fall again, she pressed 4-1-1-SEND.

"I'd like the number for a cab company," she said to the computerized voice that asked.

And she listened to nothing, imagining that some human, somewhere inside that phone, was saying: What in the world is she talking about? A cab company? But Lila had never taken a cab before in her life. For all she knew, Baltimore didn't even have a cab company. When a human did speak into her ear it asked her if she could give the name of one specific company. Then, as if dropped from the heavens, the most propitious thing happened. A tan and black cab whizzed by. She had seen these bland cars at least once a day for every day of her life. But since it was never one of those entities that touched her day-to-day existence, she never really bothered to notice it. But there it was, whizzing by at the very moment she needed it—Tan and Black. "Tan and Black Company, please," she said with surety into the phone.

The cab arrived inside of a few minutes. She must have helped to speed things along by letting them know that she was standing on a street corner with a rain determined to grow steadier, she thought when she saw the cab. And when it pulled up, enough rain had fallen to plaster her curls to her head. She slid into the backseat and was struck broadside by the fear of having nowhere to go. Home. Never. Jack simply couldn't come home and find that the only place her imagination could take her to was home. And to go to Nell's would seem far too new-lywed of her, seen in her mind in the same light as going home to mother. As for Gil, well, he wouldn't understand without knowledge of everything, and he could not know even a part of everything. But just as the cabbie turned to ask kindly, "Where can I take you?" it occurred to Lila that she did, indeed, have a place of her own, a room of her own. "The twenty-eight hundred block of Calvert Street, please."

As they took off down Gwynns Falls, Lila sighed and settled her back into the seat. She sat, watching with unfocused eyes, trying to imagine what could have happened in this cab to make such a smell. It went beyond stale, beyond an identifiable funk like sweaty feet or odorous armpits, to something strange, and she found herself searching all of what she knew of the language to find what might describe it but could find nothing. It took her over until she could think of nothing more than escaping it with the prayer that it had not attached itself, like some paranormal entity, to every fiber of her clothes, every pore of her skin, every strand of her hair, so that she just might go through the rest of her life smelling as vile as this cab. And then, as if the stench were not enough, the cab rounded onto Twenty-eighth Street, barreling headlong toward a place that she'd hoped would have disappeared by now. It had caused more pain and wreaked more havoc than any place should be allowed by law. That corner, that store, everything around it that brought to mind that day, should have been razed, like all pocks upon the goodness of humanity. Lila's heart pounded as the cab bounded closer, and so to keep it from succumbing to its own pounding and simply stopping, Lila closed her eyes and slid down in a possum's sleep until she was certain the evil had passed.

WHAT WOULD JACK do in prison? Whom would he befriend, and did he have enough of a memory of the rough world of his childhood to connect to any of those prison types? This is what filled her mind while it idled as she sat in her office in its after-work-hours silence, completely out of ideas as to what she should do next. Maybe he could get a law degree, except there'd be no pride he could find as a jailhouse barrister. And she would have to tell people with pride that her husband got his medical degree from Johns Hopkins, then under her breath and in deepest shame say he'd gotten his law degree in prison. Then again, she could leave that part out altogether. Who really needs to know? But Lila knew that no matter whether she turned it sideways, or upside down, or right side up, or held it close, or far, the line was too much of a sliver when it came to knowing which shame was worse.

Lila hadn't been at her office for a good full half hour before Jack's key turned in the lock. He threw the door open with one exaggerated motion, like some matinee hero coming to save the damsel in distress. His eyes told of his conflicted emotions, somewhere between fright and fury, but still passion. And his cloud made him totally misread Lila's stunned face.

"What the hell's wrong with you, Lila?" he snapped.

"Nothing's wrong with me. It's just . . . how did you know I was here?"

"Well, you weren't home, so I drove past here and saw the lights on." He crossed the room to where she was curled up on the sofa and stood over her. "But that is so beside the point, Lila. The better question I have is, why are you here?"

"Because, Jack, I don't have a better place to be. I mean, what is this we're doing? I don't think I even know who you are anymore. I used to know your every thought, Jack. I used to be able to look in your eyes and know exactly what you needed. Now I look in your eyes and I don't see your thoughts, I don't see anything—I just see haze, a wall, and I don't understand it."

Jack turned to find the chair behind him and sat. He unbuttoned his suit jacket and nervously scratched his chest. "I'm the same guy, Lila. If anyone has changed, it's you. You get completely wacky if I'm gone a second longer than usual. I still don't get what happened that night I went over to see Mrs. Chalm. All I know is that I came back home and suddenly I'm not sleeping with my wife."

"And that's all it was to you, Jack? All you can see from that night is that you went out, stayed a second longer than you should have, and then came home and your irrational wife storms off and sleeps on the couch?"

"That's your projection. Those are your words. I didn't say anything about being irrational."

"Well, you might as well have, Jack. I mean, that's what you meant. You used to say exactly what you meant. Why don't you say what you mean now?"

She watched Jack open his mouth to say something, perhaps to let her have truth in the raw, but then he seemed to think much better of it. Maybe it would have been wretched, or it may have even cut her to the bone, but what made her mind sulk was the possibility that he would have meant it.

So Jack put four fingers over his mouth, as if to assure that it wouldn't in any way burst, or slide out. Then he said, softly, calmly, "Listen, Lila, let's just stop all this. There's been—I don't know, just a lot going on lately. Maybe we need to get out of Baltimore, you know. Get a fresh new start somewhere else.

Maybe Virginia, where my folks are, or that hospital down in Birmingham. They've been hoping I'd take them up on their offer for a while now. Maybe with a quieter life down there we'd be able to at least have sex again."

Lila took him in with retracted eyes, a retracted heart. She could scarcely believe that she was sitting here, now, in this place of her own, in the city that would always fit her as her own, listening to the man to whom she had tethered her life talking about taking it all away from her. "Alabama? You are actually serious about moving us to Alabama?" She shrieked the steel-cold laugh of the insane or the desperately bothered. "Jack, do you really think that I would agree to not only leave Baltimore, but leave it for a place where some redneck cracker named Cleatis will use our children for target practice? Oh, you've really lost it now. Oh, and just so that you'll know, I got your passively sarcastic comment about having sex again. But just so the record can be noted, it's not the most appealing notion to have sex with a husband who spends most of his time with you miles away from you."

"Lila, there are rednecks everywhere. You can go to Maine and find a backwoods redneck."

She was glad he didn't try to defend himself regarding sex. How could he? She believed Jack knew she was right. Lately it seemed to her that Jack had been interested in sex only cursorily, for physical reasons, and those moments only came to him every now and then nowadays, even as Lila tossed and turned beside him in sexual frustration. So she left the touchy topic of sex alone, too, and said, "That may be true, but they're headquartered in places like Alabama, and I simply won't agree to living in their backyard." Lila sat in contemplation for nearly a full minute, her mind softening so that she just might have second thoughts, but then she thought about Baltimore. She thought about streets, and places, and people. Streets that invoked very specific memories, like Lafayette Avenue, the street that held the house where the mother who gave her life was born; at least this is what she learned from her brother,

who peeled off information about their mother as the memories
grew in him like layers of thin skin. But believing this made her
romanticize Lafayette Avenue, even in its present life.

Then there were places like Lexington Market, or Fort
McHenry, or the Peabody Conservatory, which polished the
brilliance of Andre Watts whom her stepmother adored; or
Frederick Douglass High School, where Thurgood Marshall was
educated. Even the view from Federal Hill stirred up a certain
pride in her, for she was proud that she was born, and lived,
and would die in the city that held these places.

And she couldn't forget the people, quirky, often with Southern eccentricities, yet contradictorily simple and plain. And the
people like her from families of social renown who bask in the
glory of their small-time, small-town fame and special blood,
seduced by it all to believe they're somehow set apart from the
plain bred; though with each snobbish slight the pure fact won't
be suppressed, particularly by Lila now in her present life, that
each and every one, the low- and the high-born, share the same
legacy. The good and the not-so-good. It was all a part of what
formed Lila, and what made him love her, she believed. This
was Baltimore for Lila, take it or leave it. She'd rather take it.

Lila unfolded herself and sat upright to face Jack, so that he
would not be able to say, at some point in the near or distant
future, that he did not hear her. "You know, Jack, my great-great-
grandparents on my mother's side were slaves on a plantation
down in St. Mary's county. And my great-great-great-grandparents
on my father's side were sold from the slave block down in
Annapolis to a plantation down in Virginia, only to have one of
his branches come back to this state and plant some pretty
impressive seeds. Why would I want to leave these roots? I'm
deeply planted in this city, in this state, and I'm proud of it." She
thought for a second of lamenting out loud the probability of
finding, in a place like Alabama, an absolute dearth of intellect,
but thought better of it when it was edited by her second
thoughts. The thought of such a thing spoken gave her the dis-
tasteful memories of her full former self. It didn't stop her,
though, from imagining being bored into a screaming rage by

endless discussions of where to buy the best live bait, or where to get the best deal on a pickup, and how Miss Sally-Mae's dress shop in town is the only one selling the iridescent orange sherbet–colored, puffy-sleeved taffeta party dresses to all the belles. No, thank you.

"Well, I'm rooted here, too, Lila. Nearly every black person in this city and in this state is just as rooted as you and I are, and rooted from the same historical moment, but does that mean that nobody should ever leave?" He scooted his chair closer to Lila, then said with imploring hands, "Look, Lila, it's just that I can't take this city anymore. I mean, I have never seen a major city with more apathetic people, where the only certainties they want to count on in life are marriage and babies that they may or may not want, and taxes, and death. If you're not married in this city then you're nobody, and you know that because the pressure's particularly intense for women. Especially the pressure to push out those babies," Jack said mockingly, as if he had the provincial thinking of someone very specific in mind. He paused briefly, so as not to say whom, then continued, "For that reason I think this city probably has more neurotic women per capita than any other city in America, except for maybe D.C. And everybody has the same damned goal—a house out in Randallstown, the benchmark for black success in this town. Lila, I've known from the moment I met you that you want more from your life than what this city dictates you should have, that you should *want*."

"I don't care what everybody else does, or what everybody else wants, Jack. All I know is how I feel, and I feel like I don't want to leave Baltimore, Maryland. And that doesn't make me apathetic, lazy, or shiftless, and it doesn't mean that I don't want more from my life than what's barely essential. It just means that I like the profundity of being born in, living in, and dying in the same city where so many in my family tree did the same thing." Lila set herself firm in her unyielding decision as she picked, with seeming nonchalance, at a fingernail. She thought of what she wanted to say next, but struggled with whether it was prudent in the moment. What the hell, is all that slid silently across her mind as she said, "And yes, Jack, I do want a baby, and that doesn't make me neurotic. It makes me normal. And by the way, there was a time when we both wanted a baby."

"I didn't say I don't want us to have children, Lila. All I'm saying is—" Jack stopped short, as if even he wasn't certain of what the complete thought might be. Then he just continued on the matter at hand. "All right, Lila," he said, getting to his feet. "So fine, you don't want to leave Baltimore. We won't leave Baltimore. Are you coming home with me, or don't you want to leave this room, either?"

She shifted where she sat and crossed one leg over the other, away from him, as if staking her own territory and closing him off from any part of her. Looking haughtily at Jack, she said, "Your sarcasm is well noted, and might I say, beneath you. But be that as it may, there are three things, Jack Calloway, that I know for sure. The first is that whether we stay in Baltimore or leave it, if this empty space between us were to get any larger and become permanent, it would be the worst thing that has ever happened to me. The second is that after coming into the world from the cloistered life I'd always known, I know that it wouldn't be the worst thing that *could* ever happen to me. And the third, Jack, is that believe it or not, I'm not so attached to this secure and comfortable life that the thought of giving it all up to have to take care of myself again could make me stay in a marriage that's slipping away from us. And three years ago, I wouldn't have believed in myself enough to know that I could shake off the security of these trappings without really missing it all and being scared to death. I know how to take care of myself now, and just three years ago, I didn't. Even though I only did it for a short while before we met and got married, I still know that I can live by myself, and only three years ago, I couldn't. So you decide what's most important to you—that wall you've closed yourself up behind, or me. You let me know, Jack, because I'm going to be okay, no matter what."

Jack studied her first for a few seconds, then revealed only an ironic smile and said, "Where's all this coming from? I mean, you lived on your own for two minutes and all of a sudden you're telling me that you know what it's like to really live on your own. Lila, you didn't live on your own long enough to even know whether you could make it through a lean money streak without having to go to your mother."

"I might have lived on my own for two minutes, Jack, but I got a crash course in life in those two minutes."

Jack stood with a deliberation that could have meant nearly anything. He turned and, looking down to where Lila sat, said, "Well, if you think you've had just about enough of me and the way you say I've become, Lila, then I don't want to be the one standing in the way of your getting on with this life you say you can live on your own. This is a burden on me, too. You're always sulking around. You're so damned suspicious of me that I can just barely go to the bathroom without you questioning where I've really been or what my motives are. And then, just to make me even more confused, you want to have a baby. Yeah, Lila, this is way too much for me to take sometimes, too."

In the seconds it took for her to know that she could have sent him back to his God, right then and there, Lila had to choose what was more important, her love or her pride. And then she decided that she didn't have to choose, because both were in a critical state. One didn't have to cancel out the other, she believed, particularly when the rest of her life was so entwined in his pride, and acts of pride. "Jack," she said, standing to meet him where he stood, "if it's too much for you, then why can't you just talk to me about it. That man dying, Jack, didn't just happen to you, it happened to me, too. For the first time in my life, Jack, I had to really ask myself honestly about my feelings, my true feelings about white people." She sat back down because the heaviness was too much for two spindly legs to hold. Reaching up, she took Jack's hand and pulled him back down next to her. "With the way I grew up, I really didn't have to think much about white people. They didn't affect my day-to-day existence in the least bit. My world kept me insulated, not only from other blacks outside of our social circle, but also isolated from white people. I didn't even run headlong into racism until that Saturday I stopped with you at that store, and even then, it somehow seemed theoretical, because I still knew I was, even with my black skin that they so abhorred, superior to them. I felt that that was preordained for me decades ago, and their words or their actions couldn't change that."

"That's because you grew up with money, Lila. You grew up with money, and privilege, and a father who had some power in this city. A man who could say his name and open doors, black ones and white ones. That makes a difference."

"I'm not going to lie to you, Jack; it does. I remember being at Western High and having white girls wanting to know me because they knew that my father was Judge Giles. This one girl told me, the second day of school, that her father was so happy that his little girl was in school with Judge Giles's daughter. Her father was sure, she said, that Judge Giles would have had his kids at Friends, or Garrison Forest, or some other prestigious private school. And you know what, it's only now that I know that that meant something regarding race relations. But back then, when she said that to me, it meant nothing to me except that it made me know for sure that I didn't necessarily need white people in my life. White girls at Western were friendly enough to me, and I was friendly enough to them. I could eat lunch with them, and laugh and joke with them in the quad, but I would not invite them home."

Jack hung his head, as if suddenly aware, as if suddenly ashamed, and said, "Well, I think I knew, from the moment I was born, that if I were to do anything that would matter in this world, I would need white people to do it. That may or may not have been true, but that's what you believe when you're born where I was born. It just kind of went right to the center of my fear when I thought that to get where I've gotten, and then to possibly move further along in life, I could have needed, or could end up needing someone like . . ." Jack stopped and put his head in his hands, as if afraid of that complete thought.

Lila went to him with only her hand, landing a fingertip touch so soft but so filled with compassion that it could have made her cry. And she would have, except that tears might have distracted him from letting himself out of the prison he'd built up around himself and he was almost free. She knew that he believed, consciously and subconsciously, that there was no better place for him to be than behind those walls. So she would only caress him for as long as he'd let her slide her hand from the small of his back up to his shoulder; that is, until he inched away from her. In his heart, she knew, he was not trying to offend, but with her laying on of hands she was about to break into a place where she was not wanted right now. And so all she could do was watch helplessly as he, with his emotions still raw, still as red as they were the day they were born, ducked and dodged any part of her that just might break through.

Lila could no longer reach him, so she pulled back her hand and said, "Jack, I have to tell you something. With that guy, I wanted him dead for what he said to you the week before he died, and that's the most I have ever felt about a white person. Ever! I didn't hate or love them. I didn't fear them, and I didn't necessarily want to be around them or not want to be around them. They held no more significance for me than a light pole. So, I can't imagine what it felt like for you who had this emotional history with white people. What did it feel like, Jack?"

"That's just it, Lila. I wanted him dead, too. But I should have risen above that feeling years ago, because in the world I come from you either wanted to kill white people or become just like them. There was no in-between. I didn't have the luxury of indifference toward them. I don't know, Lila. Should I have wanted him dead? I don't know." Jack stood and stuffed his hands in his pants pockets, as if that alone would be enough to shut off all the talk about dead white people. With the upper part of his body, but mostly with his head, he motioned toward the door and said, "I do know that I don't want to talk about this anymore, so I think we should go. That is, if you're planning to go home with me."

"Is that it, Jack?" Lila asked, too perturbed to try to force kindness into her voice. "We're just supposed to stop talking about it because you don't want to talk about it anymore?"

"That's right." And he walked toward the door, then stopped in the middle of the room. "What else is there to say, Lila. It's done, so let it be done."

"Jack, what if I need to talk about it? I am a part of this whether you like it or not."

"That's where you're wrong, Lila." Jack's voice was hard, stoned-in, and it would in no way reveal any form of tenderness lying beneath. Then, slapping both of his hands into his chest with two thuds in unison, he said, "This is mine, Lila. You can be here with me. You can't be in this with me, even with as much as you think you are, you simply cannot be, so stop trying. Now are you coming home with me or not?"

And when she didn't respond, didn't so much as twitch, Jack thought his heart just might crawl up into his throat and choke the life from him. He just knew it couldn't be like this, where life could plunge into someplace unknowable *from* someplace unknowable. All he would need, all it would take to know that life wasn't plunging, would be for Lila to move, even if it were only one muscle. Jack blew out a chest full of exasperation and lowered his head into his hands. In a southern tale, Lila would be the woman who vexed and beguiled a man all at once, which is what she was doing to him now. For as much as he wanted to walk away from her and leave her there in all her senselessness, he had no choice, no will of his own to do anything but love her. His heart beat with a desperation he'd never known, and did not want to know now, as he stood there, knowing that in some allegorical way, his longing to live was dependent on something as simple, yet life-affirming, as movement, her movement. And so she moved.

chapter eleven

BY THE TIME Lila got to the bench in front of Rash Field to sit, she was already melting under the heat of the noonday sun, blindingly pale and many hours old in its heat. She had to sit there and endure it, though, because she'd taken such a large step just by being there to meet a stranger on a bench. But now, with a slackened spine that seemed to have been made limp and slumped by the heat, she regretted not setting the meeting later in the day, or on another day altogether, and indoors somewhere.

She fanned herself briskly, forgetting it simply made her hotter. The raw prepubescent enthusiasm coming from Rash Field of young boy voices desperate to win the baseball game and parents with determination equally as candid was only a minor distraction. It was hot and seemingly getting hotter. And being near the water did not help in the least. Maybe it even added to the sogginess in the air. Then, as if something had snatched her face toward the sky, she looked up at the Harbor Court Towers.

Lila felt watched from one of those high-up windows that must make anyone on the other side feel as if they were looking through their own personal aperture between here and heaven. Anyone could have been watching her, though, she thought. Any sick nut. Lila was certain that someone was standing in their window, looking, laughing at her dissolving in the heat instead of finding a cooler, less sun-soaked place to sit. To make it all worse, they were probably sipping lemonade or iced tea, and asking her cruelly through their thick window, Want some? But before her mind could gallop further out, and away on its paranoid jaunt of some mean-spirited stranger taunting her from their cool high-rise apartment, she stopped and looked away from the building, because in spite of her poor judgment of agreeing to meet a cyber-stranger, she hadn't lost her sanity to a hasty, sun-induced mistrust of people she couldn't see, and who most likely weren't there.

Lila thought back on the day before, when she had to tell Jack that he'd be alone on his Saturday mission. There was no way she could describe his face, if she had to, as she saw it in her flashback. It was the face of a man who'd been hurt, but oddly one of benign expectancy as well, as if he knew it was coming. And except for some part of trust that was mysteriously slipping away from them, she had no idea how in the world he would have known. Still, she wasn't prepared for his hurt and sixth sense to manifest itself as anger when he learned that she was meeting a stranger whom she'd met over the computer. Anything could happen, he said. That woman could be troubled, he told her. Well, aren't we all, she thought. And it even made her laugh now inside to think how she and Jack were the very last people in Baltimore to talk about someone else being troubled.

So now, waiting, fanning, trying to keep still to catch any breeze at all, she didn't know what she'd say to Barbara after the niceties. Yet how far she'd come from her mother's daughter, she thought. Eulelie's daughter would never have left the safety of the cocoon that defined her to write to anyone on the Internet, much less make a living on it for the world to see. On this early afternoon, hot to the touch of anything, and sitting on a bench at the harbor waiting for a stranger, Lila was not her mother's daughter.

A woman approached at a clip, and though Lila couldn't tell through the woman's sunglasses, which at once shut out the sun and all human eyes, it seemed that the woman was looking squarely at her. It didn't matter, though, because even if she were to take off the glasses, the eyes would be no more familiar to Lila than the next stranger's eyes. She could have been a parent late for her kid's Little League game. She was certainly dressed for a child's game on a Saturday afternoon—Bermuda shorts, a T-shirt, and sneakers. And that was just the thing that ruled this woman out as Barbara Gallagher, because no one would meet someone for the first time wearing Bermuda shorts, a T-shirt, and sneakers. Unless, of course, they have no friends, and rarely left home, and spent sunup to sundown on the Internet. Besides, even though Lila hadn't given it much thought at all, somehow she didn't expect the woman to be white. Lila stared, her stern face set in her jaws, because there was nothing more vexing than this predicament in which she now found herself. Not knowing the woman she felt compelled to know. Then she saw the woman's lips slide into a faint smile that could have had more to do with the rudeness of Lila's gawking than familiarity. Then her smile grew less faint, more directed, nearly intimate; and that's when she knew it had to be Barbara Gallagher.

"Hello, Lila," Barbara said, with her hand limply extended for a shake.

Lila took her slack hand, seeming to be completely caught off guard. Smiling dimly, she then said, "Hello, Barbara. It's really good to finally meet you." She took in all of Barbara Gallagher as she tried to readjust her image. In Lila's mind, Barbara wasn't nearly as petite and thin as she was in the flesh. A woman who'd lived to tell of the death of a child would have to be big, Lila thought, and broad shouldered, with legs like Atlas to hold up all the pain that kept her vertical here on earth against her will with a pull stronger than gravity. Then there was her hair, which was in no way blond in Lila's imaginings, especially since she thought Barbara was a black woman. But what struck her most was not just her whiteness, but her extreme whiteness. They had to get out of that sun, Lila thought, because Barbara looked as if just the tiniest bit of sun exposure could turn her entire body into a red, weeping blister.

"Oh, it's so good to finally meet you. It seems like it's been forever to me, but I guess it's only been about a month since I started writing to you."

"Yeah, about that, I suppose." Lila scooted over to allow Barbara room to sit. Then she nervously fidgeted with her wedding rings, trying to find what to say next. That's just the thing—for as badly as she wanted to meet Barbara Gallagher, she hadn't given one thought to what she'd say. In some part of her mind where reality could be suspended, she thought perhaps Barbara would simply come up to her, spilling out her heart about everything Lila wanted to know about her life as the mother of a dead child without Lila's having to ask anything.

"So, have you been here long?" Barbara asked with an apologetic lean to her voice.

"No, not at all. Only about five minutes."

"Of course the heat must have made it feel longer."

"Yeah, I suppose that's true," Lila said with a slight giggle. So, now what? She had run out of witty and interesting observations about the weather weeks ago, and though she hadn't shared them with Barbara, the thought of repeating them again bored her terribly. Maybe, she thought, it was best to talk about the most ordinary thing strangers can think to talk about. So she asked, "So, Barbara, what do you do for a living?"

"I'm a psychologist," she said flatly. "I've been on a leave of absence since Matty died."

And so now this explained it all, Lila thought. This is how this woman is able to climb out of bed every morning and start every day as if the world had not come to an end the day her child died. She had analyzed herself, Lila believed, and gotten herself back to sound mental health. "That must be interesting work," Lila said for lack of anything else to say.

"I would say that it was far more interesting in the beginning of my career when the practice of it was still theory, for the most part."

"And now?" Lila asked, as if Barbara should have known to continue.

"And now I find the problems of other people to be tedious," she said without a hint of a smile, and in a tone that bespoke a melancholy arrogance.

"I guess I can see how that would be the case" was all Lila could say as she reflexively turned when she felt, but before she saw, someone just paces away from them. It was a thin white man, and she wondered what he wanted, so she regarded him with questioning eyes.

"Barbara," he said. "It's really good to see you. What brings you down here?"

"Hey, Stew, how are you? I'm here meeting a friend of mine." And then Barbara put her hand on Lila's shoulder and said, "This is Lila Calloway. Lila, this is Stew Parker. Lila does a show on the Internet called *Lila Lilly's Story Hour*. Your kids watch it, don't they?"

"Why, they sure do," Stew said, looking at Lila as if he all of a sudden noticed she was sitting there. "How do you do, Lila? It's a pleasure meeting you. My boys sure do love your site. Your stories have been the topic of many a dinner-table conversation at our house."

"Oh, well I'm glad" was all Lila could say, somehow too stunned for words, or at least the right ones. By her estimation, if she had any white followers she had only one, and when Barbara Gallagher walked up she knew it had been Matthew Gallagher. And so now, with this white man telling her that his white sons—who knew how many?—loved her, she suddenly thought of a brave new world, a colorless world achieved through the Internet. "Are they on the field playing baseball?"

"Two of them are; my twins. My other son's at home. If you're still around here when the game's over, they sure would like to meet you and get your autograph, I know."

Autograph? she thought. Even though she knew just how far around the world that little camera, trained on her every week-day, could reach, she certainly didn't hold herself up as a celebrity worthy of autograph seekers. This was all too much to absorb at one time. So, stammering to say something, she said, "Well, sure. That would be just fine."

"Barbara, it was great seeing you," Stew said. "Please don't be a stranger. Jan and the kids would love to see you. And Lila, it was very nice meeting you. I hope you'll be around, because my boys will be so disappointed to know they missed meeting you."

"Oh, I will certainly do my best" was all she could say. Once Stew had cleared earshot, she turned to Barbara and said, "He seems nice."

"Oh, he's okay. He's a part of that group of people who are my former friends."

Puzzled, Lila looked at Barbara, then said, "He didn't seem so much like a former friend to me. He seemed like someone who still wanted to be a friend. Jan, too, whoever she is."

"Jan's his wife," Barbara said, looking off into the distance. "Yeah, she's nice enough, but you see, what they both don't seem to understand is that when you're going through a divorce, the friends have to choose. They either have to choose me or him. They can't have us both, and so far, they seem to have chosen him."

"I didn't know you and your husband were divorced."

"Well, we're not yet, according to the law, but in my heart we're as divorced as can be. We will be soon, though, and it can't come quickly enough for me."

"Oh, well, I'm sorry, Barbara. It must be hard, nonetheless."

Barbara looked at Lila from a sideways stare, then gave her a smile that was almost sinister and said, "You have no idea just how easy it is, Lila. He's a wretched deceitful drunk and I'm well rid of him. I hate him."

Lila didn't respond, because she didn't quite know what to say in the face of such hatred. What did it mean? It hardly ever means the same thing each time it's expressed, or even felt, since it is an emotion with layers and phases, and levels within those layers and phases. In Lila's mind, for Barbara hate could have meant she disliked his habits so intensely that she could no longer take being married to him. After all, a woman can take but so many socks left in the middle of the floor. Or she could have meant that she hated him with the passion of her true love for him. And since hate is not the opposite of love, Lila thought, Barbara most likely meant, along with seemingly the rest of the world, that hate was contrary to love. So, deciding not to touch any part of Barbara's hate, she said, "Well, I guess I can understand how hard it must be to be friends with people who are also friends with your ex. It's as if you never get a moment without that person in your life."

"That's right. It's bad enough that he'll always be in my life because of the kids."

"How long after you married did he become an alcoholic?" Lila asked, more for her own sake than out of idle curiosity. What do you do when you're married to someone and then the demon of alcohol takes them over? And then there was Jack with his wine collection. Could she come home one day, she wondered, and find that he'd transformed from a connoisseur and collector into an all-out drunk? "Did you just come home one day to find an alcoholic?"

"No, that's just the thing. I knew he was an alcoholic when I married him, but that was back in the days when alcoholics were called winos, and a wino sounded less alarming, you know, like someone with a tiny annoying habit like nail biting that you can live with."

Lila thought before she spoke, approaching cautiously, then said, "I don't mean to pry, but is the death of your son what caused your marriage to dissolve or was it the alcoholism? I've heard that losing a child can be so stressful that marriages are lucky if they survive it. And both must be impossible for a marriage to endure."

Barbara looked off across the harbor as if, from all the way over where she sat at Rash Field, she could actually make out the face of someone she knew. Then she turned to Lila with an ironic smile and said, "My son's death most certainly is what ended our marriage, but it was definitely both. And every single time I see my husband I'm reminded of the day my son died."

A chill went through Lila that seemed to be fanned by her quivering heart. Everything inside her felt like jelly, and suddenly, in a way she could not explain, she was afraid, but not so afraid that she'd run away. So she said quietly, "Barbara, what do you mean?"

But Barbara wouldn't answer except to give Lila a shadowy smile and cryptically say, "I mean just what I said, Lila." She took off her dark glasses and squinted at Lila, as if the shock of the sun had taken her by surprise. Then, Barbara brightened, as if to pull herself back from the edge of an anger she did not want to release in public. She sat up straighter, cocked her head sideways, and said proudly, "But everything I do, every day of my life, keeps me close to Matty. That's why I wanted to meet here at Rash Field. That Little League team back there playing, the team in the blue and white, well, that was Matty's baseball team. Matty and Stew's twins are the same age. Jan and I were pregnant together. Those twins miss Matty something awful."

"Doesn't it make your heart ache even more to be here, see-ing these kids play without Matty, seeing how they've grown since he's died? It would just break my heart. It would darn near kill me." A snatch of blue from the corner of her eye made Lila turn from Barbara to find a group of boys from the blue and white team walking in defeat with their parents.

"Oh, no, Lila. Not at all." She was so sure, so convincing. "It's like he's sitting here with his little hand in mine, rooting his team on."

"It looks as if they just lost."

"Yeah, they're not having such a good year. Most of them are pretty bad losers. My Matty, though, he loved to win just as much as the next boy, but he always seemed to be philosophi-cal about it in his own way. 'Mommy,' he'd say, 'if you win all the time, it doesn't feel so special because you're always win-ning. But if you lose a game and then win a game, the win is going to really make you feel like a winner.' Can you believe that? He was only seven years old and he was thinking like that."

"Wow, he was a wise little boy. I guess that says a lot about what you gave him."

"I'm a good mother, Lila. I just wish I had some kids to mother. My Gretta and Sam don't want mothering anymore. You know, I watch *Lila Lilly's Story Hour* because it keeps me close to Matty, but I also watch it because it's a way for me to fanta-size about being the mother of somebody who needs me again. And I know that probably makes no sense to you at all, but I can't really explain it any better than that."

"No, I can understand, I think," Lila said, letting Barbara's feelings make more sense by the second as she figured that since Barbara was a psychologist, what she was doing to ease her pain had to be by the book. And the way Lila saw it, Bar-bara's way gave the quirky way in which she connected herself to her unborn child credibility. "I mean, it's not as if I do what I do with *Lila Lilly's Story Hour* because I don't like children. It helps me to know their hearts, and when I make one of those kids smile, boy, I can't begin to tell you how much hope it gives me for my ability to be a mother one day." Then, as if from nowhere, two little boys, one the spitting image of the other, were standing in her face, beaming. She had completely forgot-ten about Stew's twins. For two boys wearing the losing blue and white uniforms, they didn't seem to be all that broken up about the loss.

"Hi, I'm Mark," one said.

"And I'm Clark," said the other.

"These are my boys," Stew said, standing behind them, so as not to overwhelm Lila. "Knowing that you were here really gave them a boost. They forgot all about losing the game, didn't you, boys?"

And they both said no in unison.

Lila laughed, charmed by their honesty, and said, "Well, that's okay. You'll win the next game."

"Lila Lilly, do you remember the story you read about the twins and the lion?" asked Clark.

"Yes, I do remember that story. 'Brian and Ryan Play with the Lion.'"

"Yeah, that's it," Mark said excitedly. "Well, Clark and I wrote an ending that you read. Do you remember it?"

"As a matter of fact, I do, Mark, because it was the only one that I got that had actually been written by twins. It was great teamwork, you two." And Lila beamed with an excitement that was no less childlike, because it was as much of a special moment for her as it was for the boys. "I have to tell you two, I am really proud to meet you. This doesn't happen to me every day." Forget the sun. Lila could have melted away to nothingness merely from the warm sweetness of their identical smiles.

"Lila Lilly, may we have your autograph?" Mark asked.

"All we have is this paper bag that Dad's coffee was in," Clark said.

"Oh, that's just fine, boys. I can write on that." Lila took the white bag, put her purse under it for stiffness, then drew a blank. She had never, ever thought about putting her signature on anything but a check, or a letter. And now here she was, in front of Rash Field, being asked for her autograph as if she were as famous and beloved as Cal Ripken. So now what do I say? she thought. And what name do I use? Lila Calloway would mean absolutely nothing to them, so she'd have to sign it Lila Lilly. That settles that, but simply to sign her name would seem to cancel out the moment the three of them had just shared, and that moment meant something to her. So she wrote: *To Mark and Clark, who are great teammates both in baseball and in writing. I wish you lots of wins in life. Lila Lilly.*

"Wow, thanks," Mark said, taking the bag from Lila.

"Yeah, thanks," Clark said, trying to ease the bag from his brother's grip. Then he gave up on that, turned to Barbara, and said, "Hi, Mrs. Gallagher."

"Hello, Clark sweetie. Sorry about the loss. Better luck next week."

"Thanks," he said, as if unconcerned about that. "I didn't know you knew Lila Lilly." Then he turned to Lila and asked, "Did you know Matty?"

"No, I didn't know Matty, but I wish I had," Lila said with a smile that had turned sad.

"He was great," Clark said, looking behind Lila at Rash Field, as if hoping to find Matty there.

"Hey, I have a good idea," Mark said. "Can you come to our

game next week, Lila Lilly? If you can come then we can bring the ending to our story and you can autograph that."

"Oh, boys, I don't think you should impose on her in that way," Stew said. "I'm sure she's got other things to do."

Then Barbara took Lila's arm gently and turned to her, as if trying to have a private moment with her, and said, with an enthusiasm that almost felt like an order, "So what do you say? We could come next week. We'll get some lunch from the pavilion over there and watch the game. I'd love that, Lila. What do you think?"

"Well, I guess that would be okay," Lila said hesitantly. "I've actually never been to a Little League game, not even my brother's when I was a kid, so it might be fun. I'll be here." And she smiled, more to herself than to Barbara, the twins, or Stew, at the places fate was sending her on a road to wherever.

GRASS HADN'T EVEN had a chance to grow over Mr. Chalm's grave, and the dirt on his grave was still a fresh mound, when Jack got the call about Mrs. Chalm. She died while napping, and her daughter believed she must have been dreaming about Mr. Chalm, because she'd gone off to heaven smiling. At least this is what seemed to give Mrs. Chalm's daughter comfort when she called Jack at his office with the news, and Jack shared some of her comfort in the thought as he hung up the phone and smiled sadly. He could smile at the peace he had to believe she possessed when she left this world, yet the old woman's headstone had fallen on his heart and crushed it. How could it have happened that they would pass on so near each other, as if they had a pact? It was positively Shakespearean, maybe even operatic, in its magnitude, in the oddity of its fate.

And he certainly had a role in this passion play, he knew, because they couldn't have simply died without cause, or in Mr. Chalm's case, without warning. So Jack was the malevolent force who brought in death. In fact, he could have been death. His weapon, ineptness, and maybe even an arrogance that made him believe he was actually doing good for the people he believed needed him. How had he helped them if they only ended up dead beyond reason and as a result of what had to have been his oversight? Why didn't he see Mrs. Chalm's death coming? Weak heart and all, she still could have lived forever. His culpability was more than apparent with Mr. Chalm, since in Jack's mind he should have ripped the cigarettes from the old man's grip. Jack knew he couldn't have been more responsible for that man's death than if he had choked him lifeless. But Mrs. Chalm, oh, what a mystery. He'd seen the woman only days before her nap of death, yet he still managed to miss the one thing that killed her. Even though, as near as anyone could tell, she simply slept away. Death could not possibly come so simply, at least as Jack reasoned it. It had made sense to him at a time when deaths like these were at a safe-enough distance, when it wasn't close to him, when it wasn't a relative, when it wasn't a part of divine retribution leveled at him. but nobody just up and dies. So when the old woman went to the other side, she went with a heart weaker, Jack believed, than he'd been able to see. For this, he felt less like a healer than a charlatan. And so now he sees the truth in the adage that death comes in threes and this was the third, and all three were at his hands.

Jack got up from his desk and took his bag. As he walked toward the door, his beeper sounded, and though the doctor in him from days, weeks, months ago would have responded immediately, would have looked at it before taking another step, Jack shut off the lights in the office as if he heard nothing. It was only when he stepped out into the hallway that he took the beeper from his hip and stopped its racket. But before he could look at the number to see who needed him, someone called to him from the other end of the hallway.

"Dr. Calloway!" the panicked voice said.

When Jack turned, he found one of the nurses from the Cardiac Intensive Care Unit. Earlier, Jack had done a triple bypass on a patient who'd been tucked into the unit, at least for the night. Protocol. But when he saw the nurse approaching, the one who'd been his OR nurse in the bypass he did that morning, and he saw that she was positively confounded, Jack froze, because this could not be happening. "Did you just beep me?" he asked, without really wanting the burden.

"Yes, I did, Dr. Calloway." When she got to Jack it was clear that she was out of breath, which blended with her anxiety to make her seem completely out of sorts. "It's Joshua Kaplan, Dr. Calloway. Your bypass from this morning. He died. His heart seized again, and he died." Her eyes regarded him with a question, and she asked, "Did you hear me, Dr. Calloway? Mr. Kaplan died."

"Yes, I heard you. What more do you expect me to do but hear you? If he's dead, he's dead. I can't do anything about it. I can't raise him up. He's not Lazarus and I'm not Jesus." And when he turned to leave her, he felt the shame that was due him. Jack was one of the few doctors who never spoke curtly to nurses, knowing what he knew; knowing that they were more than just a doctor's sidekick. Doctors simply went the extra mile, either due to financial good fortune or sheer determination. Nonetheless, there were circumstances separating an M.D. from an R.N., but those circumstances did not warrant disrespect. He turned back to the woman to see her crestfallen face, her surprised eyes, and said, "I'm sorry, Kathleen. I'm really sorry. It's been a stressful day. I've had another patient just die on me, and in the same senseless way. Mr. Kaplan shouldn't have died, he just shouldn't have. That operation seemed to go flawlessly, and I really can't stay around here to deal with any more death. Dr. Greene assisted me in the surgery. Can you get him to sign off on it?"

"Sure thing, Dr. Calloway," she said. "And I'm sorry. I know it can't be easy. I know it's never easy for me. I was talking to him one minute, and the next he was dying. I can't find the sense in it." She then turned and walked back from where she came.

Jack walked down the hall with a calm that was eerie. When he got to the door, he kicked it out of his path, and hell's fury was risen, because whoever heard of death coming in fours?

Before Jack could open the door of his home, he was already smelling through the open living room windows what would calm him. Lila's fried catfish and red beans and rice. Either she put something in those beans and rice that drugged him, or there was some chemical compound in the catfish, like trypto-phan in turkey, that could make a man forget his troubles. Except Jack's troubles were too big to dissolve. But he'd let it distract him while it could, because after all, it was Lila's fried catfish with her red beans and rice. So he turned his key in the door, opened it, and let the smell hit him full in the face, and go to every frayed nerve to smooth as neatly as it could.

"Jack?" Lila called to him, not necessarily to confirm it was him. She knew.

"Yeah, it's me," he answered flatly. Jack put his bag on the hall table and walked into the kitchen. If he were feeling his true self, he would have been able to appreciate fully the com-fort of seeing his wife fussing over a salad while the crackle and spatter of part of his favorite meal fried up in the pan. But he reached halfway out of himself and said, "You're making fried catfish. It smells wonderful. Did you make red beans and rice, too?"

"Of course, Jack. What else would I do? I thought you could use it. I thought it might perk you up."

Jack said nothing but went to the refrigerator and plucked a Coke from the shelf. The pop of the can made him smile for only the barest second before he sat at the table and took a long swig. He let the fizzy burn subside and slide into his gut before saying, "Mrs. Chalm died today, Lila."

Lila nearly fell where she stood. She dropped the salad tongs in midtoss, looked squarely at Jack, and shrieked, "She what? She died? Oh my God! This just can't be real! She died of what?"

"She took a nap and didn't wake up. Her heart just stopped."

"Oh, Jack. This is positively surreal. Why is this happening?"

Precisely, Jack thought, but would never say. He could only look away and hope she could tell him.

Lila went to the table and sat across from Jack. She reached over and took one hand, and with the kind of calm she knew was needed just then, said, "Well, you know, Jack, I've heard of things happening like this sometimes. Two people get together and they really are together for life, and one life is really no good without the other. And so when one life ends, the other one follows, really close behind, because there's nothing else for that life to do without the other one. Geese are like that, too, you know, and chinchillas. There's something very poetic and beautiful about it, I think. At least that's what I need to think to make me understand it all."

"Lila . . ." Jack almost told her that he didn't care about geese, or chinchillas, or swans, or any other mate-for-life animal she could name. In fact, he almost dismissed her completely, but he didn't, thinking twice about just how far he was willing to alienate himself, at least in this moment when all he really wanted was to eat fried catfish and red beans and rice, and to enjoy it peacefully. "Is the catfish ready? Because I don't want to talk about death. I don't want to talk about Mr. Chalm, or Mrs. Chalm, or Mr. Kaplan, who also died today. All I want to do is sit here and eat your catfish, and your red beans and rice, and I don't want to think about anything else but how damned good it is. That's what I need to do right now."

"Who's Mr. Kaplan?"

"He was the bypass I had early this morning."

"He died on the operating table?" she asked sheepishly, as if preparing for him to snap her head off.

"No, Lila," Jack said tersely, but still willing to answer. "He died in the Cardiac Intensive Care Unit. The surgery went perfectly well. At least I think it did. Maybe I screwed something up, I don't know." Jack rubbed his head in confusion, then he realized he was talking about death. "Look, Lila, I don't want to talk about this. He died, and that's all there is to it. His heart stopped and he died. Is the catfish ready?"

Lila got up from the table and went to the counter to get her fish spatula. Then she stopped where she stood and said rather profoundly, "Jack, they say death comes in threes. This was the third, and so this is it."

And Jack merely gave her a side-cocked stare. Her sense, or

maybe even her sanity, was in question, at least in his mind. Couldn't she count? Or maybe, he reasoned, it wasn't her ability to count he should question, but the power of a tragedy that had throttled her mind into reducing that despicable man, that horrendous moment, until she could no longer see it. So if her mind had given her the gift of forgetting, why should he make her remember? Good for Lila. Jack sank himself deep into the red beans and rice and the catfish that Lila had placed in front of him, and he ate with relish, carrying enough of that day in his mind and on his heart for both of them.

chapter twelve

LILA HAD BEEN wiping the same spot on the counter, which was really no spot, no spill at all, but just the place where she concentrated all of her attention until she had the stomach required to break Jack's heart with what she'd tell him; and if her news would not break his heart, at the least it would bend it a bit. By now, she'd put her entire self into cleaning that nonexistent smudge, rubbing it in a circular motion, counter-clockwise, and with a rhythm set by her subconscious. And it was only when she looked over at Jack as he drank his coffee, seeming so trusting in the comfort of his ordinary Saturday, that she had guilt pangs strong enough to make her call off the whole Rash Field excursion with Barbara Gallagher. But she couldn't, because for a reason she could not understand, and certainly could not explain, this Little League baseball game called to her in a way Jack's Saturday medical mission did not and had not in the last two weeks.

Jack drank down the last swallow of his coffee as he stared mindlessly out the window into the backyard. "You're going to wear down the granite on that counter if you keep rubbing on that spot," Jack said, as if to let her know that he saw her with-out looking at her.

"Oh, yeah, you're right," Lila said as she stopped her compul-sive wiping and tucked the sponge back into its place on the side of the sink.

"Are you ready?" Jack said, getting up from where he sat. "We should get going now."

Lila didn't move. In that part of her mind where anything was possible, she believed if she stood there without a word long enough, Jack would simply know and leave without her. No hard feelings. But in that place where reality lived in her, she knew she had to say, "Jack, I'm not going today." And her explanation started out as a near apology but then began tumbling forth, as if the words were rolling down a hill. "It's just that I promised Barbara Gallagher that I'd meet her down at Rash Field again today to watch a Little League baseball game with her. I told you about the woman, Barbara Gallagher, who started writing to me through E-mail and how her son, who loved *Story Hour,* was killed in a car accident. Well, this Little League team was the team that her son played on, and just as *Lila Lilly's Story Hour* gives her comfort because it keeps her close to her son, so does going to these baseball games."

Jack just stared blankly at her, as if he would say nothing or everything to her in anger. He slid his chair back into place at the table and said, "You couldn't tell me this before now?"

"Jack, I'm really sorry I didn't say anything earlier. It's just that I didn't want to hurt your feelings. But, Jack, this is really important to me. I can't explain it, but for the first time in my life, there's somebody who actually needs *me* instead of me always needing everybody else. There's something about this woman, Jack, and I can't just walk away from her."

"What are you expecting to do for her, Lila? I mean, I think that this obsession she has with her dead son's activities is unhealthy, and you're letting yourself get sucked into it right along with her. The next thing I know you'll be telling me that she thinks she sees her son out there on the playing field. It's just not healthy, Lila, I'm telling you."

There was something about his judgment of a woman he didn't know, had never seen, that made Lila madder than anything in only seconds. "Well, Jack, let's just pray that we will never have to know the pain of having a child die to know whether what Barbara is doing is mentally unhealthy or not,

because, frankly, that's not for you to judge. You're wrong."
And she left the kitchen with a haste that seemed to stir up a
breeze. She went to the hall, grabbed her keys and purse, then
stopped, but only briefly, to marvel at how, without a wit of
knowing, she had made it to that mysterious place of marital
honesty where women like Cordelia reigned; women who can
say to their husbands *You're wrong* and then just walk away.
Then she felt Jack right there in the hall behind her. Most likely,
she thought, he was just standing there giving the back of her
head that impassive stare he'd come to perfect in the last several months. And she was so certain he was there, that without
having to turn around for assurance, she said, "Is there something you wanted to say to me, Jack? Because if there isn't I
need to be going."

"Look, Lila, I'm sorry I said that woman isn't healthy. I guess
everybody has got to grieve in their own way. I just don't
understand why you have to be a part of it."

"Because I choose to be, Jack. What makes you think you're
the only one with a gift to help people, huh?" She turned
around to face him, because she needed him to see her eyes to
know just how deeply this ran for her. "What makes you think
that matters of the heart aren't just as important as matters of the
body? Barbara Gallagher reached out to me, Jack, in a way she
probably hasn't reached out to anyone since her son died. Am I
supposed to just ignore that, or make light of it? Am I supposed
to spend the rest of my Saturdays for the remainder of my life
by your side just sitting there, because in a way, Jack, all I do is
sit there? I can't explain this to you any better than to say that I
just have to do this, Jack. I think Barbara Gallagher pulled me
into her life for a reason, and I need to find out what that reason is, and it may be something, or it may be nothing at all, but
I've got to know."

Jack set his jaw, as if to hold something back, then said,
"Okay, Lila. That's fair enough. But I need to tell you that I
resent your even suggesting that all I expect from you is total
obedience to me on Saturdays. There has never been a
moment, since the day I met you, when I wasn't completely

supportive of anything you wanted to do. You wanted an Internet story hour and I made that happen for you." Jack stuffed his
hands in his pockets and paced back and forth a few steps
before continuing. "And yes, I'm disappointed that you won't
be with me today, but it's not for the reasons you think. I get to
spend so little time with you during the week and Saturday is
the only day I really have to share something with you and look
at your face, so if that makes me wrong, or selfish, or whatever
it is you're trying to say I am, then I guess that's what I am. I'll
see you later." He then brushed gently past her, walking down
the hall toward the door. With a determined close of the door,
he was gone.

Lila was left standing in the hallway, feeling the loneliness of
her empty home, and wondering how, before she could even
blink twice, she had come to be wrong. So she clutched tighter
the handle of her childless-woman's purse and went to the door
to leave. She opened the door and just before she stepped
through to close it behind her, she took one wistful glance back
down the hall and fought against the guilt that she knew she
shouldn't feel. But she would leave that guilt on the other side
of the door as she closed it tight and headed down the walk to
her car, and to Rash Field.

When she got down to the playing field, there were only a
scattering of parents in the stands and three boys from the blue
and white team throwing a ball around. It wasn't until she got
to the bleachers, even after having seen the jersey up close on
the twins, that she noticed the name of the team: the Blue Jays.
They even had a little picture of the bird on their caps. She
climbed up to the center to a spot where it would be easiest for
Barbara to find her. Just before she sat, she noticed a woman
sitting a few rows back, smiling at her as if she were about to
say something. The woman had a long thick mane that looked
red and then brown and then red again, and round light brown
eyes that made her look somehow familiar, but in spite of the
woman's familiar-looking face, Lila just smiled, then turned and
sat, since she didn't think she knew the woman. Besides, she

couldn't guess what this woman would have to say to her. Then, just as Lila got herself settled, the woman finally spoke.

"You have a son on the team?" the woman asked in a heavy accent.

Lila thought for a second about the woman's accent and what it might have been. But mostly she wondered which one of those little white boys on this all-white baseball team the woman thought might have belonged to her, before turning to answer. "No, I don't."

"So why you here?"

"I'm here to meet a friend," Lila said, thinking that wherever this woman's accent hailed from, it was a place that knew no subtlety.

"Who your friend?"

"Barbara Gallagher."

"Ohhhh," the woman said in a foreboding way. "The lady whose son died. Yeah, she so sad the way she come to these games all the time. She should stop that. It make her even more sad, you know." Then the woman got up and stepped down two rows to be closer to Lila.

"I guess everybody has to grieve in their own way," Lila said, unconcerned with whether this woman, who knew nothing of the art of tact, would find her rude. "It's not for anyone to determine whether she should stay away from these games or come to them."

"I lose a child, you know. Four years ago, my daughter die."

Lila's face fell flat with a film of shock and a little bit of fear. What was it with dead children everywhere? "How did she die?" Lila asked, figuring this blunt woman would not be offended by her frankness.

"She die from leukemia. It was sad. I mourn all the time for one year, then I was done. That's what we do, us Jews. We give ourselves one year, then we go on with life. It makes sense that way."

"Where are you from?" Lila asked.

"I from Israel."

"Really? I've always wanted to go there, you know, to the Holy Land."

"Oh, yeah? Well, Barbara went there. She don't tell you?"

Lila thought for a second but realized that she and Barbara hadn't really known each other long enough for that to have slipped into a conversation. "No, she didn't tell me."

"Oh, well, she went there for Christmas. She look for her faith, you know, she lost all faith in God."

"Well, I would think that losing a child can shake your faith a little bit," Lila said distractedly, imagining Barbara walking the roads of Nazareth in the path of Jesus, feeling his power, glowing in the miracle of her renewed faith in him.

"No, it didn't shake just a little bit. She come back and say, 'There's absolutely no physical proof that Jesus ever existed much less rose from the dead.' So I say to her, 'Well, no, there's no proof you can touch, you know, but something must've happened.' That's what I believe. Something must've happened."

"Really?" Lila said, her eyes widening as she was physically reeled back by the woman's words. "You really believe that Jesus must have risen from the dead?"

"Yeah," she said dismissively. "People not crazy. All this talk and belief in Him after all these centuries, of course something must've happened. But that's not to say that I give up my faith and be suddenly Christian."

And now Lila really was confused, because this woman, whatever her name might be, was possibly the closest she'd ever come, she thought, to meeting a Jew for Jesus; but she wasn't exactly for Jesus. It was all too much for her to ponder, and that's why she brightened and the creases in her forehead flattened when she saw Barbara approaching. "Oh, here's Barbara," she said, pointing. Then she turned back to the woman and said, "By the way, my name is Lila Calloway. What's yours?"

"I'm Talia. Talia Nechai." Then she looked up to find Barbara coming closer. "Well, I'll go now. I know she don't want me sitting here with you two. It's nice to meet you, Lila Calloway." She patted Lila on the shoulder and climbed back to her seat.

Barbara got to Lila, saying, before she even sat, before she even said hello, "What did Talia want with you?"

"Oh, nothing, we were just talking. She thought I was the mother of one of the kids on the team, although I don't know which one it could have been, since none of these boys on this team look the least bit ethnic in any way," Lila said, and then she laughed at the irony.

"Yeah, this team's pretty lily white, isn't it?"

Lila's laughter trickled to an end "I guess so." Then she continued with more interest. "You know, one of the things Talia happened to mention is that you went to the Holy Land at Christmas. Tell me about that."

"Well, there's nothing to tell. I always wanted to go, and I just didn't want to spend Christmas in that house without Matty's joy. So I got three tickets and packed up Sam and Gretta, and we flew to Israel, two days before Christmas Eve. It was beautiful there, especially on Christmas Eve. It was so peaceful. It was really a silent and holy night. I went there looking for something that wasn't meant to be found by me."

And though Lila knew from what Talia had told her, she still had to ask, "So what were you looking for?"

"Peace, Lila. I was looking for peace to be put into my heart by the miracle of being in the place where Jesus was born and lived and died for my salvation, but it just wasn't meant to be."

"And so what did you find?" Lila asked in a small voice. There was an uneasiness set in her by assuming Barbara's role, by asking a question that must have been common to a woman trained to get down to the heart of the matter with a well-timed, well-placed, albeit seemingly objective question like the one she just asked. And the question had come to her so naturally that she nearly smiled out loud with the self-satisfaction she felt at finding one small key to the psyche of a virtual stranger.

"Oh, look, the twins," Barbara said, as if she hadn't even heard Lila's question.

The twins came scurrying up the bleachers with one of them, Mark or Clark—who could tell?—waving a piece of paper. Each wore the same bright, eager smile that made Lila beam. And for the barest of seconds, she thought she knew what it was like to be a mother with a child running to her out of sheer and complete joy to see her. "Hey, you guys," she said.

"Hi, Lila Lilly," Mark said.

Clark, the one carrying the piece of paper, reached her first. He shoved the paper at her and said, "Here's the ending to the story we wrote. Can you sign it for us, please?"

"Oh, absolutely, Mark," she said, then looked at him puzzledly, since she didn't know if he was Mark or Clark.

"That's Clark," Barbara said.

"Oh, I'm sorry," Lila muttered equally as chagrined as apologetic. Then she turned to Barbara, amazed, and asked, "How do you know that he's Clark?"

"Because he has a little scar on his forearm that he got one day playing over at my house with Matty." She put two feathery fingers on Clark's scar then smiled sweetly at him, then at Mark.

Lila looked at Clark and laughed, saying, "Well, I don't know you well enough to have known that you have a scar on your arm, but I hope you forgive me for mixing the two of you up."

"That's okay," he said, as if it didn't matter. "So can you write the same thing you wrote last week?"

And so she did. When she finished, she handed it back to Clark and said, "It looks like they're ready for you guys. You'd better get down to the field so they can start the game."

Clark turned to leave, but Mark took the paper from Clark and just stood there, as if in awe, and said, "Thanks, Lila Lilly." Then he hugged her so quickly, yet so intensely, that it seemed to take even him by surprise. He smiled into her face as if he wanted to kiss her or hug her again, but only said, "I love you, Lila Lilly." Then he ran off behind his brother, as if embarrassment were nipping at his heels.

He was gone too quickly for Lila to respond, and it was a good thing, too, because Lila was left to stare after him in a gape-mouthed daze. What does one say, she wondered, in thanks for a gift so unearned? And she had no idea what she had done to deserve it except to read to him the same stories she read to thousands of other children. She thought of Jack and wondered who he'd deem unhealthier—Barbara for connecting with her dead son through a baseball game, or her for feeling the love of her unborn child. So this is what the unconditional love of a child feels like, she thought, giving herself a smile. "They're so sweet," she said to Barbara as she watched them run off onto the field.

"Yes, they are. I really miss them."

Lila thought twice, but then said anyway, "But it doesn't seem to me that you have to miss them. Stew came right out and said that they'd like to see you."

Barbara turned her face away from Lila, away from the field even, and said, "It's complicated, Lila. If I talked for two days you wouldn't be able to understand loathing the very presence of your ex-husband to the point where it is absolutely unacceptable to run into him socially."

"I see," was all Lila said, looking halfway over her shoulder to see if Talia was still sitting there. Then she continued in a whisper, "So, what about Talia?"

"What about her?" Barbara said defensively.

"Well, she didn't exactly say this, but what I got from talking to her is that you two used to be friends and now you're not friends anymore."

"So then I guess you know about Talia, because that's all there is to know." For several long seconds it seemed that Barbara had said all she would say on the subject of Talia until she said, "Talia Nechai is a pushy, bossy woman who doesn't know the meaning of boundaries. She's just so doggone judgmental."

"Yeah, I kind of picked that up from her," Lila said, nodding her head, satisfied that she had figured Talia out in their brief encounter.

"And I'll bet she told you that her daughter died, didn't she?"

"Yes, she told me that," Lila said as she shifted uncomfortably at Barbara's acerbic tone.

"She wears it like a badge of honor, as if she deserves some sort of mother-of-a-dead-child award for grieving for only a year then moving on with her life. That's what she always talks about, you know."

"Yes, she mentioned that, and I thought about it when she said it. There seems to be some sort of wisdom in allowing yourself to get through the first everything after the death of anyone—the first birthday, the first Thanksgiving, the first Christmas. I guess the idea is that nothing could be worse than the first year without them."

Barbara only looked at Lila with eyes too blank to read. Then she turned to face the field. With an abruptness that indicated she wanted no more of the discussion, she said with an enthusiasm that seemed mostly forced, "Hey, the game is starting! And our boys are up at bat first. This is good. Hey, batter, batter, batter!" she yelled with her hands cupped around her mouth, seeming to shut Lila out, or at least up, for the moment.

So Lila watched the game with only half her interest while the other half thought about Barbara, and Talia, and just what the specifics were behind their rift. She had a feeling it had something to do with Talia's challenging Barbara on the matter of Jesus' life and resurrection. And how incredible, Lila thought, what a gift for Barbara to have been given a friend, a Jew and unlikely ally of Jesus, who would try to hand her back her faith. A woman who would say, I am not a believer, yet I believe and so should you. So if Barbara could not find peace in the Holy Land, she should have found it, Lila believed, here in Baltimore in Talia's belief. She listened to Barbara's whooping and cheering for the Blue Jays, and watching her, hearing her, brought Jack's words into her ears—"The next thing I know you'll be telling me that she thinks she sees her son out there on the playing field." Anyone who didn't know would think Barbara had a child out on that field. Maybe this *isn't* healthy, Lila thought. Maybe the peace that has been so elusive to Barbara is being subverted somehow by the joy she's finding in these baseball games that seem now to Lila to be an elegiac veneration for a dead son, as opposed to something in which Barbara could possibly find serenity.

After devoting her total attention to two full innings, Barbara finally turned to Lila and said, "So, are you enjoying it?"

"Oh, yes. It's a very good game," Lila said, attempting to sound sincere But the fear of falling short showed too prominently in her widened eyes.

"So, let me ask you," Barbara said, shifting to face Lila. "You know so much about me, and I know so little about you. Now, I know that you're married, but what I don't know is how long you've been married."

"Two years," Lila said.

"Are you two happy?"

Lila didn't answer right away. It's not that she didn't know how to answer, but it just seemed like a complicated question these days. It certainly was no longer one of those questions for which the answer would simply roll right off her tongue and come out as yes. So she said, "Well, I guess we've had happier times. It's not that we're unhappy, it's just that our arguments seem more real nowadays."

"Oh, I see. You two are just settling into that other phase of marriage crudely referred to as the end of the honeymoon. That always sounded so stupid to me. It has nothing to do with the end of the honeymoon. I've known couples who've been married for fifty-some years and their honeymoon never ended. All marriages have to settle in. I wouldn't worry about it if I were you."

"I'm not worried about it," Lila said, her defensiveness peeking through her tone a bit. "It just feels a little strange, that's all."

Barbara looked at her and smiled with the wisdom of a seer, then put her hand on Lila's and said, "If you don't mind me being so bold, I'd like to make the observation that you are worried. You see, I've been married long enough to know where a woman's emotions lie when it comes to her marriage. I can tell when a woman is afraid, because when she tries to talk about the good points of a marriage going bad, she doesn't quite know what to do with her eyes and hands, and her smile is as forced as her words. I can even tell when a woman has checked out of her marriage emotionally, lock, stock, and barrel, because when the marriage or her husband is mentioned her eyes glaze over and become as dead as a doll's. And this I know because I've seen my own in the mirror. But I can particularly tell when a newlywed woman like you is worried, because when you talk about arguing with your husband you seem to be suggesting that the arguing is not abnormal."

"I know that arguing is normal. It's just that he seems to—"

"Be shutting you out," Barbara continued for her.

"Yes, exactly," Lila said, relieved to know that someone understood.

"It happens, Lila, and it's not what it appears to be. He's not shutting you out, he's just taking his space. Let the marriage settle into what it will become. If you relax with it, you'll find that it will settle into something more beautiful than you expected. Once I let my marriage settle in it was a wonderful thing before it fell apart." And she smiled into only half of Lila's face.

But how could Barbara possibly know? She didn't have nearly a quarter of the story. If she had even half of it, maybe her words of wisdom would be different, or maybe she wouldn't even have any at all, because no one could know how to navigate the course Lila was trying to find her way through. And so Barbara would just have to believe that she was right, because there was nothing at all in the air down there at Rash Field that would be miraculous enough to make Lila tell her about Twenty-eighth Street. For now, though, there was the baseball game, which gave her as good a reason as any to stop talking about her life. "Wow, a home run!" And her cheers were real and comforting in the way they spun around her to wrap her in the cocoon that would keep Barbara at a secure distance.

chapter thirteen

LILA SAT IN front of the window with her chin in her palm, almost contorted in order to get the full view of Charles Street. Her freedom amazed her now, more than ever, and she recalled the first time she understood the complete definition of freedom's concept. It came to her when she was only fifteen and wide-eyed with fear as her father described to her, in more vivid detail than her stomach could take, the inside of a prison cell. He told her that a prison cell was no larger than their powder room. And so for weeks after, and now fifteen years later, sitting, possibly, in the same chair in which her father had sat when he told her to imagine living in that powder room without the frills of her mother's cranberry-colored touches, and English rose soap, and English country garden air freshener. Just a toilet, a sink, a stench of constant mustiness and stale urine. No plush mats or embroidered fingertip towels. No curtains of imported Brazilian lace, no blinds, just bars.

After her father gave her a fright like no other, Lila suddenly became fascinated with that powder room. Whenever she had to use the bathroom, Lila would always make her way to the powder room, whether or not it was the most convenient commode in the house, and then stare out the window at Hilton Street, overwhelmed by her freedom to do more than long for her freedom. That people in prison cells looked through their bars at a street on which they could never walk at the whim of their will was, in her mind, punishment enough. She couldn't think of anything more cruel than to lock a man away in a room, with the taunting of a window. And as she sat, now, remembering her father telling this story, as if it were not a made-up tale of horror but fact, she thought she could actually feel her heart trembling; quivering in the same way it quickened the day her father put the image in her mind in full color. She wondered now, as she had then, why in the world anyone would do anything wrong, ever.

Her ruminations on criminal life were broken by the pressing time, and by Jack, who was in the other room, riled by something. He was talking, actually shouting passionately, heatedly, to someone about something, and she could not imagine to whom or about what. She got up from where she sat thinking and looked instinctively out the window at passing cars, and freedom, before following the trail of Jack's ranting. "That's right!" she heard him say with authority, and then, "They need to know we won't stand for that bull!" She couldn't fathom what could have put him in such a state, and why, until she entered the kitchen to find him leaning against the counter with everything in him pasted to the television. She walked deeper into the kitchen to see what had him so riveted, and she saw Kweisi Mfume carrying a microphone around an audience filled with young people. Even though she could glean rather quickly that they were talking about that African immigrant in New York who'd been killed by four white policemen shooting forty-one bullets so long ago, she couldn't really see the point now. Except as she listened further, she learned that it had had happened again in New York. But what did that have to do with Baltimore? And why did Jack care? In fact, aside from the more dramatic cases, she could scarcely remember details.

But one thing she did recall was being struck by one word through it all—innocent. Every news reporter, commentator, editorialist, and even anchor, from Channel Eleven's Rod Daniels to the world's Peter Jennings, kept calling the dead man *the innocent victim*, and this struck her as particularly peculiar, since there was nothing about the word, or even his state of innocence, that made his death any more egregious than if he were guilty as the sinful world into which he was born. Besides, not one of us is innocent, she now decided as a footnote to her original thought, with all of us being born into worldly sin as we all are born. So why, at the hour of his death, call in his innocence to bear witness? And what would be the point, anyway, since all those bullets proved far more profound than that one word?

"Since when have you been such a militant?" she said with a resentment that she found unreasonable but somehow couldn't stop.

"What are you talking about? This has absolutely nothing to do with militancy, Lila. It's about how there seems to be an open season on black men."

"Okay, Jack, but that happened in New York. That doesn't have anything to do with us."

He gave her a patronizing glare and a sarcastic half smile that could have prefaced almost anything. "Like hell it doesn't. This isn't about geography, Lila. This is about black men dying, not just in New York but all around the country and in the same nonsensical way. And by the way, it has happened right here in Baltimore, too."

"Well, I guess what I'm trying to understand is why you're so concerned. I mean, since I've known you, you've never been a cause man. I've never seen you get up in arms or on a soapbox about anything, so why all of a sudden are you ready to start up a chapter of the Black Panthers, wrap yourself in kente cloth, and march down Charles Street?" she said, her acerbic tone making it clear that there'd be something drastically wrong with such a display of his allegiance.

Well, she knew she'd taken it too far, since it was clear that Jack had decided, had actually forced himself, not to answer her. Still, she glared at him with determined squinty eyes as he stared straight ahead with a vengeance at the television; as if, she thought, she weren't in the room, as if she weren't waiting for an answer, as if her heat were not boring into him.

Then, without either of them expecting it, without either of

them seeing the possibility that someone might make the connection, Kweisi Mfume put the microphone in the face of a
young man who said, "That's why I'm glad that that brother left
that white man to die over there on Twenty-eighth Street. And if
that brother was a doctor, that's even better. I mean, once white
folks start realizing that we can have some power over their life
and death, too, then maybe things will start to change, you
know what I mean?"

Okay, that's it, Lila's mind screamed as she nearly leapt for
the remote and clicked off the television. She'd had about as
much as she, or anyone, she presumed, could take. "We're
going to be late getting to the Rawlingses'," was all she said as
she hastily left the room.

It wasn't until they were in the car headed for the Rawlingses'
that Lila realized that it was the very first day of September
already, and so with fall only weeks away, she could see a
glimpse of hope that the summer would dissolve forever into
the past, unable ever to return in any form. The heat of the
summer had long since died, and on this day, she'd found contentment in that part of her spirit that comforted her body, and
she remembered a time when she thought she'd never find contentment in any form. But the other part, which was her mind,
and the core of her spirit, was still flying in unrest, and it was
clear in the way she and Jack drove to the Rawlingses' that the
void between them was growing, it seemed, in increments of
seconds. And it was a result mostly, she knew, of what she said
about his becoming a Black Panther, and wearing kente cloth,
and marching down Charles Street. She knew it was wrong, and
the urge to apologize was niggling in her conscience, yet she
couldn't; she couldn't because her tongue was not wicked
merely for the sake of wickedness. Lila needed to understand
why, daily it seemed to her, the true Jack was becoming
increasingly faint in every way that made her know him.

So once Jack parked and turned off the car, Lila climbed
from her seat as if in a rush to get somewhere to do something
critical.

"What's your big hurry?" Jack asked.

"Nothing," she said, turning around in a snatch as if just caught in the wrong. She couldn't move now, so she stood and waited as he locked the car door. She couldn't tell him that she just wanted to get in there and get out. She couldn't tell him that the stillness between them—whatever it was, whatever had caused it—had made these missionary Saturdays dreary. She couldn't tell him any of this because she was not at all fully aware that she felt this way herself. But one thing she was aware of, and that was the memory of days when she felt more connected to his mission through her bond to him. And now, everything seemed unplugged, right down to the wire that connected her to this Saturday calling.

Jack walked around the car, then past where she stood on the sidewalk. Without saying a word, he climbed the steps of the row house. He rang the doorbell with one quick and forceful motion, then stood back solidly and without humor.

"I guess now I can ask you what's the rush," Lila said sarcastically.

But Jack did not respond. His plain-faced, straight-ahead stare was meant to say that he did not hear her, or would not hear her. But he knew that the more seconds that ticked by before someone opened the door, the more likely he would be to answer her in some acrimonious way. It would be for no good reason, he knew, but her sarcasm would certainly warrant it.

Then the door was opened by one of the children, a little boy of about eight. Jack wasn't certain to whom the boy belonged, or whether or not he even lived in the house. The Rawlings family was so large, with people—adults and children—coming and going constantly. Some were kin, some were neighbors, some were stray friends who came with kin. There was no telling, by his estimation, why they even bothered to close and lock the door. So Jack stepped aside to let Lila walk in ahead of him, and as she stepped past him, he smiled at her apologetically, not so much for turning his shoulder coldly against her, but for his intention to aggravate while doing it.

"How're you all?" Mrs. Rawlings said from her wheelchair in the living room.

"We're just fine, Mrs. Rawlings," Lila answered, seeming to transform herself into the Lila the Rawlingses were accustomed to seeing.

"Yeah, we are," Jack said, stepping into the living room beside Lila and slipping his arm around her shoulders. Jack could feel her pull away before she was actually gone. And this was what he couldn't understand about her. So he became the Jack he needed to be and seemed not even to miss his wife on his arm. "The last time we saw you, Mrs. Rawlings, this city was smack in the middle of that heat wave. Remember? How'd y'all end up faring through that?"

"Oh, we managed," the woman said with a throaty laugh that might have been sexy on a younger woman. "But I've gotta tell you, that thing was so horrible I can scarcely remember. Blocked the dang thing right outta my head, it was so terrible. Seems like it happened ten years ago, and then to somebody else."

"Well, I'm glad you all made it through it okay," Lila said. "I was just so worried about you over here."

"Yes, I know you were, and I sure did appreciate you calling all those times you did to see if you could be of help."

Jack took in Lila with eyes that questioned her with utter and complete rawness. His surprise was laid so bare, even Mrs. Rawlings could see it in only the side of his face turned toward her.

"Yes, darling," she said. "You didn't know your wife called on us over here?" Mrs. Rawlings's tone questioned the secrecy of it all. "She's just the sweetest girl. You've got yourself a prize in her, honey."

Jack only smiled, still expecting to hear something from Lila. Not that it mattered in any meaningful way, but Jack couldn't understand the secrecy himself. He stared into the side of her face.

"Well, there was a lot going on that week," Lila finally said. "I guess I just forgot to tell Jack I called on you." She checked behind her to make sure the chair was there, and then she sat.

"Oh, well, I guess when times get busy . . ." Mrs. Rawlings's voice trailed off. "Anyway, Dr. Calloway, come on and follow me. I'll take you on back to where James is." Then she motioned to the boy who had opened the door, but he either wasn't moving fast enough for her or simply didn't know what her waving hand was supposed to mean. "Binky, come on here and push old Grandma into where Granpy is."

Lila stood to follow, but then saw, felt, that Jack wasn't waiting for her, wasn't even expecting her. So why bother? She sat back down to stew in what she was manipulating to be her hurt feelings until she realized that what she was actually stewing in was relief. So, as the three of them went off, leaving Lila alone in the living room, she settled into the chair to wait. She looked around at the sun-bleached wallpaper, and the washed-out flowers on the furniture's slipcovers, and the fading faces in the faded Polaroid photographs stuck willy-nilly into frames. Everything in this room started out as something else, some other color, she thought.

Just then, she saw that what had once been a mere crack in the doorway that led into the dining room was growing wider. Her head turned with a start to take the mystery on in full. And though there was no clear reason why, given this particular home, she was astonished to find the tiniest little girl, seemingly far too tiny to be able to walk, toddling into the room, carrying a ball divided in slices of primary colors. Every child has had this ball, and in all different sizes, Lila thought. This child's ball was just big enough—almost too big for her to grip—but she held on to it covetously, as if she'd just snatched it from another and was making a clean getaway.

The little girl gave Lila the gift of her sparse-toothed smile, and Lila's face softened from her surprise. She returned to the small girl the kind of fool's grin adults can be reduced to when in the presence of so much untainted sweetness. When the baby finally made her way to Lila, she did so with the ball outstretched for Lila to take. When Lila took it, the girl stood for some seconds, waiting for what Lila would do, then she took off running across the room and turned to Lila, laughing once she got where she was headed. Lila giggled along with her, because she was certain she knew this game, whatever it was they were playing. Then, just as quickly, the little girl ran to Lila again, snatched the ball back, threw it across the room, and ran to fetch it. And when she got there to get the ball, the child's lilting laugh had Lila laughing heartily, and quite out loud.

By now, Lila had already given this baby her own pet name—Sugar Toes—because when the baby walked and ran it was on her tiptoes. So, when Sugar Toes crossed the room again on her little tiptoes, she came with the ball outstretched again, handing it to Lila. Lila took it but again just held it there. But by now, Sugar Toes was looking at Lila with high hopes. And finally she said something to Lila that sounded like *foe*, or *fro*, or *fwo*. "Toe?" Lila asked the child, with Sugar Toes dancing in her head. "Fwo," the child said again. But Lila just couldn't make it out, even though if she'd had a mother's ear, it would have been as clear as day. So Sugar Toes, by now exasperated at Lila's ignorance, took the ball from her and threw it across the room again. And how foolish Lila felt when she realized what the game was supposed to be. When Sugar Toes brought the ball back to Lila with yet another hope that Lila would play the game, Lila, having figured it all out in an instant, took the ball from Sugar Toes and tossed it. Sugar Toes laughed and squealed and clapped, and Lila's heart leapt with the excitement of suddenly understanding life outside of her language, outside of her literal and aged mind, to communicate in the world of her newfound friend, Sugar Toes.

Sugar Toes, her giggles spilling from her pink bow ribbon lips like bubbles, tiptoed back to Lila with the ball. Again, Lila took it and tossed it, and their laughs filled the room. It was like a carnival in there, and the fun was only for them.

Then, in the same way that Sugar Toes had appeared only moments before, through the crack in the door, the opening grew wider until a large figure stepped into the light of the room. She was a teenager, Lila guessed, but her portliness gave her an older look, though sloppy-trendy clothes revealed her youth.

"Come on here, Kia," the woman snapped sternly at Sugar

Toes. "You know I told you that you ain't supposed to be in here right now." She grabbed up the baby as if she were a sack of something, and in the same motion scooped the ball up from the floor. She did not acknowledge Lila with a glance, or a half look, or even as much as a half smile. Lila could have been Sugar Toes's invisible friend, for all this woman seemed to care.

As the woman left through the crack in the door from which she'd come, Lila stared after her with the expectation that she could make some kind of contact. Lila wanted to tell her that it was perfectly okay. That Sugar Toes wasn't a bother at all. That they were actually having fun playing chase the ball. But this old-looking girl, or woman, seemed far too austere, far too obdurate, far too unapproachable for Lila even to try to reach her in any way. How could she possibly be the mother of Sugar Toes and not have had her heart softened? Maybe she wasn't the mother. Maybe, Lila hoped, Sugar Toes was only in her charge, because Sugar Toes's mommy would have to be someone as sweet as the little one. The woman never even looked over her shoulder at Lila when she finally shut the door with a determined push, closing it tight this time so that Sugar Toes wouldn't come tipping and toddling in again. Closing Sugar Toes out of Lila's life.

For the first time in this journey of hers toward motherhood, this baby, smelling of the so sweet blend of baby powder and hours-old juice and milk, had made Lila's womb ache. She had heard of this feeling before—a longing so profound that it takes over every part of a woman's body, sending an orgasmic throb to the deepest part of her being, and to let it go, to let it pass, not to embrace it, would be as unholy as ripping a baby, body and bone, from her womb.

Lila hung her head with a confliction of emotions that hit her broadside and came from someplace she did not even know her heart wanted to go. And she thought, so loudly to herself she thought she was saying it aloud: I want my husband back. I want our life back. And I want a baby.

chapter fourteen

LILA CROSSED THE backyard, struggling with the large stuffed trash bag as she went between dragging and carrying it to the large trash can that sat just on the other side of the fence, in the alley. She would have left it up to Jack, as she always did, but these days, it was hard to fathom what he would remember and what he just might forget. After all, he couldn't remember, when she pressed him on it, to whom little Sugar Toes belonged. When she asked him all he could say was that one of those girls was her mother. But he wasn't sure which one. She knew that it was nearly impossible to keep track of the many extensions in that family. Lila also knew that the only way that any of those extensions would matter enough to Jack for him to care would be if by some extension he was also related. But that didn't change the fact that two days had passed already, and Lila still couldn't get Sugar Toes out of her mind. That child had stirred not only a longing in Lila's heart, but also a tender pining in her womb. There was even a brand-new great-grandchild in the Rawlingses' home that didn't make her want a baby in the same way as did Sugar Toes.

So, Lila turned to cross back over the yard to the house, still remembering Sugar Toes's smile, still hearing her laugh, when she saw something that she hadn't seen in the moments before. And she was certain it was God, in his auspicious way, giving her the hope of having a Sugar Toes of her own someday, but most likely very soon. It was one solitary rose sprouting up from the ground, seemingly in defiance of anything that had tried to hold it back. She walked to it, trying to imagine how it had come to be. Her mother would know. Lila stood before its perfection as if before something holy, marveling at the miracle that it had come only for her. It drew her in, this rose of exquisite form. Someone could have painted it, or very painstakingly sculpted its delicacy—it was just that flawless. And then dipped it in blood. The color. It went beyond red, into a realm where red was physical. Life. The color. It was body and blood; and this red, so deep, so human, made her heart quicken and her head swoon hypnotically until in her trance she could see nothing but every layer of red God had slathered onto this mere rose. The red on this rose was life, and so it was also death. It was love, and so it was also hate that can only rise from the passion of love. That red could kill, or it could salve. That red could be every passion in her heart. The red on that rose was Lila. The rose was for her.

Lila hadn't heard Jack approach, so that's why she nearly jumped from her bones when he came up behind her and asked what she was doing. "I'm just. . . . Well, I just took out the trash for pickup tomorrow."

"I would have done that," Jack said, nearly defensive.

"I just wanted to take it out, since I don't know what time we might be getting back from Chuck and Nell's. And you may not have felt like doing it then."

Jack merely let out a quiet grunt in agreement, then asked, "Well, what were you doing just standing here?"

"I was just looking at this rose and trying to figure out where it came from. Why it popped up all of a sudden. I've never seen this before, ever. I mean, the bush blooms in the spring, but that's a whole bush of roses. I've never seen just one single rose just pop up from nowhere."

"This rose came up last year at this time. Don't you remember?"

"No, I've never seen it before."

"Maybe you just don't remember because we'd just moved in,

but I know it came up in the same way, and in the same spot last year. Anyway, what's the problem? I think it's kind of beautiful. Symbolic, in a way. One rose going it alone."

And for the first time, Lila turned her eyes from the rose to see Jack. She felt the need, the absolute urge, to reproach, because how could he possibly believe that a lone rose could spread as much beauty as a bush? How could he possibly believe that any living thing can go it alone? What was so beautiful about the world were the multitudes of facets that brought something to the beauty. What would the world be with only one man, or one lone wolf? Nothing, and it wouldn't last long, either. This was the most significant difference, she believed at that very moment, between her and this man with whom she'd vowed she'd go through life. And more than anything, she wanted to tell him so, but she didn't, because it would only serve to tether them tighter to the place they hadn't been able to leave for nearly two months now. The place where the ball of truth hung over them from a weakened cord, threatening to snap, yet all they could do was stare at it and not take cover in the solace of each other. Rather they could only stand and wait, each from their own cold and hollow space.

"Jack, what do you see when you look at this rose?"

"I see redness."

"I mean, what does it remind you of?"

"I guess it reminds me of love, you know. What else would it remind me of?" Jack looked at Lila as if searching for another answer besides his obvious one.

"Well, it reminds me of blood. It makes me think of death, of stabbing, of killing, dying. That's what it makes me think about, because a rose is not always so benevolent, you know."

"A rose?" Jack asked quizzically. "It makes you think of all that? I can't honestly say that I get it, Lila, but if that's what you see, that's what you see. I guess it's like art, huh? It's all very subjective. What one person sees may completely elude another." And Jack gave her a smile that somehow equaled the banality he brought to the discussion of the rose.

"I don't think it's really that simple. At least not for me. Not when it comes to the rose." She stopped just short of explaining to Jack her likeness to the rose and its redness, in its depth of layers, and moods, and its hidden secrets, from stem to soul. Lila turned to face him, because in looking at that rose, she knew that now was the time. They either had to talk about it now and wipe the decay of that dead man from their lives, or their lives would, like that dead man, continue to decompose until there'd be nothing left but a skeleton of what they once were, and what they once had. So she held his eyes squarely in her gaze and said, "Jack, we should talk about it now, about what I know has been bothering you. It's been between us for far too long. I can't take this silence much longer, Jack."

"Okay," Jack said, backing over to the bench and finding it with nothing but his sense of space. Once his buttocks had touched down on to it he slid back. And waiting for Lila to slide right beside him, Jack said, "Well, I guess I should go first, since it really affected me." Jack crossed his legs, crossed his arms, and settled back to tell Lila plainly the feelings he'd been keeping close. "Ever since it happened, the words and everything about that day have just kept playing over and over in my mind. I've wanted to talk to you and tell you how I felt, but it's just been so hard, Lila. Of all the things life could have thrown at me, I really didn't expect this."

"Jack, I'm so sorry about it all, and I don't know if anyone can know that their life will be rocked in the way ours has been. When someone tells you that you're not good enough just by virtue of the human being you were born to be, that's got to hurt like hell, so in that way, I kind of understand. You were thinking with passion, and that always gets in the way of clear thinking."

"Well, Lila, I don't expect you to sit here today and tell me you're sorry, because, after all, that's how you truly felt. For you to apologize for it now would just be hypocritical." He still held her in his gaze, and as he held her, she grew distant; not that she had checked out momentarily, but her eyes had drawn away from him, as if struggling, squeezing, squinting to see print too small. So he cocked his head to one side as if the sarcasm in his eyes had pulled it down, and said, "Lila, when you told me that if I had been the man who collected your garbage, you would not have married me, that just made me wonder who I married."

Lila looked past Jack to where the trash cans stood. Maybe in the heaping stench of the garbage, she could find where the sanity had gone that had been with them briefly just moments before. She put her eyes back on him and quietly said, "Excuse me, Jack?"

"What do you mean, excuse me?"

"I mean, excuse me, but I don't understand what you're talking about. This is what you think we need to talk about? That's been bothering you all these weeks? You think we need to talk about the fact that you're wondering who you married because I was honest enough to tell you that I wanted to marry my intellectual equal?"

"Well, that's not what you said back then, Lila. Back then you basically said that you wouldn't have married me if I hadn't been a doctor."

"Jack, I honestly don't remember saying that exactly the way you just put it. I remember saying that no, I wouldn't have married you if you collected garbage. I guess what I would have gone on to say is that I would have married you if you were a teacher, or an accountant, or any other kind of professional. It has to do with being my intellectual equal, Jack, nothing else."

"A garbage collector could be your intellectual equal," Jack said, with a tone as if to prove a point.

"Jack, don't do this. You know exactly what I mean. Yes, in theory, a garbage collector could be my intellectual equal."

"But?"

Lila thought about that *but*, because it would certainly come next. And she knew that once she said it, she'd be stepping on the slippery slope that would bring her down into the mud of class and all its distinctions where there'd be no sidestepping the truth. She had to say it, though, because it was dangling in midair, as if it were alive and tangible. "*But*, be that as it may, I could not see myself married to a garbage collector because there are certain other levels on which we'd have to be on a par that simply transcend intellect."

"Like?"

"Like levels, Jack. Just different levels, and some are little things, but some are big things, too."

"But these big and little things are all centered around class, right? I mean, a garbage collector is not the kind of man you drag to a soiree at the home of one of your siddity childhood friends, is he?"

"You go to hell!" Lila said as she got herself up from the bench to go off in a huff of indignation.

But Jack was right behind her. He took her by the arm to stop her in her stride. "No, Lila, you're not going to walk away from this. Now you're the one who wanted to talk about it, so let's talk."

She glared at him with a steeliness she'd never before let him see. And though she knew it meant nothing in the way that it's been meant for so many women grabbed by the arm in dangerous, sometimes murderous, rage nearly every second of the day, she said to Jack in a determined, anger-filled whisper, "You let go of my arm, Jack Calloway." And only after he let her arm drop did she continue. "Okay, you want the truth, so here it is. No, I wouldn't marry a garbage collector, regardless of his intellect, and yes, it would be a class thing. But that is not to say that I think there's something wrong with being a garbage collector, since it is honest work and Lord knows a service none of us can live without. And believe me, you'd be able to appreciate my saying that a lot more if you knew just what a leap that is for me from where I once was when it came to the matter of class, Jack. But if it makes you feel superior in some way to judge me—and I think we both know that that man you left to die on Twenty-eight Street is why you have this superior need to judge me—then you go right ahead and point your finger at me. Just be mindful, Jack, of the three fingers pointing back at you, and they have absolutely nothing to do with class, or even this whole garbage-collector-versus-doctor business you think is the point." Lila turned determinedly and left Jack standing alone in the yard, making it clear that she wasn't coming back. But before she got to the door, she said with the firmness of a woman in control, "Let's go. Chuck and Nell are waiting for us."

Lila turned and went toward the house, but when she saw he wasn't following her, she said a little louder and with an edge of irritation, "We should get going to Chuck and Nell's, Jack."

"I don't think I want to go," he said flatly.

"What do you mean? Why don't you want to go?"

"I'm just not in the mood now. I mean, do I really have to go? If I didn't go, would it be such a crime?"

Lila let out an exasperated breath that seemed to deflate her entire body. "Jack, what are you talking about? We always go to Chuck and Nell's for holidays."

"Come on, Lila. What do you mean 'always'? We've just been married for two years. How can 'always' be such an absolute for our holidays? Why don't you just say that for most of our holidays since we've been together we've gone over there?"

"Oh, what difference does it make, Jack? The bottom line is that they always extend an invitation to us for their holiday celebrations, and nine times out of ten, it seems, we've accepted without hesitation. Now, all of a sudden, you don't want to go. You must explain yourself, Jack."

He clenched his jaw as if that would keep some extreme emotion in its place. "Look, we go there, we see the same faces all the time. Nothing ever changes. It's always Chuck's loose and down-home family trying to fit like a square into a circle with Nell's more uptight family. I swore I wouldn't go back over there after last Thanksgiving when Chuck's drunk uncle spit on the turkey then threw it out in the yard. Don't you remember that?"

"Well, of course I do, Jack," Lila said with as straight a face as she could muster, considering she was trying to keep a smile and imminent laughter at bay. "Who could forget Chuck's mother standing there telling Nell to go out in the yard, get the turkey, and wash it off and it would be just fine to eat. That's why you are not about to send me off to deal with that insanity by myself."

Jack laughed with the exact heartiness he laughed with Lila

that Thanksgiving night when it was just the two of them, curled together in bed. And it felt so good for Lila, too, just being in the same air together and sharing a moment so light. She didn't want to remember the last time it had happened for fear that the precious present would dissolve. Then Jack said: "God, that was unbelievable. But what I'm saying is that I vowed I wouldn't go over there again after that, but I let you drag me back there for Memorial Day *and* the Fourth of July."

Lila wiped her laughing tears from her eyes and composed herself only slightly long enough to counter with, "Yeah, well they didn't serve turkey, did they?" And then they did laugh.

"Okay, well, I suppose we can take comfort in knowing that this will be a relatively turkey-free meal," Jack said, reaching for Lila's hand. And when he had it, they walked into the house together. Together.

LILA WALKED BEHIND Jack—who carried the pasta and seafood salad she'd made—into Nell's Labor Day barbecue. The back-yard was filled, hedge to hedge, with the sisters and brothers and cousins, and the children of these sisters and brothers and cousins, of two separate and distinct families blended by Nell and Chuck. And boy, did they all blend on this day. They blended so well that it was hard to tell who was whose kin with the exception of a few. And of course Chuck's uncle, who was well on his way to the land of the drunks, was unmistakable. Then there were Nell's sister and two brothers, who could belong only to Nell. Whenever she saw the four of them together, Lila always thought, and never failed to say, though she always determined not to, that they looked more like one another than any siblings she'd ever known who weren't hatched from the same egg. She had said it so much that by now, she thought, it must sound to them like one of those things people say when discomfort makes them incapable of saying anything else sensible. It was surely tiresome for them to hear, much in the same way it had become tedious, when she was a child, to listen to strangers at the mall or in restaurants comment on how much she and Gil and Lucretia and Linda looked *exactly like* their mother; people who were completely unaware that it was a biological impossibility for any of them to look *exactly like* Eulelie in any significant way.

"Hey, Jack," Nell's sister Brett said, slinking over in that way she walked to plant a kiss on his cheek.

Lila gave Brett a stressed smile that took some time to become lightsome. Brett was one of those women who would have offended Lila, and any man's wife for that matter, if it weren't for two points in her favor: one, she's Nell's sister, and so by virtue of blood she's granted some of Nell's integrity, and two, she's one of those flirts who spreads her charm equally between men and women. Lila always grew warm with embarrassment, as she was now, each time she remembered the first time she met Brett and the way she thought Brett was a lesbian who was coming on to her.

"Lila," Brett said, with arms outstretched for a hug.

"Hello, Brett," Lila said, accepting the embrace. "It's so good to see you again."

"I'm telling you." Then Brett stood back to take in the two of them, Lila and Jack. "I've to tell you, girl, you got the last good man in Baltimore. And gorgeous as can be, too, girl. You'd better know how lucky you are." It seemed as if she'd stop there, but then, as if it were an afterthought, encouraged mostly by the smile that was falling flat and flatter on Lila's face, she said, "And you'd better know that you're lucky too, man."

Well, now, Lila thought, if Brett can repeat herself so tritely with every meeting and without shame, then Lila could certainly comment on the identical face Brett shared with her brothers and sister. "Thank you, Brett. You know, I still can't get over how much all of you look alike. More alike than twins."

All Brett said was, "Yeah, we hear that a lot."

Lila could hear the tedium in her voice but could not stop herself from thinking how Brett should know now how it feels to be so completely tired of hearing something that if it were at all humanly possible one would cram the words right back into the mouth from which they slid and make something of import come out.

"Hey, when did you all get here?" Nell said, coming to them from behind and just in time to save the moment.

"Oh, we just got here," Lila said. She took the salad from Chuck and, passing it to Nell, commented, "I made a pasta and seafood salad."

"Oh, Lila," Nell said, genuine in her lack of expectation. "You didn't need to bring this. Besides, you know this brood. This is far too gourmet for them. We're talking a strictly burgers and dogs crowd."

"I beg your pardon, big sister," Brett said with playful indignation. "But my taste buds are quite capable of appreciating more than just cow and pig. You speak for yourself and your husband, and maybe his family." And then she laughed, as if the joke were indeed private.

And Nell joined her in their secret and seemingly never-ending comic story of Chuck's family, laughing as she warned, "Don't you dare start today. I've been doing real good so far keeping it together with these nuts running around here. I don't need you starting with me." And Nell went off for the kitchen with the salad, still chuckling to herself.

"I think I'll go help Nell," Lila said, following Nell.

Jack looked desperately after Lila. What was she doing, his edgy eyes said, leaving him there with Brett. "You need some help? Wait, I'll come with you."

"No, that's okay," Lila said over her shoulder, but it was too late, because just like that, Jack was right there beside her as she was about to step through the door. "What are you doing?" she said, surprised to see him.

"That girl makes me very uncomfortable, Lila. She gives me the creeps. She's so hungry."

"Well, she's just intense, I guess," was all Lila said. She'd never given as much thought to Brett's hunger for a man as it seemed to her Jack had given. "Look, there's Chuck," she said in that way a wife can palm off a husband when she doesn't want him around. Go play with him, she might as well have said. She waved to Chuck then continued on her path to where Nell was unwrapping the salad on the counter. And she didn't so much see as much as feel Jack finally going his own way.

"Hello, Mrs. Teague," Lila said, reaching across the counter to peck her cheek. She was consciously not staring at the hairy mole on the woman's chin, which was like a magnet to any eye, when she said, "It's so good to see you again."

"It's good to see you too, honey," Mrs. Teague said without looking at Lila. She was too distracted by her anticipation at seeing what Nell was unwrapping. "What's that?" she finally said to Nell, as if unable to wait a second longer to see for herself.

"It's a pasta and seafood salad," Lila answered.

"You brought it? You made it?" Chuck's mother asked.

"Yes, ma'am. I made it fresh this morning."

"It looks delicious. Nell, honey, fix me a plate of that, would you?" Mrs. Teague said.

"Sure, Momma, let me just get a serving spoon for it." As Nell searched the drawer for an extra spoon that would be long enough for the job, she seemed to grow nervous seeing the puzzled face of her mother-in-law as the woman stared into Lila's salad. "Momma, what's the matter?"

"Nothing, baby. What's that stuff right there?" She pointed without touching.

"That's lobster, Mrs. Teague." Lila spoke up.

"Oh my, that's *real* lobster?"

"Of course, Momma." Nell laughed nervously, embarrassed even though Lila was like family.

"And is that real shrimp, too? And what are those round white things? And I think I see some crab, too. Looks to me like you went and spent an awful lotta money on this stuff. Why'd you go and spend so much money? You coulda just made a regular salad and that woulda been fine by me. I don't think I've ever eaten so high on the hog."

Lila couldn't fathom how she'd answer such a question. She looked to Nell with rounded eyes that said she needed saving.

"Yes, it's real shrimp, Momma. There's no such thing as fake shrimp," Nell said, her voice teetering just on the edge of her patience. "The round things are scallops."

"Oh, yes, there is, honey. That stuff you buy in a can, those little tiny things, that stuff sure ain't real shrimp. I ain't never had lobster before, and I sure ain't never had scallops, but I've had real shrimp before, and I can tell you that that stuff you get in a can ain't real at all."

Lila smiled uncomfortably at the woman and said, "Well, you should like the lobster and scallops, Mrs. Teague. And I also put crabmeat in it, and the crab is also most definitely real. No fake crabmeat for my salads," she said with a laugh that felt far more genuine than her smile. "All the ingredients are fresh."

"Of course they are," Nell said, dishing the salad onto a plate for her mother-in-law with a spoon she finally found. "Here you are, Momma. Why don't you take it outside and ask Chuck to get you something to drink? I'll be out as soon as I finish getting things together in here."

"Okay, okay, honey. I'll just get on out there. I guess Lila will help you if you need anything done."

"That's right, Momma. I don't want you worrying about helping me. I've got everything under control."

"I know, I know," Mrs. Teague said as she shuffled out the door. "You always do."

Once her mother-in-law was clear out of earshot, and it was only Lila and Nell in the kitchen, she was free enough to tell the truth. "My life, girl. Between my mother and my mother-in-law I've got two extremes. Here was my mother-in-law in my face being a nuisance wanting to help, but being more in the way than anything else. Before you came in here she was asking about the price of this and the cost of that and, Why do you do it like that, honey?" Nell said, imitating her mother-in-law in a less than complimentary voice. "And can you believe she asked if it was real lobster and real shrimp in your salad?" And without giving Lila a chance to answer, she continued, "And then, just look out there at my mother, Princess La-di-da. She wouldn't dream of lifting a finger to help, flitting all over the yard as if we don't have enough butterflies out there."

"Well, if it's any consolation, you know I have two just like them. What makes me luckier than you is that one lives in Virginia and the other one in Florida, thank the Lord. But what would make it worse if they both lived here is that they'd both be in the kitchen driving me to a slow death. Jack's mother would be in there, not just complaining about the cost of things, but actually making a list of all the places I could get this or that cheaper. My stepmother, on the other hand. . . ." Lila stopped to shake her head, scarcely knowing where to begin explaining Eulelie to Nell. "Well, let's just say that she'd be in there telling me the proper way to do this and that, and then quite probably arguing with Jack's mother about why etiquette says you simply cannot entertain on the cheap."

They shared a laugh like sisters, with Lila tearing and washing lettuce for the green salad, and Nell slicing the tomatoes to go on the side for Chuck's family. The whole lot of them couldn't bring themselves to tolerate a salad without tomatoes and cucumbers. What's the point, as Chuck's mother always said, of having a salad with nothing but lettuce? It's like wearing a rain-coat without a rain hat, she'd say. "Oh God," Nell said, seeing her mother approach through the window. "Heads up. Here comes my mother."

"Lila," Nell's mother said in a shrill singsong, and without being fully in the kitchen. "I haven't had a chance to even say hello to you. You came right in and then holed up here in the kitchen with Nell." She went to Lila and kissed at her, then pulled back, as if to take a better look, fluffed the back of Lila's hair and said, "It's such a shame you won't let this beautiful hair grow out again. It was so lovely when you wore it long."

"Oh, thank you," Lila replied, feeling Eulelie's presence so strongly that she straightened up from where she slouched against the counter at the mere touch of Nell's mother's fingers. "It's just easier to deal with when it's cut short like this." Lila smiled at the woman who, with all her aspirations, always brought Eulelie to Lila's mind, along with the harsh truth that those aspirations would not get her into Eulelie's world even if she could somehow buy a ticket.

Nell's mother turned abruptly to Nell and said, "Oh, and speaking of short haircuts, honey, you need to tell Chuck's sister that short hair was definitely not the way to go for that face of hers."

"Ma, please!" Nell snapped. "Now that's just mean, what you're saying."

"I'm sorry, honey, but it's the truth. It's a darling haircut, and all, but it's not as if she's got a face as beautiful as Lila's. At least with long hair, she could give the illusion of being halfway decent-looking. Now, she's just another tall, unattractive girl with short hair. And I've said it before, and I'll say it again, that girl is truly a waste of tall and thin. She's got the graceful height of a giraffe and a face like a horse. It's such a shame."

"Ma, I'm not asking you now, I'm telling you to please stop it." Nell looked up to see Chuck cutting a path straight for the kitchen and said in a whisper, "Anyway, here comes Chuck, so just be quiet."

Chuck and Jack came back into the kitchen with an air of accomplishment in their strutting. Jack carried the empty platter that had held the steaks. Jack put the platter on the counter, then opened the refrigerator and dug through to the back where the good beer was stashed.

"Are you having a good time, Ma?" Chuck said as he went past his mother-in-law.

"Oh, of course. I'm getting ready to go back out there now." She turned to leave, then stopped and said to Chuck, "By the way, I think your sister's haircut is just darling. I was just telling the girls how darling I think that cut is. Very becoming." And then she left, but not before sneaking a sly wink at Nell and Lila.

"Now, you know that you can't take that beer outside," Chuck said, seeing Jack emerge from the refrigerator with the gold Chuck had stashed specifically for himself and Jack. He had to make certain Jack understood that he was privileged to have access to the premium beer. "Those Coronas are only for us."

"Jack, you know you must have a hallowed spot in this man's life," Nell said through a laugh. "He won't even let his brothers and sisters know that these Coronas are in here. Let one of them come in here and try to go in the refrigerator for something. Chuck guards that thing like he was being paid for it, just so they won't see them."

"Come on, quiet down. Here comes Brett," Chuck said in a sneaky whisper, seeing Brett through the window on a clear path toward the door. But from seemingly nowhere, his brother Joe and Nell's brother Lonnie were stepping into the kitchen, one behind the other behind Brett. And before they could get into the kitchen fully enough to know where they were, Chuck said, "What's everybody doing in here? The party's out there." He sounded like a man trying to hide beer.

"Well, you all are in here," Brett said defensively. "What, are you all in some kind of secret kitchen society that excludes the rest of us backyarders?"

Chuck's brother Joe went to Lila and gave her a loose hug. "It's good to see you again, Lila. It's too bad that we only get to see you and Jack when these two entertain," he said, motioning to Chuck and Nell with his head.

Is there anyplace else that would make sense? Lila thought as she simply smiled with nothing else to say except what was so inappropriately in her head. It wasn't that she disliked Joe. In fact, she found Joe to be a much more sincere man than his brother. Joe didn't impose upon people the tedium of sifting through charm to look for the true man, and for that alone, she often thought, on their rare meetings, that she'd take Joe's company any day over Chuck's.

"Yeah, well, that'll change soon, I'm sure," Chuck said, slapping Jack on the back like a pal. "Once Dr. Calloway here becomes the next head of the esteemed National Institutes of Health, I don't know if we'll be graced by his company anymore."

And the room broke into comfortable laughter, as if they knew, or as if they understood the joke. Lila, however, glared at Chuck with a smile that, in conjunction with her puzzled eyes, seemed to say that she should have known, yet somehow didn't, and couldn't. In an instant, she played through her mind all the ways in which Chuck and Jack kidded with each other. They'd joked before about being president and what it would be like for a black man. They even did a comical skit about taking the job no self-respecting doctor would want—the surgeon general. But, as her memory served her—and she whipped it into serving her well in this critical moment—there was never a time when they joked with each other about something as highly respected, and seemingly unattainable, as the National Institutes of Health. For as long as she stood there staring into Chuck's face, hoping to grasp onto his meaning, she felt increasingly twisted and constricted by some sort of deficient riddle.

The intensity of Lila's smile elicited an uneasiness in Chuck, who clearly realized he'd made a misstep of some kind, though he couldn't be expected to know what it might have been. "Ah, lighten up, Lila, will you?" he said to relieve the tension. "I'm just joking around. I'm proud of this brother, because you know that they're probably going to sift ten times through the pile of white boys they're considering before they're going to have to give it to Jack. And I know you guys would never snub us. Besides, we're going to be the ones who'll keep you two humble. You know, keep you grounded and never let you forget from whence you came." And he laughed aloud again with everyone. Everyone, that is, except Lila, Nell, and most of all Jack.

Jack stared into the salad bowl as if he might be able to crawl between the lettuce leaves and disappear. And as he seemed to find momentary comfort there, his countenance suggested one sure thing—he was wrong. Wrong for not telling Lila. Wrong for not telling Chuck that he hadn't told Lila. But mostly responsible, liable, for the damage his bad judgment was now inflicting on Lila in the way hurt, frustration, and surely disappointment showed in her face. He should have told her. When he finally seemed to find the courage, Jack lifted his head and looked into eyes that remembered the way he'd put those feelings there in the early days when it hurt her to the core that he wouldn't clean the kitchen after she cooked a meal. He'd made a vow to never put such sadness in her eyes again. But this time it wasn't just the sadness. It was betrayal, and the loss of hope and faith on yielding ground, that lived on Lila's face.

"I'm telling you, you've got to know that there isn't a person over at Hopkins who doesn't know that this is one serious brother," Chuck continued.

Nell tried to shut him up with her eyes. She tried to get him to see what was as plain as the hairy mole on his mother's chin. She looked at him with an exasperation that suggested his talking might be compulsive. "Chuck," she finally said. And she tried to bring his eyes, with her own, to see what was happening between Lila and Jack; the way they were melting down, completely and silently, right there in her kitchen.

"What?" Chuck said, annoyed that she had clipped him off in mid-discourse.

"Look, you guys," Nell said, turning to Brett, Lonnie, and Joe. "Can you go out and check on the grill for me? Just turn the steaks over." She handed them the long fork, relieved that they left without seeming to know they'd just gotten kicked out. When they were well into the yard, she snatched herself around in a fury to face Jack and said, "Why didn't you tell her?"

"I was going to tell her," Jack murmured with the quiet shame of a scolded boy fully aware of his trespasses. "I didn't think he'd make a public announcement about it." He cut Chuck an angry side glance.

"That is not what I asked you." And it was difficult to tell if Nell was reprimanding a grown man or one of her children.

"I just wanted to wait until I actually got the offer. I didn't even tell Chuck until yesterday." He turned to Lila with a plea on his face. "I swear, Lila, I was going to tell you."

Lila heard him but only walked past him, and through the swinging door, into the dining room. She wasn't at all certain where she was headed, she just knew that she couldn't be in the same room with Jack and his lies, or half lies, or undisclosed truths. Lila hadn't been able to figure out what to call it yet, since fresh truth now blended with decayed mercy. So when she reached the stairs, there was nothing else for her to do but sit on them. She was alone, and sitting on the steps, and that's exactly where she needed to be, what she needed to be doing.

Nell came around the corner in search of her, and when she found her on the steps said, "Come on, let's go upstairs," and she began climbing the stairs. Lila followed her, but so did Jack, and then Chuck, pulling up the rear of this line of trouble.

"Lila, wait, please," Jack said, taking the stairs two at a time to reach her.

And the first words Lila would speak to him since learning of his betrayal were, "And just what would I be waiting for, Jack? Waiting for Chuck to tell me something else about my husband that I don't know? Waiting for him to tell me all the details, large and small, going on in the life of the man I sleep with every night?" She reached the top of the staircase, where Nell was, holding out a protective hand to guide Lila down the hallway. But she turned from Nell to face Jack again. There was one more thing he had to hear. "You tell me all about some bullshit offer you have from some backwoods hospital down in Birmingham, or some other god-awful place, and meanwhile you keep from me something worthwhile, something actually worth considering, like this. This isn't a marriage anymore, Jack." And though she knew her last proclamation had gone too far in the direction of histrionics, she didn't regret saying it. She needed to have his reaction, which she didn't get, anyway, because she didn't bother to wait for it.

She continued on with Nell until they got halfway down the hall and Lila swung around with a will she simply could not contain and snapped at Chuck. "And why can't this runner be for the rest of your family and not just for the purpose of *your* big old corn-encrusted feet! Move!" she shouted at everyone standing on the rug. "I'm going to fix this damned thing once and for all. I'm so sick and tired of coming up here and seeing this testament to a man's selfishness." And when they all stepped gingerly off the rug to let her have her slipping-down moment, she knelt and began pulling and tugging at the runner, centering it on the hallway floor.

When she finished and got back to her feet, she was completely unfazed by the feeling that everyone else must think themselves in the presence of the insane, and the insane was she. Lila stepped onto the rug without purpose, but the mere coincidence appeared to be proving a point, and she continued down the hall toward Nell. When she reached Nell, she brushed past her and went into Nell's bedroom.

Nell said to the dumbfounded men at the other end of the hallway, "Give us a minute, okay?"

Chuck, his face still slackened by Lila's assault, managed to close his mouth long enough to say, "I know she's upset and everything, but why'd she have to go and attack something as personal as my feet?"

Nell first stared at her husband with flattened, perturbed eyes that should have let him know that his feet, corns and all, and even within the context of Lila's assault, were quite beside the point right now. But just in case he didn't understand, she only said, "Well, how many times have I told you that you shouldn't wear sandals?" And then she went into the bedroom and closed the door softly behind her.

Lila was sitting on their high bed, dangling her legs off the side as if she were a mere girl who had climbed upon her parents' bed to sulk. And by now she knew exactly what she wanted to say to Nell.

"Okay, Lila, so what's going on in your head right now?" Nell asked as she went to the bed and hiked herself up on it right next to Lila.

"At first I thought, 'Oh, well, the honeymoon's over.' But it's really not quite that pedestrian, you know. I think now it's all about whether I really knew this man at all. Things happened so fast with us. Six months we knew each other and then we were married. And he was always so forthright. I thought he had shown me everything there was for me to see that would matter to our life together. And now, here I am, sitting in your bedroom wondering why my husband couldn't tell me about something that is so much a part of who he is."

Nell said nothing for a few seconds, then looked at Lila with meaning and suggested, "Lila, did you ever stop to think that maybe he didn't think he was worthy of the position? Jack is very humble."

"No," Lila answered without really listening to the question. "But what I do think is that this is all so very familiar. This is just like my mother. The only difference is that with my mother, I could only see her with farsighted vision. With Jack, I can only see him with nearsighted vision. When I moved out of my mother's house, I could feel, I could see, that she'd never really let us know her completely. Everything I know about my mother is what I can see immediately when I look at her. She is so very good at hiding her demons, and it took my being away from her to see that. But one thing I know for certain is that there's this very intense part of her that she keeps buried so deeply that I don't even think she could find it if she wanted to."

"So, how does this all apply to Jack?" Nell asked.

"Well, in the obvious way. Jack is tortured. Tortured in his mind, and tortured in his soul."

"And are you?"

"Am I tortured?" Lila asked, her eyes squinted. "Why would you ask me something like that?"

"Because, Lila, since it happened, you have not said too much yourself about that man Jack left to die on the sidewalk. So if you're too tortured by it to talk about it, couldn't it be that Jack feels the same way? It's a horrible thing to have happen. And it's a horrible thing that shouldn't have had to happen, but it did, and now the hands that were trained to heal didn't in a moment of anger. Be in the place where he is for a second, Lila. How does he live with that?"

But Lila didn't have to imagine how Jack lived with it, because even though they seemed no longer to live the same life, at the least they were living parallel lives. She raised her head from where it hung, staring into her own lap and said, "I don't know, Nell, I just can't look at him in the light of that day, because I'm ashamed of him, and proud of him all at the same time, and that terrifies me more than you can know."

The bedroom door opened with a creak, and in the crack was Jack's face. He dared not push the door open an inch more, dared not set one toe inside the room until he got Lila's approval to enter. And when she didn't shoo him away much the way she would a pest, Jack thought it safe to bring himself fully into the room. Even though he was fairly confident of the answer, he still asked, "Lila, is it okay if I come in?"

"Yeah, sure. I'm all right now. I was just hurt, Jack. This is something you should have shared with me before you told anyone else. We should have gone out to celebrate. We should have gotten champagne. Even if you're only being considered for the position, it's still something to celebrate."

Jack seemed to feel Nell's affirmation in her silent glare. "That's just the thing, Lila. I haven't been asked, or anything. There's nothing to celebrate because nothing's certain. All I know is that I'm being considered, and I'm not even sure how I feel about that. It's flattering and all, but I have to take every-thing into account in terms of what this might mean to *our* life."

The shrill of Jack's beeper pierced the room. He checked the number with annoyance, then looked around the room until he found the phone. "May I?" he asked Nell, gesturing with his head to the bedside phone perched on the night table beside Nell.

"Yes, of course," Nell said, hopping up with the immediacy of a doctor's wife used to getting out of the way for medical emergencies.

Jack went to the phone and sat exactly where Nell had sat. He dialed the number half from memory, the other half from what was displayed on the beeper.

"This is Dr. Calloway," he said with some doubt into the phone. "I was paged." Jack listened with a peculiar distraction. Then something was said that made him shout, "What?"

Lila was startled, as was Nell, who clearly suffered the same jolt to an identical nerve. Lila could only imagine one thing that could have gone wrong. One of the interns at the hospital must have done something that only an inept intern, or an overly ambitious intern, or an arrogant intern, can do to get a response like that from Jack. And when she heard him say that he'd be there shortly, she could nearly smell the blood of the intern Jack would shortly be there to chastise.

Jack hung up the phone and didn't say anything, didn't even look at either women. He was retracted in every significant way. Then he stood, inhaled deeply, exhaled, and said, "I have to go. Mr. Rawlings died this morning. I just saw him on Saturday and . . . and . . . I'm sorry; this just doesn't make sense," he said, rubbing both temples with his thumb and fingers.

Lila got to her feet, ready to go, ready to hold her husband steady after this blow that had hit him mighty hard, she could see. "Nell, you understand that we have to go. Mr. Rawlings was Jack's first Saturday patient, and so this is hard to take."

"No, Lila," Jack said, taking a step back from her toward the door. "What I mean is that I'm just going to go myself. I'm only going by the Rawlingses' house for a minute, but what I really need to do is go to the hospital and review all his blood work and his tests. I need to see if there was something I missed." He lowered his head and turned to leave, then said, more to himself than to anyone else in the room, "It had to have been something I missed." Jack went through the door and closed it behind himself.

Lila sat stilled by what could make no more sense now than it did the previous seconds as she tried to understand, tried not to feel rejected, tried not to feel shut out, tried not to feel unnecessary. Though she fought against it, she was completely consumed by herself at a moment when she needn't and shouldn't be, and Lila felt it all in every petty, childish way it could be felt. She was his First Lady, and she should have been with him.

"It's hard when they lose a patient," Nell finally said, having sat for so long in silence Lila had almost forgotten she was there. "You haven't been married to Jack long enough to know what it's like, how hard they take it, but with that man, Mr. Chalm, being the first patient of his to die since you two have been married, you can't possibly know how long it takes them to come out of it. No matter how many times their God complex is humbled and torn down by death, the reality that they're not God socks them right in the gut every single time. It's sad, really."

Lila stood slowly and straightened imaginary wrinkles in the lap of her skirt for something to do, then said, "Well, this goes far beyond the God complex. This is about God cutting down everyone who matters to Jack, one by one, and pretty soon God will start on me, because I'm no innocent in this, you know. It's just a matter of time before . . ." She couldn't bring herself to say it, no matter how strongly she believed it. "This is about divine retribution, Nell. My Jack has already left me. I'm going home now." Lila left Nell, and Nell's bedroom, with more misery dragging in her shoes than she'd ever known.

chapter fifteen

JACK SAT AT his desk, only the solitary light from his desk lamp glowing like a small ball in the vast darkness of his office. September first had fooled him into believing that it had only stolen sky light, not time as well. But he could scarcely see or care about the darkness or the time as the desk lamp, with its yellow glow, illuminated Jack's hands, his arms, and all that paper. He'd turned page after page, reading, and then reading again, Mr. Rawlings's medical life straight through to midnight, until now, when there was nothing for him to do but sit there and let all those pages with letters and numbers and codes watch him. They watched him leap to ends to which only the guilty can find their way. They watched him go back to Mr. Chalm's life and death and blame himself for the latter without really knowing the details of the former.

Jack's guilt even took him to another patient, a mother, survived by her husband and a son and three daughters, whose life slipped, little by little, from his fingertips, as he tried to will a heart to beat that was bound to stop by something more powerful than Jack's hands. He could still see the eyes of the husband, who through grief managed to grow his arms long enough to embrace four children at once, four children whose eyes joined their father's to become one accusing glare. And even though that woman's husband said he understood that Jack had done all that he could, how could that man really know, as Jack recalled it all now. How could that man know, when not even Jack himself could know whether he'd done all that he could have done, given every ounce of his all? Jack could remember every cut, every suture he made on the heart of the wife and mother, and even though the seizure on her heart was heavy and unyielding, she should have lived. Others had lived by his hands, and under equally dire circumstances.

So Jack was in his office, sinking lower and deeper when the door opened, letting in the bright fluorescence of the hospital hallway. Jack looked up with a squint, unable to clearly see the backlit figure in the doorway until the door closed.

"Chuck?" he asked, still scarcely able to believe that it was Chuck, at this place, at this hour.

"Yeah, it's me. I figured you'd be here. Nell sent me to get you. Actually, I don't know if she wants me to get you or just tell you something." He stopped before just blurting it out at Jack. It seemed the best way to deliver the news. "Lila's left you, man. Or at least that's what Nell thinks. Lila went home, got her clothes and stuff, and now she's at her office. Told Nell that this is the only thing she can do, because she can't live with your rejection anymore." Chuck settled into the chair in front of Jack's desk, the crinkling of his nylon windbreaker being the only sound filling the room.

Jack was unmoved, and unmovable, with the news. He leaned his chair back, squeezed closed his wearied eyes, then opened them and said, "Yeah, well, that's Lila's drama. Once again she's brought it all around to being about her. It's all about Lila and what she needs and her feelings of rejection," he said, just shy of mockery. "I guess she's got to do what she's got to do."

"Maybe," Chuck said, unzipping his jacket. "No doubt that Lila's spoiled and pampered and used to things going her way. That was there long before you stepped into her life; but you still married her, so you can't fault her for that. What I'm here to say, man, is that you have been acting strange. Can't put my finger on it, but something's crawled up in you and you're not letting it go."

"It's all these deaths, Chuck. That's all. You know how it is, because you've been where I am. One after the other. Man, I'm on a roll."

"Four patients died, Jack. Three *old* patients and Mr. Kaplan, who was in really bad health, died. They were all people who had a multitude of health problems, especially Rawlings. I know that from the time he was in here. How long did you expect them to live, Jack? I mean, come on, instead of looking at it as you not doing enough to keep them alive, look at it the way it was—you gave them good health care, and a good quality of life for the time they were in your care. That's the reality, Jack."

"Yeah, but do you remember that woman with the four kids who came in here with a heart attack? I worked on her for hours, and I think she should have survived, but she didn't."

Chuck squinted past Jack and out the window, searching his memory for that woman. "You're talking about . . . ? Jack, that was four years ago. And if it's the woman I think you're talking about, she was a heavy, heavy smoker, Jack, and that wasn't her first heart attack. I know she was a young woman, but there was no way she should have even survived the first heart attack. You couldn't have saved her no matter what. You need to get some perspective. I mean, you're good, don't get me wrong, but nobody's that good."

"Well, you weren't there in that operating room with me, Chuck. You don't know how close I came to pulling her through, and then something went wrong. I just don't know what."

"No, you're right, I wasn't there. But I certainly heard about her case from others way more impartial than you, and I can tell you what went wrong. It's called the odds. When you started out with her they were already against you. Give it up, man."

Jack closed the folder that was Mr. Rawlings's life and pushed himself away from the desk. He sat sideways, looked at Chuck, and with an abruptness that said he would talk no longer about the dead wife and mother of four, he said, "So what am I supposed to do, go and get Lila from her office again? Indulge her drama?"

"Well, I think that would be totally up to you. I'm just the messenger." Chuck stood and zipped his jacket. Before leaving, though, he looked at Jack squarely and said, "My advice, coming with fifteen years of marriage behind me, for what it's worth, is that you should go get her. Take her home. That's what she wants, and so that's what will make it better."

"Well, that's what you say. What I say is that the honeymoon's over."

Chuck's laugh was far too nefarious to be sympathetic. He walked toward the door, and before opening it, before he even reached for it, he turned to Jack and said, "Well, there's your biggest mistake right there. The honeymoon's a mirage. It's not real. It's like playing anything when you were a kid where your imagination could make life whatever you wanted it to be. The only difference is that when you were a kid you had control over the suspension of reality. You could stop it and start it at your own will. And now you can't. Life doesn't suspend reality for you. I'll check on you later, Jack, but do what you need to do."

Jack stared at the door as it took its time closing, and all he could hear, still lingering in his office, coming from every corner, was Chuck's laughter. And all he could feel was the hollow chill in his chest at the knowledge that the everyday nature of life had taken from him his light-as-a-breeze life with Lila. And so, now what?

LILA WOKE IN a curl on the sofa, chilled with not even a corner of the blanket on her. It had fallen, at some point during one of her tosses or turns in the night, into a heap on the floor. She stretched and rolled onto her back, only to be assaulted by a streak of sunlight bombarding her face that made her squeeze her eyes closed and curl up on her side again. Morning light was not her favorite light of the day, and for this very reason. But she couldn't even settle into comfort. She was being chased by time. There was Nell, who'd be there any minute, maybe. More than Nell, though, more than anything else, there was something she needed to do.

Lila stumbled to her feet and crossed the room with groggy steps to her desk. Lifting the receiver, she put it to her ear, then pressed a button. The phone dialed, rang, and when Jack answered, Lila pressed another button, disengaging the call, and Jack. "Thank God, he made it home okay," she said with a smile to accompany her comforted heart. Lila had phoned home at midnight, and then at two, just before she fell into a coma of a sleep, and Jack had not found his way home by either hour. And there was a certain pride she felt with herself coming from the notion that a less trusting wife wouldn't be able to take comfort in her husband's safety due to the possibilities of where he might have been at two in the morning. She didn't want to sleep with him last night, but she did love him enough to want him to be safe.

Lila set the handset back in its cradle and crossed the room again to bring what had become her bed for the night back to its original sofa state. But just as she reached down to get the blanket from the floor, the phone rang. She froze where she stood. It was Jack. It had to be. Of course he would have known that it was she who rang him and then hung up. And so now, what would she say to him?

She dashed to the phone before it had a chance to finish a third ring. And of course it was Jack. "Hello," she said with a coolness she thought she was supposed to have, considering the circumstances. He asked her if she'd just called, and she admitted that she had. But when he asked her why she'd hung up without saying anything, all she could think to say was the truth. "I didn't have anything to say." And then he wanted to know why she'd called, and once again, she was forthright. "I wanted to make sure you'd gotten home safely last night." So now, they'd said all that could be said to each other in a phone call, and Lila confirmed it. "Okay, well, have a good day. Good-bye."

Just as she'd put the phone down, Nell was walking in the door. Lila was caught. Caught in her nightclothes, but mostly caught in the midst of her marital troubles, and airing it all for Nell to see. And even though Nell knew it all, Lila still felt shame, particularly at being caught still in her pajamas. "Are you really early, or is it that I don't know what time it is?" she said, with just an edge of annoyance.

"No, no, I'm early. It's only eight. But I thought you could use some breakfast and a friend this morning. I figure we've got an hour for the friend thing before work has to start." Nell closed the door with one hip and unloaded the bags of breakfast and a thermos of tea onto her desk. "I guess that was Jack you were talking to, huh?"

"Yeah, it was. You heard?"

"Yeah, I did. I waited outside the door until you were finished. Frankly, I thought you'd have more to say to each other."

Lila said nothing. She went back to the sofa and sat, folding her legs underneath her, lotus style. She was far from a centered place, though, and so she guessed that's why Nell followed her with the bags of breakfast. Nell believed in getting it all out, Lila knew. Sometimes it was tedious, Nell's way, but right now what Lila wanted was for Nell to pull and push and tug at her, until Lila could be completely unburdened.

"So, did you sleep?" Nell asked.

"A little bit, I guess," Lila said, digging into the bag Nell gave her. She didn't need to unwrap it to see the pink lox and the bagel speckled with garlic bits through the thin white paper. It was just what she wanted, maybe what she needed. "Oh, my favorite! Thank you, Nell. Boy, what a treat!"

"Well, you deserve it," Nell said, unwrapping her plain bagel with butter. She took a small bite, barely chewed it, then couldn't wait to ask, "So, how long are you going to do this?"

"I don't know, Nell. I'm not thinking that far ahead. All I know is that I need to be here for now. I'm trying to understand what's happening with us. I didn't expect this, Nell."

"Well, flowery expectations of marriage can end up being the bane of our life."

"That's just it, Nell. I didn't have any flowery expectations. I expected to have those kind of arguments you have when he uses all the salt and doesn't refill the shaker. Or when he leaves only a drop of milk in the carton because it's too much trouble for him to simply finish the milk and then throw out the carton.

I even expected those major and minor disagreements that can spring up around his mother or my mother. But, Nell, there was nothing, absolutely nothing, in my experience that could have prepared me for what Jack and I are going through now."

Nell took another bite of her bagel, but this time chewed it until she could swallow. "So, as you see it, Lila, how did you and Jack get here?"

"I don't know him, Nell. It's that simple. I never did know him. The day he let that man die on the sidewalk is the day my Jack disappeared right before my eyes."

"Lila, do you know yourself?"

Lila smiled distantly at Nell with thankful eyes. For the first time in her life, someone had thought to ask her. Finally someone understood the importance of this question in the context of her life. It was simply easier, she knew, for others who'd never tried to touch her inside to believe that she'd never given herself much thought. In those moments when she stood outside herself long enough to see what so many others did in her, she could not judge harshly their assumptions. But Nell knew. Nell could always see beyond.

"Yes, I do know myself, Nell. Better than anyone would have ever assumed. I have done nothing, since the day we drove away from that dying man on Twenty-eighth Street, but read my heart." She bit into her bagel and savored the salmon bursting with its own fullness all over her mouth. The picture of the solitary red rose growing in her backyard came fully to mind for its likeness of herself. Since yesterday, the first day she saw that rose, growing all by itself, but as red as anything that God or man could make, she knew something holy had put it in her backyard for her to see herself in it. Would Nell ever be able to understand?

"Have you ever looked at the red on a rose, Nell?"

"A red rose? Of course I've seen a red rose."

"Yes, but have you ever studied its redness? The rose could possibly be one of the most perfect things of beauty in God's creation, but if you stare at the red on a rose, this thing of beauty, long enough, you can see violence. And rage. You see the rage, and the fury, and blood, for God's sake! The blood of violence and rage that is born straight from passion. And it's the kind of passion that can maim or kill without wanting to. It's as if its beauty and its virtue are somehow flawed, somehow betrayed by the biggest part of it that makes it beautiful and virtuous. That's what I am, Nell, I'm the red on a rose."

Nell sat, as if in deep thought about the image Lila had just laid before her. Her brow was so wrinkled that she seemed to be wondering if Lila knew just what she was saying. "To that end, Lila, everyone is like the red on a rose. I don't think there's a human being who can actually live their life from beginning to end without ever once encountering that dark side of the self that, God knows, no one ever wants to see or admit to having. You know, Lila, the one good thing that I can think of about that man Jack left to die is that at least he lived his life in the truth of his dark side. He hated niggers. That was his dark side, and he knew it, embraced it, and lived in it."

"God, Nell, what are you saying? Are we all supposed to live in our dark selves? What kind of world are you talking about having?"

"Oh, come on, Lila. Of course I'm not talking about that. But what I'm saying is that when he felt it, when he saw what could always turn him dark, he didn't run from it. I mean, think about it. If that man were pure darkness, would he have had his son pleading for Jack to save his life? We can't believe that that man lived in pure darkness. He prayed at a church, it seems, every Sunday. He was a Boy Scout leader, and the papers said he did the grocery shopping for three elderly and infirm ladies on his block. And when his life was done he had plenty of folks come and speak nothing but kindness about him. But he lived his dark side in full."

"I think there's something to be said for keeping your dark side out of plain sight."

"Well, yeah. But I think it's dangerous when you keep that dark side out of plain sight of yourself, because when it comes out of hiding, it surprises you most of all. Nobody's all good, Lila. Not even you. Not even me. But especially not even Jack."

"So what you're saying is that I shouldn't feel guilty about having wanted that man to die like a dog on the sidewalk?"

"I'm saying that maybe you should recognize just how human that emotion makes you. Guilt is probably a healthy thing when it comes to our dark side because it's the only thing that can keep it from taking over. But I don't think guilt should be allowed to get out of hand either. It can't get so out of hand that it sends you to a place where you deny your dark side, because the darkness in us is what gives our goodness power. It not only makes us want to be better, but also makes us need to be better."

Lila sat staring at the sandwich in her lap without actually seeing it. She saw Jack and his goodness, which healed people every single day of his life except Sundays, when even God says he should rest. And up until that particular day—the day whose details, she feared, would always come back to her in sharp-focused memory—Lila thought that the Jack who healed was the only Jack, the whole of him. "Well, Jack's dark side certainly came at me from out of nowhere. I didn't even know it was there."

Nell looked at Lila and smiled with what had to be the patience conjured from her mother-nature, then said, "Lila, do you really think that was the first time Jack had the thought to leave that man to die on that sidewalk? In his fantasies, Jack had probably done far worse to that man each and every time he was slimed by that pig's vileness. In fact, just as you had fantasized about killing that man, what makes you think Jack hadn't fantasized about taking a more proactive role in that man's death? I think your expectations of yourself *and* of Jack are way too high."

Lila wrapped up the half-eaten lox and bagel and put it on the sofa. She stood and stretched so that her meager stomach, as flat as a child's, peeked out from between her pajama top and bottom. Grabbing up the skirt and top she'd laid out for herself the night before, she looked back at Nell and said with an edge of resentful sarcasm that not even she could understand, "Well, where's the goodness in yourself if your expectations of yourself aren't high? I'm going to take a shower. We need to get started on work." And that was the end of the discussion, or even the thought of the darkness living in any part of her. But not even a shower was going to let her forget the red on a rose that was every part of her.

STORY HOUR WAS only a few minutes from starting. Lila could see that Nell had everything set and ready to go, and that made Lila nervous in a way that kept her eyes trained half on the story and half on Nell. As Nell fussed over it all, and double-checked in her efficient way, Lila's doubt grew heavier over whether this was the story she really wanted to tell. When she sat down to write it, she was so certain, through everything that was her muse, that this was the story that her children should hear. They could take so much from it, from wherever they approached it. They could see how important it is to treat one another right. Or they could find the wisdom of old people in it. But most important of all, they could take from it the morality of accepting responsibility for their wrongdoings. But now, as she reread her own words, it was clear that this story was morose.

"What's wrong?" Nell asked as she watched Lila's forehead grow wrinkled.

"It's just that, I don't know, this story is so gloomy. It might give these kids nightmares. With this old craggy lady and the Block Boys who throw stones and rocks . . . I don't know, Nell. Why don't we just tell them that today we're going to our sack of books and pick a Faith Ringgold story to read, or something."

"Lila, I think the story is just fine. Besides, we don't have time to go through and see which story we want from the sack. I think you're tired—you've been yawning and dozing practically all day—and we just need to get this done so you can get some rest. Why don't you come for dinner tonight? The kids would love it."

"Yeah, I guess that sounds fine. And you're sure the story's okay?"

"All right, Lila, it's not the most upbeat story you've ever written, but it'll be fine. You've written a great ending that redeems all the morbid stuff." Nell went to the camera to make sure it was trained on Lila. "Okay, now, are you ready, because here we go."

And with that, Lila was on the spot, reading the story that from word one gave her a sinking feeling. It began with the craggy old lady putting her cookies in the window so the aroma could entice all the children from near and far to come together and forget all their differences. But then there were the dreaded Block Boys, who were so mean even the meanest dogs ran from them, and the craziest cats scurried from their path. Just as Lila came to the part where the Block Boys came to the old lady's cookie party and sprinkled Bad Boy Dust all over the cookies to make the children fight, something clumped so tightly in her throat it made her heart beat with an intensity she'd only known in those rare erratic moments when she'd been besieged by fear. She suddenly felt very aware of herself, of her words, of her hair, of the shine that may have been on her nose, cheeks, forehead. For that she felt watched, studied, picked apart. And maybe Nell wouldn't tell her that she was greasy, looking instead upon it—as Nell would—as a natural glisten.

All those mothers, she believed, had to be wondering who she was, who she thought she was, sitting there in the middle of the afternoon with her greasy face, without a child of her own to take care of, reading stories to their children. How dare she! And what if they knew what she'd done as Jack's disobliging accessory, the wife of a man on his way to prison? What right, what authority did she have?

And what will I wear to prison on visitation days? she thought, the desperation of the notion complete in her face. She thought about gingham, for some reason, a yellow gingham dress and a straw hat, white. Of course that would only be in the hot summer months. What will I wear in the winter? Cloth? Wool? Corduroy—a jumper, pants, a skirt. Definitely a wool coat, she reasoned, because I certainly can't walk into all that steel wearing the mink coat Momma left me when she moved to Florida.

Those women, those mothers of children, hate me, she believed with everything in her, because why wouldn't they? They hate me for what has to look to them to be my frivolous life; they're thinking. Isn't there something more substantial for this childless woman to do with her day than read to children who aren't even her own? If only they knew. But what mother wouldn't want to have the luxury that would let her take an hour, a whole hour out of her day to read to her child? And what must Nell think? She's a mother, and maybe she's had these same thoughts of my frivolous life all along, agreeing with everything because she needed a paycheck, paltry though it may be.

As she sat frozen, the seconds peeling off to nearly a full minute now, and leaving as its reminder nothing but silence, Lila was certain she was slowly losing the ability to breathe. She finally looked pleadingly at Nell, then managed to sputter: "I . . . I can't do this. Please . . ." But she had no idea for what she was asking Nell. All she knew was that she needed something desperately.

Nell, so quick in thought and action, so adept in the ways of an emergency, slid in front of the camera next to Lila, and in no time had Lila off the sofa and out of sight of the children. If Lila were to have a breakdown of any kind, it wouldn't be in plain sight of the children. Talk about nightmares. Nell read while never losing sight of Lila out of the side of her right eye. She could glimpse Lila, agitated, unable to keep still, but not in such a state where *Story Hour* would have to come to an abrupt halt.

When the story was over, and Nell had to talk about the story and the lessons learned, she was actually aware that she was talking without being terribly certain of what she was saying. Her distractions were manifold, the first being the actual meaning of Lila's story and then having to interpret it. Lila never scripted this part of *Story Hour* because, since the story was born from her, she could simply speak about it as if it were all so real. All Nell had was her own limited understanding of it, considering it was not a part of her. And then there was the distraction that none of Nell's drawings for the story were seen by the children because there was no one to do her job, and she worried that this had kept the children from being drawn into the story. Children were nothing if not visual, she knew from raising three of her own. Most of all, though, there was the distraction of wondering if Lila would be tuned in enough to pull the responses from the kids and parents off the computer as they came in, since Lila wasn't even aware enough to show the children the drawings.

At least that distracting fear could be dissolved, as she saw Lila hop up and over to the computer, and work like mad to get the printing of the responses started before Nell could finish. Lila was grateful for Nell's drawn-out summing up of the story, since she was nowhere near as quick on the computer as Nell. And when the last response, or at least the last response for which they had time, was handed off to Nell, Lila had gotten so far back to herself that she even did the final thing that would bring *Story Hour* to a close and shut off the cameras.

Before she would give Nell a chance to say anything, Lila said, "Nell, I am really sorry. Thank you for bailing me out. You were so, so great."

But Nell's response was absolutely no-nonsense. "Lila, I have no idea what happened to you, but don't you ever do that again. You tell me beforehand that you're about to have a breakdown, or whatever that was that happened." All of her nerves, all of the fear of being in front of the camera, came down on poor Nell all at once, as she sat there trying to rein in her racing heart and sit still long enough to let her nervous perspiration dry now that the crisis was over. Just like a mother who knows what to do and how to react when she sees blood or broken limbs, Nell hadn't taken the time to stop and admit that doing Lila's job would positively terrify her. She simply went into action and seized the situation. "What happened, anyway?"

"I don't know, Nell. As near as I can tell—and mind you, I've never, ever in my life had one—I think I had an anxiety attack. It was just everything, you know. That morbid story with those bad Block Boys sprinkling what could have been construed as

drugs onto the cookies to make the children who ate them at
the kind old lady's house act so bad. It was just all wrong. I'm
surprised that we didn't get any responses from irate mothers
saying they'll never allow their child to visit our *Story Hour*
again."

"Oh, Lila, come on. Okay, yeah, the Bad Boy Dust was like
drugs, but even so, it was presented in a menacing way. The
Bad Boy Dust made them act bad, seem horrible, not good."
Nell got up from the sofa—the *Story Hour* sofa, and for the time
being Lila's bed—and went to where Lila sat behind the computer. She leaned against the desk, took Lila's hand, then took a
deep breath for courage and said quietly, "I don't doubt that
you freaked out because you felt the story was wrong for the
kids. But I think it's something more than that swimming
around in your brain. I'm no marriage counselor, Lila, but I do
know that you and Jack need to talk."

Lila slid her hand from Nell's and pushed herself away from
the computer, away from Nell. "I don't doubt what you're saying. Just tell me where we'd start."

chapter sixteen

LATER IN THE evening, Lila was perched on the same bench she'd sat on the first day she met Barbara Gallagher for the baseball game. She chose the spot for two of the best reasons she could think of. The first being that Talia Nechai was the only parent in the bleachers, and Lila had enough on her mind without the heaviness of Talia's boldness on her. Mostly, though, sitting on that bench let her kill time while waiting for Barbara with the healing powers of the water right before her eyes. That water snatched from her mind, at least for the moment, everything that burdened it and took it to its murk. The thoughts would not be drowned, since their life force was far too strong, but for now, they could be away from her.

And there she was, quite delighted to think about absolutely nothing for a change, when some errant thought came up and claimed her. Little League baseball was over and done with, and now she was there at Rash Field for the first soccer game of the season. Soccer. What did she know about soccer? Nothing, she thought, absolutely nothing. Which brought her to the question of why she was there, and that in its way brought her around to wondering if she looked odd and out of place, a childless woman hanging out at Little League baseball and soccer games and cheering as if she cared. What would be next, she wondered, lacrosse? It made her look desperate for a baby, she thought, no different from single women who sit with want on barstools waiting for Mr. Right. Suddenly she felt self-conscious, wondering who other than Talia would remember her from the baseball games. And would she eventually appear to them to be just as odd as Barbara? So she began deflecting her face from everyone who passed in such an obvious way that the only purpose it served was to make her look as if she were up to something.

"Lila?" Barbara said as if she couldn't tell. Lila looked up at her. "What are you doing?"

"Oh, nothing, just . . . Well, nothing at all."

"You look like you're hiding from someone."

"It's nothing. Just forget it," Lila said, getting up from the bench. She looked at Barbara, struck, as if for the first time, at their identical size. We could share clothes, she thought.

"So why are you sitting out here?" Barbara asked as she began to walk toward the field.

Lila followed at Barbara's leisurely pace, saying, "I didn't want to have to talk to that woman Talia. She's too much to take when you just want solitude."

"Tell me about it. She's like a gnat on a hot day, always buzzing around. Though she doesn't bother me much anymore. She steers clear of me, and that's just fine by me."

Lila trailed Barbara on the climb up the bleachers. She threw a friendly wave in the air at Talia, who was waving frantically at her, as if she wanted Lila to come to her to share pleasantries, or maybe even sit with her. And suddenly Lila felt the prickly heat of stress in her armpits, as if she'd have to choose between these two women at odds with each other. So she decided to do what her stepmother would do and smile sweetly, blankly, as if she didn't understand. When she and Barbara got to the spot where they'd sit, Lila turned to face Barbara's probing eyes.

"I wonder what she wanted with you."

"Oh, who knows, who cares," Lila said.

Barbara laughed lightly then grew serious. "So have things gotten better between you and your husband? The arguing, I mean."

Lila thought about how to answer her. It would be good if

she could give her one answer, yes or no, and be honest about it, but it wasn't that simple. "Barbara, remember when you told me that the relationship between you and the twins' parents was too complicated to explain?"

Barbara nodded yes with questioning eyes.

"Well, that's kind of the way things are between me and Jack. Jack is my husband's name. It's not the little arguments that really get to me, it's more like the bigger picture. It seems to me that the very thing that made me fall in love with him, his strong silence and evenness, is exactly what is making my love for him shift. I'm not going to say that I'm falling out of love with him, because I don't think I am. I just think my love has shifted into another place, because I get so angry with him sometimes. I get so angry that I could just walk out on him right then and there." Lila stopped to think if she should continue, but she'd come this far. The way she saw it, she might as well tell Barbara the rest. So, she lowered her head, feeling the same shame she felt when Nell caught her in her pajamas. She said, "In fact, and I'm not proud of this, I spent last night and I plan to spend tonight at my office. I'm just so mad I don't want to see him. In fact, I'm supposed to go to a funeral with him tomorrow, and I don't want to go because there's a part of me that doesn't want to be there with him."

"Then don't go. Stay home and enjoy the solitude. That way when he comes home, you'll be in a much calmer place. But let me ask you something. If one part of you doesn't want to be there with him, what does the other part want to do?"

"The other part wants to be there with him, but only if things are normal between us, which is not going to happen by tomorrow night. It's a catch-22." Lila tapped one nervous finger on her knee, pondering the end of the tunnel and hoping that soon she'd see light.

"Well, you never know, Lila. But I just say that maybe you should take advantage of the quiet in your home to center yourself."

"That's not going to do anything for us. I'm home with nothing but silence even when he's there. That's why I'm sleeping at my office, Barbara. It's a never-ending cycle that I just don't see getting any better. I don't know how it could."

"Listen, Lila, I'm a little bit older than you, and have been married far longer. I can tell you that what you're describing is so common." Barbara stared off to where the sun was setting on the other side of the field. She chuckled ironically, then looked back at Lila. "One thing I know for certain is that you still love him, because if you didn't, you wouldn't be angry with him. Without love, you can't know anger. You can't know any kind of passion. And I'll tell you something else. I can remember the day when I realized that the love in my marriage had shifted. My husband had always been the type of person who could see a stack of dirty dishes in the sink and still only wash his plate, his knife, and his fork, and for some reason, when we first got married, I thought this was so cute. Then after about two years as his wife and the mother of his eighteen-month-old baby, I would walk into that kitchen, see his clean dishes on the counter and all those dirty dishes still in the sink, and my heart would just drop. I couldn't believe that he could claim to love me yet not care enough about me to save me a couple of steps at the end of the day by washing all of the dishes. I was so hurt, and I felt so used and unappreciated. But believe it or not, Lila, that wasn't the beginning of the end. We got past that and he eventually stopped doing it. But that incident was the transition point of our marriage where we settled into a couple. So, I'm telling you all of this to say, don't fret over whatever this thing is between you two, because it will pass and everything will be right again. It may not be the same as before, but in its way, it will be better."

Lila looked at Barbara, confounded by her wisdom. "But how can you say that, considering your marriage is breaking up? I mean, the two of you shared a horrible tragedy, yet that wasn't enough to bring you together again." Then a horrified expression that she managed to hide from Barbara took over Lila's face, and she wanted to take back all that she said. Suddenly she remembered that Matty's death was what broke the marriage apart, at least according to Barbara. "Well, I guess what I mean to ask is, how is it that Matty's death broke your marriage apart instead of healing it in some way?"

Barbara drew in a long laborious breath and blew it out. She put the palm of her hand to the side of her face as if in despair, then steeled herself to face Lila. "Lila, I'll tell you why, but you'd better make certain you can handle hearing this."

Lila stared blankly at her without a word. How would she know whether she could handle it until she knew? And her shrugged shoulders said as much.

So Barbara folded her arms, stared past Lila out into the harbor, and began, "Well, as I told you once when I wrote you, it was July twentieth of last year, in the early evening. I had dropped Matty off earlier in the day for a birthday-party cookout at Stew and Jan's for the twins, and Ben—that's my husband—was supposed to pick him up. I didn't go to pick him up because I wanted to savor the last few moments I had to myself, since Ben had been gone most of the day to God only knows where, and Sam and Gretta were gone, too, over to Great Adventure, and wouldn't be back till late. Things hadn't been right between me and Ben for a long while, and I just needed all the thinking time I could get to decide if I wanted to stay with Ben or leave him. Anyway, wherever Ben went, he got drunk; I mean, stinking, falling-down drunk. So when he got to Stew and Jan's to get Matty, Jan wouldn't let Matty go with him. And Stew was trying to keep Ben from driving altogether. It didn't stop him, though. But at least Jan got Matty out of that car and put him in a car with some friends of theirs who said they'd bring Matty home. So I get a call from Jan telling me what happened and how Ben's so drunk that Matty's coming home with some friends of theirs, the Marshes. I'm waiting and waiting, but still no Matty."

Barbara stopped and winced, as if the pain from her memories had become physical. She put her hand over her mouth, but she simply could not hold it back. She stretched out her arm to point at the field, then said, "And you see, Lila, this is the thing. If I had just gone over there right then, when Jan called to tell me about Ben, Matty would be out there on that field

right now playing the game he loved. Instead, I just stood there
at that window so mad, thinking about how I didn't give two
damns whether that drunken husband of mine made it home, I
just wanted to see my Matty. Well, after about an hour went by,
I was really terrified. I called Jan back, but she told me not to
worry. Traffic, you know. But they only live about twenty minutes away, right over there off York Road. Traffic from there to
my house wouldn't make them take that long. So after about two
hours, I was completely beside myself with fear. I called Jan
again, and this time she was really worried. So she sent Stew to
drive the route between our two homes and that's when he found
it. The next thing I know, Jan and Stew are at my door with faces
that had every word of what happened written all over them."

Barbara took another breath, then looked at Lila, whose own
puddle of tears was pooling in the rim of her lower eyelids. So
she said, "Do you want me to go on?"

"There's more?"

"What I've just told you is only half the horror. They were
only five blocks from my house, driving on Cold Spring Lane.
Matty was in the car with the Marshes and safe, but Ben was
driving right behind them, weaving all over the road. Then Ben
blacked out and drove, at forty miles per hour, smack into the
back of the Marshes' car as they sat at the stoplight at Cold
Spring and Charles. He knocked them clean into the middle of
the intersection, where they were hit by two other cars, each
one coming from the other direction. Matty was thrown. He
wasn't wearing a seat belt. The Marshes had some pretty serious
injuries, but they survived. And that son of a sea whore walked
away without a scratch. But just like that Matty was gone. He
was killed instantly. So you see, Lila, my Matty wasn't killed by
some drunken stranger I'd never seen before and would never
see again. He was killed by his father. So what was I supposed
to do?" she asked Lila with imploring hands. She seemed to be
teetering on the edge of an explosive emotion. "Was I supposed
to tell him that even though I knew he had a drinking problem
that he never tried to get any help for, and even though he
had no business driving drunk but did anyway and conse-

quently ended up killing my baby, that it was okay and that everything could go back to normal? I'm sorry, but my heart's just not that big."

"Neither is mine" was all Lila could say softly, and she was completely broken into tears. Now that she knew, really knew it all, she couldn't fathom how Barbara could wake up in the morning without making the conscious decision to scream every single moment of the day. To Lila, it seemed as if it would be so very easy for one's mind, under such circumstances, to reach that fork in the road where reason splits from madness and chooses to embrace the comfort of insanity. She let her hand slip into Barbara's where it sat limply on her lap, then squeezed it with every ounce of empathy pouring from her heart, which was more than she had ever had for anyone. Then she looked past Barbara to find Stew with a woman she presumed to be Jan, and they were headed right for them. So Lila asked, "Is that Jan?"

Barbara's head whipped around, and her mouth dropped in a way that could only mean panic.

It was only when Barbara turned around that Lila saw the tears that had been streaming quietly, like still water, down Barbara's cheeks, making tracks in her sparse face powder and rouge. But that wasn't what troubled Lila. It was in the desperate plea coming from her eyes. "Barbara, what is it?"

"Can we leave?" was all she said as she stood in haste and snatched up her purse. "Can we leave right now?"

"Of course," Lila said, jumping up with equal swiftness. "Whatever you want to do, Barbara." And she followed Barbara as she took giant steps down the bleachers. Lila looked over at Stew and returned his wave, then returned the warm smile Jan flashed her. Awkwardness, once again, just as it had with Talia, had taken over Lila as she listened to Jan beckon to Barbara twice to stop. When Lila finally caught up to Barbara, who had already made her way outside of the enclosure of Rash Field, Lila found herself wondering what she had gotten herself into with Barbara Gallagher and her tragedy, but mostly she wondered what would come next.

There was no place else to go but home, and the home they chose was Barbara's. So Lila followed her in her car only to discover that they were practically neighbors, with Barbara living on Charles Street, but closer to the piece of the street that crosses Cold Spring Lane. In the recounting of Matty's death, Barbara had told her that she lived only five blocks away from it, but it wasn't until they got closer, and Lila's heart quickened with a little bit of fear and a whole lot of sorrow, that she remembered. She would never see that dreaded intersection in the same way again. For Lila, in those crossroads she would always envision a shrine to Matty every time she passed through.

When Lila stepped into the front hall behind Barbara, it first seemed as if no one was home. Everything was so still, Lila thought. The only movement was the swinging pendulum of a six-foot-tall art-deco clock that stood guard in the corner of the living room. There was no life, except the cut flowers sprawled from a vase in the middle of the coffee table. Life, but limited. And joy, she could feel, was a memory that was no longer allowed to sing out loud. She stopped in the hall as Barbara closed and locked the door behind them, and Lila was amazed by this solemn place where no one lived, but only existed in the form of beating hearts.

"Come on back to the kitchen," Barbara said. "It's sort of the heart of my home. I guess it's the heart of every home."

And so Lila followed her, thinking that maybe in the heart she'd find life. "What a nice kitchen," Lila said as she stepped behind Barbara through the door.

"You like it, huh?"

Before she would answer, Lila looked around at all the whiteness—white everything. And its shininess seemed to make everything disappear, or at the least become an illusion that compelled double takes; a double take even of the cut flowers splayed in a dramatically thick vase on the counter. Life in a room too clean to be alive. "Yes, I like it. I mean, it's not necessarily my taste, you know, but I certainly can appreciate its beauty. And it is beautiful. It's really difficult to carry off this look."

"Yeah, this is my dream kitchen. I grew up in such a formal home, you know, and so I knew that my home would be modern and accessible in the way that antique-stuffed formal homes are not."

Lila looked around the kitchen, trying to find a way to say her truth without offending Barbara. It wasn't that she felt uncomfortable in Barbara's white kitchen. It's just that it didn't put her in mind of the kind of kitchen where secrets from the heart could be told and a few laughs shared. A woman would have to mind her manners in this kitchen. So she put it this way: "This is formal in its way, you know. It's certainly not informal. It makes you want to keep it clean, not make a mess. You wouldn't want to have mail piled up on the edge of the counter like in my kitchen. And spaghetti sauce would be my worst nightmare in here."

Barbara laughed lightly and said, "Oh, believe me, it is."

Just then Lila was spun around by the sound of the kitchen door being swung open. It stopped her heart for a second, because, as far as she could tell, just she and Barbara were in the house. And to the two teenagers before her, who couldn't have been anyone but Sam and Gretta, all she could say was, "Hello."

The young girl, as blond as could be with a golden tan, stared at Lila quizzically and said, "You're Lila Lilly, from *Lila Lilly's Story Hour*, aren't you?"

"Yes, I am. And I guess you must be Gretta," Lila said, though she knew she was correct. Then she looked to the young man, who was just as tanned but not as blond, and said, "And I guess you're Sam."

"Yes, ma'am," he replied, extending his hand. He shook Lila's hand as if he couldn't have been happier to see anyone. "Wow, Lila Lilly! Man, it's good to meet you. Mom, you didn't tell me that you knew Lila Lilly."

Barbara turned to him from where she stood straightening out the canned goods cupboard, and with eyebrows raised in some emotion that was very closely related to annoyance, said, "And I didn't know the two of you knew about *Lila Lilly's Story Hour*."

"Yeah, I log on every day," Sam said. He lowered his head with his memories and said, "I—I know a kid who really loved it. I mean loves it. I mean, loved it." It was hard to tell which was more painful, the memory of Matty or finding the proper tense in which to put him. Then he turned to Gretta and said, "So I didn't know you knew about *Story Hour*, too."

"Well, I do, but I guess neither of us should, since we're way too old for that kind of stuff," she said, laughing nervously with her head dipped in bashfulness. "But, M . . ." She stopped just short of saying Matty's name and then continued. "Well, I know that it's really popular with kids, and I checked it out a few times, and I can see why they love it, so I just kept logging on. I don't know, maybe it takes me back to my childhood, or something."

"So, what can I do for you two?" Barbara said with a near snap, halting any further discussion of *Lila Lilly's Story Hour*.

"May we use your car, Mom?" Gretta asked. "Sam's going to drop me at Lori's for dinner, if that's okay. He'll will pick me up around ten, okay?" Then she turned to Lila and said in that teenage tone that can set even a childless woman's nerves on edge. "Mom won't let me get my license."

"That's right," Barbara said in defense of herself. "I don't care what the law says, sixteen-year-olds don't have the maturity to operate a two-thousand-pound vehicle. Sam just got his license and he's eighteen. You'll just wait until you're his age. That's the law in my house."

"Okay, okay," Gretta said with the exhaustion of hearing her mother's broken record yet again. "So, can we use the car, or not?"

"Sam, what are you doing after you drop her off?"

"Nothing, Mom. I was just going to fly by the mall and pick up some CDs."

"Okay," Barbara said, getting her keys from the pocket of her purse. "Here're the keys. I expect you to be careful, Sam. I don't want a bunch of boys in my car. You know the rule.

Two friends are your limit. And I don't even have to say the rest."

"No, Mom, you don't, because you know that I don't drink, and have never had a desire to drink," Sam said, his tone telling just how offended and very close to hurt he'd grown at his mother's suggestion of the possibility. He took the keys from her and turned to leave with his sister when he turned back to his mother and said, "I've never taken a drink, Mom. Never." And then Sam, distracted, left with Gretta right behind him. "Oh, it was nice meeting you, Lila Lilly," he hollered from the hall.

"Yeah, nice meeting you," Gretta mimicked.

"It was nice meeting the two of you as well," Lila called back.

Lila studied, for an extended moment, the memory of Sam and Gretta, since she couldn't see them through the door through which they'd just left. And that emptiness created a discomfort she didn't quite know how to settle. There was so much of what was spoken, but mostly unspoken, that left her troubled. With the recent history the three of them shared in the tragedy of alcohol and automobiles, why was Barbara's trust in her son so flimsy that his proclamation as a teenager against drinking wasn't enough for her? And why couldn't Sam and Gretta say Matty's name? Had Barbara's mother-grief zapped them of all ability to speak it, and zapped her of all reasonable trust? And how could it be that everyone in the house watched *Lila Lilly's Story Hour* on three different computers, possibly for the same reason, and not one of them knew that the others were watching? It set an ache off in her heart to see how connected the three of them were in their pain, yet how great the void was between their souls. She looked to Barbara, who had busied herself as if she couldn't see, or did not want to see. "Barbara, does it bother you that your kids don't even mention Matty's name?"

"I don't know what you mean. Sure they mention his name."

"Barbara, no, they don't. They talk around his name, side-stepping and ducking under and climbing over it, as if they'll be scorned for the mere utterance of it. And, I don't know, I may be wrong, since this is my first time meeting them, but it seems to me as if they do it for you. Gretta went right up to his name, her lips had the *M* completely formed, and then she stopped herself. Are they doing it for you, Barbara?"

Barbara stopped her hands from straightening the things on the counter that were already set in their places and stared through the kitchen window into the backyard for several pensive seconds, as if summoning all the things she had to say from their hiding places behind trees, and shrubs, and rocks, to come in and take her over. She turned to Lila, with tears that seemed to come from nowhere, and said, "Lila, did I ever tell you that the day I don't watch *Lila Lilly's Story Hour* will probably be the day I will slip from my sane mind into the one that will lose itself from reality?" And without giving Lila a chance to answer, she crossed the kitchen to stand opposite the counter from Lila and looked her in the eyes with the truth. "And did I ever tell you that I am so angry with God that I'm not sure I even believe in what I'm praying for anymore? And I know I never told you that there isn't a day that goes by when I don't wish that it had been Ben in his drunken stupidity who died in that car crash and not my Matty. No matter how hard I pray, Lila, I simply can't find forgiveness for that man. And I will never forgive myself for not just getting in my car when Jan first called and driving over there myself to get my baby. If I had done that, Matty would still be alive."

Barbara looked away from Lila, as if to hide her face, as if trying to heave from herself what was most difficult to say. She put her eyes only halfway on Lila, and said, "You know, every time I go to see my priest he talks so eloquently about how death is not the end of life, but a continuation of it. I don't want to hear that, Lila. I just want my baby, right here with me. My faith has always been so solid, as solid as my priest wants it to be. I'm a good Catholic girl, capable, I thought, of forgiveness. I never questioned God, and I never bothered him for anything but his will. I wanted his will to be done, Lila, because he knows best. Right? So I shouldn't be questioning him about why he took my baby, and why I can't forgive my husband, but I have to, Lila. I have to question him, and I have to let him know that I am mad as hell at him for taking my baby. And I hate myself for being so damned weak, because my faith isn't so simple and blind anymore, Lila." Barbara broke down and sobbed into her hands, as if the shame would never leave her. Then she wailed, "Oh God, why didn't I just go and get him! What is wrong with God?"

Lila wanted to touch her but didn't know how. So she stayed in her own space and spoke timidly. "Barbara, you seem to be saying that you're a good Catholic girl who's not so good any-more because you're angry with God and you're questioning him. Well, I want to ask you, what do you think Jesus was doing when he was dying on the cross, huh? Those last words, *My God, my God, why have you forsaken me,* they weren't just the irrational mutterings of a dying man, Barbara. Those words were said in anguish, coming from the center of his being that was in physical and spiritual pain that brought Jesus to question his Father, and rail against him. And I don't know, you know, I've never been a deeply religious person aside from going to church, and all, but I have to believe I *do* believe, that to have true faith is to question. Yes, I suppose we do ask for God's will, but I think we have a right given to us by our faith to appeal that will, to question it when it doesn't make sense."

And now, Lila was able to touch her, trying her best to make everything that was in her heart heal Barbara. But then, feeling Barbara's tension under her fingertips, Lila carefully pulled back and tried again. "I think, Barbara, that if you have an intimate relationship with God, I think you will be mad with him from time to time, and you are going to question him. And I guess it's hard for you to see or understand this right now, but you are so blessed to have a profound enough relationship with God to be mad at him, yet still believe. I've never known that." And Lila fell silent, almost sad, thinking about how she so intensely needed to be mad with God right now but simply could not feel him deeply enough to have anything but a child's deference instead of a woman's faith. And her intellectual understanding of a woman's faith, of Barbara's faith, could only let her help Barbara, not herself. She felt Barbara's eyes waiting for the rest. "No, I've never known that kind of intimacy. All I do is pray and believe without asking why. And maybe that speaks more to the lack of depth in my faith than questioning God in anger speaks to yours."

"But that makes me weak, Lila. Don't you see? With every-thing I have always believed through my faith as a Catholic, I believe that that makes me weak, and I just can't take it. I can't take it when God has taken my strength away from me. I have asked for answers in every way, in every prayer, as to why my Matty had to die. And he doesn't hear me. He just does not hear me, and now, I don't know what to do, because if he's not answering me, or maybe if I simply can't hear his answer, then I'm the weakest of the flock." Barbara slumped over the counter with a wail that filled the room with a chill. She wailed until she could not breathe.

Feeling all of Barbara's desperation, and some of her own pain, Lila went to her to hold her. But Barbara snatched herself from Lila's arms, pushing her away. So Lila stood nearby, close enough to catch her, but far enough away to let her writhe alone in her pain. She looked past where Barbara sat slumped to notice the vase with the cut flowers. It hadn't magically dis-appeared then reappeared to capture her curiosity. It had always been there, holding the flowers that sliced through all that pristine whiteness with its dash of colors, but now, the ves-sel captivated her for its symbolism. It was heavy, she could tell, thick and impenetrable. Made so strong of lead, yet cut with a delicacy that allowed its facets to dance by the light of any illu-mination. It fascinated Lila, this rigid piece that had only one purpose. So she went to it, and though it seemed she was under the hypnotic spell of the prancing light in prisms, she removed the flowers from the vase and laid them on the counter. She poured out the water, watching the last drops drip, drip, drip into the sink before she turned it upright again. And then, with what seemed to be the most sinister of motivations, which could come only from a mind that had made a left turn, she held the vase in midair, then let it drop to the hard tiled floor. What a crash it made, glass shattering into a million pieces with enough thunder to raise the dead.

It brought Barbara to sit stark straight. Eyes bugged, mouth agape, she looked at Lila and exclaimed, "What the hell!" Then she looked to find her flowers laid on the counter. "My vase! Did you break my vase?"

"Yes," was all Lila said flatly.

"Why in hell did you break my vase, Lila?"

"Because I wanted to ask you something. Why do you think that vase broke?"

"It broke because you dropped it," Barbara said, her annoyance strong and inching toward anger.

"Well, some would think that the vase broke because it was weak, fragile. But that vase didn't break because it was weak, Barbara. It broke because it was too strong. No weaknesses. Inflexible. Incapable of bending or being malleable in any way. Strength, Barbara, is not the absence, nor is it the opposite, of weakness. Strength is in being able to absorb the blows, get a little bruised from it, maybe, but then continue to stay whole. Strength, Barbara, just may be the absence of the fear of those blows, because you always know that you won't fall apart, that you won't break into hundreds of pieces on the floor, like this vase just did." She went to where Barbara sat and took her hand. Leaning into a slight stoop so that they'd be eye to eye, Lila said, "Barbara, if I were to go by the strength of what I always believed, or thought I knew, I wouldn't be standing here with you right now, because I would have stayed strong in my belief that I couldn't, or did not want to, have a white woman as a friend."

Barbara stared at Lila until her face could do nothing but soften into a distant smile. Then she stood from where she'd slumped on the counter and went over to a cabinet and snatched down a broom and dustpan that hung on the other side of the door. She went to the pile of Lila's broken metaphor in the middle of the floor and did what only a mother can do right after a soul-wrenching fit; and she said as she swept, "So what do I do now?"

"Now, Barbara, you forgive yourself. You forgive yourself for being too afraid to be weak. You forgive yourself for being angry at God, because he will always understand, and there isn't a sin so great that he won't forgive us." She paused only long enough to offer up deference in her remembrance of the woman who gave her that piece of wisdom, Mrs. Chalm. "But mostly, Barbara, you've got to forgive yourself for letting Matty be in the car that your husband ran into that day, because if you don't do that, Barbara, you will never live again, and you'll completely miss what you will never be able to get back, and that's these moments with Sam and Gretta. Log on to *Lila Lilly's Story Hour* with them, Barbara. Because all three of you are living in secret with so much pain, and maybe if all three of you can share this memory of Matty, then just maybe, I don't know, there can be life in this home again. Let yourself breathe again, girl. And give Sam and Gretta a chance."

Lila listened to the twinkling of glass being swept into the dustpan. It made her come, fully focused, around to what she'd just done. She really hadn't been thinking, because it was reckless, she thought, and over the top, and right at the edge of crazy; but the sound of that vase crashing, still echoing through the room for her, had shaken her by the shoulders to bring her fully awake and fully present into her own blessing. For her heart had increased to make room for an intimacy with a woman who once would have been considered a most unlikely friend. She smiled at Barbara, who she knew could not see it, and said, "By the way, I'll buy you a new vase."

Barbara laughed from deep inside herself, then with the back of her hand, she wiped the remnants of tears that had not yet dried to salt on her cheeks. "You bet you will. But I'm not worried about that. You've just got me thinking. I do need to figure out how to forgive Ben, and I think it is going to have to start with forgiving myself. But can we make a pact? Can you also forgive Jack? I have to believe in somebody's happily ever after, and I want to believe in yours. I don't know what happened, and you don't have to tell me, but try to meet him halfway, Lila. Something in my gut tells me you won't regret it."

Lila only smiled as she filled with fear because it wasn't until now, even with the broken vase and her metaphor, which snatched Barbara from the edge, that Lila knew some of her own wisdom had to go home with her. But who would come to her home and break a vase and make her see the light, because all she could see right now was Barbara's beacon at the end of the tunnel.

chapter seventeen

T HE SMELL OF the roasted chicken from Safeway wafted through the room where Lila sat in her funeral dress, mindlessly munching a barely steamed string bean. She had drifted off to thoughts of Jack, which is where her mind spent the balance of most days since she'd imprisoned herself. He was alone and at a funeral, quite possibly the worst two places to be at one time. It was in her every thought, all the day, to be at that funeral next to Jack, but once she got into her funeral dress, the only thing she could think to do was to walk to Safeway and get a roasted chicken and steamed string beans; the same as she'd done in her single days when she lived in her safe land. And even as she savored her favorite store-bought meal, it was still not too late to get there for the actual funeral, since they were still in the middle of the wake right now. Yet Lila couldn't move. It seemed more natural to every part of her simply to sit there alone with her chicken and string beans. And think about making love with Jack.

It had been so long—one month, three weeks, and a day— since she and Jack had come together that it seemed to her there was something quite sinful about it in the eyes of man and God. More than any actual physical pleasure she remembered from that night, she saw his face. But not just his face, his eyes, in which she also saw herself and her love reflected. There was no doubt that each time they made their way to their high heights, she'd see in his smile and he'd see in hers that they'd just fallen one inch deeper in love, their souls clenched tighter to each other. And so now that they weren't making love anymore, she wondered how far their love had drifted, and how it would ever be the same, or feel the same again.

More sinful than their not making love, she believed, was her sitting there all dressed in black on the night of Mr. Rawlings's funeral, thinking about sex. It wasn't right that she'd remember the way Jack's fingertips, light as a zephyr, could take her places, when there was a dead man somewhere. It wasn't fair that someone's life was gone, while she sat in her memories of the moments when every cell in her body sprung to life in one gust of passion. And it was downright lowlife of her to remember going with Jack for the first time to visit one of his Saturday patients—Mr. Rawlings, as coincidence would have it—in their days of hand holding, and having a warmth flood her when every move Jack made, and every step he took, made her want more from him than his hand. It was only now that embarrassment hit her. Back then, shame had no place in the midst of her longing for Jack. And now, in the light of all that was new, did she long for Jack or for sex? The line between the two had somehow, to her dismay, grown far too thin.

And that's when she thought about where she was, and why she was there. And she thought of Hillary Rodham Clinton and the way that woman vowed she wasn't some little woman standing by her man like Tammy Wynette. Except that in the end, she did stand by her man like Tammy Wynette, which wasn't altogether a bad thing. When a woman is looking into the darkest night of her man's soul, there's some basic wisdom to be found in Tammy Wynette's words. In the end, that's what Lila would do—stand by her man even through all her judgment, all her contempt, all her resentment, because there'd be no place else for her to stand. She'd end up bucking up to become the cliché of a prison wife, getting her hand stamped, and her purse rummaged through, to stand by her man in prison. And she'd have to learn how to bake cookies, it suddenly occurred to her, because Jack would need something that would give him the comfort of home in his lonely hours of cell life. Though her catfish with her red beans and rice would bring the most comfort simply because that was always the one thing she could count on for his raves, cookies were far more practical for their immediate accessibility.

When the door buzzer from the porch droned loud enough to reel her backward, she nearly didn't know what it was for a few seconds. No one ever used that buzzer because anyone with a purpose for being there had the privilege of a key. She had to remember where the intercom was placed. All she could recall was that it was in an awkward place, hidden partially by something. It buzzed again, only this time with the drawn-out determination of what seemed to her to be an impatient finger seeming to act of its own will. She looked over to see just behind Nell's desk where two white buttons peeked out from the curve in the wall, just slightly behind the file cabinet. Lila got to it before the finger down on the porch had the chance to lay on it the next time.

"Yes? Who's there?" she asked cautiously.

"Lila, it's me, Gil."

She drew herself back for a full two seconds before she pressed the button that would open the door downstairs. Things must be pretty dire, she thought, for Gil to be there nosing around, getting involved. Jack must be in a bad way, because Gil stayed out of things, kept his distance, knew his place. That's just always who she'd known her brother to be. Now, here he comes, wanting to know what's going on, wanting to know why she's living rough and away from Jack. Here he comes, caring.

She opened the door when she heard him on the last step. "Gil, what are you doing here?"

"Well, it's funny, Lila. I came here to ask you the same question. Why aren't you at home? And why are you in your funeral dress?" he said, walking through the door as Lila held it open for him.

"Which do you want me to answer first?"

"Doesn't much matter. I'll be equally intrigued by either answer."

Lila closed the door and followed Gil over to the *Story Hour* sofa/bed. She could tell that this would be one of those drawn-out visits, because her sofa/bed was the most likely place anyone would go to with a mouth full of long wind. Where would she begin to explain to Gil the state of her marriage? He knew absolutely nothing about the institution, and she herself understood only slightly more. She'd have to be obscure, because, after all, that was the state of things. "Gil, Jack and I have just not been seeing eye to eye on certain things."

"Lila, come on. Lots of married couples don't see eye to eye on almost everything, but they don't move away from each other. Now, I'm asking you again and hoping for you to tell me the truth. What's going on with you and Jack?"

"How do you know anything's going on at all?" she asked like a distrustful woman with a secret.

"Because I called you the other night. Jack told me that you were staying over here at your office, and I have to tell you, that didn't sound like you at all."

"So, did you ask *him* what was going on?"

"No, I didn't ask him because I knew he wouldn't tell me. But I could hear in his voice that whatever was going on between you two was bad, and it didn't make him happy."

Lila watched her brother slip out of his suit jacket and lay it over the arm of the sofa, looking more like their departed father than their father. He unbuttoned his shirt cuffs and rolled back his sleeves, and she thought of a fight. Is this what this will become? "You look as if you're ready to dig in."

"I want to make sure you're okay, Lila. That's my job. Remember? And with you living here and not with your husband, I don't know, I just somehow get the idea that you're not okay."

She tried to hold out, and hold back, but Gil could always break her down with the way he loved like a brother, with the way he cared like a friend. They didn't stream. The tears just burst, as if something had been defying them to fall. "Oh my God, Gil, things just couldn't possibly be any worse than they are right now. I married him too fast. It was just too fast. You warned me, but I just didn't listen. And now, here I am, married to a man I never really knew." She gasped for a breath. Crying while talking can really take it out of you.

He put an arm around her and pulled her close. He said quietly, somberly, "No other woman's tears can make me want to protect more than yours, Lila. So you've got to tell me what happened."

"Gil, as much as I want to tell you, as much as I just *need* to tell you, I can't. As an officer of the court, you would put all of us in a very precarious situation. You'd be obligated to tell what you know."

Gil squeezed her closer to him, a result of his own tension, as if he wanted to know but didn't want to know, so he asked anyway, "Lila, did Jack commit some kind of crime?"

She only sat, listening to his heart beat, and feeling her own. In the moment, it was difficult to tell one from the other. "Yes," she said softly, ashamedly. "And that's all you need to know, because you would have to take him from me if I told you more."

"Lila, you've already taken him from yourself just by being here. If Jack's in trouble, he needs you more than he's ever needed anybody."

Lila pulled away from Gil to sit upright. She looked into her hands to see busy fingers of their own mind pick at a fingernail. "Yeah, well, I guess I don't want to be there loving him when the inevitable happens."

"Here, there, what does it matter? No matter where you are, Lila, you're still loving him."

"But I don't have to watch him being taken from me."

Gil stared straight down into his lap, then closed his eyes. What he was about to say went against the essence of what made him a thinking man. "Lila, this is a question I would never ask a client. And you're right, given that I am an officer of the court, it is just absolutely idiotic for me to ask you this, but I've got to help you and Jack in whatever way I can." His voice grew quiet, and sad, and his face fell flat enough for tears to slide smoothly down. Though none would fall in actuality, they flowed in every word he spoke to her. "I'm in this now, Lila, whether I want to be or not. I don't have the choice of walking away from you without your telling me what Jack did." He took a deep breath and blew it out of seemingly every orifice in his head, and asked, "What did Jack do, Lila?"

She made her hands stop their nonsense, placing them firm and flat on her lap. There were so many reasons why she should tell Gil, the least of them being that she needed somebody else's arms to hold the burden with her. But then, there was one large reason why she shouldn't tell him. Inside of an hour, Jack could be in handcuffs and on his way to a life that the circumstances of his good mind and good fortune had allowed him to slimly escape. A life where he'd find ghostly reminders of shadowy figures and faces he knew as a boy that could have portended his adult life, but of which he resembled not one as a man.

Lila looked into her brother's eyes without question, without a doubt that she loved him in spite of, maybe even because of, his obligation, and said; "Okay. But before I tell you, I want you to understand that whatever you have to do when I tell you is simply what you have to do, and I know that. It changes nothing about our love, and I would never ask you to go against your principles or your oath."

"Lila, just tell me," Gil said impatiently.

"Have you heard about the white man who died on the sidewalk over on Twenty-eighth Street a few months ago? There's this big stink about the black man who may have been a doctor but didn't do anything to help him."

"Yes, of course. Who hasn't heard about that? By all accounts, the man who died was a pretty nasty racist. Said some pretty nasty things to that black guy."

"Okay, well, that black guy *was* a doctor. It was Jack."

Gil looked at Lila as if unsure of what he was thinking, because there was so much coming at him through such a sliver of time. It may have been too much to absorb, and that may be why he asked what only the severely obtuse might ask: "What do you mean?"

"Gil, I mean that Jack was the one who left that man to die in the sweltering sun that day. He stepped over that man as if he were a heap of trash, got in his car, put down his cola, and drove off. I didn't know who Jack was that day, Gil, and to this day I can't say that I've seen my old Jack since then."

"He told you he did this?"

"I was there, Gil. I saw it with my own two eyes. He did it! But that man said some vile things to him, Gil." She lowered her head, unsure if she could even repeat such incredible nastiness. Even thinking about it made her feel freshly the shame, the anger. But Gil had to know. "He called Jack Dr. Porch Monkey."

Those words seemed to strike Gil viscerally, and he winced. "Okay, so he did that, but what's this criminal thing you're talking about that he did?"

Lila gave her brother the glare of lost patience. "Gil, have you been listening to me? I told you, he walked away from that man as if he didn't even see him dying."

"Yeah, okay, but that's not illegal, Lila. He can't go to jail for that."

Lila's entire body seemed to be lifted into midair, right along with her face, which came into a life that had been lost to it since that horrendous day. "Are you serious, Gil? Are you saying that because in your opinion you don't *think* he should go to jail, or are you speaking as a lawyer who knows the law, and knows for fact that what Jack did was not a crime? What about Good Samaritan laws?"

"What Jack did, Lila, was not a crime. It was not illegal. It was unethical, but it wasn't illegal. But Jack could have told you that it's not a crime."

It was one of those silent stares that said what no words in the language she knew could say. Apart from everything else that it was, it was mostly a shame that Jack couldn't have told her that what he did was not a crime. But then she remem-

bered. "No, no, Gil, I remember him telling me when it happened. I remember him saying that in a lot of people's eyes he's
liable for that man's death. He said that he would have to take
the consequences like a man. That means he knows he's crimi-
nally responsible."

Gil shook his head with authority and said, "My guess is that
if he was talking about what he did as a crime he was speaking
about it in a metaphorical kind of way, as in it was morally
criminal. But trust me, Lila, what he did was not a crime, at least
not in the legal sense of the word. And the only way it would
be a crime would be if Maryland had a Good Samaritan law,
which we don't have here. Now, the family of the dead man
could try to sue him civilly on those grounds but it would probably go nowhere. This wouldn't even be a malpractice case
because Jack never administered any medical treatment to him.
The only crime Jack has committed, Lila, has been against his
own conscience. And maybe—I don't know, I'm no psychia-
trist—but just maybe that's what this whole thing between the
two of you is all about."

"What it's about, Gil, is Jack and his morally criminal side.
That was perfect, the way you put it, because I've been trying to
think of exactly the right words that could explain what Jack
did. I thought it was just legally criminal, but you're right. He's
a moral criminal."

"Morally criminal, Lila, in a very narrow circumstance, not
morally deficient. There's a difference. There's a big difference.
Given the right circumstances, I don't know of anyone who
couldn't be legally criminal. I couldn't say that I could never kill
a man if conditions fell into place in such a way that it seemed
right in that moment, in that second, even. So I certainly
couldn't say that I could never have done what Jack did."

"Well, I can honestly say, Gilbert, that I could never kill a
man," she said harshly, superciliously, pointing to herself
haughtily just to make her point. "And if it had been in my
power to save that man that day, I would have saved him."

"Damn, Lila!" Gil nearly screamed at her. He was on his feet
now, and in the throes of his courtroom histrionics with flailing

arms and one pointing finger. "You are such a hypocrite! Okay, you say if it were in your power. Well, you have a cell phone in your purse, don't you? You even have a car phone. Just dialing three little numbers the moment you realized Jack wasn't going to help him could have gotten help to that man quicker than it came, probably. And you know CPR, don't you? I know you do, because I remember when Jack insisted you get certified. If it meant that much to you, Lila, you would have jumped from the high horse where you sat looking down on Jack and gotten out of that car and saved that man. But you didn't. So don't you go making Jack less than a man for doing what he did, because sometimes a black man in this world has had enough, and sometimes enough can be way too much. And let me tell you, Lila, if you would start being completely honest with yourself, you'd see that, yes, Jack was hurt by that man in a way that nobody should ever be hurt by anyone, but there's only a really thin line separating his hurt from yours. Think about that, Lila."

It wasn't easy for her to know what to say now that she'd been called a hypocrite, since no one had said such a thing to her, ever. And now, not only was she a hypocrite, but her brother had also actually made a rather winning argument against her character and moral constitution. She was a moral criminal, too, for her judgment—judgment of herself, but certainly of Jack, as well. Lila knew it was all true because her brother didn't get this passionate without cause. She knew it was all true because he never told anything but bitter truth, whether welcomed or not. Mostly, though, she knew it was all true because Gil invoked a battle cry, and she'd never, ever, in her years as his sister, as a child and as a woman, heard Gil roar for his gender, and certainly not his race. Lila looked at Gil with the clarity in her eyes that had been shaken into her heart and said softly, "My God, Gil. Those were Jack's exact words. He said the same thing that day: 'Sometimes a man has had enough.' Oh Gil, what am I doing?"

Gil didn't answer her right away; he was too deep in thankful prayer, that he'd reached her so far down where she'd descended. And he was so thankful that he had reached her before she'd gotten to the place where Eulelie, their momma, would live out the rest of her life—forever looking over her shoulder for herself. So he looked at his sister with plain eyes and merely said, "Lying to yourself."

chapter eighteen

ACK WALKED THROUGH the door, dragging with the exhaustion of the funeral, and having spent the whole of it within his head. He knew Lila was there, probably upstairs in bed already, but he wasn't rushing to get to her. There was no telling what made her come home. As badly as he needed to see her face, see her slight form just beneath the covers, he didn't want the challenge of defending himself from her pain. He didn't want to defend himself for staying on a little longer than usual at the Rawlingses' home after the funeral. Nor did he wish to endure the tedium of her blurry accusations of a misdeed, the likes of which, he was sure, not even she was certain. So he decided to stand sideways, much like a torero, and let her dash at what she presumed to be him. Until the face-off, though, he'd dawdle at locking up downstairs before his ascension into what had come to be his own personal hell.

After checking on the back door to make certain it was locked, both locks, he took a bottle of Coke from the refrigerator, opened it, and tossed the cap on the counter. No need for that, since he'd finish it in no time, maybe even before he got to the bedroom. By the time he'd reached the midway step on the staircase, Jack had sucked down half the bottle. And by the time he got to the bedroom door, there was only a swallow left in the bottle. But when he opened the door to behold his wife, he could scarcely remember that he had a bottle of Coke in his hand at all.

Lila sat at the foot of the bed, as if she'd been there for days, anticipation keeping her as fresh and lovely as spring. She wore the green chemise that she hadn't worn for her husband since the first night they were husband and wife, and it was the kind of green that, against her skin with its fusion of yellow and brown and something resembling barely ripe olives beneath her surface, made the whole of her look like an edible pleasure. Lila clearly knew what she was doing, having orchestrated the way she now lay herself before him. What she had no way of knowing, though, is what he saw when he looked at her.

Jack came fully into the room and put the nearly empty bottle of soda on the chest of drawers next to the door. He took a deep breath that did nothing to ease the tension of what felt to him the way virgin love once felt. "Hi, baby," he said quietly. Jack went and stood before her, as unsure as the first time of what he should do next.

Lila drew her legs up beneath herself to kneel on the bed, so that they were eye to eye, nearly shoulder to shoulder. "Jack, I'm sorry. I'm sorry for that awful thing that happened to us both back in July. I'm sorry for the silence that almost killed us. But most of all I'm sorry for not loving you the way I needed to during the darkest hour of our lives."

Jack slipped his hands around Lila's waist and pulled her to him. His hands slid over the satin of her chemise, bringing him back to a place of which memories were sparse, but he did remember that with Lila, satin and skin were indistinguishable. Jack closed his eyes and breathed into her neck as he felt her holding him, as if to let go would be to fall to a despicable place, and he held her as fast. And he prayed that she could hear all that he could not say.

"I know we should, but I don't want to talk now, Jack. All I want . . ."

Jack hushed her with the devotion of his kiss, which was deep, and hard, and unrelenting. And when his lips did relent, they did so only long enough to slide to that spot on her neck where they always knew to go. He heard her moan and felt her tremble in his arms, and then grow flaccid, as if she'd gone into a cold faint. Jack wasn't certain if it was actually Lila whispering in his ear, or the memory of her whisper echoing through him from their first time, when he heard Lila say, "Don't you remember? Don't ever go to that spot on my neck unless you're completely prepared to make love to me." But he did remember, and that whisper, real or imagined, only made him stronger. He scooped her in his arms from where she knelt and laid her flat. Sitting on the side of the bed next to where she lay, he drank in her soft and faultless beauty, which put him in mind of a painted satin dance-hall doll, existing only for her loveliness. But oh, how Lila existed for far more than her loveliness. She was now, and would always be, his everything.

Lila reached for him, and he came to her in every way. When his fingers slid between hers, the intimacy of that unadorned connection closed her eyes and sank her deeper inside him. With his lips finding her place again, she felt the weight of her love for him in all the parts of her body it had rushed to, filling, and then drenching; so that when he spoke softly in her ear of just how much he loved her, there was nothing she was able to say, having lost the ability to speak, and her eyes were still fastened on him with, and inside, and from, desire. And when she came to see him again the bond put a heaviness on her heart, the kind that makes a woman unsure if she needs to weep for her ethereal joy, or scream to the heights of herself in earthly rapture. Now, they were back to their fundamental life, skin on skin, eye to eye, soul within soul, each inside the other. And they loved each other with equal strength and passion to the end.

BY THE NEXT afternoon, Lila was positively useless. Through the morning, she'd drifted in and out of a grinning haze that had her staring blankly off into the night before with Jack. Love-making with Jack had never been without intensity, but last night, Lila felt the two of them soaring higher even than their wedding night, which reigned. Mostly, she was worn down, completely drained from the energy she'd expended into dread and despair. She wanted to move, she wanted to do more than simply sit there staring at her unfinished story, at the unfinished sentence her mind left when it took its last journey back to the night, remembering Jack in yet another way.

She particularly needed to get moving since today she wouldn't be able to work right up to the minute before *Story Hour*. At two-thirty, a reporter from the *Sun* papers would be there to interview her and see her in action, not for anything having to do with *Story Hour*, her own impressive life's work if she were to thump her own back, but for an article on Jack's possible appointment to the National Institutes of Health. Still, with that bearing down on her as every wasted hour went by, all she could seem to do was sit behind her desk, slouched in her chair, not necessarily seconds from sleep, but definitely overcome by the same heavy-eyed paralysis. Who knew peace could leave indolence in its wake?

Even with guilt bearing down on her as she watched Nell be the drone, Lila couldn't move. She watched Nell go back and forth from her drawings to doing something on the computer that Lila could not fathom, mostly because she didn't feel like thinking much about anything, much less about what Nell was doing on the computer. So Lila said, "Nell, I'm sorry I'm so out of air today, and I know I should be working. I just can't get it together."

"Well, good sex can leave you that way, unable to think or move," Nell said through a wry smile.

And Lila did perk up then and said with an embarrassed chuckle, "Nell, how did you know?"

"Lila, please. I've seen you lethargic from worry, sadness, fear, and good sex. I can tell the difference. So, what happened? And why didn't you tell me about it as soon as you walked through the door this morning?"

"Well, because, Nell, I'm not even sure I know what happened. I think it was about forgiveness, mostly of myself, but of what else I'm not sure. What I do know for sure, though, is that it was beautiful."

"So, you two talked about what happened?" Nell asked with a certain skeptical tone that said she was fairly certain that they hadn't, but she asked anyway.

"No. No, we didn't," Lila said, fairly ashamed of herself. Then she tried to explain. "But that has to happen when we're both ready. Last night was just about us reconnecting." Lila let out a blushing laugh after hearing Nell's sly chuckle, as she peered into Lila's impure mind through devilishly dancing eyes. "You know what I mean, silly," Lila said, playfully throwing a paper clip so that it would land on Nell's desk.

"Yes, in fact, I do know what you mean." Nell was serious now. Then she continued, "Love without pride always has a way of bringing a woman back to what's basic, because that's just how women love when they really love—without pride. The difference between husbands and wives is that a man can stop making love to his wife for weeks if she cuts her hair, or lowers her hemline, and he'll truly think he's justified—as if she's broken some sort of sacred marital commandment, like Thou shalt not take scissor to hair, or add fabric to hemline. But us wives, we're completely different. A man can do the most dastardly thing, totally egregious, and we can always find our way back to that basic part in us that lets us make love to him from the first day."

Lila savored Nell's sentiments briefly, but deeply. "I've never thought about it in those terms, but I think you're right. There's no doubt that Jack and I need to really talk about what happened that day, but I have to tell you, last night was wonderful. I mean, we were back, just me and Jack, we were back to that place where we will always know we love each other. It's pretty awesome, Nell." Lila let her head drop onto the back of the chair to marvel, once more.

"So, who's this guy coming here today to interview you?"

"Oh, some reporter from the *Sun*. I don't know about this interview, because over the phone he's already asked me the most ridiculously trite question in a reporter's bag of questions.

He asked me if I was proud that Jack might be the first black director of the NIH. What kind of question is that? I'm just proud that Jack might be appointed to head the NIH, period. Why do people do that—you know, make such a big deal out of the first black this or the first black that? I thought those days were gone."

"No, they're not gone, and they won't be gone, as long as color still matters in America."

"Color sure has put a whipping on America."

"Now that's the truth," Nell said, finally coming to sit down behind her desk and breathe. "I remember the first time I realized what God had done to this world by coloring us all so differently. It was my junior year in college, and I had this roommate named Yolanda. Yolanda was one of these girls who could always find the dark side of life. I mean, if I woke up in the morning and said, 'Wow, what a beautiful, sunny day!' she might say something like, 'I wonder how many people will end up with skin cancer because of this day.' That kind of darkness. Anyway, one night I came in from a date, and Yolanda had fallen asleep in the middle of the floor. But lying on her stomach was this picture she had drawn in colorful chalk. She had drawn all these faces of women—a white woman with blond hair, a white woman with red hair, a white woman with brunette hair, a Japanese woman, a Chinese woman, a Filipino woman, a Latino woman, and then black women. But just like she had white women with different color hair, she had the black women in different shades, but only different shades of light skin. The darkest black woman she drew was of my coloring. And at the bottom of the page she wrote: THE OBJECT OF EVERY BLACK MAN'S DESIRE."

Nell stopped, because to remember, even after all this time, was still hard. She looked as if she just might cry for her long-ago friend. "Okay, so that was weird enough, but when I turned the paper over, there was another picture, this time of just one woman, with beautiful, round eyes, perfectly formed splayed nose, and lips as plump and luscious as strawberries, but this woman was blue-black, and underneath *her* face, Yolanda wrote: THE OBJECT OF EVERY BLACK MAN'S IRE. I wanted to cry, Lila, because I knew then that she looked at my light brown skin and her fudgy brown skin and didn't even consider us to be the same race because our lives were so different based on color. *I* was the girl guys asked out on Friday and Saturday nights. *She* was the one they merely spoke to distractedly and then only out of sheer social protocol. It's when I think of that moment that I wonder most about God's plan. But more than that, for the first time I really understood, I mean *really* understood, the pain color inflicts on this world. Yolanda's feelings about herself and about the way black men feel about her are probably the most repulsive relative of racism."

Lila couldn't speak on it right away, since most of what she'd come to know about the hierarchy of color within her color she learned from her stepmother, Eulelie, and it was an education that would give truth to Yolanda's feelings. And she knew it was wrong, what she'd learned, yet knew if she tried spouting off against it, she'd sound like one of those parlor liberals—the kind who talk, in parlors where it can be intellectualized, of a brave new world of inclusion and tolerance, yet live in the secluded world of their own kind. She'd been called a hypocrite yesterday, and she couldn't bear to hear it again so soon. After all, Nell married Chuck, a black man whose skin was pure with the hue of Africa, so she walked her talk. Lila, on the other hand, married Jack, and did not cross that other color line to do it. But now, in the dim light of that dead, fat redneck's porch, where every black man and woman in the spectrum all sat as monkeys, it was clearer than ever that the variety did not matter.

And it all—the assortment of black skin, porch monkeys, dead racists, Yolanda—made her think of her mother, and the innocence of babies. Her baby. The baby she wanted. But she did not just want any baby. Lila wished for a baby that would reach all the way back and snatch the black off of Jack's grandfather, and then cover itself in it from head to sugar toes. And then she would take her chocolate baby straight to Florida and put it in her stepmother's arms, and defy Eulelie, not in words but certainly in airs, to say one word against her baby's black skin. Lila fantasized of making sure her mother would know that the misinformation she'd given Lila on the pecking order of black skin had been replaced with the truth: if Eulelie were ever to find herself face-to-face with a redneck on a street corner, she'd be equally as black as Lila's little black baby. There would be no differences. There would be no acceptable hues of peanut butter, or honey-dolloped, or red-bone, or even damned near white. Yet, even after all her fantasizing of the revenge of the darkies on her mother, all Lila said to Nell was, "Yolanda's story is sad. I wonder if it ever got any better for her."

"Probably not. That kind of thinking is deep-seated, and comes from a very tenuous place in her psyche." Nell seemed to be looking off into a time where she could see Yolanda, feel her sadness as if she were still back there with her and those drawings. "But I pray for her, every single time I think about her."

The buzzer from the front door sounded, startling both of them, and Lila thought of Gil. "Oh, goodness, that must be the reporter. Is it two-thirty already?"

"Yes, it is. Time sure does fly when you're daydreaming about sex, doesn't it?" Nell said, with an infectious laugh she passed on to Lila.

"Okay, okay," Lila said, trying to stop her runaway laughter. "I've got to be serious. He's here to interview the wife of the man who just might head the National Institutes of Health. He can't come in here and find a buffoon, so let's get serious. Oh, and by the way, I've invited Barbara Gallagher and her two kids to come and watch us do *Story Hour* today," Lila said as she pressed the button that would open the downstairs door. "I hope you don't mind."

"No, I don't mind. When did all this come about?"

"Yesterday. She called me just before I left here and asked if they could come. I don't know what happened between the three of them, but the fact that they're coming here together says that at the least they sat down and talked. And I feel a little bit responsible for that. It feels good, you know."

"Yeah, I'll bet it does. They've got a long road of healing

ahead of them, and it's great that you set them on the right path," Nell said, smiling before her face grew serious. "But do you think it's such a good idea to have them here today with the reporter coming and all?"

"Well, I don't think it will matter. I don't think they'll be in the way."

"I guess you're right," Nell said with eyes half full of doubt.

Climbing the stairs with the burden of three flights, Lila heard more than one pair of feet, so she opened the door before anyone could knock. "Hi," she said brightly to Barbara, Sam, and Gretta. "I wasn't expecting you this early."

"Oh, I'm sorry," Barbara said, stopping on the last step. "It's just that Sam had early classes today, and Gretta only had a half day. We can come back later, if that's better for you."

"Oh no, no, no," Lila said, pulling Barbara into the room. "I'm glad you're here early. It's just that I didn't expect you. Come on in." She stepped aside for Sam and Gretta, who pecked her on the cheek awkwardly, yet somehow sincerely, as they passed by. "This is Nell Teague, who helps me make *Lila Lilly's Story Hour* possible. Nell, this is Barbara, Sam, and Gretta Gallagher."

"It's really nice to meet you, Barbara," Nell said as she got up from her desk to greet them. "Your letters to Lila were very inspiring to us."

"I meant every single thing I wrote, Nell," she said, taking Nell's hand into both of hers. "I think what you two are doing for children is just wonderful."

"Thank you," Nell said.

"And your illustrations are awesome," Gretta said. "I wish I could draw like that."

"Do you draw at all?" Nell asked.

"Yeah, I fool around a little bit," Gretta said with a bashful head tilt.

"For all the money we've put out in art lessons for you, you'd better do more than fool around," Barbara said with a good-natured chuckle that pulled everyone in.

"Well, come on over here, Gretta," Nell said, taking the girl by the hand. "Maybe you can help me put some finishing touches on the illustrations I'm working on for next week."

"Oh, cool!" And she went off eagerly behind Nell.

"Mind if I check out your computer equipment?" Sam asked Lila.

"Help yourself," she answered. And when Sam was completely out of range, she turned to Barbara and said with a smile so wide each end seemed to want to reach her ears, "I'm so glad you brought them with you. This really makes me smile."

"You were so right, Lila. I really did need to reach out to them. Every time I walked into the kitchen and saw that empty spot where my vase sat, I thought about everything you said to me that day. I realized that I had lost one child, but by closing myself off and keeping Matty's memory all to myself, I was slowly losing the children I have left."

"So I guess the three of you talked?" Lila asked as she walked with Barbara over to the *Story Hour* sofa.

"Boy, did we ever!" Barbara said, letting herself flop onto the sofa as if to take the weight of the thought off. "We talked, we cried, we yelled at one another, we accused one another. I'm telling you, Lila, it was all-out holy hell in my house. But it was so enlightening. I can't even begin to tell you how much lighter I felt after we talked with the kind of honesty we shared. And can you believe that my Sam said he actually believed that I wished it had been him who was killed instead of Matty?"

Lila gazed quizzically at Barbara at first, uncertain as to whether she was expected to answer. Considering the events of the last few months of her life, Lila thought, she could believe almost anything, particularly when it came to life, and love, and death, and the passion connected to it all. So she said, "I suppose I can believe it, Barbara, but not because of you. I guess it makes sense that Sam would feel that way because I think there's probably a lot of guilt for a surviving child."

"Survivor guilt," Barbara said quietly, as if she'd never had the thought till now. Then she stared for a flash into a far-off place and said, "Well anyway, Gretta told me that I was selfish and that I had turned our house into a cold tomb where no one laughed or even lived. And then when she told me that she's started counting the days to when she'll be able to leave home forever, Lila, I nearly died right there. What have I done? I had to ask myself." She smiled softly at Lila, took her hand in a vise of a hold, and said, "Lila, I still haven't worked out all this God business as it relates to my Matty, but I have to believe that he did work through you to bring me back to my children and them back to me, and that includes Matty."

In her mind, Lila was falling to her knees in praise for, and in deference to, something she did not completely understand, and was not certain she ever would. It was hard for her to know what had happened with this woman, who under the ordinary circumstances of her earlier mundane life she would not have let through the door. And so now here they sat, one hand in the other, and it was only in those moments when her eyes squinted, and she turned her head first this way then that, that she knew the color of what covered Barbara's was not like that which covered her. In these days since Twenty-eighth Street that once seemed to be the end of days, when the distinction in skin was to Lila as significant as the difference in two names, she was certain that something divine had been infused into that great part of her heart where color mattered, and it had come through Barbara. So she thought of this moment in which they now found themselves and the profundity of her comfort with it, and that's when she knew she need not say a word. That somehow Barbara knew in that way a mother, by virtue of the miracle of childbirth, has the mystical gift to know all.

"You don't have to say anything," Barbara finally said. "I didn't mean to choke you up. I just wanted you to know that I'm grateful for your wisdom, for your gift, and for your friendship."

"Well, thank you, Barbara," Lila said shyly. "And I thank you for something I couldn't begin to explain. Maybe when we know each other better I can tell you."

"I look forward to that."

Their moment was broken into by Sam, who asked, "Say, Lila, what kind of a resolution do you get on this printer? I'm looking to buy one to do some design work on it, but this one here looks pretty high end."

Lila stretched her smile tightly, and as her embarrassment was revealed, she said, "Oh, Sam, to tell you the truth, Nell is the techie around here. Anything technical you're going to have to ask her. I just barely know how to get and send E-mails. I'm what you call a talking head," and the hearty laugh she had at herself pushed her chagrin away.

Just then the door buzzed again and its harsh honk startled Lila so that she nearly leaped off the sofa. She looked over to Nell, who stood talking with Sam, and said, "Nell, could you buzz him in, please?"

"Sure," Nell said, leaning over to press on the button. "What did you say this guy's name is?"

"I can't remember his name," Lila said, her eyes narrowing in a panic. "He told me, but I just can't remember. I think it's something really plain and simple, though."

"Oh, that's all right," Barbara said. "He'll say it when he walks through the door, most likely. By the way, are you sure you don't mind us being here?"

"I'm positive I don't mind."

Barbara only smiled thankfully.

The reporter walked into their office with a comical, wide-eyed, fast-walking eagerness that made him appear bright green with inexperience. He was the type who looked intensely into eyes, taking eye contact to the extreme. His name was George Snodgrass, he said, and boy did he ever look to Lila like a George Snodgrass. He had the kind of cornpone bearing and pasty whiteness of someone born and reared in a place like Nebraska or Iowa. Definitely someplace wholly white, and smack in the middle of the country, where two stores on one street made it a city. Baltimore was the big city to this guy, Lila presumed. And how sad would that make his life? Lila crossed the room to greet him, and when he looked at her, the heaviness of his stare as he shook her hand forced her to look away, her eyes seeking refuge over at the file cabinet. When he freed Lila's hand, finally, from what seemed to her an interminable shake, she smiled sneakily at Nell as the man turned his attention to her.

"So are you the one who draws those incredible pictures for Lila's stories?" he asked Nell.

"Yes, that would be me," she answered while receiving his hand.

"You're really good," he said, almost deferentially. "What did you do before you started doing this?"

"I was the art director for the children's magazine *Baltimore's Kids*."

"Wow, what a talented woman you are," he said, gushing.

Nell smiled, as if confused by his enthusiasm, then humbly said, "Thank you, George."

Lila looked at George without the expectation she was actually feeling. What happened to her kudos? What happened to the praise of her talent? Was he really here to interview her about Jack, or was he really here to do the story on Nell? It wasn't that she felt Nell didn't deserve the praise. Much to the contrary. Lila believed that *Story Hour* would sound like blah-blah-blah-blah without Nell's illustrations. But, after all, her own talent was worthy of his admiration. "So, George, we should get started with the interview, because right after *Story Hour,* my husband will be giving a live interview on Channel Eleven about the NIH and their interest in him. It might be nice for all of us to watch it," Lila said proudly.

"Do you think he might announce his acceptance live on the air?" George asked with far too much interest for it to sound anything but self-serving.

"I would doubt that, George. That would presume he's been offered the position, which he hasn't. And even if he has been offered it I don't think he'd make an announcement of any sort without talking it over with me first. But I guess you just never know."

"No, I suppose you don't," George said. "But it will still be interesting to be here with you as you watch him."

So Lila led him over to the set of *Story Hour* and sat on the sofa.

Barbara had moved to the chair just outside the set but was still near enough to the sofa. She looked as if she felt odd, out of place, so Lila said, "George, this is my friend Barbara Gallagher—" Then she stopped dead in midintroduction, struck dumb by that word *friend*, which had slid from her mouth as naturally as breath. She hadn't given an extra thought to what else she might have called Barbara, but right now she had to push it away, because if she thought any more about it, she'd most certainly be unsettled by it. So she continued, "Barbara, this is George Snodgrass."

"It's a pleasure to meet you, George," Barbara said, getting up from the chair without coming to a full stand.

"It's nice to meet you as well," George said taking her hand. "Do you have children who watch *Story Hour*?"

"Well, yes," she said with a nervous chuckle. "Those two big kids over there are mine, Sam and Gretta." She paused, then looked squarely at Lila with deep eyes that spoke in their own language of glints and near squints. "I have another son who loved *Story Hour*, but he was killed last year. He was seven." And that's all she said as she set her back firmly against the chair, as if proud, very proud.

"I'm so sorry to hear that," George said with as much empathy as a detached reporter can give. "How was he killed?"

"In a car accident."

Lila lowered herself onto the sofa to distract George from trying to sniff out the story of Matty's death and its connection to *Lila Lilly's Story Hour*. Sitting all the way on the end, she gave George enough room for his pad and his tape recorder and himself, enough room for him to spread out and be comfortable, thought it never occurred to her that maybe she'd need to be relaxed as well. And she would see to that when, just as he informed her that he was about to turn on his tape recorder, Lila said, "Before we start, I'd like to set some ground rules. I will not answer questions about pride in Jack being the first *black* doctor to be asked to fill the post. I will also not answer any personal questions about our married life. It's nobody's business."

And with her rules thrown down before him, George looked positively stricken, as if he were rewriting every single question he had for her. Then, in hesitant agreement, he said, "Okay, well sure, Lila. That's not a problem." He paused as if with second thoughts, then said, "So, tell me something, why aren't you interested in discussing your husband as the first black man to be appointed to the post, if indeed he were to be appointed? It seems to me to be quite an accomplishment."

"Because it's simply not a pertinent issue," Barbara said, speaking without being spoken to, but clearly vexed. "Why do you people always want to make race an issue? If he were white, would you be writing about how he's the fiftieth or sixtieth white man to be appointed to the position?"

"Of course not, because a white man would be expected to have that position, and that's exactly my point. Finally blacks in this country are being considered as equals in professions like medicine. We don't make it an issue, Mrs. Gallagher. It's already out there as an issue, and that's not going to change."

"Well, if blacks are indeed being treated equally in professions like medicine, then by your own argument things have already changed, so why do all you media types need to exploit it?"

George laughed nervously, as if what he was about to say was not what he wanted to say. "Exploit it? I think those are pretty harsh words, which people have become far too comfortable at tossing around cavalierly. We write about it because it's a fact of life that yes, while blacks are making strides in certain professions, this country still has a long way to go to make race immaterial, and until that happens, I think people like myself have a duty to this society to write about it. By your own argument of race not being an issue, should the *Sun* papers not have reported about what happened over the summer with that racist who was essentially killed by his own hatred?"

"That's different," Barbara said, as if praying that he would not ask how.

But he did. "And how is it different? It's about a white man who could have been saved by a black man who may or may not have been a doctor. That's how race is still lived in America, Barbara."

"But that's vileness. That kind of contemptible thing could not go unheard."

"All I'm saying," George said, first to Barbara, then turning to Lila to continue, "is that Jack Calloway, a black man, being appointed to the National Institutes of Health is the victory at the end of what happened over the summer."

Lila thought about Barbara's word *contemptible*, and in her forehead creased the question of on which man Barbara had cast her contempt. But before it could set her own heart against her new friend, she put the thought aside for another day and said, "It's an accomplishment, George, because he's a talented and dedicated doctor who's loyal to his patients and to his profession. His blackness is merely a happenstance of birth and nothing for which he can take credit. And anyway, why does it matter? Just as Barbara said, the fact that you write about it, make a big deal about it, makes it more important than it needs to be. It's a throwback question, throwing us back to the days when men like Jack were considered anomalies by white standards. Well, my husband is not an anomaly, George, and he's far too gifted a doctor to have this whole experience reduced to his color."

"Lila, there are a lot of people who would say that we're still living in throwback times, that nothing has changed. Like that guy who died over there on Twenty-eighth Street a few months back. That's a man who, by the way things seem, caused his own death because of the nasty things he'd said to that man who might have been able to save his life. Maybe if he hadn't reduced that man to nothing but his color that racist would still be alive, but he did reduce him to nothing but his color, so your husband being so strongly considered for this post is, I must tell you, a big deal, and his color does play a large part in it. What happened over the summer goes to show just how big a part being black plays in all of this."

Lila disengaged from him without even knowing what was happening to her, without knowing for certain that she had floated away. She wanted George and his thoughts on the matter of color as far away from her as that dead fat man had gone. Why, in the grand scheme of simile, did he have to go back to what happened on Twenty-eighth Street, particularly this man, of all people, whom she'd known for all of fifteen minutes? She looked across the room at Nell to find Nell's eyes panicked, checking to see if Lila was okay. So to show Nell, and to show herself, Lila said, "So we can start whenever you're ready."

At that, George turned on his tape recorder and asked Lila his first question of how *Lila Lilly's Story Hour* was born. And even though she thought about how the article was supposed to be about Jack, she assumed the question to be for background. So Lila spoke of the birth in such a measured way that it was clear she had told the story far too many times for it to hold anything exciting and new for her anymore. As the questions piled one on top of the other, her mind wandered further away—to Jack and his imminent interview, to what he might say, to whether he would come home later and tell her he'd be accepting the NIH position. And between those moments when she was fully present for George, she'd even let herself wonder if they'd have to move to Bethesda, which she'd always considered a no-man's-land whose name alone made her think of cows and horses. She imagined this for absolutely no other reason except for the fact that she'd never been there.

So now, when George asked her why she didn't just publish her stories the traditional way through a publishing company instead of putting them out there essentially freely on the Internet, Lila wanted the interview to be over right then and there.

But she replied, "Well, George, I've never published in the traditional way because I feel that by putting my stories on the Internet, I can reach more children, and after all, that's what this is all about for me: reaching children and making a difference in their lives."

"And so what about children? Tell me about your love for children, because that has come across loud and clear in everything you've said to me."

With this question the interview took a turn in a direction that came closer than any other to stirring her. "I love children, George. That's why I became a teacher. That's why I do this. Children are the only creatures on this earth that give you the rawness of their hearts in the form of truth. We need to watch and learn from children to see how we can keep that part of us that we're born with. Do you know how much ugliness could be eliminated if we only kept intact the child's heart that we were born with?" She stopped, not to wait for an answer, but to think about what she'd said and how it would read. The answers to previous questions, she thought, seemed like so much puff and fluff simply because the questions were. And it made her imagine that the interview was for some trifling section of the paper that didn't dig too deep or ask too much, but kept things light and trite. That's why she couldn't fathom, even as the words were tumbling from her mouth, how she could say, "More than anything I want children. I sometimes think about what I'd do to their little imaginations, and how I'd guide them in such a way that they'd never let their child's heart fade away."

But now, it was clear that she was talking from outside the space of reason within the context of what she was supposed to be doing. Yes, she'd asked him to steer completely clear of personal questions, and what did she do? She brought him right into the most personal part of herself. No one else would ever have done something so stupid. Wearing the rawest part of her heart on her sleeve, she thought, had turned her into her own worst enemy, and she was stabbing herself in the back. So as she hovered her flattened palm over the tape recorder, as if that alone would erase what she'd just said, she asked, "Can you strike that part I just said, the part about me wanting children? I really don't want something that personal to appear in the article."

"Sure, Lila," George said, as if he knew she'd gone further than she wanted to go. "That's no problem."

Just then, Nell had to interrupt. It was time for *Story Hour*. So Lila asked George if he wouldn't mind moving, not expecting at all for him to scamper from the sofa as if he'd just been scorned.

And as she began *Story Hour*, she felt her nerves as she had never felt them before. She felt watched as she had never felt watched on ordinary days when she knew that millions of eyes were on her. But just having four extra pairs of eyes expecting her to shine set a squall off in her innards. Then, after a while, with them being so still and mute, they became to her like mannequins, and eventually furniture.

As she brought *Story Hour* to a close, she saw that George seemed somehow inspired. It was clear to Lila from the corner of her eye that he had been riveted all along to her every word, either for the story itself, or for the novelty of what she was doing. Whatever it was that drew his fascination, it was obvious that she had charmed him.

Once Nell had turned off the camera and Lila was off the air, or off the Net, as the case may be, George said, "Lila, that was just fantastic. And I mean that."

"Oh, Lila, it really was wonderful," Barbara said. Sam and Gretta agreed in unison.

"What I want to know is, why don't you take it to the networks, or at least to the local stations?" George asked. "Or how about Maryland Public Television? It seems to me that they would love something like this. An interactive *Story Hour*. I mean this could really go places."

"George, do you know how much control we'd lose if we were to do any of that? It would become someone else's. Right here in this room, we're small, and it's just us, and it's a lot of work, but we're in control. Besides, the Internet is the way to go. Eventually, the Internet won't be an alternative to television, it'll be a competitor, if it isn't already."

"You may quote her," Nell said with a chuckle at the way Lila's words seemed to insinuate profundity.

"Oh, no!" Lila said frantically, jolting the laughter in the room to a dead stop. "It's five past five. Turn on the TV. Jack will be on soon. Channel Eleven."

George's reason for being there, to talk about Jack, had never been fulfilled, and this was clear as he seemed, now, just to be hanging around without purpose. And then he found his purpose. "I would really love it if I could stay and watch the interview with you. I mean, after all, it would be a very intriguing part of the story, to have your reaction, your response, in your exact and immediate words as it happens."

"Okay," Lila said without a second thought. "That sounds reasonable." Just then, some commotion in the hallway outside the office distracted her. "What on earth is that?" she said as two determined knocks came at the door. Her heart jumped, not so much with fear, but with a certain amount of alarm. After all, this was certainly not the norm.

Nell went toward the door, as if she was certain, she knew who might be the source of the mishmash of the muffled commotion. She opened the door, and just as a mother always knows, there was not only her daughter standing there, but also the rest of her brood, and her husband, too. "What in the world are all of you doing here?" Nell said, surprised, but not unpleasantly so.

Chuck walked behind the boys through the door, whose long faces told that they were still simmering from an argument with one another. "Get in there, and stop acting like this. I'm sick of the two of you fighting," Chuck said sternly.

"Chuckie started it," John-David said of his older brother. "He's always acting like he's the boss of everything."

"I am not, John-David. Why don't you just shut up, because you're the one who—" They were both cut off by their father.

"Knock it off, you two!" Chuck snapped, in his no-nonsense voice. Then his face was brought to a smile by little Adia, the youngest of them all, who had gone to Nell's desk and tucked herself quietly out of the line of her brothers' fire.

"What is it with those two this time?" Nell said to Chuck.

"Oh, the usual. You don't even want to know."

"You're right, I don't. So just keep me blissfully ignorant," Nell said, pecking Chuck quickly on the lips.

"Well, what brings us here is that I finished up early at the hospital and thought I'd come home, give the baby-sitter a break, and you, too, by taking the kids to dinner. Even these ruffians," he said, cutting a shameful eye at his sons. "Anyway, I thought that since you have to eat, maybe you would want to come along. Make it a family night out."

"Well, I would love that. But do we have to go right now? Jack's going to be interviewed in a few minutes on Channel Eleven, and I kind of wanted to hang around to see it."

"Oh, wow, that's today? I completely forgot. I'm glad we came by, because I'd like to see it myself." Then Chuck turned to his sons and barked the orders that would force a truce. "Chuckie, you go over there and sit at Lila's desk. John-David, you go over there and sit on the sofa. I don't want to hear a peep out of either of you." And he stood firmly as they followed his command.

"Daddy, is it all right if I play *Reader Rabbit* on Mommy's computer?" Adia asked sweetly.

"Sure, baby," Chuck said.

Then John-David mocked his sister with an exaggerated baby voice under his breath, but clearly with the intention of being heard. "Daddy, is it all right if I play *Reader Rabbit* on Mommy's computer?"

"I'm warning you, John-David. You'd better knock it off," Chuck said.

"John-David, will you just do what your father tells you?" Nell said. And with her boys' ire settled down for the time being, she made introductions. "Barbara, Gretta, Sam, George, this is my husband, Chuck, and my two sons, Chuckie and John-David, and my daughter, Adia."

"Adia," Barbara said as if it conjured a memory. "That's such a beautiful name. It makes me think of the song by Sarah McLaughlin."

Nell only smiled without a clue and continued, "Barbara is a friend of Lila's and a fan of *Story Hour*. George is from the *Sun* papers. He's here to interview Lila for a story about Jack."

"He's on," Lila bellowed across the room, as she scooted over to make room for John-David.

"Boy, is he handsome, Lila," Barbara said.

"Yeah," said Gretta, blushing with new pubescent hormones.

As the interview began, Jack seemed at ease and in control of himself, which calmed Lila, since this was the first time she'd turned on the television in months without a fear that they'd still be talking about what happened on Twenty-eighth Street. And so when she saw him smile, so did she, mostly because he was speaking of himself so presently, so truthfully, speaking of himself as the healer, not the Jack who left someone to die. After all the healer is the full man, and the food of his full spirit was his joy in healing.

"Lila, you look so proud," George said.

"Of course I'm proud," she said without looking at him. Then she snatched her eyes from Jack briefly, only long enough to say, "But not for the reasons you may think." And she laughed, barely.

"Hell, we're all proud," Chuck said. "We'd be proud even if we didn't know him. To have a black man's dedication to his work recognized in this way is a hell of a thing."

And George only looked at Lila with a self-satisfied grin that he was careful not to let her see.

Lila was riveted, anyway, so even if he were in direct eye-shot, she wouldn't have noticed his self-righteous grin at all. She was with Jack all the way, and with every question. She was so deeply planted in his mind that she answered every question he was asked, nearly word for word, but only in her own mind. It was as if she gave him thoughts telepathically. And then they reached a point where she was stumped, and she just knew Jack had to be as well.

The interviewer asked Jack, and unknowingly, Lila, "Your career has brought you to this point, but what I'd like to know, Dr. Calloway, is that with your stellar and unbelievably impressive record as a doctor, is there anything in your career you regret?"

And without wasting a second of airtime, Jack answered, soberly, clearly, and without a trace of emotion. "Well, yes. We all have regrets, don't we? What I regret most is leaving that man to die a rather inhumane death on Twenty-eighth Street back in July. That was me. I was the one who left him there, and if I were to be granted that day to live again, I definitely would have done what I could to help him live." Then Jack just sat there staring into eyes that had frozen on him with shock.

"What?!" Chuck said, his voice echoing through the room so loudly it almost reached a high-pitched scream.

"SSSHHH," everyone said, even John-David.

So, in what seemed to be an act of kindness to his interviewer to stave off dead air, Jack continued, "So, now you can understand why I've been so evasive in your questions about whether I will accept the post at the NIH if it's offered to me. As much as I would like to make a commitment, there's a larger issue that needs to be sorted out before I can do that. And now that everyone knows that I was the doctor with the questionable ethics, or the hero who helped rid the world of one more deplorable redneck, depending on your perspective, we'll have to wait and see if I'm still the golden boy in the light of tomorrow."

Jack had given the man just enough time to recover, so he asked Jack next, "So, Dr. Calloway, what happened that day?"

"I let my bruised ego and my pride stand in the way of my Hippocratic oath. I let a man's vile words break my spirit to the point where I forgot why I'm here, and why I do what I do." And perhaps that's when Jack decided that he didn't want to, or maybe shouldn't, say another word. So he stood up, took his microphone off his lapel, and said, "If you don't mind, I'd like to end this interview. I hope you understand." He was gone inside of a second.

"Okay, now," Lila said, chipper and upbeat, and it wasn't at all an act. She felt as light as her voice. "So now we all know, and we can put the mystery to rest. And, George, I'm sure you've seen probably more than you expected, so we'll let you get on your way to write your article."

"Lila, come on," George said, pleading like a man used to begging. "You've got to talk to me. This is some pretty big stuff that just happened, and I need to know if you knew."

"What is it they say?" she asked, turning to Chuck.

"No comment." Then Chuck, using nothing more than his

demeanor, walked toward George to escort him away from Lila and toward the door.

And Sam was right behind Chuck with the strength of his determined youth bound to protect Lila Lilly.

"Can you just tell me if you knew?" George asked.

Lila remained silent.

"No comment, George," Chuck said, still trying to herd the man out the door. "Maybe next week she'll call you and answer your questions. But *she'll* call *you*."

"Will you, Lila? Can you at least call me next week?" George said, willing to accept that scrap of hope if only she'd tell him so.

But Lila only nodded that she would, then gave him a faint wave good-bye with three fluttering fingers.

As soon as Chuck closed the door, he locked the dead bolt, as if he were taking prisoners, then said, "Lila, what the hell was that? What was Jack talking about, he was the man?"

"For God's sake, Chuck," Nell said, annoyed at something. No one could tell what. "What didn't you understand in what Jack said? He said it plainly enough."

"Nell, I understood him. Okay? What I'm not understanding is how he could walk around here for all these months and not tell me something like that. And judging by the fact that you don't seem so surprised, Nell, I guess I can assume that you knew, too."

Lila pressed her eyes into Nell, who only looked down at her shoes, as if feeling her due shame at keeping it from her husband. It was difficult to fully know, but Nell seemed mad to Lila, and Lila knew exactly why. Of all the ways even Lila had imagined Chuck's finding out—and most of them were visions of Jack sitting Chuck down and just telling him—this had to have been the worst way, considering all that Jack and Chuck had been to each other. Friends, school chums, roommates, colleagues, best friends. And it all came down to Chuck's feeling a hurt, she believed, he could not possibly comprehend fully.

Lila crossed the room to get her purse from where it hung on the standing coat hanger. Barbara followed her, with Gretta

lagging behind them both with a slackened jaw and a stupe-
fied stare. Barbara said, "Lila, I'm so sorry. I had no idea you
were living with something so painful. What a thing to have
happen."

And Lila still couldn't be sure of Barbara's loyalties, and it was
more critical now than it was an hour before for her to know.
So she turned to face Barbara to find Gretta's eyes peeking at
her just over Barbara's shoulder. "Barbara, let me ask you something. When you called what happened with that man and Jack
a contemptible thing, where were you putting your contempt,
with Jack or that fat racist?"

Barbara stared flatly at Lila, as if she had shut off every emotion in her with a blink. "Lila, I think it was contemptible that
that man had to die the way he lived, and I think it's contemptible that Jack made the choice he made. All of it is shameful if you ask me. I'm sorry, and I know this isn't what you want
to hear, but the way I see it, there's no one side or the other
with this."

All Lila could do right then was respect her, and love her
from the morsel that was growing with every day they shared.
How easy would it have been, she thought, for Barbara to give
her one of those Milquetoast answers, telling her what she
wanted to hear. Instead Barbara shared her truth in spite of consequences unknown. Friend. So Lila simply said, "Okay." More
words would have been untrue to what she really felt. She
smiled softly and then said, "Well, I have my life back now, so I
was thinking that you and the kids should come have dinner
with me and Jack some evening. I haven't been home yet to
know for sure, but I have a hunch my house has life in it now."

"I would love that, Lila. I really, really would," Barbara said,
leaning toward Lila for an embrace.

"Me, too," Gretta said, touching Lila's arm, as if she wanted in
on the hug.

Lila released herself from Barbara, slung her purse on her
shoulder, turned to Chuck, and said, "Chuck, I'm sorry you had
to find out about it like this, but if it is any comfort to you, any
comfort at all, Jack didn't even tell me, and I was there." Then

she smiled contentedly, leaving him with quite the conundrum to ponder. Then to Nell she said, "Can you shut down everything and lock up without me? I'm going to be needed at home, and very soon."

"Sure, just go," Nell said.

And she did go, taking with her the vision of Chuck's eyes as she closed the door. They were mixed with the confusion, and hurt, and shame, and pride that she'd known far too well, and for far too long. And it all took flight and left her forever on the wings of Jack's words that went out all over Baltimore. Free.

chapter nineteen

JACK STOOD AT the door with his key frozen only inches from the lock, wondering if going in would actually be the most prudent thing for him to do. Certainly, he did not want what Lila was certain to have waiting for him, considering how he had, just an hour before, taken away their freedom of anonymity, turning them into fodder for anyone within earshot of Baltimore to lambaste. He might find her in an enraged state of confusion, or he might find her totally defeated. Then again, he thought, he just might not find her at all. The chances were good that she had run—run to her office, or to Nell, or maybe even to her mother in Florida. It didn't much matter as long as her escape let him suspend her inexorable fury.

Just as he took his blind comfort in stepping into an empty house and was about to slide his key in the lock, he felt commotion nearby and could tell it was for him. All he needed was a half glance over his shoulder to see a camera pointing at him from the sidewalk, on its way down the path to make him turn that key and open that door, as if he were trying to escape with his life intact. On the other side, in the comfort of safety, he turned both locks swiftly, their hard thwacks showing his determination.

"I've already closed all the blinds and curtains," Lila said, from where she stood behind him. She didn't intend to give him a fright and make him jump nearly clean from his shoes, but then she seemed to have no idea that his mind had sent her and what he presumed to be her rage away. "We'll be prisoners in here for a few days, then somebody else will do something and they'll go crawling off to feed on them. You'll see."

Jack took his time turning to see her. Her words were benevolent, her voice soft and without antipathy, but her eyes could still attack, as they had for months, and then launch the contempt, in thought and deed along with words that would come hard and fast, shot from where they'd been pent up for all this time. So, when he could finally see her, he could not identify the surface of what he felt, but fear, or something very close to it, was the very next layer. And what she'd say is not what frightened him as much as his belief that what he did in front of Baltimore in the name of cleansing his soul would ultimately end up breaking Lila—from herself, and from that part of him where she was always present. Then there would have been no point to his purge at all, because his life would be over.

"So I guess you saw the interview today," he said quietly.

"I did. And so did Chuck, and so you're going to need to deal with him soon. He's really pissed at you," she said, unable to choke back a laugh. "He doesn't understand why he was the only one of us who didn't know about it. Oh, you should have seen him. He was so pathetic. I'll tell you, Nell has got something on her hands tonight with him."

"So you told Nell?" Jack said, surprised that she'd betrayed her own confidence in such a way.

"No, I didn't actually tell her. It's somewhat of a long story, but she just figured it out."

"Well, you've got to remember to tell me that story in its entirety, because I can't even begin to imagine how she could have figured it out."

"Well, she did." Lila went to Jack in two steps and took his hand. She led him into the living room, over to the sofa where she seemed to have to force his body, apparently stiffened from the shock of everything, to sit with her. "Anyway, I'm glad you did what you did. I know it must have been the most difficult thing you've ever had to do."

"Actually, Lila, you want to know something? It wasn't. It just came out. I hadn't planned it, hadn't planned it at all. I was just sitting there, and it came out just as naturally as my name." Then he settled back on the sofa, taking Lila with him in his arms. "And I want you to know, baby, that that's what happened that day. What I did, leaving that man to die, seemed as natural to me as anything else I do in life, and that was wrong, I know now, but in that moment, Lila, it seemed so right. I wouldn't have tried to save the life of a dying roach, because there'd be no point to it, and that's exactly where my head was that day. That man was like a roach dying on its back with its feet up in the air, needing only for someone to flip it back on its legs so it could go on living. But who in their right mind would flip a roach over so it could live? And that day I thought, Who in their right mind would let this vile thing live? I was emotional, I was passionate, and I wasn't thinking, and the only forgiveness that matters to me is yours. I just hope you can forgive me for doing this to us."

Lila burrowed in closer to Jack, inhaled deeply, taking in a strong whiff of hospital, then blew it out. At first she didn't think she'd need to answer, because certainly he'd know he was forgiven. "I forgive you, Jack. And I forgive myself, because for as much as my self-righteous resentment said that you should have done what was right, most of me that was wrapped up in anger and hurt left him there to die, too. I was just so. . . ."

"Let's just leave it at that," Jack said evenly. They had already lost so much of their time, of themselves, of their love, wallowing in this, and to spend another minute down in the dredges of the details of their emotions seemed equally as wasteful. "We should just enjoy this tranquility that we have right here, because our lives are going to get very noisy before we'll hear this much quiet again."

And they sat in the still oasis of the room and each other, hearing but not hearing the sounds of the increasing pack forming on their front lawn. Lila had thought of everything. Every blind was drawn—every one except the ones in the kitchen.

She thought to rush in there in that moment and make their iso-
lation complete, but right here beside Jack was where she
belonged. She had remembered to unplug every phone; she did
not want the wrong person getting through to them, but mostly,
she didn't want to hear the shrill of her stepmother's voice, who
was certain to hear all of it within the hour. There were enough
people whose judgments weren't worth a nickel to her; but Lila
certainly didn't need, and positively could not accept in that
raw moment, Eulelie's judgment.

The seclusion made Lila feel safe from what she could hear
and imagine. Every now and then, the mutterings of reporters
with no other story to chase would drift in and out of her consciousness, and she envisioned them staring desperately at the
door, pathetically clutching their microphones at the ready for
something that would simply not happen. There was something
fun about it, and it filled her with the excitement of not knowing what might happen next. It was Lila and Jack against the
world. She even thought she heard one of them at the back
door. They were totally surrounded. This was the closest she'd
ever come to being a bad girl, and it gave her an odd, yet still
vicarious, out-of-body thrill. Then, without any warning, she
was jolted when Jack sprung forward with an immediacy that
gave her a genuine fright.

"Did you hear that?" he said.

"Hear what?"

"Somebody's at the back door."

"It's probably just one of those reporters. You know how they
skulk around everywhere, like gutter rats, trying to get fed." But
when the back door opened, she was stilled by a terror that
knew positively no bounds. "Jack, that I heard."

But Jack was already on his feet and in a combative,
confrontational, ready-to-shove-a-microphone-somewhere-unspeakable
deportment. "Who the hell is it?" he said, his pumped-up chest
going angrily before him as he stormed into the kitchen.

"It's me, man," Chuck said, his hands in midair like a perpe-
trator or even a useless burglar. "We drove by earlier and saw

the camp-out on your front lawn. I dropped Nell and the kids off and thought I'd come by to see what you need."

So, with Jack now breathing again, he said, "Oh, wow, Chuck, thanks, man. To tell you the truth, I don't know what I need right now. I just know that I need them away from my house, but there's nothing you can do about that."

"Well, don't be so sure," Chuck said, locking the dead bolt in the kitchen. He then went to all the kitchen windows and drew the blinds closed. "It'll only be a matter of time before those idiots realize there's a back to the house and then start swarming out here." When he finished, he turned to Jack, folded his arms, and leaned against the counter. "Now, I wouldn't be so sure that I can't help with getting them out of here. You may not be ready to talk to them right now, but I can certainly go out there, you know, like the family friend, and give them a statement from you."

"That actually sounds reasonable, but I'm not sure if I have anything more to say to them than I've already said over at Channel Eleven. What more do they want me to say?"

"I don't even think they know. I guarantee you, if I go out there and read a statement, lo and behold one of them will ask a question that was answered in the statement, or that you already answered on Channel Eleven. But you've got to give them something."

"Yeah, but they're like alley dogs in a situation like this, man. You feed them once, and they're right back a few minutes later looking for another treat." Jack thought for a second, then started to leave the kitchen. "Okay, I guess you're right. I should give them something. Maybe Lila can help."

When they got into the living room, Lila was already settled back onto the sofa, since she'd already figured out that it had been Chuck who disturbed their silence and entered their sanctum. Somehow, she felt even safer, calmer, with Chuck there. Something about him told her that he'd take care of things. This is where his charm would really work for good, and not for vanity. "Hi, Chuck. How'd you give them the slip?"

"I grew up streetwise, Lila," he said, laughing to add something light to the midweight air. "I know how to sneak in and out of the backs of places. Nobody's back there, though, you know." He sat near the window, seeming a bit disturbed by the drawn curtains, since the view of Charles Street from his seat had never been hindered by drawn curtains. "Damn those reporters," he said beneath his breath. "Okay, do you want to write it down, what you want me to say, or is it just going to be a few lines that I'll be able to remember?"

"I guess you can just say . . ."

But Lila stopped Jack before he could get to the business of shooing reporters away. She whispered, even though Chuck could hear her. "Jack, don't you think you should talk to Chuck and explain why you didn't tell him about this sooner?"

"Ah, listen, I was pissed off before," Chuck said, embarrassed by his earlier display of shock. "But Nell and I talked over dinner, and I understand now where your head must have been. There's no need to explain anything."

"No, Chuck. Lila's right. I do owe you an explanation. And the best one I can give you is that I wasn't even sure what I would say to you. How I would explain it. There was a part of me that didn't believe I could have done what I did."

"I can totally see that. I was telling Nell, and I said it even before I knew it was you and what he said to you, I know that my scruples wouldn't have been able to pass a test like that. Some racist son of a bitch is going to stand there and call me Dr. Porch Monkey and then expect me to save his life a few minutes later? I damned sure would have wielded my power."

"Well, that's just the thing, Chuck. I didn't wield any power, not really, by leaving him there. I didn't prove a damned thing, except that maybe when it comes down to it, I'm really no different from that man in the way that I allowed my disgust of him to keep me from seeing him as a human being."

"No, Jack. His status as a human being is still in question, if you ask me."

Jack didn't say anything for a few seconds, and it wasn't clear if he ever would. Then with slowness he said, "I guess you have to live through it and come out on the other side to understand." He stood up for no apparent reason and continued. "Okay, so listen. Why don't you go out there and just tell them that what I did by leaving that man to die was a regretful episode in my life, and that I am haunted by the wrongful choice I made that day. Tell them that I send my deepest sympathy to his family and I hope this incident is something that, in time, we all will be able to learn from and heal. That's it." Jack sat back down next to Lila and took her hand.

"I think that sounds good, Jack," Lila said. "Very sincere. They can't expect any more than that."

Chuck was scribbling something on the back of a piece of paper he'd taken out of his jacket pocket. He stood and went toward the hallway but stopped just short of leaving the living room to turn and say, "So, you're sure this is what you want me to say for you?" His eyes were skeptical, his reflexive near smile equally so, as if he didn't agree, or believe, or respect.

And Jack saw it all. "That's the truth, so that's what I want to say." He watched Chuck until he disappeared behind the wall. When the door opened, the voice of someone yelling with far too much enthusiasm skittled into the room. "The door's opening!" And shortly after Chuck's voice followed. And Chuck read from his script, syllable for syllable, word for word, but without one hint that his heart or mind had grasped any of it.

When Chuck came back into the living room after shutting and latching the door, he sat down in the chair farthest from the sofa where Jack and Lila sat and said, "Well, that's over with. I guess now we just wait and see what the rest of the fallout might be. Why don't you turn on the television and let's see what they're talking about."

Jack took the remote from where it sat on the edge of the coffee table and clicked on the television. "Which channel?"

"Eleven. That's where the story first broke, so they probably have the most coverage."

Jack flipped channels until he came to it. He narrowed his eyes, then looked sideways at the old white-haired, white-faced, pink-nosed man whose face filled the screen. "Who's that?" he asked, as if Lila and Chuck would know what he did not.

"I don't know," Lila said. And then, as the camera pulled away from the man's face, Lila sat straight up from where she slumped and pointed. "But look at those two men standing next to him. That's the son and the other man. Remember?"

Jack only nodded. "So what's going on?"

"Turn it up a little," Chuck commanded, as if it were urgent.

And the reporter was saying, ". . . so I am here with James Potite Sr., the father of James Potite Jr., who has shocking and baffling news coming directly on the heels of Dr. Jack Calloway's admission that he was indeed the doctor who left this man's son to die on Twenty-eighth Street last summer. Mr. Potite, you say that Dr. Calloway was not the man who denied assistance to your son as he lay dying on the street?"

"That's right, and I can prove it. These here are my grandsons, and they was right there, him wit his daddy and him wit his uncle till the moment my boy died. They seen it all, and I don't know why Dr. Calloway would say such a thing. Maybe he's trying to take the blame for somebody else, or maybe, just like me, he wants y'all to just shut up 'bout this already and leave it alone. Now y'all keep talking 'bout this and that and how the autopsy was showin' if this Dr. Calloway had used that difib . . . whatever you call that thing, then my Jimmy would still be alive. Well, I don't know, and y'all don't know neither. Don't nobody know for sure and can't nobody really say but God whether he'd still be alive. But I do know that that Dr. Calloway ain't the one y'all is lookin' for, ain't that right, Ernie?" and the old man turned to the man standing closest to his side whose expression was too undefined to read.

And then, without looking at his grandfather, without even looking directly into the camera, and as if he'd just gotten the Pavlovian command that would prompt him to speak he said, "Yeah, Grandpa, that's right. He ain't the one."

The camera stayed on Ernie, since his face was where the truth lived, while James Potite Sr. said, "And so now, if y'all had any sense at all, you'd just leave it alone. My boy's gone and that's that. Findin' that man ain't gonna make one bit a difference and doin' all this talkin' 'bout how Jimmy could still be alive ain't helpin' nothin' in the least. God knows who the man is and he knows what he did, and I believe in his justice, not yours."

That was all James Potite Sr. had to say. So the reporter wrapped up. "Well, that's it from here, Rob. Back to you at the studio."

Jack turned off the television without saying a word. Lila and Chuck were on him with their questioning eyes and would not let him go, but they still weren't powerful enough to get from him the words he didn't have to say. He got up from where he sat and looked out the window to find all the reporters who'd just moments before seemed as if they'd be permanent fixtures in his front yard scampering into their news vans and onto their next prey, like gutter rats to the next trash heap.

Lila broke her eyes away from Jack to see Chuck, and then she simply didn't want to see either one of them. It couldn't come together for her; except that all of it had only made sense to her existentially, ever since that day on Twenty-eighth Street when Jack's free will and free choice rose up against a microcosm of a harsh world, with that one unique episode happening in the grand scheme of life, only to her and Jack. But with James Potite Sr.'s proclamation just now to all of Baltimore, she and Jack could easily have been living all this time in a parallel universe. That's the only way that Jack could possibly have not been the one they saw. That, though, only happens in film noir, she thought, where anything unrealistic goes. What she and Jack had lived was very real, with a smell, and a touch, and a taste, and an image, all of which taunted. And now, here come these men, two of whom smelled, touched, tasted, and saw just as she had, saying that it wasn't Jack. And if Jack's contribution to the death of a redneck was all in his mind, and if Jack was not who the men saw, then what about her mind and her eyes?

Then through the silence Chuck said so softly it may not have been meant for anyone but him to hear, "I will just be damned. What the hell was that?"

But as Jack walked to the room's aperture, the only thing he would say was "Well, now." And he went up the stairs as if his feet weren't touching the earth.

BY THE NEXT day they were back like locusts, those reporters. Not in numbers as large as the day before, but still with a thinned-out presence that made them seem both diligent and pathetic. Lila had made herself believe that with the twist James Potite Sr. had put into their lives, not one of those microphone wielders would know what to think, what to say, what to ask. She believed this until the cool light of dawn along with the ringing of her doorbell at seven in the morning slapped her in the face. And even though no one had ever rung their bell that early in the morning, Lila still went skipping down the steps as if she knew exactly who'd be on the other side.

When she swung open the door, sweeping it wide in welcome, a woman whose face she knew but whose name she couldn't summon smiled with fakeness, then let it evaporate and said, "Mrs. Calloway, can you tell us why your husband says he was the doctor who left James Potite Jr. to die on Twenty-eighth Street back in July, yet James Potite Sr. and his grandsons say he wasn't there?"

Lila stood there too dazed to do what she needed to do. All she could manage to extract from her mind to say was, "Uhh, uhh, I just—" But then she heard a commotion behind her and saw a commotion coming toward her, and stillness overpowered her. Then she regained some part of her equilibrium when she realized the commotion behind her was Jack.

"We have absolutely no comment," Jack said strongly as he slammed the door so close to the woman it was a wonder her toes weren't poking through the bottom of the door. "Are you all right?" he asked Lila as he took her in his arms.

But she didn't know what to say immediately, because there

was still the haze of the commotion that had been coming toward her. She thought it was her mother, but it couldn't have been, not at seven in the morning and among a half-full yard of hungry reporters, and especially not, she believed, she hoped, without sufficient notice. Perhaps it was only her mind playing tricks, as it would if she were desperate for water in the middle of a desert, but in that moment, she was certain her mother was trying to get to her.

The doorbell rang again as Jack was trying to usher Lila into the living room. And before he could see to it that she was tucked away on the sofa, a series of frenzied pounds fell on the door that drew Jack to it with angry steps.

But before he could get there, the voice coming through the cracks said, "Lila, Jack, it's me, Mother. Let me in."

"Jack, it's my mother," Lila said as if he couldn't hear for himself. "I thought I saw her out there, but I wasn't sure. Let her in."

Jack opened the door only wide enough for a body the size of Eulelie's to slide through. Once she was through, he tried to shut it right up behind her but met with resistance. "Come on!" Jack yelled. "This is our home! You're going too far!"

But then the voice from the other side said, "Jack, it's me, Gil."

And Jack let the door give enough to let Gil in, then shut and locked it. He followed them into the living room without asking the obvious question.

"Momma, Gil, what are you two doing here at seven o'clock in the morning? Momma, what are you doing in Baltimore?"

"Well, I'm here for the two of you," Eulelie said. "Where else would a mother be at this time? Of course, I thought we'd be able to beat the reporters here."

"What are you doing here this early in the morning?" Lila leaned over her lap and put her forehead in her hands. "I'm just so confused."

"I got a flight out yesterday as soon as I heard. Gil got me from the airport and I stayed with him last night," Eulelie said.

"She insisted on coming up," Gil said to Lila, almost apologetically.

"Now Gil told me everything that happened, and I think it's horrible that you had to go through that, Jack," Eulelie said, going to Jack with a sympathetic hand on his shoulder.

"Well, it wasn't all that awful, Eulelie," Jack said plainly as he moved himself away from her touch. And if anyone had been listening carefully to the layers of his voice, they would have heard that he was just barely on the other side of being annoyed with Eulelie's presence. "I mean, after all, I'm not the one who's dead."

But Gil seemed to get Jack's true feelings, as he was the only one who lowered his head and chuckled lightly where no one could see him.

"Now don't you start talking like that," Eulelie said. "There's no reason at all why you should feel guilty about that man's death. He brought it on himself. So this is what I think we need to do, now that that man says it wasn't you. I think—"

"Momma, what do you mean by *we*?"

"I'm here to help, honey. What do you think I mean?"

"I'm not sure. But if you've come all the way up here to help us devise some sort of plan, you're so wrong. This will go away in its time, but we're not about to engage in a game of talk volleyball with the press. The truth is what it is, Momma. That's one thing that's not going to change. We're happy with that, and we don't need to say another thing."

Eulelie let out a massive sigh, then said, "Honey, all you're doing by being so passive is giving them the leeway to come up with their own answers. Now, the way I see it is that you can go ahead and take the high road and not say anything, or you can back up what that man's father said and come up with a story as to why Jack made the admission. In doing that, Jack will still be able to move on to that post at the NIH. That's the prize, Lila. You've got to keep your eye on that prize." She stopped, then walked across the room, peeked out the drawn curtains, and sat in the chair in front of the window. She looked at Jack and said, "They're still out there. Now listen, the way I see it, that man's father gave you the best way to back up what he said and slide out of that crazy admission of yours, and that is to say that you just wanted the whole mess to come to an end, and you thought that by confessing to something you didn't do, you were putting an end to it all. You were being honorable for the sake of peace and goodwill in this city. That's your best way to go."

Jack went over and sat in the chair opposite his mother-in-law. He crossed his legs, uncrossed them, stood back up, and said, agitated, "Eulelie, I think Lila just told you that the truth is what it is. The reason I did what I did in that interview yesterday was because getting back to the fundamental truth in my life was long overdue. Now you come all the way up here and tell us that I need to suck that truth back in and keep it, letting it blacken my conscience for the rest of my life. No one, Eulelie, or at least no one decent, lives like that."

Eulelie stared at him straight, without flinching, without blinking, and she said, in a voice as if she were speaking in defense of her life, "Let me tell you something about truth, Jack. Truth is changeable and hardly ever knowable. It is subjective. And it can be benevolent or spiteful, but what it will be is always conditioned upon who is manipulating it, and there is always someone manipulating the truth to their gain. All I'm saying is that the dead man's father has manipulated the truth to your gain. You might as well take it and run, and help yourself."

Gil looked at his mother with a stare that would not let her loose. He narrowed his eyes and even halfway smiled as he said, "Momma, that's a pretty bleak picture you paint of truth. By your thinking, it would be impossible to know who was telling the truth, or maybe even if anyone is ever who they say they are." Any trace of a smile had vanished.

Eulelie softened her hard line only long enough to look at Gil contritely and say, "Gil, honey, all I'm saying is that Jack is still a young man with the rest of his career, a good number of years, still ahead of him. There's no point that I can see in letting this thing stop his progress. You can understand that, can't you?"

But Gil never answered. He only stared directly ahead, as if to look clear through his mother.

Lila watched Jack go sit at the writing desk. She looked on as he slid a piece of paper from the drawer, picked up a pen, and began writing before she asked, "Jack, what are you doing?"

"I'm doing exactly what your mother said I should do. I'm going to give those people out there what your mother said I should give them," Jack said.

"Jack, are you crazy? You actually listened to that crap my mother was spewing? What in the world is happening?" Lila was on her feet and desperate for someone in the room to show reason. This, she thought, was how natural disasters devastate lives. They come, as did her mother, without warning and without reason, and slam into all that had been calm and safe and life affirming, making a mess of everything. She paced in the narrow aisle between the coffee table and the sofa, then turned to her mother. Cocking her head as if she truly questioned, Lila asked, "Who the hell are you?"

"What do you mean?" Eulelie said with equal surprise.

"I mean, how do you come in here, as a mother, and tell your child to lie? How do you look at a situation like this and not seem to have any empathy at all for the family who lost a son?"

"That's for that family to work through, Lila, and they obviously already have. But I don't know how it is you can't see that the real tragedy is that Jack, an upstanding surgeon at one of the finest medical institutions in the world, had to be reduced to his color. That's the tragedy, Lila. Somebody needed to take that stand, and I'll bet that now crackers like that will think twice before letting that kind of evil come out of their mouth when they're thinking it." Eulelie paused, as if uncertain if she'd say the rest of what was on her mind. Then she got to her feet and stood like a statue in the middle of the room with one finger righteously raised and said, "If you really think about it, Lila, what Jack did is really no different from what Rosa Parks did when she refused to move her tired and wearied self to the back of that bus. In his way, Jack took a stand for the civilized treatment of every black person in this country, because he let white folks know that they just never know who they might need to save their sorry lives."

"Momma, but Rosa Parks didn't refuse to go to the back of the bus and then lie about breaking the law." Then she looked at Gil and smiled with a memory of that night in her office when his knowledge eased her fear of Jack's going to prison and his wisdom sent her back to her husband. And when he smiled back at her, as if to endorse what she was saying to their mother, she continued. "The only reason why Rosa Parks has any importance all these years later is because she lived in her truth. That's all Jack and I have been trying to do. It does not matter, Momma, whether all those reporters out there on the front lawn and all those people sitting in their homes listening to those reporters, all wrapped up in this story, believe the truth that Jack was the doctor, or whether they believe the dead man's father. Jack told his truth, the real truth. And another thing. If Jack did indeed stand up for the civilized treatment of all black people by leaving that man to die, then the only way it can ever have that significance is for Jack to stay true to his admission. I'm just not going to have you come in here with your warped version of reality and put a different ending on this story."

She sat back down on the sofa, right on the edge of it, looking as if she could topple forward, head over heels. Thoughts were fast and furious, the way they flew at her. But Jack's father, Dub, had brought his sizeable bottom into her mind and sat it right down in the middle of everything. And so with her mother tangible, and Dub only a recollection, she thought of the mind-boggling riddle of how two vastly different people could be so much alike. Dub most likely knew by now what Jack had done, and though it would be an ignominious gain for Jack, Dub was certain to be proud, offering up his respect to Jack on a silver platter; or at the least a paper plate, in Dub's case. So why hadn't they heard from him? So she asked, "Jack, have you heard from your father?"

Jack looked over at Lila, his eyes saying that he did not want to speak on the matter. But she wouldn't release him from her questioning gaze until she knew, so under that pressure, he said, "Yes, he called last night very late. You were sleeping."

"So what did he say?"

"He said 'I'm proud of you,' and then he hung up. That's all he said."

"Smart man," Eulelie said.

But Lila took her in with narrow eyes. "Smart man?" she questioned. "Well, I guess you would think he'd be smart for being proud of Jack, but the truth is this, Mother. There is absolutely no pride in what happened. Can you understand that?" She stood to pace again and continued. "So you know something, I can't do this. I just can't. I have spent practically all of my life trying to peek inside that vault you keep the real you penned up in, only to discover that there was no way you were ever going to let me see in there. Because, you see, it doesn't surprise me that you would think lying would be the best way around this, but what I don't understand is why and how you've come to put so much faith in lying in such an unyielding way. Everybody lies, I suppose. I've lied, you've lied, we've all lied. The difference is that for most people lying is a desperate and unreasonable way out that rips at the conscience. But for you it seems to be a reasonable solution."

Eulelie slapped her leg, as if she had some clever thought that just wouldn't wait, but then she only said, "Lila, you'd better be very careful of what you're saying."

"I don't have to be careful, Momma, because I'm in my own house. And this house will not be a house of secrets and lies. Our children, mine and Jack's, will not come into this home wondering when they'll be let in on the secret. You lie without a conscience, Momma, and you do it with a righteousness that only makes sense when put up against your warped set of ethics and morals. And so do you want to know why you think Dub is a smart man?" And before she gave her mother the opportunity to say one way or the other, Lila went to where Eulelie sat and stooped, to see her eye to eye, so that Eulelie would really hear her. "You think he's a smart man, Momma, because you're just like him. You are just like a bigoted, chauvinistic, projects-born-and-bred fat black man with a tenth-grade education. You two are cut from the same cloth, and so the next time the two of you are here together and you're sitting there gloating in the superiority you think you have over him just remember that maybe you have to feel better than him in order to stomp down that part of yourself that's just like him."

Eulelie looked without emotion at Lila and said patronizingly, "Lila, my dear, you've gone too far, and the only reason Momma is going to be understanding and not get upset is because I know that you're overwrought with everything that's happened."

"I may have gone too far, Momma, but I went there in truth. Now if you say that you understand that I'm overwrought, then you will leave right now, because like I said, I just can't do this. You are too messy, Momma. I love you, but you're way too messy for my life at this moment, so I need you to leave and give us the space we need. I'll call you when I'm ready, but you need to go, because I can't be here with Jack, who is trying to get our life back on an honest track, and have you on my shoulder spouting the glory of lies." Then, she turned to Gil with pleading eyes and said, "Listen, I'm sorry to do this to you, but would it make things easier for you if you left out of the back?"

"Yeah, we can do that. No problem. Come on, Momma." Gil leapt up, heading out of the room before Eulelie had even gotten out of her seat.

Then Jack said as he put down the last word of what he was writing, "Wait a second. Eulelie, I want you to be here for this. Lila, turn on the television. Channel Eleven, probably." He got up from where he sat behind the desk and went toward the door.

"Jack!" Lila said frantically. "What are you getting ready to do?"

So he went to her and showed her what he'd been writing. She skimmed his scrawl long enough to get the gist of the whole from the few words she could read. Then she looked at Jack and smiled big, then said, "Do it." Then she took Gil by the arm and said, "Sit down, Gil, Momma. You should hear this."

Gil crossed the room and sat, this time on the sofa, and Lila followed to sit next to him. As she was reaching for the remote, she looked up to find Gil mouthing to her *I'm proud of you*. She only smiled, knowing that he had every reason to bestow on her his pride, for she was proud of herself.

After a few minutes SPECIAL REPORT was emblazoned across the screen, a blond woman's face popped up who said her name was Dina Napoli just before it appeared at the bottom of the screen. She had interrupted the *Today* show, of all shows, with Jack's news. How had it come to pass, Lila thought, that Jack had the sway to shut Matt and Katie out of Baltimore, if for only a few minutes, so that he could have his say? Life was moving at top speed.

Before they knew it, there was Jack, and the front door, and the shrubs framing the stoop that had grown far too wild. Why, Lila wondered, did she have to notice this at the same time all of Baltimore must have been saying, Would you look at how that woman keeps her shrubbery? But the obsession over the bushes vanished once Jack began, slowly, measured, speaking of his belief in truth. And that led him to say that his truth from the day before was no less true today, then he'd say no more on the matter.

She was amazed at how much of what he was saying he'd already committed to memory in the short time between the writing and reading of it, as he spoke more to the cameras than he did to the paper, particularly when he reached the climax of what he was there to say. And as he eloquently took himself out of consideration for the post at the National Institutes of Health, he admitted his frail, human desire for the prestige of the post for nothing more than personal gain. But then, what he'd say next had Lila beaming with the comfort of knowing that without question, the Jack she'd married had just been given back to her. And so the last thing he would say to those cameras, which Lila heard as if he were saying it only to her, was that prestige and personal gain were not the reasons why he took the Hippocratic oath. So the last two lines of his speech, Lila could have said with him, since, in that way that they could know each other's every thought in a glance or an obscure smile, she seemed to know each word only a second before he spoke it.

"So, it is with no regrets that I take myself off the list because nothing should keep me from what I was really meant to do, and the work I do on Saturdays with Baltimore's black and neglected elderly is ultimately more meaningful to me and the oath I took than a long-term tenure at the NIH. But I am humbled and honored by the consideration, and I thank everyone who supported me for the post." Jack turned, and before anyone knew it, he was back inside.

He walked into the living room after latching the door. He went directly to the middle of the room, smiled shrewdly at Eulelie, and said, "How's that for truth?"

Eulelie looked at Jack as if she'd just been blindsided by a two-by-four, and said, "I don't know what to say, except to say that I think you're being foolhardy. You're taking this noble stand, and for what? To help people who aren't going to bring you anywhere near the kind of satisfaction that a prestigious place like the National Institutes of Health can bring you. I'm sorry to have to say this, Jack, but you're being stupid, and I thought you were smarter than that. I just don't get it at all."

Lila stood blowing out the deep, premature breath of the relief that was to come. She walked to the aperture of the room and said, "Well, Momma, I guess it's a good thing for you that you don't have to get it, but you do have to leave. So come on, I'll let you two out the back door." She was halfway down the hall and about to go into the kitchen when she heard her mother's hurried footsteps leaving the living room.

"Lila, you can't be serious about this. You're actually going to ask your mother to leave?" she questioned as she pushed open the door to follow Lila into the kitchen.

And Lila waited until Gil had come into the room before saying, "Momma, I've never been more serious about anything. For all of these months since that man died, I have been trying to figure out a way to keep me and Jack from drowning. And so now we're on dry land, and I'm not about to let you pull us back out and under the deep. Can you get that?"

"Lila, are you telling me that you're choosing your husband over your mother?"

Lila slumped against the back door to think about such a

harsh notion, to question whether it was actually in her to make the right choice. So in the few seconds it took her to answer, she was certain she'd have no regrets when she stood upright again, opened the door wide, and replied, "Yes, Momma, I guess that is what I'm doing. I'm choosing a life with my husband over a blind obedience to you that I never really understood from the very beginning." She opened the door a few inches wider, as if to make certain Eulelie understood it was open, and her time there was over. "Bye, Momma. This isn't good-bye for good, but it has to be good-bye for now."

Eulelie passed through the door and out into the backyard, seeming too disconsolate to let her eyes fall on Lila. She looked halfway back, but still not seeing Lila fully, and said, "I'm the only mother you've ever known, Lila, and I've loved you with a passion that would have been no different if I had brought you into this world myself. This hurts, Lila."

"Momma, this has nothing to do with my love for you. You *are* the only mother I've ever known, and I love you, too, but most of the time, like right now, I simply don't like you, Momma. I don't like you because I don't know you, and I cannot work all of that out now, and I don't know if I'll ever want to. But what I have that's real is what's between me and Jack, because for as much as this whole thing made me doubt it, I do know him, and I always have. I'll call you when you get back to Florida." And that's all Lila had to say.

So she watched her mother go toward the gate to leave the yard, and then Gil as he went to follow her. But first he took Lila's hand and kissed it, and in his eyes she saw the pride he felt in her stand. She closed the door, and the harshness of what she'd just done hit her again but then was overcome when she looked up to see Jack's smile.

As IT HAPPENED, their lives hadn't become terribly noisy. It took only a few days for the cameras and microphones and tape recorders, along with the moving lips behind them, to dwindle little by little and then vanish completely, since there was eventually no story for them and no one was talking.

Now with a week passed, Lila missed it all—the excitement of the cameras and the lights, the drama of the questions, the rush of being the object of the city's attention, canonized by some, demonized by others. But even as her minutes of fame waned, she could still feel the relief of having her free will back. And Lila was certain, as she walked through the sliding door of Johns Hopkins, that she'd never again take for granted the privilege of just being able to leave home without the machinations of a plan.

But in walking the halls that she'd walked hundreds of times before, the worst half of herself sat on her shoulder whispering, making her unsure if familiar faces were speaking and smiling for the mere sake of familiarity, or for what they now knew. Or maybe, she thought, they were laughing through their smiles at the wife of the doctor who turned down a position at the National Institutes of Health before it was even offered to him. It was a horrible feeling to have, not knowing who was laughing and why, and she wanted it nowhere near her. Faces came at her like leaves in a wind tunnel, one after the other, saying nothing but hello, but meaning so much more. And what would

they say, she wondered, even if they were to garner the gump-
tion to walk up to her and speak their opinions. Hypocrites,
every single one of them—the way they smiled in her face and
then whispered their cast-down rulings on her and Jack when
her back was against them. So she tried to force herself to give
them not one extra thought as she stood at the elevator bank
locking eyes with no one.

As she approached Jack's office, perspiration grew in her
dark corners, and she felt that heavy thing again; that heavy
thing that took her over and sat inside her in the middle of that
one *Story Hour*, and kept her from breathing right. They'd be
there, his scrub nurse Kathleen, and Judy, his secretary, and
God knows who else. And each one of them, on an ordinary
day, could interminably chat her up with mundanely unnecessary small talk. Today, though, they'd have something very specific to say about something quite particular. She picked up her
step. If it seemed as if time were nipping at her, they'd know
she'd have no patience for a chat. *I'm in a rush. I'm in a rush* is
what she chanted to herself as she sped past with a quick smile
and hello. But it wouldn't work.

"Lila," Judy said, pushing herself away from her computer.
"Oh, gosh, it's so good to see you."

And then Kathleen stepped out from the supply closet where
she was hidden, and it was all over. "Hey, Lila, how're you
doing?" she said with a pity-filled head cock. "I have to tell you,
I am so proud of Jack."

Lila couldn't begin to fathom what she meant by *proud*, but
what she knew for certain was that she would not ask. Lila
merely smiled big, and fake, and said, "Oh, yeah? Well we all
are, in our own way. Is he in his office? We're running late for
dinner reservations," she said as she headed for his door. Then
she noticed a man and woman approaching, both gray, old, he
barely carrying his heft, she with sure strides on sturdy legs.
And he was flushed with more pink of the unhealthy kind than
she'd seen on any white man since—that day. He seemed dis-
oriented to her, or at the very least turned around. The woman
equally so, but still following the unsteady man. As they got

closer, she could see that lost was the least of their problems. The man was haggard, and bedraggled, and had the soaking sweat of a man who had fought all his life with the world. But the woman had the sensibility to match her purse to her shoes, and because Lila had searched for anything that would give her ease with these motley two, the woman's matching purse and shoes would have to do. And he would have been just fine to her, the cause of no alarm at all, had he not been so flushed, and seemed so lost, and kept one hand suspiciously in his pants pocket. She wouldn't wait for the secretary to ask. "May I help you, sir? You seem lost." And then as she got a good look she knew him—father of the dead redneck.

"Oh, well, yeah, now that you asked. I'm lookin' for Dr. Jack Calloway's office."

"Well, you've found it, sir," Judy said. "But Dr. Calloway doesn't have any appointments scheduled now. He's about to leave."

"Well, I won't take but a minute of his time, ma'am. I'm sure he'll wanna see me."

"I'm really sorry, sir, but I'll have to make an appointment for you to see him, perhaps tomorrow."

"Can't you please make an exception?" the woman said. "We've come all this way across town, and my husband here don't walk so good."

Then the man went to say something, but Lila stepped in on his behalf. "Judy, it's okay. I really think this man needs to see Jack." Then she turned to the man and extended her left hand for a formal greeting, so as to get his left hand out of that pocket, but he wouldn't free that hand even for the sake of politeness. So she took his right hand in an awkward clasp, more certain than she'd ever been about anything that this man was desperately ill, and said, "I'm Lila Calloway, Dr. Calloway's wife. I'll take you to him."

"You're Dr. Calloway's wife?" the man said, studying her from head to foot. "You a pretty thing, ain't you?"

Lila smiled awkwardly then stole a sideways glance at his wife to find her expression unchanged, flat. There was nothing in the woman's face that spoke of his impropriety. Still, there was something in what he said and the way he looked that made her feel unclean. Or perhaps she'd imagined it. Nothing was as it seemed for her anymore when it came to white people, particularly white men, particularly ones over a certain age. Nonetheless, she took the last few steps to Jack's office slowly, waiting for the old man to make his way to the door. Lila swung the door open wide enough to let the man walk through first, and when she entered after him, she had to answer the question in Jack's eyes. "Hi, honey. This man and his wife were looking for your office. I think he really needs to see you." She paused, then said, just in case Jack didn't recognize him: "This is Mr. Potite."

Jack stood and stared, his eyes frozen on the man just with curiosity, and then immediate recognition. "Jack Calloway," he said flatly. "I've seen you in the news. You look as if you need to sit down. Why don't you have a seat?"

And Lila went over and sat on the love seat, next to some of Jack's files that were always piled there. She was relieved, though, as she lowered herself, and rested her purse, and she took comfort in seeing that Jack obviously saw a physical frailty in the man as well. But she noticed that the man sat in such a way that he still hadn't removed his hand from his pants pocket, and that troubled her more than anything. His wife sat right beside him, somehow seeming to Lila to be off to the side, if not physically then certainly in every emotional way; isolated, as if tangency was her place of comfort.

The man said, "This is my wife, Shirley."

Jack looked at Shirley with a smile that was not full and said "It's nice to meet you, Mrs. Potite."

"Well, so you know that that was my son that died over there on Twenty-eighth Street over the summer. I just needed to come here and see you. My boy didn't die by your hands, but it's true enough that he wouldn't have died if you had just helped him. And when I found out that you was a heart doctor, well, that just broke my heart all over again."

So Lila knew, now, why that man had his hand sunk firmly into his pocket. He clutched a gun, and so this is how she and Jack would die—in an avenger's rampage. A tear welled and fell, and she understood helplessness and true desperation for the first time in her life. Would it help to beg for their lives? She wouldn't even know where to begin, because fear had wrestled from her mind its ability to form words into anything intelligible. Of course he would kill her first, she thought, because in the mind of an avenger, she presumed, the profundity of taking the life of their enemy's love first would be powerful. If she were an avenger, that's exactly what she'd do, she thought. What she didn't know was what his wife's role would be in this drama. And so, she thought about dying, and whether she'd see her father right away, or some time later. But the most pressing question she couldn't answer about her death was: will I know my mother's face when I see her?

"I'm unsure of what I can do for you, Mr. Potite," Jack said.

"Like I said, I just needed to come and look in your eyes and know whether or not it was the devil who took my boy away from here."

"I'm not the devil, Mr. Potite. I'm just a man who made a mistake," Jack said softly. "I don't expect you to like the mistake I made, but I sure hope you can understand that it was a mistake, and a weakness."

"Dr. Calloway, can I tell you something about me?" James Potite said. A profuse perspiration had soaked his head and was dripping into his eyes and down his face. Without knowing what terror he'd set off in that office, James Potite drew his clenched hand from his pocket.

That's when Lila drew in a breath of terror that she could not release. And only when she saw the white handkerchief did she exhale with a distant smile, relieved that reality had not gone to the sinister places her mind had gone in immediate flashes. But her face grew sober when she saw that quite obviously against his will the man's hand shook without ceasing. Trembled as if with the fear she'd just now vanquished. And it occurred to her that keeping it tucked in his pocket was the best way, the only way, to control its palsy.

The senior Potite patted the rag to his brow, then said, "Now

I'm an old man, and old men like to tell stories, so I'm gonna tell you one."

"That's fine," Jack said in a benevolent, indulging manner.

"I want to tell you somethin' about me, Dr. Calloway. You know, I raised that boy up to be who he was, and my daddy raised me up to be who I was, and I ain't proud of none of that. I ain't proud of what I sent back to the Lord. But by the time I realized what I had done to that boy, it was way too late. There wasn't no changin' him at all." He sopped the rag around his neck with his trembling hand, then shoved his hand, the rag still in its clutch, back into his pocket.

"Take it easy now, James," Shirley said with narrowed eyes and worried brow.

"I'm all right, Shirley," he said as if her concern was burdensome. "Anyway, my life got straight in one day. You see, 'round about fifteen years ago, I was comin' out from a bar down in Fells Point wit some of my drinkin' buddies. Of course, back then Fells Point was just about to change from bein' a place where dockworkers and steelworkers could go for a cold one at a simple joint to bein' what it is today wit all these fancy places and such. But we was a rowdy bunch anyway, we was, and we was just a bunch of guys wit way too much drink in them lookin' for some trouble. So along comes these black fellas, and they was young, and just a bit too cocky for my likin', at least for the man I was, if you know what I mean."

Jack only nodded as he kept his eyes trained on the man as if waiting for the moment when the story would get somewhere.

So James Potite continued. "Anyways, we're stretched out all across the sidewalk, and these two black fellas want to pass, 'cept they think they too good to step off the sidewalk for us, so they just keep walking. They was polite and everything when they got to us, sayin' excuse me, and all. But still we ain't likin' their attitude in the least bit. So my buddy Shimmy, he say, 'Go on 'round us,' and then he calls them the n-word, you know. But these fellas, they ain't wantin' to move at all."

The distraction of his perspiring head was enough to make him stop his story before it had even gotten started. He took his shaking hand from his pocket and mopped his face again. "So anyway, they commence to pushin' and shovin' and such, and then, Jesse—that's Shimmy's brother—he pulls out this knife. Now I gotta tell you, I ain't had no idea that Jesse carried 'round this knife. But he pulls this knife, and everybody's pushin' and shovin' and then before you know it, it's a full-out fight. So we're swingin' and punchin', and I have to admit, I got my share of socks in, too. But then, the next thing you know, one of those black fellas is pushed into the middle of the street and the next thing I know, he done been run over by one of those fish delivery trucks. Thing ran completely over him."

"Did he die?" Lila asked from across the room, only vaguely recalling the incident from all those years back.

"You betcha he died. Died right there on the spot. So we was all taken in, even though every witness on the street pointed their fingers at Shimmy and Jesse as the ones who pushed that fella under the wheels of that truck. The rest of us was charged as accessories to the murder because they also found out that not only did Shimmy and Jesse push him, but Jesse had gone ahead and stabbed him. So there I was put on trial, scared as can be 'cause I ain't never been in trouble wit the law for one day of my life up till then." He stopped to mop his face once more, sweating with what could have been the heat of those memories along with whatever was happening inside his body to produce so much excessive moisture.

"So anyway," he continued once he'd put his rag and shaking hand back in his pocket, "I was found guilty, of course, 'cause I was. But it was what that judge said to me as he was sentencin' me that made me think. He looked me right in these two eyes of mine and said, 'Mr. Potite, I remember this city when black people had to be careful which part of town they found them-selves in. And I remember this city when blacks couldn't go into department stores, or ride in the front of the bus, and even had to worship only in the backs of churches. I remember this city when the only high school black children could go to was

Douglas High School. Yet black men and women in this city still managed to rise up in spite of it all and become doctors and lawyers and teachers and own businesses and anything else you can imagine, and so could their children. And so now, Mr. Potite, you're standing here before a man who holds the fate of your life in his hands. A man who has the choice of imposing several years of living hell on you to avenge all of those social injustices that people of his race had to endure just because of skin color or of sentencing you to the best education of your life.' And then he paused, you know, and I thought I would just about swallow my tongue and teeth all at once, 'cause I had no idea what this judge was going to do to me. But then he said, 'Mr. Potite, I'm going to choose education here. I'm sentencing you to three years in prison, suspended, for five years of parole and community service.' " Then James Potite looked over at his wife who sat there as if the heaviness of the memories from those days, and the weight of a dead son on her face had been smoothed over by grief. That's when James Potite said to her, "Remember that moment, honey?"

"Yeah," was all she said plainly.

"So anyway, then he says to me, 'Your community service will be done with Bea Gaddy. Do you know who she is, Mr. Potite?' And I says, 'Yes I do, Your Honor. She feeds homeless people at Thanksgiving and Christmas.' And he says, 'She does that and a whole lot more. She's like Baltimore's own Mother Teresa. So what you're going to do, Mr. Potite, is you're going to work every day with Ms. Gaddy, doing whatever she needs you to do. And when you look into the faces of all those people of so many different colors you'll see in the course of your day with her, Mr. Potite, I want you to see if there's a difference between a hungry white man and a hungry black man. I want you to see if there's a difference between the way a white mother loves her hungry children and the way a black mother loves her hungry children. And if you can find those differences, Mr. Potite, then I want you to send me a letter detailing those differences for me. If I don't get a letter from you, I will have no choice but to believe that my gut instinct about you was right. And what my gut tells me is that hidden away in a lonely corner of your mind is the belief that all men, me a black man and you a white man, were created in the image of God and therefore are his children.' And that was all he said before he adjourned the court."

Mr. Potite sat staring with a peaceful smile at Jack who stared back at him with eyes of disbelief. "I'll tell you one thing, though, I'll never forget that judge. Those words he said to me opened my mind up and changed it before I had even left the courtroom. I ain't never had nobody talk to me like that." Then waving his one good hand as if to disregard all other words that had come before the judge's, he continued, "People have said things like we're all the same, and love thy neighbor as you love yourself, and stuff like that. But maybe it was the whole experience of bein' on trial and facin' prison and then havin' those words said to me that did it. I don't know. But on that day, my life changed, my heart changed. And that judge, and I'll never forget his name, Gilbert Horatio Harding Giles the second, is the one who changed it."

Lila, gripped not only by amazement, but also by the magnificent poignancy of fate, had nearly lost her ability to speak. She rose from where she sat and slowly made her way toward the old man. As she took that walk across the room, she thought about the hand of God in all its mysterious ways, and knew then and there that she would know for the rest of her life the futility in questioning it. And when she reached Mr. Potite, she stood with one hand outstretched to take the man's hand. When she had it, she finally, quietly said, "Mr. Potite, that judge was my father."

The old man looked at her with questioning eyes that slowly brightened as his smile grew larger. "What'd you say? He was your father?"

"He was my father," Lila said, her head now whirling in a laugh of release. She turned to Jack who looked as if he'd just been let out of a spinning room. "Jack, can you believe this?"

"I'm trying to, Lila," was all he said.

And by now Mr. Potite was laughing with abandon from every place in him. Then just as quickly as his laughter came, it left as he sank his head into the palms of his hands, as if in

thankful awe of a sudden brightness into which he could not
look directly. And he wept. When he lifted his head to show his
tear-streaked face, he said, "Shirley, do you hear this?"

"Oh, I sure do, James. I sure do," and she gave Lila a smile
that was of equal intensity yet completely opposite of the dour
face with which she'd come.

James Potite took Lila's hand again, patted it gently like a
father would, then let it go, saying, "You had yourself a great
daddy, young miss, and you went and married yourself a real
good husband who's on the road to his own greatness."

As he regained his composure and dried every tear pridefully
with his rag, he said to Jack, "I'm an old man, Dr. Calloway, and
it took a lotta livin' and a lotta mistakes for me to understand
what I know. My boy Jimmy he ain't never got old enough to
understand why he lived wrong, or that he lived one part of his
life wrong. You a good man, I know that from all that stuff I
read in the papers 'bout how you take care of poor people,
people like me, without askin' for one red cent. And I just hope
that you know that I'm a good man, too, and I ain't hardly here
for vengeance. Don't get me wrong. I loved my boy, and I'd rip
my own heart right outta my chest if I thought it would bring
him back, but my boy died the way he lived—filled with hate.
And that's why I wasn't 'bout to let you throw yourself to the
lions like that and tell them that you was the one who walked
away from Jimmy. No use in you losin' your life and livelihood
to my son's hatred."

"But what about your grandsons?" Jack asked. "They were
there. They know I did it, now they're saying I wasn't the one.
Why aren't they telling the truth?"

"Because I done made them see, Doc, that God struck down
your enemy for you. That's the way it works, ya see. I run my
family like a righteous man, like a man who lives by the word
of the Bible, and those boys had to be shocked into seeing the
light by seeing for themselves the way hate can strike down a
man. No siree, those boys know now that Jimmy had them livin'
wit the devil, ya see."

Jack didn't see, because this was the part of God, and faith,

and the way a man can live and die by the Bible, that completely eluded him. As an educated man, he felt as if the hearing and understanding of it all should be simple—simple faith.
But perhaps it was far too complicated in its simplicity for an
educated man, with all his reasoning and his belief on the
periphery, to comprehend. So he wouldn't ponder James Potite
Sr.'s faith in God's wrath against the unrighteous any longer,
since it had become for him a conundrum that had gotten more
twisted and more conflicted with each thought Jack gave it. He
looked expectantly at James Potite for the rest, even though it
seemed as if he were finished.

But the old man's eyes were searching the air for what he
would say next, and how he would say it. He had it, and his
brightened face spoke before he could. "Now I heard you turn
down that big fancy job out in Bethesda a couple of weeks ago,
and I'm just hopin' that it ain't cause of what happened wit my
boy, 'cause if it is, then you in need of some serious forgiveness, and I want you to know that I forgive you."

Jack had taken all of what the man had to say, even his forgiveness, and stored it in a corner of his brain where he could
go back and get it at a time when he wouldn't be so distracted
by everything physical about James Potite. He wasn't certain if
fate could possibly be so absolutely preposterous, but this man
before him, the man who created the life that Jack himself
vengefully watched fade out, was in desperate need of help.
James Potite could have been dying, Jack believed, and he
wouldn't have it—not in his office, and not on the heap of all
the other death that had come before him. "Mr. Potite, I thank
you for your forgiveness. But I've got to tell you, you look to
me to be a very sick man. Would you mind very much if I just
listened to your heart for a minute?"

The old man, his mouth agape in awe, could only agree. He
tried with his nonshaking hand and his palsied hand to unbut-
ton his shirt, but not even paired with a good hand could the
other do the job. "Dr. Calloway, if you don't mind, I'm gonna
need some help with these buttons."

Jack knelt beside him, and after loosening the first button he

had to force himself to keep his mind clinical and not let any of
the disgust seep in that he felt from the man's soggy shirt,
which had completely dampened Jack's fingertips. "Mr. Potite,
how long have you been perspiring like this?"

"Oh, I guess a few days now. It's been hot all summer."

"Don't you lie like that now, James," Shirley said. "It's been
way longer than a few days."

"How long?" Jack asked her.

"Goin' on two weeks. That's the only reason I wanted to
come here with him today, Dr. Calloway. My husband needs
help."

"Well, you're right about one thing, Mr. Potite. It was a hot
summer," Jack said as he put the stethoscope in his ears. "But
the temperature is nowhere near as hot as it was in the middle
of the summer, and this room is air-conditioned and you're still
perspiring a lot." Jack put the stethoscope to the man's chest
and listened. He moved it, then listened again, and when he
took it away, his face said all that he would need to say. "I'm
going to need to take your blood pressure." So he went a few
steps to the corner and got the blood pressure cuff. And when
he stooped and took James Potite's blood pressure, he sprang
up as if some other force moved him and was in full emergency
mode. He said to the man quickly, "Mr. Potite, are you on any
blood pressure medication?"

"I was," the man said, still seemingly unaware that he was
in the throes of an emergency. "I stopped taking it, though. It
was too expensive. It's a terrible thing when a man has to
choose between taking care of his family and taking care of
himself."

But Jack wasn't necessarily listening to the man's gripe. He was
too far gone in the planning of James Potite's care. "Judy!" Jack
yelled from where he stood. And she answered his beckon as if
she were standing at the door waiting. "I need you to call down
to the C.I.C.U. and tell them we need a gurney up here stat. This
is Mr. James Potite and he has to be admitted right now."

"Yes, Dr. Calloway," Judy said, leaving with the called-for
swiftness of the moment.

Lila, who had stepped aside for Jack, now went to Mr. Potite and put one hand on the man's sweaty shoulder and said, "Mr. Potite, everything's going to be just fine. Jack will see to that."

But Shirley Potite's face had grown positively ashen when she said, "Dear God, I knew something like this would happen." And then with an anger that made it seem as if she were two words away from cursing him, she added, "He is the most pigheaded fool ever put on earth!"

Jack looked up from what he was writing only when the two men for whom he'd had Judy beckon swung open the door. "Good, you're here," Jack said, getting up from where he sat. He picked up the page where he'd written everything that was required to stabilize the old man and handed it to one of the men. "These are the tests that I want to have run on him. Tell Dr. Greene that I'll send all the official paperwork later, but right now, this is what Mr. Potite needs, and right away."

"Now, just hold on a minute," James Potite said. "Dr. Calloway, I ain't got no insurance. I'm a drywall man, and I got a family to take care of, and I ain't got the luxury of bein' laid up in the hospital for days and weeks. If I don't work, my family don't eat. It's as simple as that."

"You damned fool!" Shirley Potite screamed at him. Who knew she had quite that much fever in her? "If you don't let Dr. Calloway fix you up, you ain't gonna come home to a family 'cause you gonna die. Can't you see that's what he's tryin' to tell you?" She got up from where she sat and went to where Jack was behind his desk.

"Dr. Calloway, I know you must be 'bout sick to death with the Potite family just about now. I'm a Christian woman, Dr. Calloway. I've always known right from wrong, and I've always in my heart known that people is people. And right now I wish so many things. I wish I had my son back. I wish you could have seen into your Christian heart to save my son, because I know you have such a heart. More than anything I've ever wished for in my life, I wish I had led this man right here away from his hatred and into the light when I married him. But I was a weak woman, just like you was a weak man the day you let the evil way that was in my son overpower your way to do good.

"Ya see, I believed that with as hard as my husband's heart was against the blacks, my Christian ways wasn't gonna make a bit of difference to our children, who was up against his hate. He was gonna pass all that hate right on down, and he did, and even though you could have saved my Jimmy with one shock of that machine you doctors use, you didn't, and we had to put our son in the ground. James is all I have. I need you to help us. Yes, we was Jimmy's parents, and yes, my husband with his ugly ways and thoughts, and me with my silence helped make Jimmy who he was. But no, we don't have no insurance, or nothin'. We just as poor as the black people you reach inside your Christian heart on Saturdays to help for free. Can't you help us?"

"Naw, now, Shirley, you think of what you sayin'," her husband noted as he tried and failed, like a newborn foal, to get himself on his feet. "We ain't never taken a lick of charity before, and we ain't 'bout to start. Now, what you do 'round town on Saturdays with them other people, well that's just fine for them. I'm a proud man, and what I can't pay for I just do without. It's as simple as that, Doc."

Jack moved with the wind around his desk and stooped in front of the man, so that he'd be right in his face. "Mr. Potite, your blood pressure is dangerously high. I'm amazed that you were even able to walk through the halls of this hospital to get to me, much less get all the way over here to the hospital. Now, if you don't go with these men and let me help you, you're going to die. It's as simple as that." He stood up and perched his buttocks onto the edge of his desk. It may have been unfair to say, but he said it anyway, "Your son died, possibly, probably, without my help. I'll be damned if you're going to do the same thing."

James Potite looked at the two men and silently let them know that he'd go where they'd take him. He hoisted himself up with their help, and with the help of the two men plus Jack, plus Kathleen, got onto the gurney. As they wheeled him through the door, he looked up at Jack and said, "Hey, Doc?" And when Jack turned to see him, he said through a small smile, "I ain't gonna die on you. Maybe one Potite died spreadin' hate so's another one could live to spread somethin' good. If you'll have me, you've got yourself another old man to see on Saturdays."

All Jack would do was smile while the man slowly vanished behind the closing door. He went to Lila and consumed her with his arms, melting into her. In her tightened back he felt the dense weight of everything. With his head pressed against hers, it was as if, in the quiet of the room, he could hear what she thought, as she thought it. His hand covered her back with love that soothed until it softened. There was no way for Jack to measure how far she'd brought him, or how. All he knew was that she'd led him where, he was positive, he would not have gone without her. And even as the need to put his thanksgiving for her life into words, her eyes pulled at him. Instead, he put it directly into her mind, so that it would be planted forever for her to see, and feel, and believe with every moment she'd live. "I am so glad you said yes."

And what he gave her did not need another word, not from him, not from her. Quietly, with steps as light and faint as newborn down, he had come back to her. She held him, with everything gone that had once taken him away from her and her from him. From a distance, dimly, were the days when fetid heat made the world so cold and cast her from her belief in its goodness. But now Lila beamed with the peace that had once been so elusive, and held tight to her life with gratitude. And she held fast to their fresh, days-old life that was coming to the earth like a dove in a time of newfound faith, in the truth of the human spirit, and in the promise of life—life a mother can always feel—growing in her, moment, by moment, by moment. And it was fated that the life, from the moment it drifts from womb to world, will come to be called Matthew.